Shad's Awakening

Shad's Awakening

A Novel

Helmut W. Horchler

authorHOUSE®

AuthorHouse™
1663 Liberty Drive
Bloomington, IN 47403
www.authorhouse.com
Phone: 1-800-839-8640

First published by AuthorHouse   07/18/2011

ISBN: 978-1-4634-0579-3 (sc)
ISBN: 978-1-4634-0578-6 (dj)
ISBN: 978-1-4634-0577-9 (ebk)

Library of Congress Control Number: 2011908243

Printed in the United States of America

By the same author:

HELP! I have been promoted . . .
A JOURNEY WELL TRAVELED
NATIVE FRIENDSHIPS
MAJA'S CAT TALES

Prologue

Los Angeles, 1957/1958

He couldn't take it anymore. His stepfather's whippings had become too vicious and too repetitive. The angry red welts and cuts on his buttocks and back had not healed properly yet from his last beating, and here was the man, his face suffused with blind anger and determination, reeking of alcohol, leather belt wrapped around his hand, ready to lash the perceived insubordination out of his stepson once and for all. His latest 'crime' had been harmless, he felt, overstaying his curfew by an hour because he had lost track of time while cruising with his friend Joe.

Tears and the specter of intolerable pain would no longer render him powerless, he swore to himself, seething with barely controlled resentment. At age seventeen he had become big and strong enough, he was sure, to take on his stepfather. The many hours diligently working out in the school gym had added inches to his height and added pounds of muscle to his previously slim frame. Over the past months his intimidation had become more psychological, based on years of unmitigated abuse, rather than physical. What he had been lacking so far was enough courage to fight back. But no more. Something had snapped in his psyche; had given him needed self confidence in his superior strength. This time he was not going to be docile.

1

Los Angeles, 1957/1958

Running away from home had been a frequent temptation for him, but he could not abandon his mother and leave her behind to suffer alone. He knew she loved and needed him. Terrified as he was of his stepfather, he accepted the moment had come for him to act no matter what the consequences.

His private hell had boiled over; he could no longer keep a lid on it. He had anticipated the looming, ultimate showdown with his stepfather and was prepared. He did not think of the future; knew he would not have one if he did not take measures into his own hands to put a permanent stop to the abuse to which his mother and he had been subjected for years.

The long kitchen knife he had absconded was hidden within reach in his room, ready to be used if it came to that. His mother, knowing what her son had to endure, continued living in her own world of terror and denial. She had secreted herself in the back of the house, in her room, where she could pretend to be oblivious to his screams. She knew she would be next if she so much as made a sound.

If his stepfather noticed he was not cowering as he had always done, he gave no sign.

"Did I or did I not order you to be home by 11:00 o'clock?" he hissed, his lips stretched into a mean thin line. "Did you think I was kidding? What the hell is wrong with you, you little piece of shit?"

The boy did not answer; refused to take off his shirt and lower his pants when told to do so. Instead, he stared at his stepfather defiantly. It threw the man momentarily off stride.

"I guess I have been too lenient with you, haven't I? Well, that can easily be remedied," he said, raising his arm, ready to strike, his face contorted with whiskey driven rage.

"Don't you dare!" the boy croaked his warning, barely hanging on to his new found determination not to accept what his stepfather was so fond of dishing out. His heart beat wildly; sweat poured down his back. His hands shook. His blond hair was plastered to his scalp. He was deathly afraid; could already feel the lash of the belt and the bite of the buckle and instinctively turned away and raised his arms to protect himself, but there was nothing he could do about his exposed back.

His stepfather's wild roaring shattered the ominous silence as the belt whistled down. The boy couldn't help himself; screamed in pain as the metal buckle struck his elbow, nearly paralyzing his left arm. Blind outrage consumed him. He rushed his stepfather, both of them tumbling to the floor. A leather wrapped fist found his face and stars exploded. He managed to scramble to his feet in the tight quarters, his stepfather, still on the floor, holding on to his ankle, determined to pull him down.

They struggled. Grappled. His stepfather was caught off guard by the stepson's unexpected defiance and show of strength. A knee drove into his groin, the full weight of his stepson behind it, and he curled up, gasping for breath. He wrapped an arm behind the boy's leg, reflexively holding him down while his roundhouse connected with the back of his head. The boy's fist smashed into his nose. Blood spewed and he bellowed with rage and pain. The boy took advantage of the man's momentary incapacitation to drag himself within reach of the hidden knife.

His stepfather, with blood smeared face, stared at the gleaming knife in shocked surprise. "You wouldn't dare use that," he taunted before scrambling up and launching himself at the boy, his arm with the belt ready to slam down once again. But he was too slow. The boy had stepped into the attack and plunged the knife high and deep into his hated stepfather's midsection.

*   *   *

In the emergency room of the hospital photographs were taken of the boy's latest injuries and his mother's barely healed scars, documenting their persistent abuse and the wounds he had suffered in defending himself. The man had died on the operating table, the surgeon unable to stop the profuse internal bleeding in time.

His mother had been totally supportive, backing up his testimony of years of severe physical mistreatment through her second husband. Before their 911 call they had agreed to tell the police her husband had brought the knife along and the boy had wrestled it away from him in the fight. With the man dead, no one could dispute the chain of events by which the knife had gotten into his room or explain why his stepfather had brought it along.

It was all plausible, given their difference in height and strength. Since the knife had come from the kitchen both his stepfather's and his fingerprints had been identified on the handle, corroborating his version of events. The amply documented, clearly visible scars on his back and buttocks confirmed the abuse story, as did the angry red welts on his mother's body. The severe bruising of his elbow and the lump on his head from his stepfather's fist had been further evidence of his self defense claim.

The printing business the family owned was profitable enough to allow them to hire a good criminal attorney when the grand jury indicted him, and yet he had not been able to prevent the boy being convicted of involuntary manslaughter. He had fought for self defense or justifiable homicide, while the prosecutor had argued for pre-meditated murder, trying to convince the jury that the boy had brought the knife to his room. At the end a plea bargain had been struck which required the boy to serve three years in prison. The first year was to be spent in a juvenile detention center, with subsequent transfer to state prison upon attainment of his eighteenth birthday.

*   *   *

The juvie center had in some ways been worse than his stepfather's beatings. He didn't believe he would survive his initial incarceration, let alone two more years in state prison. He had little hope he would be paroled much earlier, based on the terms of the plea bargain. He thought constantly about escaping and starting his life over, but how? Lying awake on his bunk, he thought feverishly about how to get out but could not come up with a viable plan.

He had all but given up hope when an escape opportunity came about unexpectedly. During the transfer from juvie detainment to state prison, a short period of confusion suddenly arose. He was among a group of fifteen juvies loaded on a bus with only one guard sitting in the back in addition to the equally armed driver. They were not considered high escape risk prisoners, given their age, short sentences and criminal histories. Halfway to their destination, a brief pee break at a truck stop had become necessary. The toilet facilities were limited. There were too many prisoners to be effectively controlled off the bus by only two guards. Following a short discussion among the guards, they decided one group would stay in the bus with the driver, while the other half went inside, with the second guard patrolling the vestibule and supervising the prisoners' entry and exit to the toilets themselves.

It astounded the boy that the guards were not more vigilant in keeping a tight rein on their charges. They should not have let more than two or three at a time off the bus, to be escorted by one guard while the other one remained in the bus with the balance of the prisoners.

But the guards were old and overweight and less than diligent. No one had ever made an attempt to escape on these routine transfers.

When it became the boy's turn to relieve himself, he found both urinals already being used. He went into the single stall and when he looked up, discovered a small window above the toilet, wide open. It dawned on him a unique opportunity beckoned. Their guard had opted to remain in the hallway, rather than the smelly facility itself. Before he could think the ramifications through or lose his courage, the boy was standing on the toilet seat and shimmying up to the ledge of the window. He could just squeeze through the narrow aperture and let himself drop to the ground. He looked around quickly and noted he could not be seen from the bus out front. He started running and disappeared into the wooded area behind the rest stop.

His absence was only discovered when the bus had been reloaded and the headcount showed one short, but by then he was nearly a mile away, running wildly through the sparse underbrush. By the time an alarm could be raised and search teams mobilized and dispatched to the truck stop he figured he would be miles away.

He had no more than the vaguest idea of where he might be. He was isolated, alone, and both scared of what faced him and elated about his successful escape. He had no money; no food, water or shelter.

Nothing beyond the clothes on his back. He didn't know what to do now that he was free but presumably already being hunted. He knew his mother would help him, but how to reach her? Even if he would have known how to get to her house, it would surely be the first place the police would look for him. He hoped it would take them some time to find her new address. He needed to get in touch with her before her phone was tapped or her incoming mail monitored. He needed money and her help to disappear. The only positive factor he had going for him was that he was wearing civilian attire, his juvie uniform having been discarded at the center in anticipation of being issued strident orange state prison overalls following his transfer.

The past year had made him physically stronger and added to his height. He was lean and fit and felt he could walk briskly forever, but he worried about the police tracking him with dogs or conducting a helicopter search. Was he as an escaped juvie prisoner important enough to the authorities to have them mount a full press search? He had turned eighteen days ago and was not sure he was still categorized as a juvie. Perhaps technically, since he had not been checked into the county jail yet. He had been a model prisoner, never complaining, never causing problems, and could not possibly be seen as dangerous, he felt. But escaped he had and they would want to recapture him expeditiously. It would be a matter of principle for them, he assumed.

Miles later, still no pursuers in sight, he came across a narrow paved road cutting through a huge orange grove. Heading south would bring him further away from the juvenile detention center and the truck stop, so this was the direction he chose to follow. He was hungry and thirsty but had no choice except to keep on walking, keeping to the side of the road, checking his surroundings regularly, ready to duck at a moment's notice. He lost track of time, plodding along automatically.

He heard the motor before he saw the vehicle coming up behind him. He crouched low by the side of the road until he could just make out the approaching conveyance. It did not appear to have a light bar on the roof. He was tempted to hide as best he could and let it pass, but he was exhausted and dehydrating rapidly and knew he had to cover more ground quickly, as well as to hide his tracks from the dogs which might have been put on his trail by now. On the spur of the moment he stood up slowly, ready to scramble for cover as the pick-up started bearing down on him. He stuck his thumb out before he could change his mind.

The engine rumbled throatily as the driver took his foot off the gas pedal. The sun reflected off the windshield, making it hard for him to see the driver, but he thought he recognized a woman behind the wheel. She was looking at him uncertainly, studying him with rather apprehensive eyes as she slowly rolled past him, no doubt surprised to come across a hitchhiker on this lonely stretch of road. He smiled at her, trying to look unthreatening, and was relieved when she came to a stop and lowered the passenger side window several inches. He noted the door remained locked.

He saw penetrating eyes mustering him suspiciously. "Where are you heading, young man?" she asked as he rushed over to her.

He hadn't thought of a specific destination. "Pasadena," he said, where he used to live.

"Well, I can't take you all the way there. I am only going as far as Glendale, but I guess you are welcome to hop in if you want to go there."

"Thanks. I really appreciate it. Glendale will be fine. I can call my Mom from there to have her pick me up."

The woman reached over to unlock the passenger door and he climbed in. She drove a few minutes in silence before curiosity got the best of her.

"What brings you out this way?" she asked. "I drive this road every week and hardly ever see another car, let alone a hitchhiker."

He didn't have enough time to invent much of a credible story. "I was out on a hike in the woods with some friends and somehow got separated from them when nature called and they inadvertently left me behind. When I tried to catch up with them, I got lost."

"I guess that can happen. This area can be tricky, no doubt. You are lucky you found this road and I came along. You would have had a long walk ahead of you."

He nodded his agreement. "I suppose I should have just waited where we got separated, so my friends could have retraced their steps and hopefully would have found me."

"Yeah, that would have been the smart thing to have done all right."

"Say, you wouldn't have a bottle of water I could have, would you? I had to abandon my backpack a while ago and I am dying of thirst."

Instead of answering, she reached behind her and came up with the water. He drank greedily while he studied her out of the corner of his eye. She looked to be in her fifties, her face tanned and weather beaten. A farmer, he thought. Her demeanor was open and friendly. She had strong hands, he noticed. A plaid man's shirt was tucked into her jeans, the sleeves buttoned around her wrists.

"I'm Maude," she said. "What should I call you?"

"Roger. Roger Stevens," he said truthfully before he remembered the police was searching for him. By the time his faux pas had dawned on him, it was too late to retract and he felt relieved when she did not react to the name. If an all points bulletin for him had been issued, she had apparently not become aware of it. Her radio was turned on to a country and western station.

She was driving fast; well above the speed limit. It made him nervous. He wanted her to slow down, afraid they might be stopped by a sheriff's cruiser, but when he asked her about this risk, she waved him off.

"Don't you think those folks have something better to do than patrol this lonely neck of the woods for speeders?" she dismissed his concern.

He was tempted to point out to her that there was always a first time, but he did not want to make her suspicious. He focused on listening to her explain her weekly overnight visits to her daughter in Glendale, on her way to sell her produce at the Saturday farmer's market in South Pasadena.

"Do you think I might be able to use your daughter's telephone to call my mother?" he asked.

"Sure. I guess she wouldn't mind."

A few more miles had passed before she interrupted his thoughts. "So tell me about yourself, Roger. What do you do when you don't get lost in the woods?"

"Not much right now. I just turned eighteen and graduated from high school, so I am still on vacation. I am trying to find a job, but I am also thinking of joining the army. I already visited their local recruiting office, and they seem eager to sign up volunteers."

He could not have explained why he came up with this fiction so spontaneously, but it appealed to her, and they discussed what three years in the military might mean for him. Her husband was a retired marine, she told him, and went on to extol the advantages of the marines versus the army. But he demurred; pointing out to her he would then have to sign up for four years instead of three.

As soon as they had arrived at Maude's daughter's house and the introductions had been made she invited him to use the phone.

"Mom?" he said when she answered, "are you alone? Can you pick me up? I am here in Glendale."

"What in the world are you doing there, Roger? And yes, I am alone, but I thought you were in the county jail by now? What's going on?" She sounded worried and confused.

"I'll explain when I see you. I can't talk now. I am calling from a friend's house." He gave her the address Maude provided and asked his mother to hurry.

2

Decision time, Shad Cooper thought. The recently opened Tranquil Towers Retirement Center in La Jolla had been an immediate success and if he wanted to buy in, the time to do so was now. He had been procrastinating long enough. *Being* old, he concluded—not for the first time—was a lot worse than *getting* old, and much harder to accept than he had anticipated. In fact, he had to force himself to acknowledge being old; to see himself the way others did.

He was sitting across from the marketing manager of the Towers, studying her while trying to focus on what she was saying. She was attractive. Youngish, as everyone he saw these days seemed to be compared to his own age. The slight smile playing around her pink lips was professional; did not come from her heart. An aspect of her sales talk. Sybil Delatour read her name tag. The long sleeved pink blouse, with its collar turned up, complemented her tight black skirt and black pumps nicely. Her stylishly coiffed blond hair fell naturally over her shoulders and went well with her blue eyes.

She was as good in selling as she was pretty, extolling the many advantages of the Tranquil Towers, much as she had done when he had first visited her with his wife Veronica and their friend Thomas Grady more than a year before. And just as he had done back then Shad idly wondered if he would fantasize about her later when he was alone again. No, he concluded, she was not his type.

It occurred to him that at 68 he was too old to pursue such speculations, and yet he tried to imagine how she might be viewing him. As simply another potential customer? A senior but still handsome male? A wrinkled old retiree? Wondering what sort of person he might be?

He felt slightly discomfited that she would read his mind and found it hard to concentrate on her sales pitch.

He was being stupid, he reminded himself. Close to forty years separated them and she wore a wedding ring. Why should she see him as anything other than a rather senile old man? He knew he looked his age. One glance at the mirror as he shaved in the morning sufficed to tell him the truth he was reluctant to accept, namely that despite his trim figure, tall upright posture and almost full head of grey hair, he could not deny the encroaching years. He could not hide the age spots becoming noticeable on the back of his hands; the sagging of the skin around his face, the bags under his eyes visible to anyone who cared to look closely. The wrinkles around his neck had gotten deeper and more pronounced.

He pushed himself to pay attention to what she was telling him. There was nothing new in her informal presentation; nothing so far he had not heard on his previous visit. It all sounded so attractive—the communal dining room, open for breakfast, lunch and dinner. The health club facilities with massage service. The indoor swimming pool. Sauna and whirlpool. The many group activities. The Towers' weekly speaker's program to keep the residents entertained or to enhance their knowledge of topical subjects. The limo-on-demand availability to take one shopping, dining or to the theater or concert. The wireless internet connectivity throughout the buildings. Maid and laundry service. The barber shop. In house mini-market and library. The proximity to the center of town. The magnificent view of the ocean and the coastline from many of the units. And critical, given his age, the assisted living option or full time care being offered meant he would never have to move again should he decide to become a resident.

"What I should also point out," Sybil went on to explain, "is that in building this facility, we have tried to take the future health status of our residents into account—the day they reach the point where little considerations become important in maintaining a safe environment for them. To this end, we have installed three separate, strategically located panic buttons in each unit with which immediate help can be summoned. The showers have an extra wide door and no sill so they can be entered in a wheelchair. Sturdy handicap bars are in both the shower and throughout the bathroom. All doors in the apartments are designed for wheelchair passage. Even the light switches and climate controls are low enough to be handily accessible from a wheelchair."

Shad listened silently, absorbing the information but unable to get excited. It sounded too familiar. Not only had he heard this from her before, but he had also browsed through the Towers' website. While impressed by how well thought out everything seemed to be, the talk about wheelchairs depressed him. He knew all too well that the elucidated amenities could eventually stand him in good stead; that he might not be able to live without them in some hopefully distant future. He also knew he should decide to move *now*, while still healthy and in full command of his mental capacities. Time and again he had read how critical an early decision was on coping with old age's infirmities; not to wait until he could no longer make an informed and sound decision on his own behalf.

He attempted to change subjects. He felt too dynamic and healthy to seriously entertain dire prospects, but Sybil was not to be deterred.

"We want our residents to feel alive," she assured him. "To force them, if you will, to make daily decisions on what gives them the greatest pleasure and satisfaction. To think about whether they want to attend a lecture, play shuffleboard or a board game, go for an escorted walk, or take our bus to a museum or shopping center. The Towers are not in any way comparable to the older retirement facilities you may have seen. We have positioned ourselves to be a Continuing Care Retirement Community, going way beyond the obsolete perception of an old age home. We cater to the 62 and older people who want to downsize and have maintenance free, carefree living. When you reside here you should feel as if you were staying in a five star luxury resort hotel, but without the hustle and bustle and traffic and anonymity of such a complex. We are a vibrant apartment community where seniors are surrounded by their peers and enjoy themselves in innumerable ways, but still have the privacy of their own residence. We go to great lengths to make sure people don't just sit in their rocking chairs waiting for their end to come."

She smiled brightly at him. No doubt she believed every word of what she said, but Shad's thoughts had wandered.

"Is the massage service you mentioned only available in the health club? Or also in the apartments?"

"I suppose you could have one in your unit, if our massage therapist was willing, but the residents who avail themselves of this service tend to combine it with their work-outs and make use of our specifically designed massage room," she said.

"I see. And what types of massages do you offer?"

"What types?" she echoed. The smile had left her face. She didn't like questions she could not answer knowledgably.

"Yes, could I have a choice of, let's say, Swedish? Thai? Whole body? Deep tissue? Hot stone? Relaxing? Sport? Japanese? Oil?"

Her body language showed she was uncomfortable with this line of questioning. "I regret I really don't know," she said. "I am not sure I knew there were so many different ones. No one has ever asked. I would have to assume it would be the traditional kind of therapeutic one you could get in many health clubs, but then again I expect this would be up to the masseuse and her qualifications."

Shad enjoyed seeing Sybil squirm. He smiled, giving her to understand he was deliberately baiting her. The subject awoke memories of the massages he had enjoyed throughout his years of traveling, going back to his early military days in Asia, suddenly remembering Mai, but these nostalgic ruminations were just another irrelevant distraction.

"What else can I tell you that would help you to make the right decision?" Sybil asked. The smile was plastered back on her face. "Any concerns I can address?"

"Not really," he said and lapsed into silence.

Why am I hesitating? Shad asked himself for the umpteenth time. When his friend Thomas had faced the same situation a year ago, he had pushed him to accept the offer, telling him that as a recent widower he would be much better off in this senior citizen community than in his sprawling single family house on the slopes of Mount Soledad he had called home for the past twenty years. Shad had pointed out to Thomas he would no longer be alone. That he would not have to drive anymore, with his deteriorating eyesight and hearing and slower reflexes. That he would not have to take care of cooking his own meals; he could eat in the dining room of the Tranquil Towers. No more grocery shopping. Being able to travel without concerns of what might be happening to his house and garden in his absence.

Thomas had hesitated as much as Shad was doing now, similarly procrastinating endlessly, coming up with one silly reason after another not to move. Shad had not understood Thomas' irresolution then, but now that he faced the same turning point in his life, he did. What had finally led Thomas to moving into the Towers? Had he convinced himself the time had come, or had he merely bowed to the pressure of his adult children and friends? Shad made a mental note to ask him.

As for Shad himself, the sudden death of his wife Veronica eight months ago had changed his own circumstances dramatically. A year ago, with her by his side and both of them apparently healthy, it had been easy to conclude that a move into a retirement home was premature. Now, alone and still mourning, he was telling himself the same things he had told Thomas, and yet, just like Thomas, he found it extraordinarily difficult to wrap his mind around uprooting himself.

"The one thing that has changed since you were here last year, Mr. Cooper," Sybil intruded, "is our fee structure."

"Prices have gone up?"

"Not really, but we have learned that the 'one size fits all' approach is no longer ideal. We have introduced flexibility into our one time entrance fee to meet the diverse wishes of our customers. Depending on how long you expect to live—rather than actuarial life expectancy—you can choose among various options. If you pay the maximum entrance fee, it is fully refundable to your heirs upon your death. At the minimum level—fifty percent of the maximum—it becomes non-refundable. Intermediate steps are also possible. The same individuality applies to the monthly charge we levy. While the basic fee can increase by two to three percent per year, depending on cost of living indices, the actual amount you would have to pay depends on what you would like to have included."

Shad frowned. "What does that mean?"

"For instance, you could have needed nursing care covered, but some clients prefer to take out a stand alone insurance policy. Or our meal plan: you could opt for anything from zero to three meals a day. Or you could pay as you go. Whatever best suits you. The complete new pricing structure is outlined in this brochure."

Ms. Delatour pointed to the price scales of the brochure, highlighting the various options before once more emphasizing the proximity to restaurants, grocery stores, shops and the "downtown" area.

The Towers were expensive, even by La Jolla's high standards, as Shad already knew. It wasn't a question of money for him, however.

Hadn't been for Thomas either. Both were fortunate enough to eliminate fees as an issue.

"You may need a little time to decide which payment option would work best for you," Sybil said when he did not react to the pricing table in front of him. "I would also encourage you," she went on, "to query some of our residents personally to see how they like living here and what they think of our organized activities."

"Good idea." He hesitated momentarily before continuing. "Tell me, I find the sight of so many residents shuffling along on walkers or being confined to wheelchairs rather depressing. Have you ever considered establishing separate wings to keep the independent occupants apart from the physically impaired?"

"We have, because we understand the matter, but the Department of Justice has ruled this would violate their Fair Housing policy, so we are legally prevented from doing it."

He was still listening to her with only one ear. He kept analyzing his indecisiveness instead. It was his fear of giving up familiarity. Exchanging the known for the unknown. The significant downsizing and with it, having to give up so many of his prized possessions, collected from around the world over many decades. His extensive library. The feeling he would be parting with his freedom and independence. The trepidation at the thought of having to pack and move. The heart wrenching difficulty of deciding what to take along and what to abandon, and what to do with the latter. In short, the same subjective struggles he had helped Thomas to resolve. And yet he suspected the time was right for him, just as it had been for Thomas. He needed to be among people. He spent too much time being alone, feeling sorry for himself and despondent in his isolation.

Looking at himself as dispassionately as he knew how, he had to admit he was at risk of becoming a hermit; a complete recluse. It had been his wife Veronica who had made and cultivated their friendships. The number of true friends he had was marginal, with Thomas—ten years older—at the top of the very short list. Seen as an extrovert by outsiders, only he knew how inherently shy he actually was and how difficult it was for him to initiate and maintain friendships.

"Why don't we look at a couple of the units still available?" Sybil suggested, interrupting his meanderings.

Shad nodded and stood up. It took a moment for the persistent ache in his right thigh to abate so he could walk comfortably, without limping. Perhaps his pain was the result of asking too much of his aging body by running every afternoon.

Sybil's incessant chatter started grating on his nerves. There wasn't anything new she could tell or show him. The revised pricing philosophy would need to be considered, but for now, he much preferred to be left alone with his thoughts. He already knew which apartment layout, if any, he wanted. The corner penthouse design, with its nearly 2300 square feet and its two large balconies running around the sides, was all he was willing to entertain. From one side he could enjoy the view of the pacific to the west and the magnificent north shore, with Scripps Pier in the distance. From the other veranda, off towards the northeast, he could gaze upon the low mountains with their cluster of magnificent houses rising up from the long La Jolla Shores beach, hugging the slopes and interspersed with lush vegetation. Yes, these would be views he would never tire of, no matter how long he would sit outside and stare at the water and the breaking waves. The constant stream of walkers, joggers and bikers passing by, the surfers patiently riding their boards, waiting for the right wave, and the captivating scenery would always enchant him.

Of the three units Sybil insisted on showing him, only the penthouse met his expectations, just as he had known it would. He told her so.

"How much time do I have to decide?" he asked when they were back downstairs, standing in the lobby.

"Quite frankly, I don't know. Several people have expressed interest, but no one has made a deposit yet. It could happen today or tomorrow, or it could be weeks. I would urge you to play it safe and make a commitment soonest. With the payment of a $100,000 deposit, we could hold it for you for three months, and if you then decided not to take it after all, your money would be fully refunded. Does that sound fair to you?"

"I guess so. Let me think about it," he said. He was pleasantly surprised at her honesty. He had expected her to tell him that a decision had to be made immediately. That the unit was as good as sold to someone else unless he acted at once. "I am going to see if my friend Thomas Grady happens to be at home," he added. "I want to talk to him."

"I understand. I think you will find he is quite happy here now, after his initial misgivings. Why don't you take this informational material with you to study, and then you can give me a call with either questions you might still have, or—better yet—to set up a meeting so we can finalize the paperwork for the option. I know you would absolutely love living in the Towers."

With that she gave him a dazzling smile, turned, and set off towards her office. Shad's eyes followed her. She had nice legs and he liked the lithe swaying of her hips as she walked away. He continued watching her as he waited for the elevator to arrive until she had turned the corner of the hallway and was out of sight. He rode the elevator up to Thomas's apartment.

"Hey, Thomas," he said when his friend answered his doorbell. "I hope you don't mind my dropping by unannounced."

"No, no, not at all. Come on in. It's always good to see you, Shad. How have you been?"

"Ok, I guess. I just took another tour of the building with Sybil. She is really pushing me to make up my mind."

"Yes, she can be rather persuasive, can't she? Which unit are you considering?"

"The penthouse next to yours. Same layout as yours, as you probably know, except that it faces west and north, so I can see the ocean and the hills and houses rising up from La Jolla Shores."

"Well, you can't beat the view from up here, that's for sure. The whole facility does indeed offer all the advantages and amenities Sybil outlined. And it goes without saying that it would be great to have you as my immediate, adjacent neighbor."

Shad smiled. "Do I detect a 'but' in your statement?" he said.

Thomas hesitated before replying. "Yes, I suppose so. The problem is that it still doesn't feel like *home*, if you know what I mean. At least not for me, not yet after nine months. I still catch myself occasionally wondering whether or not I shouldn't simply move back into my old place. This is no more than an apartment, after all, a place I essentially rent—not own—and despite the fact that everything is taken care of and available, I miss my house. And my Pam. I still find myself talking to her; wondering how she would like living here."

"Well, I can relate to that, what with Veronica no longer by my side. If Pam were still alive, I suppose the point would be moot. You would most likely still be in your old house; just like I wouldn't be considering moving if Veronica was still here."

"Probably. What I struggle with is that just because there are lots of other people in the building, this does not mean I am not lonely. On the contrary, I would almost say. The more surrounded I am by people, especially couples, the more I realize how alone I am. Oh, I mean it's nice to be able to go down to the dining room and eat with other residents when I don't want to go out for dinner, but overall I find the whole atmosphere tends to be somewhat depressing. You walk down the hallway to the dining room, and everyone seems to be on a walker or in a wheelchair or at least using a cane. I mean, the people here are *old*."

Shad struggled to suppress a smile. He looked at Thomas and saw him for what he had become: an old man. Mentally alert and physically able to enjoy life, but seemingly to have shrunk with age. His sparse white hair barely covered his skull. He had lost weight and was no longer just slim, but skinny to the point of being a collection of skin and bones. He was wearing a short sleeved shirt, and when he raised his elbows, the skin under his upper arms sagged down loosely; flabby and severely wrinkled. His posture still straight, he had apparently lost a couple of inches in height. In short, he had become a small, frail gnome and when Shad saw him walking around, he constantly worried that Thomas would stumble and fall. Only his ready smile and charming demeanor had not left him, and he still dressed impeccably. It was typical for Thomas to think of himself as being too young to fit in with the walking dead inhabitants of the Towers. Just as Shad thought of his own age.

"Sure they are old, Thomas, but then you have to remember that we are too."

"Not *that* old," he protested. "I certainly don't feel I belong here, age wise; I feel too young."

Shad understood. He didn't doubt that strangers who saw him also considered him to be older than he felt. He remembered his mother, when she was well into her upper sixties, driving and complaining about those "old ladies" behind the wheels of their cars with their erratic style. Neither he nor his siblings had had the courage to point out to her that she too was an old lady.

"And then there is this name tag rule," Thomas continued, "every time you leave your quarters you are supposed to be wearing your name tag. I mean, it can be helpful, but it's also a not so subtle reminder that everyone is presumed to be too old to remember the names of the people they see."

"I follow you. It's like being a visitor rather than a resident."

"Exactly," Thomas said, "it's all part of living here, but not being at home."

"So what do you think I should do, Thomas? We have known each other for more than twenty five years now and you know me better than anyone. Tell me the truth. Do you think I could be happy here?"

"I wish I knew, but it's just too hard to say. You could stay where you are and consider doing what you always pushed me to do: hire a factotum who could drive you around as needed, cook some simple meals for you, take care of your shopping, maintain your yard, and generally look after you. I think that some of the issues I have to deal with here would apply to you as well. You are still ten years younger. That probably makes you more flexible than I am. You would have more time to get used to a new lifestyle, so you might have fewer difficulties adjusting to this radically different environment than I am having, but whether you live here or at home is not going to make much difference when it comes to the feeling of solitude. Let's face it: we are both widowers and alone, no matter where we live. The key difference is a technical one. Living in your own house means having to take care of a lot of things, giving you responsibilities and chores, rather than sitting around here with nothing to do."

"I understand that," Shad said, "but by the same token, as you mentioned, our age difference would give me more time to get used to apartment living again. I would guess that the older I get, the fussier I would become, and the more difficult it would be for me to adjust to new surroundings."

"That's what I meant about you being more flexible," Thomas interjected.

Shad nodded. "I am not really crazy anymore about having to take care of house and garden," he admitted. "It's quickly becoming onerous. Maybe residing here would even address one of my biggest concerns, namely facing the day when I can no longer drive anymore. The thought of losing my independence, having my car keys taken away from me, terrifies me. Living here, in the center of things, so to speak, might make it less painful not to be allowed to drive."

He paused, gathering his thoughts before continuing. "But I guess that's something we all have to come to grips with sooner or later in any case. I know you are struggling with it right now. Anyway, I am wondering if you could tell me where you see the biggest advantages of living here, Thomas, now that you have been settled in for some months."

"Sure. That's easy to say. Most important to me is the safety issue; safety in the sense of knowing that help is just the push of a button away. Being able to page a nurse, if needed, at a moment's notice. People checking up on you regularly to make sure you haven't died. Then there is the meal service. You know I can't cook, and when I don't have a date or don't feel like going out to eat by myself, it's great to be able to go downstairs and have lunch or dinner—or breakfast, for that matter. And I like the feeling that I can just lock my door and leave if I want to go on a trip, without having to worry about house or garden. Plus, the people who live here are actually quite nice."

"And the disadvantages?" Shad said.

"Like I said, it doesn't feel like home yet. The overall atmosphere of the building can be depressing. Dinner service ends at 7:00pm, whereas I normally would not eat before 8:00 or even later. It's an apartment, not a house. I miss the high ceilings we had. The relatively small sizes bother me—remember it's only half the square footage I used to have."

"But surely it's more than adequate for someone living alone," Shad said.

"Yes, of course," Thomas acknowledged, "but I am spoiled and used to the wide open spaces of my house. And then I miss having my old neighbors around. I worry about turning my TV or stereo on too loud; when it's quiet, I can hear my neighbor's television or music. You have to remember that three of the four penthouses up here are now occupied. There is a certain lack of privacy because I can sometimes hear my two neighbors coming or going, and I am sure they can hear me. And living here hasn't dispelled my loneliness. I don't know. Sometimes I go so far as to ask myself whether or not it was right of me to have left Hong Kong in the first place. I loved that city. Maybe I should have moved back there."

"You grew to love New York and La Jolla as well," Shad pointed out. "In any case, I think you did the right thing by accepting the promotion to the home office in New York all those years ago, especially since you hadn't gotten over Jade's sudden death yet. At the time and under the circumstances, the move was the best thing that could have happened to you."

"You may be right. It certainly put me on the track to financial independence, and if I had stayed in Hong Kong, I never would have met and fallen in love with Pam so soon after Jade's death."

Thomas paused, lost in memories, before finally continuing. "Anyway, this has nothing to do with what you were asking me about the shortcomings I see of living in the Towers. Does any of what I said make sense to you?"

"Yes, it does, and it worries me," Shad said. "It reminds me of why I still have problems getting used to being retired, even though I haven't worked for more than four years now. Having first given up my job and still adjusting to that and then losing Veronica so soon and unexpectedly has really messed up my life."

"Well, I certainly understand all too well what you mean about Veronica, but you also still miss going to work?"

"Depends on what you call going to work. I certainly don't miss being awakened by my alarm clock and having to be in the office every morning, or attending endless meetings, or having to deal with company politics and all the bullshit that goes on there. But I miss the traveling. Working with our people overseas. The sense of responsibility and accomplishment. The feeling I did something which made a difference. The growth and development of people. The problem solving—especially from the human resource side. Plus having a purpose in life." He paused briefly. "I think that's the hardest part," he went on, "not knowing what I want to do with the rest of my life; asking myself why I am still around. What difference am I going to make to anyone in the next years now that Veronica is gone? Who am I going to "touch", as obituaries so frequently mention?"

"Oh, come on, Shad. Don't get all depressed on me. Surely it's not *that* bad. It's time for you to enjoy life, rather than being morose. Appreciate your freedom and independence as I do. Be happy you are totally free to pursue what you like without having to explain or justify. Be glad the pressure you were under all your professional life is history now."

"I do appreciate all that. And I am not really depressed. More like sad. Lacking in purpose. Asking myself why I should stay in shape and watch my health. Would any woman take notice of the fact that I am physically fit? What difference would it really make—and to whom—if I were to suddenly die?"

"I think you are way off base, Shad. People need you, and appreciate you, much more so than you realize or give them credit for. Believe me, I know your friends and I know what you mean to them."

Shad shrugged. "Perhaps," he said, "but I keep being reminded of something I read somewhere years ago, namely that a person needs three things for happiness: someone to love; something to do; something to look forward to. I guess I would add a fourth point: to be loved by someone. I know this is a gross simplification, but the more I think about it, the more I feel it applies to me. I know I am fortunate enough to love and be loved by my relatives, if no one else. Where my problem comes in is with points two and three. The last one gives me the biggest headache, and as a result, I guess I am unsure of how much I still enjoy life, beyond the simple daily pleasures of a good meal or a glass of wine or walking along the ocean. I see only emptiness ahead. I stare into a void, a huge sphere of nothingness. A never ending tunnel. I look into the future but I see only impenetrable fog. No challenge. No reward. No satisfaction. When I stopped working, I didn't realize I would not just retire from my job, but also from my friends, the Far East, traveling, a lifestyle, exotic restaurants, luxurious hotels, first class flying, and recognition. It was a shock for me to have to accept that so many of the friendships I thought I had were strictly related to my job and position."

"That's certainly a shame," Thomas said, "but that's a fact of life you have to accept. As for the traveling, there is nothing stopping you from continuing to do that, and in the same style you are used to. You can afford it, after all. What you need are some engrossing, time consuming hobbies or interests so that you don't have time to feel sorry for yourself because you are too bored."

"You are right," Shad conceded, "but I haven't been able to come up with any. I could never develop enthusiasm for golf. I am not all that crazy about movies or watching TV. I have never developed a passion for opera or ballet, and one or two concerts or plays a month are more than ample for me. I can't think of anything I would like to start collecting. I don't want to tie myself down by volunteering for some organization which would require me to be at a certain time and place every day or week. I never liked studying, so I don't want to go back to college. You are right about the traveling, of course, and yet I hesitate because I am not sure that traveling by myself would be all that much fun. I've thought about going on a group tour, or a cruise, but I never could stand those organized excursions. They shepherd you around, lecture you on what you are seeing and then take you to some local shop or factory where they want you to buy touristy souvenirs. So that only leaves me with reading, which is the one thing I have always enjoyed, but even that has its limitations. I mean, how many hours or days can I spend reading? And what do I do when my eyesight becomes too poor for me to read?"

"Start buying audio books," Thomas said, chuckling. "You also enjoy good restaurants and wine, and there is no shortage of those around here."

"That's true," Shad laughed, shaking off his despondency, "but whenever I eat a good meal these days I think about how to get rid of all those calories I am taking on. Anyway, I have been talking too much. It's a side effect of spending so much time alone with no one to listen to me. The moment I get an audience I seem to develop acute oral diarrhea."

Thomas laughed. "Not to worry, Shad. It was good to hear you have the same issues to contend with I did."

3

Los Angeles/Korea/Vietnam 1958-1964

From the cheap studio apartment he had rented in Los Angeles, using the money his mother had clandestinely given him, he studied the daily obituaries until he found a deceased that met his criteria. The eighteen year old Shad Cooper staring back at Roger from the newspaper had died in a tragic traffic accident. Physically the two bore little resemblance to one another, but Shad's obituary included the background vitals Roger needed to apply for an official duplicate birth certificate: names of parents (both deceased); date and place of birth.

Roger began implementing his plan of becoming Shad Cooper. For all practical purposes, Roger Stevens ceased to exist. Using a typewriter in the local library he labored over the right words with which to request a duplicate of Shad Cooper's birth certificate. The letter, explaining that his parents had died and he could not find his original birth certificate needed to register with his local draft board, together with a $15 money order, he sent off to the county registrar.

He concentrated on thinking of himself as Shad Cooper and waited impatiently for the essential document. He had no idea how long it would take. He worried endlessly about questions coming back. He watched nervously every time a car pulled up to his apartment complex, fearing a visit from someone coming to verify the legitimacy of his request. The occasional police car cruising through the neighborhood made him apprehensive. No one except his mother knew where he was hiding. His escape had not been covered by the press except for a brief write-up under the heading of "Police Blotter" in the local paper.

Nevertheless he only went out after dark to buy groceries. He did not frequent any restaurants; did not have a car. He had not learned to cook. Dull hunger pains were steady companions. He longed for a decent hot meal instead of the endless parade of sandwiches facing him for lunch and dinner. Only when he considered the alternative facing him—county jail—could he overcome his depressions and nervousness.

He was endlessly grateful that neither Maude nor her daughter had given him up. He speculated whether this was due to some exaggerated sense of independence, a liking for him, or if they simply had not heard about his fugitive status. After all, neither of the two guards responsible for allowing his escape, nor their supervisor, were likely to be nominated as Deputy of the Year. Instead they would have a vested interest in keeping his escape as low key as possible.

He was elated when the birth certificate, duly notarized as being an official, true and correct copy, finally arrived. His transformation to Shad Cooper, not wanted by the police, had been legitimized. He wasted no time calling his mother from a pay phone to ask her to meet him at the Department of Motor Vehicles with her car so he could take his driver's license road test. He did not want to take the risk of his mother being followed by the police if she picked him up.

He arrived early enough to study the driver's handbook to refresh his memory of the applicable laws. By the time his mother arrived he had taken and passed the written examination and was awaiting his turn for the road test. No problem. He knew how to drive and what infractions the examiner looked for. A temporary license was issued to him at the successful conclusion of the test and his permanent one would be mailed to him within a month, the clerk assured him.

He assumed the original Shad Cooper had been a law abiding citizen and had therefore registered for the draft immediately after celebrating his eighteenth birthday. Roger wrote to the draft board as Shad Cooper, enclosing a photocopy of his birth certificate and temporary driver's license, and advising them he had lost his wallet and with it, his Selective Service registration card. Would they please issue him a duplicate, since he was toying with the idea of joining the Army? The new card was sent promptly.

With the draft card he now had Shad Cooper's social security number and he requested a duplicate card, his original having been lost. The administration complied.

One final item was still missing to complement his personal background. Shad's high school was accommodating when he requested a notarized copy of his diploma and school transcript. Shad had been a good student, as his grades attested. The school did not question his story of how the original had been inadvertently tossed out with his old school papers.

He marveled at how suspiciously easy it had been for him to obtain the vital documentation proving he was Shad Cooper. He had feared there would be safeguards or routine checks to prevent fraud. But he was not about to complain. He had no idea whether a methodology was in place for bureaucracies to cross check reported deaths against requests for duplicate documents.

His assumed identity was established. Within three months of his escape he had become Shad Cooper, properly documented. He found a new, non-descript apartment. He did not leave a forwarding address, adding another safety layer to his existence. He felt reasonably safe for the first time and his outlook improved dramatically.

He continued to be careful about staying in touch with his mother. The police had visited her periodically and made follow-up phone calls to her but had to accept her assurance she had not heard from her son and had no idea where he might be living, assuming he was still alive. He could not imagine her phone being tapped or being under surveillance. But he erred on the side of caution and did not visit her and insisted she only call him from a pay phone if she needed to get in touch with him. The money she continued to provide was handed over personally in a busy post office, at a time and date previously agreed upon. The amounts of cash varied and were given irregularly so as not to create suspicion if the police were to check on his mother's bank account activities.

He was ready to continue his incarnation as Shad Cooper. The endless days of waiting, while painstakingly establishing his identity, had given him ample time to consider his short term options and what they might lead to long term. Unlike so many of his friends in high school, he had never had a clear vision of what he wanted to do with his life; which profession he wished to pursue. And that was before his life took a turn he could never have imagined when he had ended the torture his stepfather had inflicted on him. Now, as convicted felon and escapee, but with a new and—he hoped—ironclad identity, he was even less sure of what might appeal to him in the way of work. Many hours of soul searching had led him to conclude it would be safest if he submersed himself in a huge, largely anonymous organization, and there was none more so to the outside world, he felt, than the military.

The army recruiter was happy to sign him up. The "police action" in Korea was officially over but the US maintained a huge military presence in South Korea. No one knew when the negotiated cease fire might be violated, with renewed hostilities flaring up. Waiting to be drafted and sent to Korea as part of the infantry was not something normal eighteen year olds anticipated eagerly. Consequently, the recruiter was delighted to have a volunteer willing to join the infantry. The paperwork he submitted was copied and accepted as being in good order. He concentrated on being called Shad and responding unhesitatingly to his new name.

Joining the army had not been an easy decision for him. Doubts had existed. He worried about having to deal with the strict discipline the military would impose on him. He was still painfully aware of how he had finally snapped under his stepfather's punishments for perceived insubordination, and he would surely be repeatedly exposed to unsavory orders as a soldier. Harassment, especially in the critical first months, was inevitable, and he wondered if he could accept this stoically. Had he gained sufficient maturity to handle whatever the army drill instructors might throw at him? Juvenile detention had forced him to learn how to survive in a strictly regimented environment, and he believed nothing the army could do to him could be worse than what he had already endured.

This attitude stood him in good stead as he went through basic training in Fort Ord and then advanced infantry training in Fort Hood. He received the highest possible ratings in both courses.

It had taken him longer than anticipated to accept his new identity as second nature. During his first weeks in uniform he occasionally failed to react promptly when his name was called out. Awkward moments had arisen when unexpected questions were raised by new friends regarding his background and family. He had learned to answer spontaneously with whatever lies came to mind and hoped to remember what stories he had invented.

By the time he left Fort Hood for Korea, his new name had become firmly ingrained and Roger Stevens had all but been forgotten. It did not even feel strange to him when he received mail from his mother addressed to Shad Cooper. What he could not forget was what he had done. Neither his killing nor his escape, and both continued to weigh heavily on him whenever he had time to reflect. He had committed the gravest of sins. A guilty conscience had become his steady companion, a burden that would not go away. No amount of rationalizing helped him. Had he really been justified in doing what he had done? His mother thought so; she had been tempted more than once to do what he had done, suffering from her husband's abuse as much or more as he had. She looked ten years younger now, almost a year after the event, and had a steady boyfriend who treated her well.

But he agonized over his personality incessantly. He had read that only a psychopath acted without thinking of the consequences of his actions. He had acted impulsively, without considering what this would mean for him. Psychopathic behavior? The guilty conscience now plaguing him would seem to preclude this, as would the fact he knew he had sinned in the worst possible way, and yet he was unsure of what he was.

He became nearly obsessed with the desire to find out if there was a statute of limitations on prison break and how long that might be, if indeed there was one at all. But he did not know how to find out and was afraid to ask. To try and forget, Shad plunged into military life with a vengeance and became a model soldier. Military life was frequently harsh, but usually fair, he thought.

While the military and political conditions in Korea were still tense, he loved being stationed in Seoul. Everything was strange and exotic, and just strolling through Itaewon on a Saturday afternoon and studying the crowds pushing their way through this shopping paradise thrilled him. Unbelievable selections of merchandise at even more unbelievable prices. Name brand knock-offs were stacked to the ceilings of stalls and shops. Traders showed they were willing to be flexible on pricing at the slightest hint of interest by a potential customer. He bought more than he needed, it was so much fun.

And then there were the local girls. He had never seen so many absolutely beautiful young women and he made no secret of staring admiringly at them. Predominantly short skirted, with lustrous long black hair and promising black almond shaped eyes, incredibly white skin and carefully made up faces, there was an exotic oriental beauty to them he found unbelievably appealing.

Eventually he learned that many of these girls worked in the dozens of bars along the narrow side streets, catering to American soldiers, but this did not distract him from looking at them longingly.

The only thing he could have done without in Korea was the extreme weather. The fiercely cold winter, with heavy snow and an icy wind whistling down the Han river penetrated even the warmest clothes. Spring and fall were beautiful, but the suffocating heat of the summer was as hard to escape as the numbing cold of the winter.

His twelve months tour of duty in Korea passed all too quickly. It was tough for him to say good-bye to Jun, the tearful Korean girl friend he had found and who had loved him so tenderly and unconditionally. He swore he would come back to her as soon as his three years in the army were up. Less than eighteen more months, he told her, and she promised to wait for him.

The next twelve months, based at Fort Riley, Kansas, were a bore after the excitement of Korea. The end of his initial enlistment period was approaching and he did not know what he wanted to do. What sort of job might beckon to him upon discharge? How risky would it be for him in civilian life, with the police presumably still looking for him? He felt safe and at home in the army.

After months of soul searching, he decided to re-enlist and volunteer for Ranger school. Jun, waiting for him in Seoul, had swayed him. He wanted to be with her again, and since he did not have the means to have her come visit him, he hoped the army would send him back for a second deployment. If that happened and their love remained unabated, he wanted her to apply for US residency. Contemplating a life together would only be realizable if he had something to offer her, and the security of a military career beckoned as his most viable option. Applying for Ranger school was viewed positively. His re-enlistment and becoming a Ranger proved to the army he was serious about a long term commitment.

There were many days during Ranger training when he regretted his decision, but they were quickly forgotten when he graduated among the top of his class. For the first time in his life he was truly proud of something he had achieved. The hardships and trials of the ranger course had been like atonement for the crimes he had committed. A down payment on his debt to society.

He volunteered to be sent back to Korea, but the army had other plans for him. The need for Rangers in Korea was minimal; an urgent requirement existed in Vietnam.

He was dismayed when his orders came through to join the Military Advisor Group in South Vietnam to help train their army. He had barely enough time to write Jun with the disappointing news before shipping out.

Although continuing to pine for Jun in Seoul, he quickly found Vietnam and its exotic environment and people exciting. He embraced the challenge of working with the local military—not that he could comprehend the, to him, strange mentalities and attitudes he had to deal with on a daily basis. Once he finally realized he had to accept them for what they were—different; not better, not worse—he got along with them famously and became a highly respected member of the training group. This helped him to distinguish himself and he was encouraged to apply for the Special Forces then coming into existence when the end of his twelve months tour of duty loomed.

It was not that difficult a decision for him. He still had nearly two years to go on his re-enlistment. He liked being in Vietnam. His girl friend Jun in Korea had found someone else and he had fallen in love with a beautiful Vietnamese girl, Mai, in Saigon. Signing up for the Special Forces would mean he could be back in country within months, and surely Mai would wait for him? He knew he did not have exclusive rights to her, since she worked in the health club of the Rex Hotel and gave provocative massages to whoever wanted one, but their relationship was somehow special, he felt.

The club had been recommended to him by a friend, and after his first visit he could understand why. After enjoying her adroit hands for an hour and talking to her, she had agreed to meet him after hours, and for a generous tip to cover her taxi fare back home had taken him to a one hour hotel. He was sure he had arrived in heaven. Now he saw her whenever he could come to Saigon from his field assignment, and she swore she loved him desperately and exclusively. The way she treated him made this easy to believe.

While he considered the Special Forces, he also reminded himself that he was still wanted by the police and wondered how actively they might be searching for him. The military career he had embarked upon, he was sure, remained the best option in protecting his freedom.

What he didn't know was whether he could survive Special Forces training. He had learned they had an incredibly high wash-out rate. But even if he didn't make it, he concluded, he would still be a Ranger. He applied, was accepted, and six months later graduated, ready to return to Vietnam.

By then, President Kennedy had increased America's presence in Vietnam to 16,000 troops, and Shad was recruited into the Delta Force through the CIA as a member of its clandestine Special Activities Division. He was embedded with the Montagnard tribesmen being infiltrated from Laos into Vietnam. He would have preferred to be closer to Saigon and Mai, rather than in the highlands close to the 17th Parallel, but he took comfort in the fact that the CIA had surely checked his background thoroughly before inviting him into the vaunted Delta Force and had come up with nothing suspicious. This was a tremendous relief to him and he was sure now the police would never find him. But fighting and living alongside the Montagnards in the mountain jungles of Vietnam was so demanding and dangerous he often wished he had served out his time in prison instead.

Shad distinguished himself within the Special Activities Division and as a member of the MAC-V "Studies and Observation Group" to which he had subsequently been delegated. Although officially under Army command, the CIA field operatives supervised the strategic action plans and Shad had come to their attention. Apparently they liked what they had observed. As a result, at the conclusion of his second tour, he was asked in 1964 to go on special assignment to Iran, officially as a member of the Army Map Service, but actually for clandestine activities orchestrated by the CIA.

He accepted with alacrity despite having to leave Mai behind and maybe never seeing her again. As much as she had given him and the happiness she had provided with her unmitigated passion, he was realistic enough to recognize they had no meaningful future together. Culturally and mentally they were worlds apart. She was not devoted exclusively to him. He knew he would get over her almost as quickly as she would forget him.

And he was unable to think of an alternative existence that would keep him off the police's radar screen. How better to be shielded than to be working secretly for the CIA? And it might even eventually offer him an entry into civilian life, with service for the CIA and a distinguished military career on his CV.

4

While talking with Thomas, Shad became aware of the afternoon drawing to a close. A long walk along the ocean beckoned. He stood up to leave.

"Be sure to stop by when you come back to see Sybil again, Shad."

"I will. As soon as I make up my mind or have something else to discuss with her." He bid his friend so long.

As he left the building his legs took on a life of their own, leading him around the Towers complex to the sidewalk skirting the shore line. He was lost in his memories of a world he no longer had. He found himself remembering Jun in Korea and Mai in Saigon and speculated on where life might have taken them. He felt vindicated for having abandoned them in favor of his military future, which had eventually allowed him to become successful in business and brought him to where he was today: financially secure. If he had not chosen the army career when he did, who knew if or when the police might have caught up with him? How his life would have turned out if he had been sent back to jail for who knew how many years?

As it was, he felt safe from pursuit and kept on walking, trying not to think of how old and out of the mainstream he had become. He was of no interest to anyone anymore, he felt, except maybe Sybil Delatour, for whom he was a potential customer.

He asked himself how he could go about making some new friends; where he could go and what he should do to meet people. It did not seem right to him to hang out in bars. That had never been his style and now he was too old to begin. He was not interested in joining one of the many senior citizen social circles beckoning. He couldn't just start chatting up women he encountered on his walks or in the supermarket. He would not have known how to go about it.

Thinking it through, it became self evident that residing in the Tranquil Towers was the logical answer to his dilemma, and he decided he had nothing to lose by making the required deposit. Although he continued to struggle with the age issue—he being so much younger and full of vitality compared to the current residents—he would be among people who did things. Took an interest in life. Were not bored. Went to concerts and the theater and on excursions. Had meals together where they could talk and laugh. Were apparently at peace with their world and accepted their health and age for what they were.

Signing the option Sybil had offered would give him three months to definitively make up his mind while protecting his right to the penthouse. What would he risk? His deposit was refundable. As soon as he was home and before he could change his mind he called Sybil. He knew the longer he waited before making a written commitment, the more he would vacillate. By signing up now he could begin to anticipate achieving the tranquility he hoped for in the Towers.

"I am sure you are making the right decision," she said when he took the visitor's chair across from her desk a day later. "You will not regret it."

She sounded extremely confident. He wished he could share her certainty. "We'll see. Don't forget I am only signing up for the 90 day option."

"I know. I have prepared the agreement. It's our standard boiler plate contract, and I have merely filled in the blanks to cover your specific requirements. Please read it through to make sure all your concerns are addressed and that you understand it."

It was not unduly long. It did not specify his payment plan of choice and Shad glanced through the legalese quickly. He only dwelled carefully on the clause outlining the terms and conditions governing termination of the agreement.

"Looks fine to me," he said when he had satisfied himself that the contract included no unacceptable risks or conditions. He signed the two copies. He wrote a check for the $100,000 deposit.

The ninety day deadline was etched on his mind. He felt the pressure mounting and his doubts returning. Had he made the right decision?

"I guess that's it then," Sybil said. "Congratulations, Mr. Cooper! We look forward very much to having you here as our resident. You are buying a beautiful unit."

"Thanks. You are assuming I will exercise my option." The doubts in his voice could not be overheard.

"Of course I am," she said, ignoring his tone. "In fact, I feel so sure that if you don't mind, I will initiate the mandatory background check on you right away so we won't have any delays when we finalize your purchase."

"Background check?" he mumbled inanely, hoping the sudden thumping of his heart could not be heard by her.

"Yes," she said brightly, "it's only a formality, of course, but we owe it to our existing residents to make sure no . . . what should I call it? Unsavory characters? Drug lords? Retired Mafia types? Whatever. That no one like that moves in here. It's really in your own best interests we do this. You have nothing to worry about."

"No, of course not," he said, hiding his concerns. He knew the re-opening of cold case files had become all the rage with law enforcement agencies throughout the states. What if some eager beaver had already started looking into the escape of a Roger Stevens again? Shad had never been able to get a definitive answer on possible statutes of limitations on prison breaks, and with the wide spread use of computer data bases, who knew what might come up? Just because the CIA had found nothing untoward nearly fifty years ago did not mean that today, living in the advanced electronic age, he would still be absolutely safe. But there was no way he could refuse to agree on the check, unless he retracted the just signed option agreement. That did not seem prudent. What sort of red flags would that raise in Sybil's mind? No. He had to believe his true past was buried so deep it would never be unearthed.

"Is there anything else I can do for you?" Sybil asked solicitously.

"What if I wanted to make some changes to the interior of the apartment?" Shad asked to distract her from any nervousness she might have sensed.

"You could do pretty much whatever you wanted. For all practical purposes, you are going to be the owner. The only difference between outright ownership and what we have here is that you can not bequeath the unit to your heirs. But as mentioned, your heirs will inherit all or part of the money you pay, depending on which entrance fee you decide on."

He nodded in understanding. "Yes, I just wanted to be sure I could make modifications."

"As soon as you have signed the final purchase agreement and financial obligations have been met, you can bring in an interior decorator and do whatever you wish. We want you to be comfortable in your new living quarters and to feel right at home."

"That's what actually worries me the most," he said, "whether or not this would feel like home."

"Well," she said, "I think you need to be realistic. It's unlikely this is going to happen as of Day One, no more so than would be the case if you bought a new house. You will need to give it a little time."

He liked her frankness, but was not sure he agreed. When he had bought his house up in Muirlands with Veronica, they had both felt truly at home the moment they had moved in. It had felt somehow right immediately.

"Yes, I understand that," he said, "but I guess I am just wondering what a 'little time' means."

"I am confident it will happen faster than you now think, based on my experience with our other residents. They feel totally at home and are very happy living in the Towers. What else can I do for you?"

"Nothing right now, I suppose." Then he reconsidered. "Oh, yes, you could do me a small favor and call Mr. Grady to see if he happens to be at home."

She did and he was, and after saying good-bye to Sybil he walked over to the elevator taking him up to Thomas' floor—soon to be his as well, he assumed, having just parted with $100,000.

"Shad, come in! What a pleasant surprise. I hadn't expected to see you again so soon," Thomas greeted him.

Shad grinned at his old friend. He felt strangely self conscious. Relieved he had made a commitment and burdened by the clock now ticking and the final decision that would be forced upon him within a definitive time frame. And worried most of all about the background check now being initiated.

"I need to talk to someone," he said. "I saw Sybil just now and signed an option agreement and gave her a check for $100,000. And I don't know how I feel about it."

"Welcome to the club. Do you think I felt any differently when I signed the papers?"

"I suppose not. But tell me, do you ever regret having done so?"

"Only about half a dozen times a day. But I still think it was the right thing for me to have done. If I hadn't, I would no doubt regret *that* as often as I do having bought in here."

"Emotions fighting facts?" Shad said.

"I guess you could call it that. But seriously, despite the downsides of living in an apartment, I firmly believe you would be doing the right thing by moving in. Eventually you are going to wind up in a retirement home anyway, assuming you live long enough," Thomas said with a smile to take the sting out of his words, "and if you view the Towers as what they are, namely a sophisticated long term retirement facility, you would not find a better one. Whether here in La Jolla or anywhere else. And the sooner you move in and adjust to your new environment, the better off you will be."

Shad wanted to believe Thomas was right. It just did not make him feel any better. He sat down and stared out the window at the distant horizon and thought of how the Pacific reached all the way to the other side of the world, to Asia, and remembered how happy he had been on his travels there, starting with his tours of duty in South Korea and Vietnam and continuing on to his very first business trip to Hong Kong and Singapore, and then the vividly memorable first journey to Beijing.

Even now, more than twenty years later, while his recollections of Korea and Vietnam had faded in details, those long ago visits to China were still so crisply alive that he had to force himself not to keep dwelling on them. The early struggles of trying to get a business started had presented him with nearly insolvable problems, but now that the high pressure times were behind him, he missed the excitement of meeting new people, visiting new countries, and making difficult decisions. Four years into retirement, no one cared anymore what he had done and achieved; remembered the challenges he had had to overcome. The personal trials he had gone through.

His life had changed dramatically. There were new and difficult personal choices to resolve that would determine how he would spend whatever time was left to him and how happy he would be. The one thing that had not changed was his struggle to see the future clearly. He recalled never quite knowing what he had wanted to do with his life after he had killed his stepfather. During his twelve years in the military he had thought he would eventually retire from the army, but after Iran, military life had become a bore and he had opted out. During his 25 years with AmeriDerm and the ten prior years with his previous employer he had tried, without success, to define what career path he wanted to pursue.

Rather than planning his future, he had let events and circumstances dictate it. Changing over to AmeriDerm—in retrospect the smartest move he could have made—would not have occurred if he had not received that fateful phone call from the headhunter at just the right time. It had been his luck—rather than good planning—that the move to AmeriDerm had been the right one at the right time. That success and fortunate circumstances had brought him promotions and recognition—and eventually financial independence—did not change the fact that he was frustrated at having left his life more to chance than to a long range plan.

He was tempted to blame this on the tragic events of his youth, which had forced him to keep the lowest possible profile and to maintain a life of secrecy and duplicity. He had lived in such latent fear of his past coming to light that he had not even dared to attend his mother's funeral when she had passed away in 1995. The only real plan he had ever had, he mused, was not to get caught, and so far at least that had worked out better than he could have hoped.

"Where are you, Shad?" He heard Thomas asking, interrupting his reveries.

Shad laughed somewhat ruefully. "Back in Beijing," he equivocated. "Remember that first visit of mine when we met with Ning Chang? How little I knew back then! I don't know if I ever told you what your help meant to me. Without you, I would have been totally lost."

"I doubt it. You would have found your way eventually. Maybe it would have taken you a little longer, and maybe AmeriDerm in China today would not be what it is, but let's face it: you were born to open up new markets. You would have succeeded without me. You were equally successful in Thailand and Korea and Taiwan and the other countries, without any help or support from me."

"That's very kind of you," Shad said, "but you give me too much credit. If I had not been able to learn from you, I would not have made it. The insights you provided into Asian cultures, business methodologies and mentalities, were invaluable to me."

"Perhaps, but I think you had a unique talent to find just the right people to work for you. Your people skills were what made you so successful."

Shad shrugged dismissively. "I think I was just lucky. Just as I was lucky to have found you when I came to Hong Kong."

"That just proves my point. You were able to tell I was the right person to help you get started. And you were always willing to listen and to ask questions. The right questions," Thomas said and glanced at his watch. "And to establish your credibility. The respect you never failed to show for foreign cultures and people was unique and not exactly typical for an American businessman. People accepted and trusted you, and without that you would not have succeeded in Asia."

"What can I say? Those feelings were genuine."

"I know," Thomas said. "Listen, I am hungry. Dinner is being served downstairs. Why don't we go there and have a bite to eat? It will give you a chance to see what the meals here are like."

"Sounds like a plan."

He got up and waited while Thomas gathered his wallet and keys.

*   *   *

The dining room on the ground floor had a pleasant décor. Large windows faced the ocean. The horizon was so clear it appeared to have been drawn with a straight edge. The sun was just touching the water. It slowly sank and began radiating its rays upwards. Perfect conditions for the famous but all too rare green flash phenomenon, Shad thought.

Fewer than half the tables were occupied. Shad had the impression that women outnumbered men by at least three or four to one; perhaps fifteen percent were couples. Very few individuals were sitting by themselves.

The tables were round, seating anywhere from four to eight people. A significant number of diners were sitting in wheelchairs. Walkers and canes were in evidence; enough to depress Shad. Everyone was wearing their white name tags. Lively conversations filled the room. Hearing problems appeared to be the norm, as evidenced by the hearing aids sprouting from people's ears. There was a steady coming and going to the buffet line, with a number of waiters hovering around it, ready to help guests in need of assistance.

Shad again thought he was too young to fit in with this decrepit population. He was still interested in more than just existing, waiting for death.

The fact that dinner was buffet style came as an unpleasant surprise to him. He had eaten at more of them than he cared to remember, and had learned that the food never tasted as good as its appearance promised. He wanted his food prepared fresh. The menus he had seen on the tables had led him to believe there was a choice of items to be ordered, and he was disappointed when he saw they merely listed what was being served at the buffet.

"Let's go over there," Thomas said, having looked around, and walked to a table facing the ocean.

"Shad, let me introduce you to a couple of friends of mine," he said when they had settled down. "These are the Radfords; Kenneth and Jerri. This is my friend Shad Cooper. He is thinking of moving into the Towers."

"Nice to meet you, Shad. Please call me Kenny." The Radfords continued eating. Thomas led Shad over to where the buffet had been set up.

It did not look bad at all, Shad had to admit, with an elaborate salad bar and among the main courses a choice of beef, fish, and chicken. The latter two were both deep fried. The dessert section was the one most devastated by the early dinner arrivals. Desserts were obviously highly desirable items.

Shad helped himself to small portions of various dishes to get a feel for the quality and taste of what was being offered. He wondered how long the food had been on the serving line and when it had been prepared.

"How long have you been living here, Kenny?" he asked when they were back at their table and the waiter had taken their order for a bottle of wine.

"Since early this year," Jerri answered on Kenny's behalf.

"And how do you like it?"

"Oh, we think it's a fabulous place. We just love it here. We couldn't imagine being anywhere else anymore," Jerri said. Kenny nodded his agreement.

"And where did you live before, if I may ask?"

"In a large house over in the Barber tract; close to La Jolla High."

Shad knew it as a comfortable area. "You seem considerably younger than most of the residents here," he observed. "Couldn't you have simply gotten a gardener or a housekeeper to look after you, rather than moving into a retirement home?"

"I suppose we could have," Kenny said, "but we talked about it and eventually concluded we did not want to leave it up to our married daughter to decide when we should take this step, and where we should go. We are in our mid-sixties and we thought this was a good age at which to get used to a dramatic change in our lives. By the time we are in our seventies, we figured, and the time came when we could no longer be alone, we might have resented whatever decision our daughter would have made, and might not have wanted to move. Fights and acrimony could have resulted. We know people where this situation has led to a permanent schism between child and parents. This way, it was our decision, and now we have enough time to get used to our new surroundings and our daughter won't have to do what could have been very difficult for her and for us."

"They take such good care of us here," Jerri added, "and there is always something to do. We love the lectures they organize a couple of times a week and enjoy so much being among people. Back in our house, it seems like we were always alone, and we didn't have any time consuming hobbies to keep us occupied."

Shad nodded thoughtfully. Their thought processes matched what he was thinking. "What about getting used to living in an apartment?" he asked. "Don't you feel rather boxed in?"

"Yes, at times," Kenny said. "You can never forget you are living in an apartment, rather than a house. There are moments we feel cooped up. But on the other hand, our unit here has the biggest balcony of the whole place. We just love to sit out there and look at the beautiful scenery and the people walking by, and when we lean over the railing, we see a little of the ocean. You should come to visit. We would love to show you how we live."

"Thank you. I would appreciate that."

"How about you, Shad?" Jerri asked. "Do you live in La Jolla now?"

"Oh, yes," he said, "I have been a resident for many years. My house is up in Muirlands, with a nice ocean view."

"And what about your wife? I assume you are married?" Jerri wanted to know.

"I am widowed."

"I am sorry," she said immediately. "I should not have pried."

No, you shouldn't have, Shad thought, but before he could say anything, she continued. "If you are alone, I think you would find this place particularly enjoyable. All you have to do is look around you to see how many women are by themselves, if you know what I mean."

He *had* seen, and had not been tempted by the possibility of hooking up with some lonely widow or divorcee his own age or older. It had only been less than a year since his beloved Veronica had unexpectedly passed away and no one could ever take her place. He was not remotely considering trying to replace her.

"I am not in the market, Jerri," he said.

"You might not think so, Shad, but I would be willing to bet that you would have a girlfriend here within weeks of moving in."

"You scare me, Jerri. If you are right, I better not buy in. I wasn't kidding when I said I was not about to date anyone at this stage of my life. I still see my wife everywhere I look."

"Well, in that case I won't belabor the point," she reluctantly conceded, but Shad could tell by the look in her eyes that she thought he was being foolish.

Shad did not blame her. How could she know he had been truthful about not being tempted in getting to know someone romantically? It would require an effort he was too phlegmatic to undertake. And yet his loneliness weighed heavily on him. He was tired of being by himself. He needed companionship. He was not cut out to be a bachelor. The silence in his home—especially in the evenings and late at night—had become deafening. He had to admit to himself he didn't know if he would actually be able to resist persistent overtures by some attractive older woman. He hadn't thought much about it. He did not have any plans to look for one. He remained silent, his thoughts private and not to be shared with people he had barely met.

Thomas came to his rescue. "Kenny is right, you know," he said, ignoring Jerri's comments, "their terrace is huge."

"Nevertheless," Kenny said, "the point you make about living in an apartment is a valid one. We had not lived in one for more than twenty years, and it did take us several months before we got used to it. It has become our home now, despite the occasional ambiguity, and our neighbors are nice and don't bother us. And we love to come down here for lunch or dinner so Jerri doesn't have to cook all the time."

"So you like the food?" Shad said.

"Sure. It's obviously not consistently gourmet quality, but it tastes fine and is supposedly prepared with a healthy lifestyle in mind. Low on calories; no trans-fats when they deep fry. None of that unhealthy stuff you keep reading about," Jerri said, and Kenny added: "You know how it is with buffet food. It looks attractive and often tastes good at first. But eventually you get tired of it. It has a tendency to all taste the same over time. No matter how good you think the food is the first time, it gets old all too quickly. When we first moved in we probably came for lunch or dinner six or seven times a week. Now it's more like four or five times."

Shad had the impression Ken was less enamored with the food than was Jerri, but he liked their honesty. He could not picture himself becoming quite so enthusiastic about living in an apartment, even if he was glad to learn that someone at least did not regret having moved into the Towers and liked its lifestyle. Maybe he could adapt as well, he thought.

It was still not quite dusk after he said his good-byes and walked out. He needed more time to think and did not want to look at the Radford's apartment just then. Instead he felt a long stroll home would do him the most good. He enjoyed the peaceful tranquility of the village as he made his way south to Nautilus Street and then followed the gently rising hill towards his home. He recalled the first time Veronica and he had seen the house and had found it so immediately enchanting.

He shook the memory off and kept walking.

He reflected on his state of mind, trying to determine why he had become prone to often feeling miserable. It wasn't that he was unhappy. He was just not happy. Throughout his adulthood he had enjoyed health and happiness. He was still healthy, but happiness had become elusive. Why, he could not identify. He knew it was unjustified. He had always thought you had to be one or the other, nothing in between, and his life had mirrored this. Great happiness for days on hand, followed by hours or—seldom—days of unhappiness. Now he knew better. Intermediate stages, neither happy nor unhappy, existed and could go on forever. Like he had been feeling for months now, and he could not understand this ambivalence. He thought it might be related to aging. He accepted—intellectually—that he was getting older. *Was* older. That his body no longer responded or behaved the way he wanted, but emotionally he had the biggest problems accepting himself as he was. He rejected the word 'old' in conjunction with thinking of himself.

From a practical point of view, he had every reason to be happy, starting with the all important health issue. He had enough money not to have to worry. Nothing materialistic was missing in his life: a beautiful house; an expensive car; all the electronic conveniences he was able to master. Whatever he wanted, he could buy. Except, of course, the unmitigated happiness he sought. And that's where his problem came from. It was a mental issue. Something was preventing him from being happy, and he didn't know what it was. It helped little that he was also not truly unhappy.

*　*　*

Shad was perspiring by the time he unlocked his front door and walked inside. The exercise had done him good, and so had his introspections, inconclusive as they had been. He felt more at peace with himself, at least temporarily. He was not yet ready to worry about tomorrow.

He opened his panoramic windows facing the distant ocean below him and let the cool evening breeze envelop him. Lights shimmered on the downward sloping hillside and on the Beach Barber tract, and pale moonlight rippled like an inverted funnel across the dark sea. Stars studded the cloudless night sky, beckoning him. He stood there admiring the view, as he had done so many times in the course of the years, until very recently with his wife by his side. He took the photo of her from the piano and studied her familiar image longingly.

"I hope you can see the ocean you always loved so much from where you are now, Veronica!" he mumbled quietly.

He kept holding the photo for a few minutes before setting it back. If he were to move, Veronica's piano would not go with him, he decided. He could not play, and looking at it every day only created melancholy in him and reminded him of how much he had always enjoyed listening to her playing. He missed it.

As he walked into the kitchen to get himself a glass of wine, he passed the row of bookshelves holding his decades' worth of reading that meant so much to him. He tried to picture the lay-out of the optioned apartment and thought about where enough shelving could be installed. There was no way he would be able to take all his books.

He started agonizing over which ones to take along. Leaving any of them behind would be very painful for him, and almost reason enough not to move. Wouldn't it be better to simply take a chance that he would remain healthy enough to take care of himself until the day he finally fell over, dead, from a stroke or heart attack? The whole idea of moving into a retirement facility was based on the premise he would need care for medical reasons at some point, or that he would become too decrepit to look after himself or become a menace to himself or others. Was this likely to be the case? He didn't think so. He hoped not. He could not see himself facing a prolonged period of illness or a debilitating physical or mental handicap; much more likely he would go quickly when the time came.

He settled down in his favorite easy chair, his wine by his side, and tried to stop thinking. It was so much easier to dwell on memories, instead of trying to guess what the future held in store for him.

5

Iran, 1965-1968

Shad had expected his first glimpse of Iran to be more exciting than the bleak landscape he saw through the airplane's windows as his flight approached Teheran. A pale, dull, dusty, uniformly brown monotony completely dominated the countryside. The low dwellings in the vicinity of their flight path were nearly indistinguishable from the bland terrain, the few roads, and even the sparse trees covered with a layer of dust. Looking into the distance, everything appeared arid; no bright colors; no green to be seen, as if it had not rained for ten years.

Diametrically opposite to the jungles of Vietnam in which he had lived and fought, or Saigon with its myriad white structures, or lushness he had seen in Korea. He was not sure he was going to like this country, much as he had looked forward to leaving the hated jungles of Vietnam behind with their pervasive humidity and hostile environment.

Once he was in the terminal proper, he stared at the incredibly chaotic scene of passengers scrambling for their luggage. An overwhelming number of people were milling around, looking for friends or relatives.

While he waited for his bags to appear on the slowly turning carousel, he scanned the crowd, studying their appearance with undisguised curiosity. Uniform of the day for the men were baggy trousers, collarless dirty looking shirts with unbuttoned vests over them, and colorful turbans perched on their black hair. Scruffy, worn out footwear completed their wardrobe. The men were unshaven. Gesticulating wildly. Shouting. An unmistakable odor of unwashed bodies hung in the air. The few women were standing off to the side while men kissed and held hands. The women were indistinguishable from one another in their long, flowing *chadors*. How disappointingly different from the white, exotic *Ao Dais* the girls in Vietnam had worn!

Fighting his way towards the exit with his luggage, he was relieved to see a US Army sergeant, dressed in fatigues, holding up a sign with the names Shad Cooper and Neil Clifford. He walked up to the sergeant, hoping no offense would be taken at his wearing of civilian clothes.

"Hi," he said. "I am Shad Cooper."

"Jack Erskine. Have you seen this other guy?"

"I don't think so. I didn't know there was another trooper on this flight."

"There should be. Let's give him a few more minutes. What a fucking mess this terminal is. Can you believe it?"

"Is it always like this?" Shad wanted to know. He studied Jack out of the corner of his eyes. Almost as tall as he was. Sloping, muscular shoulders. Short light hair combed forward. Aquiline nose. Tanned. Maybe in his late twenties. Looking a little frustrated.

Jack shrugged. "I guess. I think the whole country is like this. Or at least Teheran is. You'll see soon enough."

They stood around silently, watching the masses swirling around them.

"I am surprised they have a sergeant pulling airport pick-up duty," Shad said, trying to be friendly.

Jack grinned. "I drew the short straw. But apart from that, we don't have anyone less than E-5's here in country."

"Should I have come in uniform?"

"No. In fact, generally speaking, uniforms are discouraged. We keep a low profile and as a member of the Army Map Service out in the field you will be in civvies full time. Only here in Teheran, when on official business, are you expected to wear fatigues."

A man finally walked up to them and introduced himself as Neil Clifford. He looked like a friendly, outgoing type, Shad thought. A few pounds too many around his middle. Wearing civvies just like Shad. Two or three inches shorter than he.

They introduced each other and Jack wasted no time escorting them to his jeep. They managed to pile their bags behind the driver's seat and took off.

Shad was glad the canvas cover was up over the jeep. The sun blazed down mercilessly and despite the wind stream he quickly broke out in a sweat. Traffic was monumental, and just like in Saigon, there seemed to be no rules of the road. A cacophony of car horns assailed his senses. Goat herders drove their flocks down the middle of the street, impervious to the car horns blasting at them. Both the sidewalks, such as they were, and the road had to be shared with heavily laden donkeys.

People were napping in the shade of buildings, oblivious to the traffic rolling past. On both sides of the street ran open, narrow channels of water. Women were washing laundry in the slow flowing water while others were bathing themselves. Shad caught himself shaking his head in disbelief at the strange scenes unfolding before his eyes.

Drivers—mostly of taxis—were patently suicidal. They drove with utter abandon, their foot on the gas and their fist on the horn, stopping for nothing except a potential passenger, in which case they came to a screeching halt wherever they happened to be. The most basic driving courtesy seemed distained and scorned.

If he ignored the vehicles, Shad felt as if he had been transported centuries back in time. It was as if he were in a movie or a book set in ancient times. He couldn't help but admire Jack's driving, with his calm unflappability in the face of such adversity. How he managed to avoid accidents was beyond Shad.

"This street is named Takht-e-Jamshid," Jack shouted at them over the incessant noise of the traffic. "The US Embassy is right up the road. If you are looking for women to fuck, this is the place. As soon as it gets dark, you will see them walking the street. The way you recognize them is that they briefly flash open their *chador* so you can see their face. When you stop, they hop in, and off you go outside the city. Once you are finished, you bring them back here. Just be careful. The whole thing is obviously illegal, so if you see men around, don't stop."

Grinning hugely, Jack turned back to maneuvering through the traffic. Shad wasn't sure he believed him. Streetwalkers next to the US Embassy?

Jack dropped them off at a rather large, non-descript apartment building. A number of military vehicles were parked out front.

"You'll find our company clerk in the offices on your left. He'll assign you to quarters and get your paperwork squared away. Get some rest. You are free tomorrow to look around. Wednesday morning at Oh eight hundred hours you have a meeting with the MAC-CO, I understand. The clerk will tell you where to find him. He is in this building as well," Jack advised them. He drove off in a cloud of dust and the accompaniment of blaring horns.

"How long are we going to be in this fucking place?" Neil asked rhetorically as they picked up their bags and entered the building.

An hour later, having been duly processed, they were in a large room on the third floor. It felt like a barrack. Twelve bunks were lined up in two rows, with lockers along the walls and an assortment of footlockers at the foot of the beds. Several of the beds were occupied. Clothes were scattered about. It was hot despite the wide open windows. The traffic noise was hard to ignore. They found two bunks with folded bedding and claimed them.

"I don't know about you, Neil, but I am starving to death," Shad said.

"Me too. Let's go find some chow."

The small dining room on the ground floor offered sandwiches. To their surprise, beer was for sale as well, and this they drank greedily.

Their trip had been a long one. Between the number of hours they had spent in the air, the time difference, and now the beer consumed too quickly, they were both exhausted and went to their quarters to sack out.

Their day off passed uneventfully. Shad wandered around, exploring his new surroundings. He felt conspicuously foreign, unable to relax while soaking up the local atmosphere. He did not find the sights greeting him impressive. If the whole country was going to be like this, it would be a very long year indeed.

The following morning he and Neil knocked on Colonel Sutherland's door at the appointed hour and saluted when asked to enter.

"At ease, men!" Col. Sutherland ordered. "Sit down. This is Bob Perkins from the US Embassy," he said, pointing to a civilian sitting off to the side, "and Captain Harry Stark. Captain Stark is the CO of the Army Map Service group stationed here of which you are a member."

They nodded their acknowledgment.

"Now then," Col. Sutherland resumed, "you have a difficult assignment. You will be sent to western Iran, into part of Kurdistan. You will go there ostensibly to participate in developing updated maps of the area. This is extremely important because we feel the Russians may one day try to occupy Iran again in order to have year around access to vital ports. You have both successfully completed the courses as topographic surveyors and will provide the field measurements to be used by headquarters staff in Washington in drawing the detailed maps we require. Any questions?"

"No, Sir!" Neil and Shad answered simultaneously.

"Good. Captain Stark, what would you like to add?"

"I will provide more information in a separate meeting. Suffice it to say at this point that you will be operating in an extremely hostile environment, both geographically and population wise. Much of the terrain is inaccessible to anything except man and animals—donkeys, in your case. You will not be in uniform and will receive a *per diem* allowance, in cash, since you will have to live off the land, so to speak. Also hazardous duty pay will be added to your monthly paycheck. No support from the army, except for a monthly supply flight which will drop off your mail, money, tobacco, alcohol, etc., which will be charged against your allowance. The first months you will both be working out of Rezayeh with an experienced surveyor to show you the ropes. Thereafter, you two will work as a team and be among the Kurds most of the time. Questions?"

"No, Sir!" They again answered in unison, not having a clue as to what was truly expected of them or how to get started.

"All right," Col. Sutherland said, "now to the second part of your assignment. Mr. Perkins, if you please."

"Thank you, Colonel Sutherland and Captain Stark. First of all, welcome, and thank you for volunteering for this task," Mr. Perkins said. Shad, having worked with the CIA in Vietnam, recognized immediately who was facing them. His looks, his suit, his behavior and mannerisms all readily identified him as a spook. "Permit me to expound briefly on what Col. Sutherland alluded to regarding the Russians. The Iranians are understandably nervous about Russia's intentions as they pertain to the Persian Golf, both because of the huge oil reserves there and the attraction of gaining access to a year around port. Plus, they already occupied parts of north western Iran a few years ago. This means it is not just paranoia on the part of the Iranians, but also a historically driven legitimate concern. The US government shares their fears and is additionally worried about Shah Reza Pahlavi moving closer to the Russian sphere of influence. Then we have the permanent friction between Iraq and Iran with one being predominantly Shi'a, the other Sunni. Oil, of course, plays a major strategic role for the US and we have to balance our interests in Iran against those we have in Iraq with their huge oil fields in Iraq's Kurdistan. We can not afford to alienate either country. Right now, the situation in Iraq is extremely tense, and we have it on good authority that the military junta under Abdul Karem Kassim may be overthrown at any moment. Abdel Salam Arif has apparently positioned himself to be his successor as head of the Baath Socialist Party. In other words, the political situation in Iraq is highly unstable and unlikely to bring the two countries closer together. We are determined to project the role of the benevolent intermediary, facilitating peaceful coexistence between Iran and Iraq. And with Turkey as well, for that matter."

"Perhaps you could get to what we expect of these men, Mr. Perkins," interrupted Col. Sutherland. "I am not sure they need all this background."

Mr. Perkins, visibly unhappy at being brought up short, nodded almost imperceptibly before continuing. "There is one other aspect I need to cover, which brings me right to what we expect of you gentlemen. This is the issue of Kurdistan itself, straddling north-western Iran, north-eastern Iraq, and the extreme southeast part of Turkey. While Iraq and Iran officially tacitly tolerate the Kurds somewhat, armed clashes break out periodically between the so-called PKK, the Kurdish Worker's Party, and Turkey. The region populated by the Kurds, many of whom are nomads and follow the grazing grounds of their sheep and goats across the international borders, is highly unstable, with violence flaring up periodically. In Iraq especially, the Kurds, led by Mustafa Barzani, have been engaging in bitter fights with the military. Here in Iran, the Shah has brutally suppressed all opposition."

Shad tried to concentrate on what Perkins was explaining but found the history and circumstances difficult to follow. Both Sutherland and Stark looked bored.

"Perhaps you could tell us just what you expect us to do, Mr. Perkins," Shad ventured to say.

"I was just coming to that. Your official and primary duty will be the topographic surveying of course, which Captain Stark has outlined. For that part of your assignment, you will report to him. For the rest, I will be working with you. If conflicts arise about priorities, you will advise us and Captain Stark and I will resolve them. As part of our clandestine activities you will be one of two dozen teams we will infiltrate through various covers and through different locations and means into the major areas of so-called Kurdistan. Your and the other teams' assignment relates to two areas: the political aspects of Kurdistan—how they pursue their desire to establish an independent country, to which country their loyalties, if any, lean, who the leaders in the various factions are and to make an assessment of their strengths and weaknesses. The other aspect is the . . . what should I call it? The potential military ramifications. You will be expected to advise and secretly train the Kurds and help them get away from the terrorist image they now have and towards an organized militia, ready to step into action or be an effective controlling force if nationalism ever does come about. We want the Kurds to be on our side without us unduly antagonizing the three host nations, so that all possible options remain open to us. I will coordinate the teams to make sure you don't overlap or work at cross purposes to each other. All communications must flow through me."

Silence greeted his words. Shad was tempted to ask, "What the fuck are you talking about?", but he had learned to keep his mouth shut. Despite having worked with the CIA in Vietnam, being directly exposed to its agents always made him uncomfortable. No way could he take the chance of alienating them and risk having his background researched again, and thoroughly. Whatever he would actually have to do in Kurdistan would be immeasurably preferable to being exposed as a prison escapee.

*　　*　　*

A week later, orders came through for Neil and Shad to report for their flight to Rezayeh. Captain Stark provided additional insights and background on their survey mission.

"We have six surveyors based in Rezayeh, including two who will come out on the flight that will take you there," Stark had explained. "None of them know of your dual role, and it is imperative you do not discuss this in any way. Although we—the USA— enjoy good relations with the Shah, his government has never forgotten—or forgiven—our involvement in toppling the very popular Premier Mossadegh in the 1953 coup. Both British Intelligence, having worked with us on the coup, and the CIA have been viewed with great suspicion ever since, and it is critical that any CIA activities today remain below the radar screen of the Iranians. Is that clearly understood?"

"Yes, Sir!"

It would be the last time they would hear Captain Stark mention the ominous initials in their presence. The subsequent time they spent together was devoted to the technical aspects of their deployment.

"Sir," Neil asked, "what about weapons?"

"As members of a foreign military force, by law you are not allowed to carry weapons. But I know these are readily available in any of the bazaars you will find." The voice in which he shared this information did not invite follow-up questions.

When their wake-up call came at 5:00am of their departure day Shad felt nauseous and dreaded the upcoming flight in the little single engine L-21.

His mood did not improve when the pilot helped them strap on parachutes before letting them board the aircraft. Just as a precaution, he assured them; no need to get nervous.

The flight was bumpy and Shad had problems keeping his breakfast down. The landscape unfolding below them was desolate; scrub brush interspersed with tiny villages for the first hour, then mountains in the distance and finally the sight of beautiful Lake Rezayeh. Shad recalled what Stark had told them. They would be only thirty miles from the Iraqi border in Rezayeh, and twenty from Turkey. The Russian republic of Armenia was a mere one hundred miles to the north. Thirty thousand people called the city their home, predominantly Kurds who had given up their nomadic lifestyle.

An Iranian soldier, driving an ancient US Army ¾ ton truck, met them and exchanged their belongings with what his two passengers, who were returning to Teheran, had brought along. He loaded the supplies from the aircraft into the back of his truck, which had no backseat. Neil and Shad had to squeeze in next to the driver.

The city looked drab and was covered in dust. The streets were laid out in orderly blocks; it was the only modern thing they saw. The buildings, the roads, the restaurants and small hotels they passed and the whole environment looked uninviting. Only the inner city streets were paved. Vehicle traffic was sparse. Horses pulling carriages or wagons, heavily burdened donkeys and bicycles were the rule. Open gutters lined the streets. Laundry and dishes were being washed in them. Coming down with amoebic dysentery, as they had been warned, was to be expected.

The house to which they were taken looked reasonably new. It had eight large rooms, Shad quickly learned, and he and Neil agreed to share one. There was little in the way of furniture. The big disappointment was the sanitary facility. Iranian style: a hole in the ground of the garden, enclosed by a tin shack. No toilet paper. Instead, a full watering can with a long narrow spout was available, to be utilized instead of paper. There was no running water in the house. A hand operated pump was installed in the backyard, as was the shower. This was a surplus 50 gallon oil drum with a jury rigged shower head on its bottom and was mounted on a wooden scaffold. Their houseboy ensured refilling of the drum. Welcome to Rezayeh, Shad thought.

Two members of their small group were out running a survey line and would not return for two weeks. The senior sergeant nominally in charge of their group showed Neil and Shad on aerial photographs and a large scale map where he wanted them to begin working. Supported by six Iranian army soldiers, they would go by truck to a town named Haseynuh, roughly 70 miles south of Rezayeh, where they would hire a man with three donkeys to carry their equipment and personal belongings while they surveyed the mountainous region stretching from Haseynuh to the Iraqi border. Contrary to what they had been told in Teheran, no one was available to break them in. It made them uncomfortable, but not as uncomfortable as the careless way the soldiers handled their rifles. Shad hoped their old M-1's were not loaded.

*　　*　　*

They came across an encampment of nomadic Kurds for the first time three days into their assignment. Neil and Shad had finally found a promising place to make camp for the night. It was level, free of rocks, and off the camel caravan trail that meandered along the narrow brook of clear water. A single large tree offered welcome shade. Not far away they saw a group of five simple tents—more like awnings—made of rough dark brown woven wool stretched over outward leaning poles. Sheep, goats and donkeys grazed on the surprisingly lush grass around the tents. The only English speaking soldier explained that these Kurds would stay in their present location until the available grass was gone, whereupon they would seek out a new valley for their flocks.

As they were unloading the donkeys, an old man approached them from the tents.

"Salem aleykum!" he greeted and gave a slight bow.

"Aleykum ah-salam!" replied their translator.

"Haale shumah shetoreh," came the response.

At Shad's request the translator, Mehdi, explained to the elder who they were, what they were doing, and that they wanted to spend the night under the tree, under the protection of his people. This so honored the tribesman that he proceeded to call his whole family over to greet the guests. They came, straggling, hesitant to approach, but then stared unabashedly, especially the children with their dark, lustrous eyes, the younger ones hiding behind the billowing skirts of their mothers.

Despite their obvious poverty they insisted on inviting Shad and Neil for dinner. The meal was a simple one, consisting of rice, *nan*, raw onions and self made goat milk yoghurt. The two uncooked sheep's eyes nestling on top of the boiled rice did not do much for Shad's appetite, but when he saw Neil spooning the delicacy and swallowing it with aplomb, he followed suit, concentrating on not choking.

Shad was acutely aware of their parallel assignment and wanted to question the elder but knew he could not do so in front of their translator. As it was, he was impressed by the hospitality and friendliness of their hosts. Endless tea kept being served to the point where Shad feared he would float away. It became apparent that getting along with the Kurds would not be a problem if they could converse with them in English.

Later that evening he raised the subject with Neil. "How in hell are we supposed to make some progress on the political or military front with the Kurds if we can't talk to them without an army translator?" he said.

"I have no clue. Either we just keep on plodding along or we try to contact that arrogant pisser Perkins and ask him to tell us where and how to reach the right people."

"I say we wait a while to see who we meet. We can't call Perkins from here anyway."

Two weeks later, back in Rezayeh, they felt totally frustrated at their lack of progress. They had not found anyone with whom they could speak confidentially. They send a telegram to Perkins asking him to get in touch with them. His answer, through Captain Stark, was to order Shad back to Teheran.

*   *   *

"Any ideas?" Perkins asked when Shad had explained what they were up against.

"Not really, since we have not met anyone who could tell us who the Kurdish powers are or where they might be found. I am sure they are deliberately reticent with foreigners. The Kurds seem to be a very close knit group of people who are graciously hospitable and friendly, but can not really be prevailed upon to share their thinking with strangers. A veil of secrecy surrounds them, either for security reasons, or because of tradition."

"Possibly a combination of the two, I suppose," Perkins opined. "So where do you propose to go from here?"

"I was hoping you could tell me. The other teams must have the same problems, if they are in place already."

"Maybe. If I knew how and with whom to get in at the leadership level, I would not have needed you. I didn't expect you or the others to come up with initial successes within your first few weeks. You need to give it time; let people hear about you, get to know you. I would certainly expect word to have gone up the chain of command by now, even if only with questions about who you might be and what you want."

"Yes. I have been thinking about this whole scenario, of course, and one thing is clear. We have the biggest problems communicating. Our Iranian soldiers make the Kurds highly suspicious, and in order to talk to the elders, we have to use our interpreter. But I am sure there is no way anyone is going to tell us anything in the presence of an Iranian, who—for all they know—could well be a member of the Iranian intelligence service. If you want Neil and me to make some progress, you have to make sure we can go to the Kurds without a bunch of soldiers tagging along."

Perkins nodded thoughtfully. "I'll talk to Col. Sutherland to see what can be done. It's politically sensitive. The Iranians no doubt want to be kept directly abreast of what we are up to, but maybe Sutherland can make it palatable to his counterparts."

"You would also need to cover for us with the Army Map Service, because if we are going into the field and live with the Kurds, we are not going to get much surveying done. We don't want questions coming back to Tom Klein, our team leader, as to why we are not providing survey data."

"Understood," Perkins said. "I will speak with Captain Stark to make sure there are no problems from the AMS side or this Tom Klein fellow."

No plane was available to take Shad back to Rezayeh that day, and when he checked into MAC quarters for the night, he ran into Jack Erskine from the airport pick-up. They had spent some time together during Shad's initial stay in Teheran, and when Jack invited Shad to an informal party at his house that evening, he gladly accepted.

Several friends of the Erskine's were already sitting around the expansive patio when Jack and Shad arrived. Shad had not known Jack was married to an Iranian he had met soon after his deployment to the country. They had been married for six months now and lived in an elegant villa provided by his wife Azadeh's father, a high ranking military officer. Jack made the introductions. Apart from himself and Jack, there were no Americans present.

Azadeh was a lovely woman, perhaps in her mid-twenties, with coal black hair matching the color of her eyes and a very outgoing personality. She made Shad feel comfortable in what could have been somewhat intimidating circumstances, with many of the men present obviously Iranian military. There were only two other women in evidence. One was older; Jack's mother-in-law, he was told. The other one was a beautiful young woman, distinctly similar to Azadeh. This, he learned, was Nellie, a younger sister. Shad was immediately enchanted with her, her black lustrous hair reminding him of his former girlfriends in Korea and Vietnam, but Nellie was taller at perhaps 5'5" and heavier without being overweight. Beautiful skin with just a hint of tan gave her an alluring appearance.

"Nellie doesn't sound very Iranian," he said, smiling at her when they were introduced by Azadeh.

She did not return his friendliness; remained rather neutral, as if something were troubling her. It occurred to him she might simply not like Americans. They were not always the most popular people in the Middle East.

"It's not, of course," she said. "My name is actually Naghmeh, but when I went to London to study, I found the name too difficult for friends to remember, so I abbreviated it to the more familiar Anglo name Nellie."

Shad tried hard to keep a conversation going with her, but she made it obvious she was not all that interested in him and after a while, she drifted away. He felt disappointed. It was only later, as Jack was driving him back, that he learned Nellie had recently been divorced. While in London, she had met and fallen in love with a fellow Iranian student and they had married. Hardly back in Iran, her husband had divorced her, for reasons Jack either did not know or did not want to talk about.

"She doesn't pine after him anymore." Jack explained. "In fact, she probably hates him now, because as a divorcee in Iran, it is next to impossible for her to find another husband. She is quite beautiful, as you saw, and really a fun girl when you get to know her. But Iranians generally insist on marrying only virgins. The rare man tempted to look at a divorced woman is leery, since she has to have been at fault. She has become tainted goods. Men can get a divorce very easily; for women it is next to impossible, so it's taken for granted there is something wrong with her. Why else would her husband have sent her away? That's why Nellie seems so reserved. She is only twenty-three but worries she will never get married again and have the children she wants."

"A sad story," Shad said. He could not get her out of his mind.

Jack shrugged. "That's the reality here."

It would be six months before he would see her again.

*   *   *

Not to be accompanied by the Iranian soldiers made all the difference. Their team leader, Sgt. Tom Klein, had thought it was foolhardy for Shad and Neil to go out into the field alone, but after having voiced his concerns, and a word from Teheran, had let them go.

They hired a large jeep to take them to Piranshar, the closest city to the Iraqi border from Rezayeh. There they rented two donkeys for their equipment and personal belongings. The owner, prodding the donkeys along, was happy for the unexpected business. They had no clear destination, other than to find Kurdish encampments that would welcome them.

*   *   *

Within six months, returning only briefly to their base in Rezayeh every two to three weeks to pick up mail and supplies, they had established solid contacts to leaders of the Kurdish fractions. One tribal elder they met early on facilitated a secret visit to Mosul, the Kurdish capital in northern Iraq. They crossed the border illegally, without a visa, making Shad and Neil hesitate, but their Kurdish hosts assured them there would be no problems. At the elder's request they became members of a nomadic Kurd family. Dressed in native clothing bought from their 'family', they saw no sign of Iraqi border patrols. In Mosul, they met with Kamal Mustafa Bakir, reputed to be one of the up and coming leaders.

Bakir, a charismatic, moderately practical man, was young enough to be open to new ideas, but old enough to be respected. Shad and Neil worked on gaining his trust and shared parts of their mission with him. The USA, they explained, had a vested interest in helping to establish a stable, independent Kurdistan. To that end, they and the other teams would assist in military training of Bakir's followers to prepare for possible armed conflicts with their three neighboring countries. Politicians, in the meantime, would be working with those countries to advance the Kurd's territorial claims through diplomacy. Bakir found this appealing but needed to consult other senior leaders before implementation.

What Shad did not reveal was that he personally harbored serious reservations about the bizarre idea some brilliant strategist in the State Department had concocted, namely to position the USA as the peace making intermediary. By first fomenting dissent and armed struggles between the Kurds and their host countries, diplomats would subsequently step in, hopefully negotiate bringing friction between the fractions to a halt and then ordaining themselves as saviors of what could otherwise have easily become a major conflict. The US secretly planned on playing both ends against the middle: clandestinely furthering the threat of warfare while brokering peace behind the scenes. How anyone could ever hope to make this work was beyond Shad's comprehension, but he and Neil proceeded with the limited role assigned to them.

It was a nightmare for Shad and Neil. Their safety was often at stake. They were afraid of getting caught in the middle. They kept as low a profile as possible. Shad was only glad he was so caught up in the intrigues being played out that he had no time to think about the police back home possibly honing in on him.

Shad and Neil succeeded in remaining officially largely anonymous and no one except Bob Perkins knew of the pivotal role they and the other teams played in the high stakes and dangerous strategy of establishing the USA as friend of both the Kurds and the three countries from which they wanted to wrest an independent nation. While it remained questionable that statehood would be achieved, it was agreed significant progress could be seen and Shad and Neil were asked to continue with their clandestine assignment until Perkins got a message to them that they should return to Teheran for ten days R&R whenever they could cross the border unobtrusively with a roving band of Kurdish tribesmen.

* * *

"How about inviting me back to your home, Jack?" Shad asked when they met up in Teheran.

Jack grinned wickedly. "Sure. Can't wait to see Nellie again, can you?"

"That's right. I have thought quite a bit about her while working out in the field."

"Ok, I'll talk to Azadeh and see what she says. But I wouldn't get my hopes up if I were you. You saw how Nellie acted when you met her. She is still like that."

"That's all right. I just want to see if she actually looks the way I have been picturing her in my mind."

She did, Shad thought when he saw her a few days later. If anything, even more beautiful and alluring than he had remembered. But no friendlier than she had been before. He wanted to invite her out but did not know where to go where he could safely be seen with an Iranian woman, at least not without a chaperone. He was culturally restricted to being with her at Jack's house. He and Azadeh were sensitive enough to leave them alone on the patio while preparing dinner.

To his surprise, once they were by themselves, he found it easy to talk to Nellie. She told him about her years in England and her former husband, with only traces of bitterness occasionally coming through. She had become a lecturer at Teheran's Women University and enjoyed her work and had made friends—all female—with whom she could go out in the evenings. She lived with her parents again. They were supportive, but a little too protective, she felt.

During his ten day stay in Teheran, Shad spent every evening at Jack's house with Nellie present. By the time he left, he was pretty sure he had fallen in love, even though they had not so much as kissed. Perhaps it was precisely this physical remoteness that made her so desirable. He longed to take her in his arms and hold her; could virtually feel her pressing against his body, and yet he did not dare touch her. They talked about everything except how they felt about each other, and when it was time for him to return to the field, the most he could get out of her was her assurance that she would be waiting eagerly to see him again.

*   *   *

The next months were long ones. During his absence Jack and Azadeh must have been promoting him to her sister. How else to explain that she came into his arms so readily when he returned and she was at Jack's house to meet him? A first, tentative kiss followed as soon as they were alone, and it was everything Shad had hoped and dreamed about. He was elated. The idea of marrying her was firmly established in his mind when he had to leave her once more and only grew with each day he was gone. The lonely and harsh living conditions he endured in Kurdistan solidified his overpowering desire for the distant Nellie, and in his imagination she became lovelier and more coveted with every evening he tossed and turned in his sleeping bag. If he had seen anything in her he did not like or gave him pause, it receded through their separation to the point where she became the perfect woman in his mind. He knew she was the one he wanted to be with for the rest of his life.

When he finally saw her again he proposed. He couldn't believe his luck when she accepted, and together they went to the US Embassy to complete the mountainous paperwork required for marriage. He could not remember ever having been so happy, and the lingering concern in the back of his mind about his fugitive status dissipated when no questions came back regarding the paperwork he had submitted. The ambassador himself married them.

6

No feedback from Sybil on the background check. A week had gone by and Shad speculated silently whether the lack of news was good or bad or indifferent. He wondered if he should give her a call but concluded she might become suspicious. It was, after all, just routine for her; a checkmark for her to make on a list. But for Shad, there was no such thing as routine when it came to someone probing into his past. He was still an escaped felon and risk of exposure and subsequent arrest preyed on his mind.

Coincidentally, while he was thus waiting nervously, his monthly social security check arrived. He had never given this money much thought. It was not a large amount, but since he had contributed to the fund ever since joining the army, he had not hesitated to apply for the benefits due him upon reaching age 65.

Now, with the initiated background check, these retirement payments took on a potentially sinister aspect. He thought about the fact that if his real identity should ever be discovered, he might well be pursued for fraud, in addition to the other looming penalties threatening his comfortable existence. Roger Stevens had never paid into social security and was not entitled to collect. Shad Cooper, the real one long deceased, cashed the checks. Could this be construed as fraud? If yes, it would be a federal offense and he would be liable not only for restitution with interest and penalties, but also subject to time in a federal prison. He was sure lawyers would have a field day sorting this out, if it ever became known.

The thought alone made him shudder with apprehension. His whole life would unravel, and instead of having to worry about the wisdom of moving into the Towers, he would have to worry about staying out of the penitentiary. He once again considered seeking legal advice but quickly rejected this as being premature; no point in getting all excited until he knew what information on him might come back to Sybil and what she might then decide to do.

But he could not entirely shake his fears, and in an effort to allay them, he invited Thomas for lunch.

"This is an unexpected pleasure, Shad," Thomas said while they were studying their menus. "What brought this sudden invitation about?"

"No particular reason, Thomas. I just keep struggling with this Towers issue. It's driving me nuts, and I thought a little chat with you about the good old days would distract me."

"Well, we can certainly do that. That's what friends are for, aren't they?"

"My thoughts exactly," Shad agreed. "By the way, speaking of the Towers reminds me. Sybil surprised me by asking if it was all right for her to initiate a background check on me. Did that happen to you as well?"

"Oh, sure. They do that routinely to keep the riff-raff out of the building."

"Funny," Shad said, but he was not laughing. "I would have thought the exorbitant prices alone would ensure only wealthy, upstanding citizens would be qualified to begin with."

"True enough. The down and out are automatically disqualified. But they also want to make sure your money did not come from illegal activities. They would not want to risk the police or FBI or Immigration swooping down on them in search of some money launderer or retired Mafia kingpin."

"I hear what you are saying. Do you happen to remember how long your background check took?"

"No idea. I never asked, knowing they would come up with nothing. I assume they would tell you soon enough if something didn't look right."

"Yes, that would make sense," Shad said.

"Why all these questions, Shad? You aren't worried, are you?"

"Not really," Shad hastened to assure his friend who knew nothing about Roger Stevens. "I was merely caught by surprise and wondered if you had to go through the same thing."

Thomas accepted this at face value and they lapsed into an easy silence while they ate. Shad didn't know whether he should find solace in what Thomas had related or would have to continue to worry, not knowing when or if he might hear from Sybil.

He looked up and saw Thomas studying him questioningly. "You look as if you weren't quite here, Shad."

Shad chuckled. He had learned to become a proficient liar in response to unexpected questions. "I guess I wasn't. My mind was drifting. Talking about this background check reminded me of how nervous I was about going through immigration in China the first time I went there, and I started reliving those early days when I met Veronica and fell in love with her and then flying to Hong Kong to see you and you pushing me to go to China. So long ago, and yet I remember it as if it had been only yesterday."

Thomas nodded. "In retrospect," he said, "I am still a little surprised that you picked up on my suggestion about China so quickly."

"Well, all I really concluded initially was to fly to Beijing to see if I could get a feel for the market environment," Shad said. "But I was worried. I was operating on a shoestring in those days, as you may recall, and I worried that Dave would only let me buy a one way ticket."

"Yes, I still have to smile when I think back to those beginnings. I can see why you might have been concerned about possibly having to spend years in China, trying to get enough orders to pay for your trip back home," Thomas grinned.

"Maybe it wasn't quite that bad," Shad said, "but I do distinctly remember sitting across from Dave, trying to explain why a trip to China was advisable. I had my own doubts, and Dave was downright skeptical. More than anything, I think, he too was afraid of the imponderability and the veil of secrecy hanging over the country. He didn't know a single person who had ever tried to set up a business there. For all I know he was even worried about my personal safety."

"Yes," Thomas said, "that was typical for US companies in the 1980's, and it was the main reason why I urged you so strongly to get in there ahead of everybody else. I knew the risks were going to be great, but so were the potential rewards."

"That's precisely what I told Dave, and I pointed out to him that our initial risk was only a few thousand dollars—my travel expenses.

I had to assure him I would not make any commitments or decisions without first consulting him before he agreed to the trip."

"You could have fooled me," Thomas said. "I was sure you could make decisions right away, and that it was your decision alone as to what to do or with whom to work."

Shad smiled. "I know. It was always a part of my management philosophy that whoever I worked with had to be convinced there was no decision I could not make. None I had to kick up to a higher level, even when I knew I had to clear it with Dave or legal or another corporate entity. Whenever I was called upon to make a decision for which I knew I did not have the proper authority, I would say I needed time to think it over, and when I had the necessary approvals, I would announce *my* decision. This way I maintained what appeared to be absolute authority and it kept people from trying to second guess me or going over my head."

"Smart thinking," Thomas said.

"The one thing Dave was adamant about was to have me analyze the pricing scenario. Diversion was becoming an issue, and since we would have to source our products for China out of our US factory, with US labeling, he was quite worried that if our China prices were too low, products shipped there would come back into the US illegally and undermine our pricing structure here."

"A valid concern," Thomas said.

"Well, I am just glad I wasn't aware of these pitfalls back in '85, or I probably would have never gone to Beijing."

"Which you would have regretted forever," Thomas assured him.

"That's for sure. But at the time, I almost had second thoughts when I found out how difficult it was to get a business visa for China—not knowing back then I could have just gone in as a tourist, with a tourist visa I could have gotten in Hong Kong while transiting through there. I even got a tetanus booster shot in case I injured myself."

"Yes, well, as I told you in Beijing already at the time, you should have asked me for advice."

"Obviously," Shad agreed, "but it turned out to be a valuable lesson for me. I learned to ask questions of people in the know."

"Yes. And it's no wonder you appeared to be so nervous when you arrived in Beijing."

Shad laughed. "Yes, almost as nervous as I am now at having to make a decision about moving into the Towers." And as nervous about getting caught by the police, he added silently.

"No reason to be nervous," Thomas said. "Keep in mind you can always move out again. It's not an irreversible, life long decision. Look at me. I kept my house for almost six months after settling down in my penthouse. You could do the same. And while I still don't feel quite at home, as I said, I am beginning to get used to the comforts and conveniences of the place. I have even learned to use the remote control for my new TV, and to set the thermostat."

Shad didn't laugh. He knew this had been an issue for the technologically challenged Thomas. "I am glad to hear that, Thomas," he said. "Now all you need to learn is operating the oven and dishwasher." He smiled, taking the sting out of his words. "Anyway, I think I ought to go now. I want some quality time to think more about my future, and these reminiscences about China don't help me."

Not only did they not help, he realized, they rekindled his earlier bout of depression. How exciting his life had once been.

They exited the restaurant and Shad let his feet lead him down to the sidewalk along the ocean. If there was one thing that could lift his mood it was a stroll along the water. And he needed a lift. He was disgusted with himself for feeling so morose. There was no good reason for self-pity. He had choices when it came to how he lived his life. He could bring changes about. If he wanted it to be different—and he did—then *he* would have to do something to make his life more meaningful. But what? At a point in his life where he had needed Veronica the most, she had left him and he was adrift. It occurred to him that his ongoing grieving could be the root cause of his recurring depressions.

And try as he might, he could not forget the risks associated with his background check. He shook his head, trying to force out his hang-ups.

When he had retired at age 64, he had been advised by Personnel that—actuarially speaking—he had seventeen more years to live. Of course they could not predict how healthy he would remain; only that his heart would likely continue beating for this number of years. It had sounded like a long time then, seventeen years. He had looked back on what he had done and seen during the preceding seventeen years; the first years of retirement. He had held up rather well, he thought, and wondered if this would continue to be the case during his predicted remaining thirteen years. One thing was certain: he had to make the most of them. For that, he had to shake his loneliness and depressions.

7

It had begun innocently enough. Long before moving to La Jolla, Shad made a critical decision. He was still in the army; still in Iran. Serving for twenty years would mean retirement at age 38. Only eleven more years. But retire to what? And live on the few hundred dollars a month pension the government would pay him? What sort of life would that allow? How would he be able to support Nellie? Maybe kids? And the Damocles sword of being a fugitive would still be hanging over him. His exploits in Iran were hidden, buried deeper than deep in inaccessible CIA archives, neither usable as reference nor as springboard for a civilian career. He thought about switching fulltime from the army to the CIA, assuming they would take him, and if they did, without further in depth research into his pre-army past. The background check they had presumably run on him before utilizing his talents in Vietnam had most likely been perfunctory, since they did not recruit him as an employee but rather as someone who had been delegated to them by the army. What might they discover if he applied for regular employment? Would someone not become suspicious when, it turned out that by odd coincidence all his identity paperwork happened to be in the form of copies? Was there some central registry where they would see Shad Cooper had died in 1958? That the police might still be looking for Roger Stevens? Could trace Shad Cooper back to Roger Stevens?

These thoughts kept pestering him as his time in Iran drew to a close. It had been relatively easy to decide to re-enlist before, but this time was different. He was no longer the young fugitive in love with the adventure of serving in Korea and Vietnam and feeling—optimistically—safe from the probing eyes of the law. He was 27 now and married. His responsibilities went beyond only for himself. He had to think thirty and forty years ahead. Think about a career as a civilian, with a long term future and working towards financial security and a family.

His closest friend, Neil, had shown him a way by becoming a sales representative for a pharmaceutical company upon his discharge, and he encouraged Shad to embark on the same path. Such a position offered job security, a decent income, and would allow him to start working on a college degree. He would have enough time, Neil thought, to attend a community college before switching to a university where he could enroll for evening and weekend classes at, for example, the University of Texas, close to Fort Hood. All he would need was to be hired by a reputable company for the right sales territory.

Nellie had not been crazy about the idea of leaving Iran. She wanted them to stay in Iran and have Shad search for a job as an expatriate there, but there were no open positions for which he was even remotely qualified. Alternatively, if it had to be the USA, she pushed for a glamorous metropolitan area like New York or Chicago, with large Iranian communities, but these cities did not appeal to Shad. He liked the idea of working in the thinly populated Texas, where people were judged on what they accomplished, rather than their heritage or right connections.

The army wanted to keep him, but Shad was not seriously tempted. The army could not offer him anything except perhaps security; no future that would satisfy his desire of achieving a meaningful and reasonable life style.

The army had been good to him, he knew. They had given him a safe haven when he desperately needed one. He had survived the hazards and dangers of fighting clandestinely with the Montagnards in the highlands of Vietnam. He had thrived in the double crossing environment of Kurdistan and had succeeded in sowing agitation and fomentation among the Iranians, Iraqis and Turks, to the benefit of his country. He felt he had repaid a good part of his debt to society; much more so than he would have by languishing two more years in prison.

When he looked at what was happening in Vietnam he was grateful he had been so lucky in his timing, spending his military career during the years between hostilities in Korea and now the all out war in Vietnam. Who could tell what might have happened to him if he had stayed Roger Stevens? Not killed his stepfather? Been drafted? No, the anonymity of the army had been ideal for him, but now it was time to start the next chapter of his life.

He waited patiently for his discharge date while applying for a job as salesman with every pharmaceutical company Neil had recommended.

He was about to give up hope when he was invited for interviews with Rigopharm and was subsequently offered a position as junior salesman in Houston. He was elated and accepted with alacrity.

The transition from the highly structured military life to the independence of being a sales representative was more challenging than he had anticipated. But he was tough, hard working, disciplined, and determined to succeed.

What proved to be his ultimate challenge, however, was not his job or surviving in the civilian world, but rather being married. Not marriage itself, but being married to Nellie. Their deep cultural and religious differences became more pronounced with every day that passed. She was unhappy. She was bored and missed her friends and relatives. Their apartment was too small. With her black hair and eyes and dark complexion and her accent she was often mistaken for a Mexican and looked down upon.

They had been married for hardly more than a year and had spent little time together in Iran while Shad had been working in Kurdistan. Once they had started living together, problems began surfacing quickly.

For him, they started in bed. At first he had been so in love and starved for sex he had taken Nellie's passivity for shyness and did not complain. He thought it would only be a matter of time until she became comfortable in actively participating in their love life, but this was not to be. Frustration began to settle over him. He wanted more from her than she was able to give and he finally worked up the nerve to share his unhappiness with her.

He chose his words carefully, and yet she was obviously hurt. "I am sorry, Shad," she said, "but that's just how we are. Iranian women, I mean. We are taught to lie still, not to move, because we should not distract the man from his pleasure and are not supposed to experience any feelings ourselves. Iranian men do not want their women to move; to be active. They are in charge. We serve them and let them use us as they see fit. But I have never ever turned you down or complained when you wanted to make love, have I?"

"No, and I really appreciate that. It's not that you don't let me have all the sex I need. It's that I love you and want to do more than just being allowed to be on top of you. You have such a beautiful body, and yet you go out of your way to make sure I don't get to see and admire it. I want to make love to you spontaneously, wherever we might be in the apartment and whatever time it may be. I'd like to take a shower with you, wash you, dry you off. I long to try different positions with you. I'd like you to hold me and take me in your mouth. I sometimes feel as if I had you, but not all of you. Not your emotions. It's as if you were forcing yourself to hold back, purposefully not showing how you really feel. Afraid you might reach pleasures you are not supposed to have. It shouldn't be just me. I would like to see you occasionally take the initiative; to show me what you would like me to do. To let me sense you like it and need it as much as I do. As it is, I can never tell whether you are merely complying or are enjoying yourself or are indifferent. That makes me feel inadequate; that I am not good enough to unleash your passions."

"You are," she assured him and promised she would try to change. To become the way he wanted her to be. He promised he would be patient.

Neither one of them, it turned out, could live up to their commitments. The schisms in their background became more and more difficult to overcome. He had only known the army and was a mere high school graduate. She came out of the sheltered and spoiled life of a rich family and was a graduate of Oxford University. She had culture and loved the arts; he did not think much about either one. He was immersed in his work and was successful. She could not overcome her boredom of being alone at home every day and living in a cultural desert.

Something had to give, and it was their marriage. They parted amicably. She was eager to return to her homeland and the environment in which she had grown up. He had his work. There were no children, and for that—in retrospect—they were grateful.

With the single-mindedness Shad had devoted to his military assignments, he was now even more determined to become the best salesman while getting a higher education. He was promoted to senior salesman and eventually territory manager, but still had enough time to work on his degree at the University of Houston. Only two factors saddened him: there were no family members to witness his graduation with a degree in business administration, and he was not as proud of the products he was selling as he felt he should have been. He needed a company with life saving drugs and more definitive career advancement opportunities than Rigopharm offered. He was ready for a change and seized an offer when it came his way.

What he could not have foreseen was that the family owned and managed company he joined had unique limitations as well. It took him ten years to finally accept this fact.

He arrived at the demoralizing conclusion he was not going to advance any further in this tightly knit environment. He had distinguished himself as one of their top sales representatives and had been promoted into a product management position after only two years. His subsequent elevation to first, Group Product Manager, and then Marketing Director, had followed rapidly. Since then—despite his undisputed successes over four long years—nothing. Senior management was too entrenched and totally dominated by family members who were either too old to show the dynamism needed to grow rapidly or too young to know what they were doing. Shad had to live with the realization that without the right family name—the one on top of the headquarters building—he was destined to remain at the director level forever. He found this to be too limiting and in stark contrast to his personal ambitions. While not sure where exactly he wanted to go in his career, he could not face the thought of having the same job and responsibility indefinitely. He needed more challenges, and completely new ones.

The call he received one morning from a headhunter was timed perfectly. He had just come out of a long term strategy meeting which had once again shown him the limits of his sphere of influence. He felt totally frustrated.

The job described by the recruiter as Area President, Asia Pacific, had immediately appealed to him. He wanted to know who had recommended him, but the headhunter was not at liberty to say. Just like he didn't want to reveal the name of the company until Shad had agreed to be interviewed. They were interested in him, the recruiter explained, because of his successful track record on one hand, and his overseas experience with the army on the other, which—they felt—gave him the right perspective and sensitivity to working with foreign nationals. Shad had no idea where the recruiter had dug up this information and worried briefly about what else they might know about him. Not his fugitive status, he had to assume, or he would never have been contacted.

When he finally learned who was recruiting him, during his first interview through the headhunter, Shad had eventually talked to a number of friends in the industry to ask them for advice. Should he really leave the security of an established, large, albeit rather boring company to take his chances with an upstart? His buddy from his military days, Neil Clifford, had been very straight forward: "Join the company or live to regret it," he advised unequivocally. "They will go public in a few years, I am sure, so be sure to negotiate some stock options up front."

His interviews by AmeriDerm at their headquarters in San Diego had gone well and he had been hired in early 1985 with the mandate of establishing a business for its dermatological products in Asia. He would have the authority and a great deal of autonomy in setting his own priorities and in selecting which countries to enter, and in what order.

He had found the challenge of starting a new venture in an environment he was unfamiliar with from a business point of view spontaneously appealing, and the thought of living in beautiful San Diego and traveling to a part of the world he had learned to admire had been an added attraction. Any reservations he might have had about leaving the security of his present employer to cast his fortune with what was still basically a small operation were quickly dispelled by the opportunities described to him during his interviews. The promise to have freedom to operate, restricted only by his own sound judgment and common sense, had been the irresistible clincher.

The one negative he could see, and which did give him pause, was that AmeriDerm, being a young company, did not have a lot of money to invest in new markets. Operating profits, primarily from its break-through melanoma treatment product *Melavict*, were being plowed back into research. From the marketing side, focus was clearly on expanding their presence in the huge US market, followed by an initial, somewhat tentative foray into Canada and Europe.

The founding partners of the company had a long term strategic vision of becoming a global player in the highly lucrative market for skin care products. Only a modest number of companies had seen fit to specialize in this segment, and opportunities were rife. As was the case with nearly all forms of cancer, treatment options for melanoma were severely limited, and AmeriDerm's bio-engineered *Melavict* had become a critically acclaimed alternative to previously available therapies. It had become the door opener to the medical profession for them and had then allowed AmeriDerm to successfully introduce a range of products for more mundane skin conditions—from acne to dry skin—in need of treatment.

As chance would have it, his hiring process had coincided with the World Congress of Dermatology, held every four years, this time in San Diego. His new boss, Dave Hardee, the CEO of AmeriDerm, had suggested he attend this important meeting, since it would provide good insights into what was happening in the world of dermatology globally.

It was a huge event, with nearly 15,000 dermatologists from all over the world attending lectures and visiting the elaborate exhibition booths of companies marketing products the physicians required for their practices. At least the same number of industry representatives staffed the displays, with the result that the exhibition area was a beehive of activity.

Shad had difficulties trying to figure out where to start in his search for a better understanding of this business. He wandered around, staring open-eyed and in amazement. He had had no idea that this relatively small segment of the industry had such a large presence. He felt even better about having joined AmeriDerm while also realizing that the competitive circumstances would be much tougher than he had anticipated.

His first morning at the convention centered on his new colleagues at AmeriDerm's booth. He introduced himself and developed a feel for who he would be working with and the products he had been hired to launch. He liked his fellow employees immediately and was impressed by the extent of their knowledge in all things dermatology.

Perhaps two hours into his get acquainted endeavors with AmeriDerm's staff members, he was called over to the small meeting room in the back of their display area.

"Mr. Cooper," he was told, "there is a gentleman here who wants to talk to you about business opportunities in Asia."

"Thanks. What can I do for you?" Shad asked, turning to his visitor.

"My name is Charles Lee," the man said and handed Shad his business card.

"I am sorry, I don't have a card yet. My name is Shad Cooper. I have just joined AmeriDerm as Area President for Asia-Pacific."

"It's an honor to meet you, Mr. Cooper. I wanted to talk to you about what we could do for your company in the Far East."

Shad studied the card he had been given more closely and saw that he was speaking with the CEO of Pan-Asia Import/Export Company in New York. He had never heard of the company.

"You may not have heard of us, Mr. Cooper," Mr. Lee said as if reading Shad's mind, "but we are a significant player in the distribution of pharmaceutical products throughout Asia. A number of our principals are represented here today, but we also work with European companies not in the dermatological business."

"I see," Shad said. He wasn't sure how relevant this was. "You wanted to tell me what you could do for us," he prompted.

"Yes. You see, there are not that many companies who could help you enter the Asian markets. We have well established organizations in nearly all the Asian countries, from South Korea in the north to Singapore and Malaysia in the south and everything in between. We have been operating in that part of the world for several decades and understand the ins and outs of doing business there. And as you may know, the conditions in Asia are rather unique, which is why even huge companies like Merck continue to make use of local distributors in countries such as Taiwan."

"Well, I have to confess my business knowledge of Asia is still very limited," Shad admitted, "but as soon as I have gotten my feet on the ground, so to speak, I plan on traveling to the Far East to see first hand what we might be able to do there."

"May I suggest you first take a close look at Hong Kong and Singapore?" Mr. Lee said and went on to explain his rational for this recommendation.

Shad listened closely. He was eager to learn. What Mr. Lee told him seemed to make a lot of sense. They continued talking at length, and at the conclusion of their discussion Mr. Lee offered to provide Shad with the names of their local managers and contact information for their Asian subsidiaries. He would let his people know Shad might contact them shortly and offered whatever help and advice his managers could provide. Shad accepted this gladly and assured Mr. Lee he was looking forward to hearing from him.

Shad was pleased with this initial contact. He had a starting point now and thought his meeting Mr. Lee had been fortuitous.

*   *   *

In the course of his two days' attendance of the congress, Shad met two other potential distributors who were interested in working with AmeriDerm, but neither one of them offered the multi-country presence that Pan-Asia Import/Export did. He kept the information they had provided for possible follow up when he would travel to the markets in which they were strong.

With so many people attending the congress, the surrounding restaurants were crowded to overflowing during the lunch hour, and Shad decided to stroll over to the nearby Sea Port Village in the hope of finding a table there during his second day. It was a beautiful respite to walk along the harbor and watch the people milling along the broad sidewalks. The sun was shining brightly; the water with its many ships a brilliant blue. A little further out, North Island Naval Air Station was visible with its steady stream of Navy fighter jets and helicopters taking off or landing. He had heard of this facility, where naval aviators practiced aircraft carrier take offs and landings.

It was pleasantly warm and the slight breeze felt good. He took off his jacket and draped it over his shoulder as he sauntered along, keeping his eyes peeled for an inviting restaurant.

It quickly became obvious that his choice of food was going to be determined for him, not by him. It would have to be the first eatery where space was available. It did not look promising. He reached the end of the Village before seeing Anthony's Fish Grotto's fast food outlet. He was hungry and went in.

Even here he had to wait nearly fifteen minutes just to place his order, and then another twenty before his tray with his grilled fish sandwich was handed over. He took it and walked out to the patio in search of a place to sit down. The only place he could spot was a small table at which a woman was sitting by herself, reading a magazine while munching on her fish and chips.

"Excuse me, but would you mind terribly much if I sat down here?" he asked when he stood next to her. "There doesn't seem to be any other table where I could park myself," he added. He didn't want her to think he was trying to pick her up or wanted to intrude on her space.

She glanced up from her reading and appeared to study him for a few seconds before nodding and saying, "Sure, be my guest, Mr. Shad Cooper." She smiled fleetingly at him.

He was momentarily puzzled she knew his name before realizing he had neglected to remove his congress name tag.

"I guess I should have taken off my tag before leaving the convention center," he said, smiling a little sheepishly, "but at least I don't have to introduce myself now."

"That wouldn't have been necessary in any case." Her eyes were back on her magazine.

"Right. But as long as you know who I am, would it be okay for me to ask who you are?"

Again she studied him with probing eyes. Her oversized sunglasses made it hard for Shad to see the color of her eyes. He continued to smile; trying to tell her he was just curious, not pushing her. He noticed she was not wearing a ring.

"Veronica Madison," she finally answered without stopping her reading, leisurely pushing a French fry into her mouth and ignoring him.

"Nice to meet you, Ms. Veronica Madison."

"Thanks," was her laconic response.

He focused on his eating while watching her surreptitiously. She was attractive in that typical southern California way. Lightly tanned, trim body, modestly made-up, friendly, wearing those ubiquitous sunglasses and a colorful dress with a flower design, buttoned down the front. She had her legs crossed modestly and had slipped her heels out of her white pumps. Good legs, he noticed. Her hair was auburn and pulled back in a ponytail. The top two buttons of her dress were open, exposing enticing cleavage. He thought she was in her mid thirties and probably divorced, given her age and that she was not wearing a ring.

"Are you finished studying me?" she asked suddenly, her eyebrows raised questioningly.

"I am sorry. I didn't know it was that obvious."

"It was. But that's okay. I don't blame you. I might even have wondered if you hadn't."

"Wondered about what?"

"How I look. If I could still attract the roving eye. Did I at least pass muster?"

"You certainly did. But I think I was doing it automatically; sort of a male thing. I didn't mean to make you uncomfortable," he said. "I hope I didn't offend you."

"No, not at all. I told you it was okay. If it had bothered me, I would have gotten up and left."

"I am glad you didn't. I enjoyed looking at you. You are very attractive."

"Whoa . . . slow down!" she said, raising her hands in what was meant to look defensive. "What are you doing here anyway?"

"Having lunch. Attending the dermatology congress in the Convention Center."

"Obviously. I meant when you are not attending a congress."

"I have just taken a job with a local company over in La Jolla and am in the process of moving here. Being at this meeting is part of my familiarization. What about you? What do you do?"

"Trying to enjoy my all too short lunch break, actually. But I work for an advertising agency downtown, as a copywriter."

"I envy you," he said. "I mean, not because of your job, but because it allows you to come over here for lunch. I couldn't think of a more pleasant environment in which to sit down and enjoy a bite to eat. At least as long as strangers don't just sit down and start bothering you."

She returned his smile. "I should have known better than to come here during a convention. It's always a mess when these meetings take place, and there seem to be more and more of them all the time. Normally I avoid the whole area on days like these, but today I forgot what was going on."

"Well, I am glad you did. It was my good fortune."

She glanced at her watch. "I am afraid I am going to have to go," she said and stood up. "I enjoyed talking to you and hope you have a good convention." She put her magazine into her oversized purse and walked over to dump her lunch wrappings into the trash container.

She offered him her hand to say good-bye.

"I enjoyed meeting you too," he said and added spontaneously: "Perhaps we could continue our discussion some other time?"

There was no mistaking the hope in his voice. She hesitated, looking him over frankly before settling on his eyes. "Maybe," she finally said. "Let me think about it. Why don't you give me a call if you are serious?"

"I will."

He wrote down her phone number and was told he could call her anytime after six.

He was elated and looked forward to seeing her again. What an unexpected pleasure, he thought, to have met such an attractive woman in his first days in San Diego.

* * *

After the congress Shad briefed Dave Hardee on what he had seen and learned at the convention and shared his initial conclusions with him. Dave advised him he would have to operate on a shoestring and fund day-to-day start-up activities by immediately generating sufficient sales to cover most—if not all—expenses. As Dave put it so succinctly: "I am buying you a one way ticket to the Far East, Shad. When you have sold enough products to pay for your return flight, you can come back!"

Shad had laughed, thinking Dave was surely joking, but his new boss had remained serious.

As it turned out, it hadn't been quite that bad, but the message was unmistakable: You are on your own; concentrate on markets where you can generate sales promptly; profit margins supersede market share during the first years. Only by making sufficient profits in one country would he have the necessary funds with which to enter another one.

* * *

He pondered the financial limitations of his mandate that evening, back in the small apartment AmeriDerm had rented for him while he looked for permanent dwellings. He would have to learn to work within the given parameters. For now, he decided, the smart thing to do was to call Veronica.

"Hey, Veronica," he said when she answered her phone. "It's me. Shad."

"Well, hello there," she said. She sounded glad, if not gushingly enthusiastic, to hear from him. "I wasn't sure you would actually call."

"Why wouldn't I? I am not in the habit of breaking promises, and besides, I am eager to see you again."

"Sounds good to me. What would you like to do?" She was rather direct.

"I was thinking we could have a drink together, and then, depending on how we feel and how hungry we are, we could have dinner someplace."

"That would be fine. Do you want to meet somewhere? Or would you prefer to pick me up? I live over here in Pacific Beach, if you know where that is."

"I'll find it and pick you up at 7:30," he said, and she explained how to find her apartment.

He debated with himself what to wear. He didn't know where they might wind up but thought a pair of gray slacks and a blue striped, long sleeved shirt would be appropriate enough for wherever they might go. On the way to Pacific Beach he stopped at a flower shop and bought a small bouquet.

She looked almost a little embarrassed at receiving the flowers but was obviously pleased. She asked him to wait a moment while she put them in a vase.

"Thank you so very much for the lovely flowers," she said when she had rejoined him. "That was very thoughtful of you."

"Don't mention it," he mumbled. "Is there any place in particular where you would like to go?"

"I don't really spend a lot of times in bars," she said. "What about going to a restaurant with a bar? That way, if we wanted to stay for dinner, we wouldn't have to drive anyplace else. Or am I jumping too far ahead?"

"No, no, not at all. It's a great idea. Do you like fish? I was taken to this place called The Fishery over on Cass a couple of days ago, and the food was outstanding. Plus, they have a small bar area."

"I don't think I have been there, but I do like fish, so let's go."

Shad hadn't noticed how tall she was when she had been sitting across from him in Sea Port Village. Hardly a couple of inches less than six feet, he thought. He liked the way she looked, wearing tight fitting hip hugger jeans, high heels, and a starched white long sleeved shirt. Elegantly casual.

They exchanged some pleasantries while he drove.

"I hope you don't have a steady boyfriend," he said when he had a chance.

"If I had, I wouldn't be going out with you," she said. "But maybe I should tell you I am married. At least legally," she added before he could react. "I have been separated for a couple of years already, but my divorce won't become final for probably several more months." Her tone was matter of fact and Shad wondered whether he should probe but decided it was none of his business. It was enough to know she was willing to go out with him.

"I am sorry to hear that," was all he could think to say.

"What about you, Shad? You are not married, are you?"

"No, I am not. I have been divorced for more than ten years. And no, I don't have a steady girlfriend either, in case you are wondering."

"So you can appreciate what I am going through," she stated, and Shad speculated silently this could have meant either her divorce proceedings or not having a steady boyfriend.

There was no vacant space at the bar when they entered The Fishery, but a table was just being bussed, and this was given to them. The question of having dinner together had become redundant. Shad was glad. He enjoyed being with Veronica.

They ordered. They ate. They talked. The food was outstanding. The conversation flowed easily and before they knew it, they found themselves the last customers remaining in the restaurant. Shad called for the bill. The second bottle of wine they had ordered was almost empty when they got up to leave.

"Are you sure you can still drive, Shad?" she asked, a note of worry in her voice. It was clear she was feeling the wine.

"I am okay," he assured her. "I wouldn't get on the freeway like this, but a few blocks along these residential streets are not a problem. But if you are worried, I would be happy to call us a cab."

"No, I guess it's okay. But please drive carefully."

They made it safely back to her apartment and he brought her to the door.

After she had unlocked and opened it she turned to him and offered him her lips. He embraced her tightly while responding to her invitation. She tasted good and did not object when he used his tongue to open her mouth. He felt her breasts pressing against his chest, her nipples hard.

Suddenly she pushed him away, gently but determined.

"What's the matter?"

"This is too dangerous. It's too good and if we continue, I might be unable to stop," she admitted.

"Nothing wrong with that," he smiled, trying to pull her to him again. She would not let him.

"Yes, there would be. As a matter of principle I never ever go to bed with a man on the first date."

"And with a woman?" he had the presence of mind to joke despite his disappointment.

"Not with a woman either," she assured him, sounding serious, and there was something in her voice that made him wonder.

"Okay." He conceded defeat gracefully. He did not want to push her to do something for which she was not ready. He wanted to see her again and believed a longer term relationship could well develop, but he did not want to jeopardize this possibility through a one night stand. "I understand," he added. "I am not going to push you to do something you don't want to do."

"It's not that I don't want. I just don't wish to rush. We just met. I want to see you again. I enjoyed this evening tremendously. But I drank more than I should have and that clouds my judgment, so I think it would be better for us if you went home and called me again tomorrow or whenever. I had a great evening."

This time her kiss was chaste when he bid her good-bye and she closed her door.

8

Hong Kong, 1985

Shad, based on information he had gathered, concluded Charles
had been right in identifying Singapore and Hong Kong as offering the
best short term prospects for AmeriDerm's products. The countries were
small, but so were the risks. They offered few barriers to market entry
and had high prices compared with other Asian countries. Necessary
government approvals of health registrations were still relatively
easy in 1985. There were few import restrictions for most ethical
pharmaceutical products, and the markets were free of corruption—a
critical factor in a part of the world where corruption, he had been
advised, was prevalent.

He had been working on trip arrangements. He hadn't thought
much about a passport until his first trip approached. Had, in fact,
inexplicably forgotten he would need one. His previous passport,
required for Iran, had been a diplomatic one, obtained through the
auspices of the Army Map Service. Unfortunately, it had been revoked
upon his return to the States. Now he was nervous about going to
the post office to apply for a regular one, not sure his duplicate birth
certificate would be accepted without questioning. He should have at
least kept a copy of his diplomatic passport as proof of citizenship, he
chastised himself, but it was too late.

To his great relief his application went through without problems
and hardly three weeks later, the document arrived. He could relax
once again.

He was eager to see and experience the Asian environment again. He had read much about these two countries he was now scheduled to visit and looked forward to his trip. The anticipation pulsing through him was so palpable he could not sleep on the seemingly endlessly long flight. Although the route from Los Angeles to Hong Kong was to have been non-stop, the headwinds over the Pacific were so strong that Cathay Pacific had to make a non-scheduled refueling stop in Taipei, adding almost two hours to his trip. Consequently, it was approaching 8:00am upon his arrival in Hong Kong.

The flight path into Kai Tek airport was awesome. Swooping in over the teeming tenements of Kowloon at an altitude already so low that buildings on both sides of the aircraft appeared to be higher than the 747's, the pilot made a sharp right turn at the last moment. As Shad looked out the window, the buildings they flew past were so close he thought he could see what people were having for breakfast.

Moments later the plane touched down and the pilot braked sharply on the short runway built into the harbor. More than one aircraft, he had read, had not been able to stop in time, and he was glad their pilot had made it. When their plane made a sharp turn off the runway onto the taxi strip leading to the terminal, Shad saw that only a few hundred feet of concrete separated them from the water.

Standing in line to get through immigration, Shad couldn't help but feel nervous at the thought of his name showing up on a list of people 'wanted' by the police. It was his first entry into a foreign country as a civilian and he didn't know how closely countries cooperated in the search for fugitives. But his crime had apparently not warranted an international alert for him, and he was whisked through without any questions.

In the chaotic area behind immigration and customs of Kai Tek airport he needed time to find the area where the hotel cars were standing by, as he had been advised, but once he was ensconced in the limo the Hilton Hotel had waiting for him, the drive through Kowloon and the central tunnel was mercifully short. He had difficulties deciding where to look; everything was strange and new and exotic, and there was little to remind him of his arrivals in Saigon or Seoul years ago.

The Hilton turned out to be the most luxurious hotel he had ever frequented. A two story escalator took him to the main lobby, richly and elegantly laid out with teak, comfortable seating areas, sparkling chandeliers dangling from the high ceiling and rich carpeting. A beautiful young hostess accompanied him to his room, checked him in, and showed him what he needed to know about his surroundings.

He rationalized that after spending the better part of a day and a whole night traveling it would be irresponsible of him to engage in meaningful business discussions on his day of arrival. He wanted a long nap, but found himself too restless to sleep and too brain dead to work. He called his contact at Pan-Asia, Thomas Grady, to confirm his safe arrival and their scheduled meeting for the next morning. Thomas would send a car for him, he was glad to hear.

After a quick shower and a change of clothes, he exited the hotel and set out to explore his immediate surroundings, wandering along aimlessly. To his surprise, Hong Kong's population seemed to be totally Chinese. He had expected to see more foreigners. The few he saw were dressed in conservative business attire, despite the sweltering heat and oppressive humidity. Shad, wearing only a short sleeved shirt and shorts, was already perspiring in the jungle like weather conditions minutes after he left the air-conditioned comfort of the hotel. He thought the men he saw risked turning into puddles on the sidewalk.

As he ambled along he quickly realized the shortest distance between two points was not a straight line in Hong Kong. The jumble of narrow streets curved over and under each other. Metal rails prevented pedestrians from crossing at will; instead, elevated walkways had to be used. The sights—except for the many architecturally stunning office towers—were uninspiring. Concrete everywhere.

Without a clear destination in mind, he thought of Wanchai and its seedy night life he had heard about from his fellow soldiers who had been sent to Hong Kong on R&R from Vietnam. He was curious to see what it looked like in daylight.

It turned out to be disappointing. Night club after night club beckoned with bright neon lights, but there were no garishly made up girls beckoning customers to come inside. The district looked empty; desolate. No hawkers. Instead, only geriatric vendors were vociferously peddling their merchandise. He had expected excitement from the area. Perhaps, he thought, Thomas Grady could take him there one evening and show him around. Surely he would be familiar with the most popular night clubs.

Small shops catered to local residents with fruits, vegetables and groceries. Tiny noodle shops abounded and were crowded with customers noisily slurping their soups. He felt lost and conspicuous. Perhaps the harbor would be more interesting, he thought, and set off in its direction.

The pavement was blistering hot. Just breathing was an effort.

He discovered that sky bridges connected many of the office towers, which all appeared to have small shopping centers on the ground floor.

More by accident than plan he found his way to the harbor and followed its waterfront sidewalk past the British Navy headquarters, with its own small and well sheltered private harbor, past Queen's Pier, and over to the Star Ferry terminal. He stood and watched the ferries shuttling back and forth between Central and Kowloon in a seemingly endless procession.

Turning away from the harbor, the Hong Kong and Shanghai Bank building dominated the sky line. An incredible edifice, stunningly unique, making him think of what he had tried to build with his erector set as a young boy. Its ground floor was open space and was being used by pedestrians to take a short cut from one side of the building to the other, saving them a two block detour. Long, steep escalators took visitors to the banking level.

He followed the crowd and emerged on Queen's Road Central, across from the Hilton. He had been walking for nearly three hours and was hungry, sweaty, and exhausted. After a quick lunch in the hotel's coffee shop and a shower he went to bed.

Later, he felt too groggy to do more than take the short ferry ride to Kowloon. A quick stroll through the huge shopping center that greeted him there underlined why Hong Kong was a shopper's paradise. There was little else to do except to go shopping or eating. He returned to his hotel.

The driver sent for him picked him up the next morning and drove him to Causeway Bay, a bustling industrial area with less than impressive offices and warehouses. Stepping out of the car's air conditioned cocoon, Shad looked around and was dismayed at how different these surroundings were compared to Central. This was a working part of Hong Kong, with a no nonsense atmosphere completely dissimilar from what he had seen the previous day. It was crowded with drab, uninspired buildings characterized by functionality rather than architectural distinction.

The narrow streets and alleys were dirty, littered with trash and discarded plastic bags. The smell of rotting garbage permeated the air. The buildings had proper names instead of street numbers. Offices and warehouse space encroached on each other.

Shad's driver took him through a freight door into a non-descript elevator that lumbered up to the fourth floor of Warwick House, where the Managing Director of Pan-Asia, Thomas Grady, awaited him.

Shad was led through a cluttered open office area into Mr. Grady's small private office. It was a glass enclosed cubicle from which warehouse racking could be seen in the background. Shad was shocked when he noticed how tiny the employee's desks were, and how close together they stood. With the prevailing noise level, he was surprised anyone could conduct understandable telephone conversations.

Thomas beckoned Shad to sit down. "Welcome to Hong Kong, Shad," he said. "Please call me Thomas. Can I assume this is your first visit to the country?"

"Thank you. Yes, it is, and I find it fascinating, I must say. Not at all what I had expected," Shad said, and told Thomas about his previous day's walking experience and gave him a summary of his background.

Thomas laughed. "Yes," he said, "it does take some getting used to."

Thomas, Shad learned, was British born, raised in Hong Kong, and with a degree in business from Leeds University. From the moment Thomas and Shad met, a solid friendship started developing. Shad was impressed by Thomas' low key style. He was quiet, self confident, and an impeccably dressed man who loved golf and was fond of holding business discussions in the venerable Hong Kong Club. Not tall, slim, with a ready smile, rather sparse blond hair and those chiseled gentlemanly good looks, he personified what Shad thought was the quintessential Hong Kong businessman.

Shad and Thomas concluded a tentative distribution agreement and, to celebrate, Thomas invited Shad for drinks in the lobby bar of the stately Mandarin Hotel. His lovely wife, Jade, joined them. During the subsequent dinner together Shad learned to admire Jade. Obviously Hong Kong upper class, she exuded a charm that was contagious. Not fashion model beautiful, but with a grace and sophistication that made her instantly appealing, it was easy to understand why Thomas was so enamored with her.

Shad recalled his walk through Wanchai. "Thomas, you must know the best bars in Wanchai." He glanced somewhat apologetically towards Jade as he said this. Thomas' eyebrows shot up.

"Best bars in Wanchai? Are you kidding? There is no such thing. If you want to go to a bar, stay out of that area. The only reason for visiting it is to find some girl or watch a sex show. I have to tell you I absolutely hate those girly bars. When I get visitors who insist on going there I send one of my managers with them."

Shad decided to drop the subject.

In the following months, AmeriDerm's entry into the market proceeded smoothly. The salesman Thomas had hired to work for AmeriDerm's product line excelled. Orders started coming in to the extent that an entry into Singapore became possible.

He could not have foreseen that Hong Kong would eventually bring some of the happiest moments of his life, while leaving him with the most agonizing memories.

*   *   *

Some months later, as Shad's second visit to Hong Kong drew to an end, Thomas suggested it was time for Shad to look at China. While immeasurably more complex, it represented the largest potential by far, and the earlier AmeriDerm got started, Thomas explained, the greater the chances of long term success. Health registrations were negotiable; salaries low; expenses modest.

"The thought of going into China makes me nervous," Shad admitted, frowning. "Combining a centrally planned and controlled economy with pervasive corruption would seem to be a recipe for disaster. Why should we be a pioneer venturing into such troubled, risky waters?"

"You are too Americanized in your thinking. Economic unpredictability is blamed on corruption in all too many countries. Generally speaking it does not apply to Asia. Look at what is starting to happen in China. Look at Taiwan, Korea, Thailand. All terribly corrupt, and yet they grow dynamically. As to communism, which scares the shit out of western nations, it does not have to be that bad economically. When you try to govern a country with more than a billion people, it has its uses. Contrast what is happening in China commercially against the world's largest democracy, India. The Indians spend so much time on endless series of elections that they are at least a decade behind China in developing urgently needed infrastructure and a larger middle class. And India is just as corrupt as China. No, mark my words, China is on its way to becoming an economic powerhouse, and now is the time to get on this train before it leaves the station. Be on board from the beginning."

Shad knew too little about China to disagree and let Thomas continue.

"There are problems involved, of course," Thomas went on. "Only government owned import/export companies with access to hard currencies are licensed to import foreign pharmaceuticals. You have to find a distributor with strong connections to such an importer."

They were sitting in the sedate Hong Kong Club, enjoying a light Chinese lunch of delicious Dim Sum while envisioning the future.

"And you could help me with that?"

"Yes. I think I know the ins and outs of the market. We don't distribute third party products there, but I know reputable companies that do."

"So your China business is limited to what you produce in Hainan?"

Thomas nodded. "A lot of people today probably think local manufacturing is stupid, Shad, but it works for us. Hainan is an economic free trade zone, so we save a lot in taxes. And China is changing rapidly. The pharmaceutical factories you see there today will disappear, to be replaced by state of the art facilities, meeting or exceeding international standards. I firmly believe that the day will soon come when companies will source some of their products out of their plants in China for global distribution. It's only a question of time before the Chinese authorities will enforce Good Manufacturing Practices. Then they will get FDA approval for these plants. In the meantime I know a lot of decision makers and could help you smooth the way."

"You mentioned sales to hospitals, Thomas, but you know that our target audience is the non-hospital doctor. Our bread and butter creams, ointments, lotions and tablets are primarily used by privately practicing dermatologists. Patients with skin ailments normally don't go to a hospital."

"I am aware of that," Thomas said, "but China is different. Oh, I see you smiling and thinking: where have I heard that before? It's the claim that every country makes, isn't it? But China really *is* different. All doctors are government employees, working in state owned hospitals. That's where the patients go. A few doctors have set up clandestine private clinics recently where they see a few patients after they finish in the hospital at 3:00pm, but these clinics are not legal and generate very little business, although everything is treated there. The government is ignoring these set-ups so far, and I think it will be years before private practices are sanctioned. In any case, if you can convince the doctors in the hospitals to use your products, and they are happy with the results they get, they will automatically sell them to patients they see privately."

Shad gave this some thought. It was a way of doing business he was not familiar with. He was not convinced that the time for China was right. He worried it was too soon and too risky. Too many unknowns. Too soon after the Cultural Revolution. Too corrupt. He was inclined to look at other, more promising large markets first, like Korea, Taiwan, or Thailand. But he didn't know these countries either, had no contacts there, and did not know what market barriers they had erected.

But if Thomas felt the time was right for China, who was Shad to argue?

"You know what I think you should consider strategically, Shad?"

Shad shook his head. His thoughts had been drifting. "No. What?"

"Go into China with *Melavict* as lead product and establish a trustworthy reputation. I seem to recall reading somewhere that China has more than 200,000 cases of melanoma per year, and if you could capture only 20% of that market—which I think is possible—and given the prices for cancer treatments, you could generate enough revenue to expand your business with the more mundane products used on out-patients. *Melavict* would serve as the locomotive pulling your train with the other products. If you are at all interested, we could visit China together for a few days and arrange some meetings with potential distributors."

This offer made China much more palatable. With Thomas by his side to guide and advise him, a fact finding trip seemed justifiable.

"That's good input, Thomas. It's kind of you to be willing to go there with me. I wouldn't have a clue as to how to get started by myself. Let me think about it and see if I can fine tune this a little before I try to sell the idea to my boss."

The longer Shad thought about it, the more he began relishing taking a personal look at the market. Wasn't this one of the key reasons he had joined AmeriDerm? To face new challenges? To overcome obstacles? Having Thomas introduce him to potential distributors and visiting selected hospitals seemed opportune. A courtesy call on the Ministry of Health could also be arranged, Thomas assured him.

"One other thing you need to keep in mind," Thomas said. "China is an unbelievably huge country, and what you see in Beijing is no mirror image of the country as such. Don't be misled by the modernity of the capital. China is still an incredibly backward country. It has dozens of cities with a population of more than 5 million that I guarantee you have never heard of, and you will not find a hospital there that you would want to frequent, so even the largest companies rely on a network of distributors, sub-distributors, dealers and wholesalers to extend their reach into the more remote areas."

"And yet, despite these problems, you think the time is right for us?"

"Absolutely. These issues are not going to go away, and the longer you wait, the more difficult it will become. New restrictions. Tighter health registration requirements. Rising salaries and general expenses. More competition."

"Well, Thomas, you have certainly whetted my appetite. I will confirm the dates of my next Asia trip and will plan on including Beijing on my itinerary. You have been more than helpful and given me a lot to think about. I hope to see you in Beijing next time."

9

San Diego, 1985

It was not Shad's style to initiate conversations with strangers. It made him uncomfortable and he feared inadvertently revealing more of himself than was prudent. But in meeting Veronica, it had happened incidentally and the words had come easily and naturally. Perhaps because it had been just a chance encounter with a lovely, self confident woman he thought he would never see again. He had been surprised when she had offered to give him her telephone number, encouraging him to call her.

Their first date had been an amicable start and he had had to fight off his disappointment at not being invited into her apartment. He had not expected it to happen, but after her passionate, promising kisses, his hopes had been raised. When she hadn't been willing to take the next step, he had accepted her principles in good grace, confident the next time would be different. He had deliberately waited a couple of days before calling her again, not wanting to seem too eager.

When he did speak with her again he invited her out for another dinner, and she was straight forward in accepting. He made a reservation at Sante's, an excellent Italian restaurant he knew to offer an intimate, romantic setting.

The table they were shown to upon their arrival was in a little alcove facing the street. It was a Tuesday evening and not crowded.

"What a lovely place," she said after sitting down and looking around at all the photos on the walls of the owner posing with famous personalities who had dined there.

"You haven't been here then, I take it?" Shad asked, and when she shook her head, continued, "I think you will like the food."

They gave their dinner orders to the waiter and toasted each other with the wine Shad had selected.

"I am very happy to see you again, Veronica. You look beautiful." She had her rather long hair down around her shoulders, a pink silk scarf tied loosely around her neck, and was wearing a pale blue blouse tucked into a deep maroon, short skirt. Just the right amount of make-up highlighted her green eyes. She looked demure and radiant at the same time.

"I was a little worried you might not call again after I sent you home the other night. I know you wanted to stay," she admitted.

"I did," he said, "but I like someone who has principles and sticks to them. I might even have misunderstood if you had invited me in on our first date."

"You mean you would have thought I was an easy lay."

He saw the smile in her eyes. "Not at all," he assured her, reciprocating her smile. "I would have thought you had just found me irresistible."

She snorted. "Oh, sure!" But then, after a moment's hesitation, went on thoughtfully, "I actually did find you attractive. Not irresistible, as you had to find out, but it wasn't all that easy for me to turn you down. Physically, I was more than ready and wanted you to stay. I was horny. But I wasn't sure whether it was the alcohol or something else that had me so excited. I certainly didn't want to take the chance of waking up the next morning regretting I had done something only because I had had too much to drink."

"So would I stand a greater chance of getting you into bed if I made sure you stayed sober?" he joked.

She laughed. He liked the sound of her laughter. Not loud, not forced; just a natural, spontaneous reaction. "I am not going to help you there. You'll have to find out for yourself."

"That's okay. Maybe I will find out tonight."

"Don't take things for granted, Shad. I am rather unpredictable. What works one time may not work the second time. And don't think you can control how little or how much I drink."

"I was afraid of that," he said with a little sigh, "but I can assure you I am not taking anything for granted, okay?"

"Don't be worried," she assuaged him and put her hand lightly on his. It felt good. It was warm and soft; a tender caress. Her eyes, when he looked up, were sensuous; sparkling.

Only when their waiter had cleared the table and they were drinking an espresso did they resume their conversation.

"Do you mind my asking why you are getting a divorce?" Shad asked.

"I don't know if I do or not," she said, letting the words hang in the air.

"What do you mean?"

She hesitated. "I don't really mind talking about it, but it might turn you off. It has caused not only problems with my soon to be former husband, but also with other men I have dated since we separated."

"That sounds pretty mysterious," he said. He was puzzled; wanted to probe further but afraid he might not like what she would say. He almost regretted having asked, and yet was unable to bridle his curiosity.

She looked pensive and glanced around their alcove as if to see if anyone could overhear her. "I might as well tell you," she said, sounding reluctant, Shad thought, "before we become more involved and you find out and don't want to go out with me again."

"I can't imagine that happening," he said. "I know for sure I want to see a lot more of you."

She studied him with inquisitive eyes. "You may change your mind. It's only our second date, and I may shock you enough to drop me. So you better not jump to any conclusions, Shad." She paused for a moment before going on. "You remember the other night when I told you I never go to bed with a man on a first date? And you thought you were being funny when you asked whether I applied the same principle to women?"

"Sure," he said, frowning slightly, not knowing where this was going.

"Well, you couldn't have guessed it, but your question hit closer to home than you might like."

"Oh, oh," was all he managed to say, beginning to suspect where her confession was going.

"Yes," she acknowledged. She looked both embarrassed and defiant, her chin jutting out. "I answered your question honestly, but what that answer implied is also true. There have been times I have enjoyed being with a girlfriend."

He wasn't sure how to reply. He was caught unawares; maybe shocked. Certainly interested in confirming what she meant. "You mean you had sex with them?" he asked, rather incredulously. And before she could answer added: "Are you telling me you are lesbian? That's hard to believe. You were much too passionate and willing, I think, when we kissed."

"Don't be so dense, Shad," she admonished. "No, I am not lesbian, but I am somewhat bi-sexual. More straight than bi, if there is such a thing, and I have been in situations where I found another woman absolutely irresistible."

Now he *was* shocked, he had to admit to himself. He concentrated on not looking or sounding judgmental. "And let me guess," he said flatly, "your husband found out and couldn't handle it,"

She nodded. "I guess men just have some fundamental problem with a lover who occasionally likes to have sex with another woman. It must give you a feeling of inadequacy. Maybe an inferiority complex; the impression you do not meet your partner's expectations. That you are not good enough to satisfy her; to fulfill all of her sexual needs."

She stared at him expectantly, waiting for him to say something. She hadn't really asked him a question, but he found himself responding. "I guess I have never really thought about it," he admitted. "I haven't run into someone with these proclivities, so I don't know how I would feel. Perhaps it might take a little time to get used to."

"Well," she said, "you have now. And knowing what I just told you, are you still eager to see me again? To take me to bed?"

He thought he might have blushed slightly at her outspokenness but recovered quickly. "Absolutely," he assured her. "Let me pay the bill and I will prove it to you."

He really did want her. There would be plenty of time to consider her lesbian tendencies later. They did not impede on his immediate desires. What difference did it make if she also liked women?

"I was only asking rhetorically," she warned, "so don't get your hopes up."

But he thought she looked ready. Maybe she wanted to test him, to see how he would react to having to compete sexually with a woman; whether it would turn him off.

In any case she made no attempt to delay him when he asked for the bill and paid.

Once they were in his car he thought about asking her where she wanted to go, but then decided it was better not to force the issue. Instead, he drove towards the ocean and then followed the shoreline to Pacific Beach and up to her apartment. They drove in a relaxed silence, both preoccupied with their respective thoughts.

Talking with Veronica during dinner had absolutely delighted Shad. She was obviously as comfortable with him as he was with her, he reflected, or she never would have confessed her sexual diversity so readily. She appeared to trust him and was interested enough in him to preempt later surprises. If they were about to start something, she wanted him to do it with eyes wide open and knowing what he would have to accept about her. That was fine with him. He couldn't imagine her propensities for occasional female sex being a problem for him.

What she was thinking as he was driving, he had no idea. He parked in front of her apartment and stepped out to open the car door for her. She walked towards her door and he followed her. When they were standing in her hallway she turned to him and said, "I worry I shouldn't have told you what I did."

"Why ever not?" he answered. "I think it's a compliment for me that you did."

"I don't know. Maybe now you think I'm weird or all fucked up, just because I like to have a woman now and then. But I can assure you what I do is not all that unusual. Every woman I have ever known has either had a sexual encounter with another woman, or has fantasized about having one. Or at least idly speculated. I bet the same probably holds true for men."

He doubted it. He had certainly never entertained the idea. "Maybe idly wondered," he finally said, in the spirit of the openness she had shown, "but never considered, and I don't know of a single straight man who ever has."

She shrugged her shoulders dismissively; whether in disbelief or indifference, he could not tell.

"Are you sure you want to do this?" she asked when, still standing in the small hallway, he took her in his arms. Strange question, he thought. One *he* should be asking *her*. He answered by kissing her and cupping one of her breasts in his hand. She groaned. He wasn't sure whether this was a sign of desire or inevitability.

She tore herself away from him and walked into her living room with a shake of her head. He could see her chewing her lips, uncertainty written all over her face. When she sat down on the couch he sat next to her. She did not object, not even when he draped his arm around her shoulder and pulled her closer to him.

"Isn't this where I am supposed to offer you a drink or a cup of coffee," she said, a self conscious grin on her face, "while I disappear into my bathroom to make myself more comfortable?"

"I don't want you to do anything you don't feel is right, Veronica. If you don't want me to stay, or are worried about what might happen, just say so and I'll leave and hope for better luck next time—assuming you would want to see me again. I can assure you what you told me is a non-issue for me."

It really was, he realized. He wasn't just saying it to get into her pants. The more he thought about it, in fact, the more exciting he found the idea of her going down on another woman. He pictured himself being allowed to watch and found the scenario highly erotic; a hitherto deeply buried fantasy coming to life. He found the thought of two women kissing provocative.

She did not say anything; did not ask him to leave. Did not protest when he started unbuttoning her blouse. She also did not help him; continued to sit next to him with her hands clasped in her lap. He reached inside her pale blue lace bra and caressed her breasts, then pulled them out and saw her nipples stiffen. He kissed them and sucked them gently. After long moments of passivity she put her hand behind his head, pulling him against her, and pushed her breasts harder against his mouth. She had apparently reached a decision. She got up suddenly and took his hand and led him to her bedroom.

In seconds they had undressed and she pulled him into her and it was everything and more than he had hoped for.

They stayed in bed, closely entwined, breathing heavily and wet with perspiration.

"Will you spend the night with me?" she asked after a while, sounding utterly content but sleepy.

"Of course. But I have to warn you: I have to get up early so I can stop over at my place and take a shower and change clothes before I have to be at work by 8:00."

"That's fine. I have to leave shortly after 7:00 as well. Traffic is a bitch going downtown."

She set her alarm clock for 6:00, but it was not the alarm which woke him up. It was Veronica, nuzzling him and playing with him. He felt himself responding, and she was ready for him. By the time they had showered together, they had to hurry to leave.

*   *   *

During the next weeks they saw each other regularly. He had told her at length about growing up in Los Angeles, but it was fiction. What he described for her was what he imagined Shad Cooper's life had been like, not the bitter and agonizingly painful reality of Roger Stevens' childhood and teenage years. Fiction and truth only merged when he talked about his decision to join the army, and his experience as a young soldier in Korea and Vietnam. He couldn't tell her about his activities in Iran, those being classified.

When he told her about Nellie one day and the break-up of their marriage, she listened sympathetically.

"Isn't it odd," she said when he had finished, "that we have a divorce in common, both for similar reasons? Sexual incompatibility?"

"I guess you could call it that," he agreed somewhat hesitatingly, "although it might be more accurate to talk about different desires. From what you have told me, you and your ex were not sexually incompatible, and neither were Nellie and I. But both you and I wanted things from our partners they did not give us and, over time, we could not deal with that."

She did not argue the point. It was irrelevant.

They were falling in love and began talking about the future. She had been notified that her divorce would become final in one month, and they went out to celebrate. They routinely engaged in lively discussions where no subject was off limits, and yet her bi-sexuality had been tacitly avoided. She remained apprehensive about what it might do to their burgeoning relationship. He did not want to intrude and waited for her to come back to it. During their celebratory dinner she finally did.

"You know, Shad," she said suddenly as dessert was being brought, "we have been avoiding discussing my occasional sex with a woman. I don't think that's right. Not talking about it, I mean. If we are going to have any kind of future together, I think we need to address the subject and resolve it one way or another. I assume you have been giving it some thought?" She looked rather worried, her eyes having problems meeting his.

"Sure I have," Shad said. "I even went so far as to wonder whether you were faithful to me while I was gone last month. It was a long time for you to be alone, wasn't it?"

"No longer for me than for you."

"Well, I didn't do anything while I was traveling, if that's what you are implying. And I'm sure you didn't have another man, but what about a woman?"

"I saw my former room mate and best friend Caitlin," she admitted, unnecessarily defiant.

The look in her eyes challenged him to get mad or jealous or pass judgment, but he remained impassive. He waited for her to continue, and when she apparently had nothing to add, he said, "So what does that mean exactly? How was it?" He tried not to smile or sound too eager to hear all the details.

"That's not fair. You shouldn't ask. I didn't tell her how it was with you either, and I wouldn't have even if she had asked."

"So she knows about us?" Shad asked.

"Sure. We talk to each other all the time. What would be the point of keeping our relationship secret? She knows I like men and normally prefer having sex with them. You and I are going to be spending a lot of time together, I hope, which I might otherwise have spent with her, so I thought the sooner she knew, the better it would be."

Shad couldn't help but agree. He was looking forward to meeting Caitlin. "I think you did the right thing," he conceded.

"You are not jealous, are you?"

"Not really. I know I can do things with you and to you that she can't, but not necessarily the other way around. I don't see myself competing with her. There is no reason for me to get jealous, is there?"

"No," she confirmed.

"But I could not stand the thought of you being with another man, that's for damn sure."

"Don't worry. That is not going to happen—ever. No other man could make me as happy as you do, Shad, or satisfy me more," she assured him.

"It's sort of strange," he said. "I know so much about you now, but this sex thing—if I may call it that—hasn't come up again until just now. I have been curious, I must admit, but I didn't want to pry and figured you would talk to me about it when you were ready."

"I thought maybe you had forgotten about it," she said and watched him smile at this unlikelihood, "or you thought you were so good that I wouldn't be tempted by a girl anymore. I guess I was wrong on both counts."

"When did you discover that you are bi?" he asked, ignoring her teasing barb. He was truly interested. He found it hard to understand. He could accept her inclinations and was definitely not jealous, but understanding them?

In thinking about Veronica's split sexual predisposition the past weeks he had been reminded of a couple of former girlfriends who had shared with him their secret fantasy of one day making love to another woman, just like Veronica had claimed to know. But these women he had known professed never having done anything about it, for whatever reasons. Perhaps from lack of opportunity or courage to ask, they had explained, or an inability to find the right partner.

He had surmised there was a direct correlation between a woman's sex drive and her latent lesbian fantasies, because the ones who had shared their dreams with him had been the hottest girlfriends. Surely this couldn't be a coincidence?

He saw Veronica shrugging. "I can't put a date on it, if that's what you are asking. My first sexual experience, when I was a young teenager, was with another girl. I was going to this school in Guam and lived in a dormitory while my Dad was based in Guam as a Marine. My roommate and I started experimenting. Challenging each other to see what sexual arousal was like. We were too young to do anything with boys and thought playing with each other and experimenting was pretty harmless. But then I discovered I really liked it when my roommate went down on me."

He nodded noncommittally. The story sounded all too familiar. He encouraged her to continue.

"Eventually my Dad was transferred back to Camp Pendleton and I was enrolled in high school in Oceanside. I became a cheerleader and all the boys were after me. Well, one thing led to another and I fell in love with this hunky football player and one evening he managed to seduce me. Maybe because he was giving me such great oral sex. He made me feel so good and made me realize how much I had missed my girl friend. When I came, he was very proud of himself. He wanted more, of course, and became frustrated and upset when I didn't need anything else and didn't let him fuck me. I was still so young and inexperienced it never occurred to me to give him a blow job, which might have satisfied him, I suppose. He kept pushing himself on me and begged me to let him do it. He promised he wouldn't come inside me, because neither one of us had a rubber. Eventually he made me feel so sorry for him, and made me so horny again, that I let him do what he wanted. To my surprise I discovered I liked having him in me. Totally different from what I had experienced before, but definitely great."

"Did he keep his promise of not coming inside you?"

"Yes," she said, "although I had to remind him continuously."

"And you have been playing both sides of the field ever since?"

"More or less. I became predominantly male oriented after that initial episode with my football player. We were together regularly until I went off to college and rediscovered the joy of having sex with a girl once in a while. It's been that way ever since. I don't mind telling you that I need a good fucking by a man fairly regularly, but then I have times when I crave a night with a girlfriend. I guess I have two very different sexual needs, and I find both of them deeply satisfying and would be unhappily frustrated if I only had to rely on one," she said. "It's quite hard to explain, actually, because I have problems understanding it myself. It's not like I need sex every day or every week, whether it's with a man or a woman, but I do need both kinds. No matter how happy and satisfied a man might make me, I sometimes, inexplicably, get this irresistible, all consuming craving for a woman. Do you think that's terrible? Am I a bad person?"

"No, I wouldn't think so. What you do is not illegal. I don't see it as being abnormal or perverse. It is done between consenting adults. It's probably beyond normally acceptable conventions and would shock people if they knew. But being different is not a question of being good or bad, but rather exactly what the word means: being different. You have accepted it for yourself, and I believe I can accept it as well, without being able to truly understand it."

She nodded. "Well," she said, "I certainly do appreciate your open-mindedness."

"Didn't your husband know what you were like before you married?"

"No," she said. "I thought I could keep it a secret forever. He might never have found out if I hadn't been stupid enough to admit it. We had only been married a couple of years when we had a big fight over some sexual issue. I don't even remember what, but I was so mad I wanted to hurt him and without thinking told him he was not as good in bed as my girlfriend. It wasn't really true. I was furious and out of control. After that, of course, it was all downhill. He was dumb founded; couldn't get over it. I wanted to discuss it with him; explain. To let him know it had nothing to do with him. That he was a great lover. That my lesbian cravings were something else entirely, but he refused to listen. He pouted and sulked and was so jealous and felt so inadequate he couldn't see straight. Wouldn't fuck me for months and told me to go see my girlfriend if I was horny."

Shad weighed this fight in his mind. "Well," he then said, "I guess if I put myself into your husband's shoes, I am not sure how I would have reacted. It's one thing to know up front that you like to have sex with a woman; it's an entirely different situation when you have been married for a while and then learn your wife is bi-sexual. And tells you her girlfriend is a more satisfying lover than you are. It might have been all right if you hadn't thrown that in his face."

"Maybe. But since we separated, I have met men who were seriously interested in me, and when we became intimate and felt comfortable enough to talk openly about my disposition, they disappeared. Never called again; dropped me as if I had a contagious disease."

"I would have thought that history would have made you hesitant to tell me, but it didn't. You told me nearly right away," Shad said, puzzled.

"Yes. I made a deliberate decision. I thought we had something going for us and concluded it was better to face the issue head on, rather than waiting until we cared enough for each other to risk a painful breakup. I thought by confessing to you, we would either never have another date—no harm done—or you would accept me the way I am and we would take it from there."

"I think that was a smart decision. I am glad you were so open with me," he said. "You were right. I don't know how I would have reacted or felt if I had discovered your proclivity for women later on. As it is, I think I am falling in love with you just the way you are."

"So you wouldn't try to change me?" she said, doubt still in her eyes.

"Why should I? My job requires me to do a lot of traveling; being away from home and you perhaps weeks at a time. I would much rather you saw your girlfriend while I am gone than for you to have an affair."

"Fair enough," she said, apparently satisfied, "and I can promise categorically never to go with another man."

They held hands across the dinner table, happy with each other. He wondered how many men she had inadvertently driven away by admitting her bi-sexuality, and was glad she had done so. He didn't like the thought of her having had too many lovers.

"You know," he said after a while, "I have to admit I am a little . . . curious, I guess is the right word."

"About what?"

"How it actually is when you are with a woman. How I would feel if I saw you making love to one. Whether I would be shocked or jealous after all, or dispassionate or aroused."

Veronica grinned lasciviously at him. She was looking at him with bedroom eyes, and he knew exactly what she would have liked to do at that very moment.

"There is an easy way to find out, you know," she whispered.

"Do you think your girlfriend would agree?"

"Yes. We have fantasized about it and discussed it. We'd both love to have a threesome with you. I say that even though Caitlin and you haven't met yet, but I am sure you would like each other and would enjoy participating."

"Aren't you afraid I might fall in love with her?" he teased her.

"No. First of all, I have enough self confidence to believe I could keep you. You have already seen what I can do in bed, and I doubt if Caitlin is better than I am. Secondly, I trust your love for me. And thirdly, Caitlin is much more lesbian than bi-sexual. She would be willing to get fucked by you, I think, or watch you fuck me, but she is not interested in finding a steady boyfriend, let alone a husband."

"I have no desire to fuck her," he said, "and I can't believe you would be willing to let me do it and watch."

"Why not? You would only be doing something I asked you to do. It would not be love or unfaithfulness. I would take it as a sign you are willing to do anything for me."

"Veronica, I honestly don't think I could do that."

She shrugged. "Let's wait and see what happens. No reason to force the issue. But you were serious about participating?"

"Yes, of course."

"Okay, I will talk to her and see when we can get together. Then you can fulfill one of my favorite, unrequited fantasies. I can't wait to see what it will be like."

"Not to worry. I am open-minded," he reiterated, wondering which fantasy she had envisioned.

"You know, Shad," she said, inadvertently distracting him, "I am so happy we met. Here I am, thirty six years old, divorced, and had just about given up hope of ever finding a man who was willing to accept me the way I am. Who would not be turned off by what I like. Someone with whom I could fall in love and who would make my wildest dreams come true."

"Maybe your fantasies are not that far removed from my own," he mused. "But anyway, I love you and would do anything for you."

"Except fuck my girlfriend," she pointed out.

"Well, yes, there is that. I am sorry."

"What about any other woman?" she wanted to know.

"What do you mean? I don't need or want anyone else," he said, almost angry she would think this would even occur to him.

"Don't be upset," she said, trying to placate him. "I only ask because you will be traveling a lot, and I know you are going to meet other women. I also know you need sex regularly. What are you going to do if you don't see me for a couple of weeks and get so horny you can't stand it anymore?"

"Masturbate, I guess," he offered.

"That's always an option, of course," she said, "but I can't believe it would be a satisfactory alternative."

"Maybe not, but that's all I would do. I certainly wouldn't go out and start looking for another woman. I love you too much for that."

"But another woman might look for you," she kept arguing.

"I doubt it. But what if?"

"Well, that would depend on what kind of woman we are talking about. If it was just some prostitute, and you were really hurting, and you protected yourself, I don't think I would mind. Not that I would necessarily want to know. But I wouldn't get all jealous on you and make a scene if you had an emergency and just succumbed to some whore."

"You are crazy, Veronica," he said, "you know that? But you are truly incredible. Nevertheless, I can't picture ever getting so hard up that this would happen, and I have no intention of relying on your tolerance."

"Okay. I admit I am glad you feel that strongly about it, but I really meant what I said," she assured him. "As to Caitlin and I, we will think of something that will make us all feel good without you having to compromise your principles."

*   *   *

Almost coinciding with Shad's return from his second trip to the Far East was the end of his probation period with AmeriDerm. It had been largely a formality, he felt, but it was significant in that it not only changed his employment status to 'permanent', but also triggered a clause of his contract under which he was entitled to a company loan. The interest rate would be favorable and, even more importantly, he could repay it with the annual executive bonus to which he was entitled, subject to his meeting or exceeding agreed upon performance criteria.

He had fallen in love with Veronica and La Jolla in tandem. Perhaps one had contributed to the other. He enjoyed his new job and company tremendously; nothing had made this clearer than his first trips. What he had seen and done had exhilarated him, and he was looking forward to China, the big and mysterious unknown.

In the meantime, he found time to look for permanent dwellings. Nice as his company leased apartment was, he was eager to move into something he could call his own. He had already learned enough about the local real estate market to know he could hardly go wrong.

He had set himself an upper price limit of $300,000, based on what he had saved, his income, and the company loan he would receive, but hoped to find a house for less. Several weekends in a row he had taken Veronica and looked at open houses. While they were not officially engaged yet, he felt certain they would marry in the foreseeable future. The first threesome Veronica had arranged with Caitlin had exceeded his wildest dreams and had removed whatever doubts he might still have harbored about living with Veronica's bi-sexuality. Now he wanted to make sure whatever house he decided to buy, she would like as much as he did, confident their lives would be permanently joined.

They settled on a beautiful three bedroom ranch style house with more than three thousand square feet, soaring ceilings and panorama windows looking out over the ocean from its Muirlands neighborhood. The purchase was a dream come true for both of them and Veronica quickly agreed to give up her apartment and move in with Shad.

He had never been happier in his life. He felt safe from possible pursuers.

10

It could only be old age creeping up on him, Shad thought, that increasingly kept him from staying awake once he had settled into his recliner with a book and a glass of wine. The pages would begin to blur in front of his eyes. It would take a conscious effort to force his eyelids to stay open; his thoughts would drift uncontrollably until the noise of the book falling off his lap startled him awake. Keeping his eyes open then was a fight he could not win. Deep slumber would overpower him, endless dreams flickering through his mind.

Insufficient motivation to get up, he rationalized. There was nothing for him to do that required immediate attention, so who cared whether or for how long he napped? Besides, it was so pleasant to dwell on ancient memories rather than the dreary present.

This evening was a case in point. He awoke from his sleepy reveries, momentarily bewildered. He looked at his watch and saw it was dinner time. He wasn't hungry. The combination of the $100,000 deposit on an apartment he was by means certain he wanted to have, his long walk home and the subsequent jog had been more exhausting than expected.

What now? He asked himself. Too early to go to bed; too late to stay up. He reached for the book he had been reading but couldn't concentrate on the text.

His mind kept wandering, returning to his memories of Beijing—and Apries. She kept intruding on his grieving for Veronica. He couldn't understand it. Was it old age that made long term memories more vivid now than short term ones? He knew from friends suffering from dementia or Alzheimer's disease that this difference in memory ability was typical for these illnesses, and he worried he might already be exhibiting early symptoms himself. How else to explain why he was suddenly so overwhelmed with 22 year old memories of Apries, whom he had known for a mere short six months, rather than with the happy lifetime he had shared with Veronica?

To this day he found it hard to believe Apries had come to his room in Beijing so unhesitatingly. Much as he knew about her, she remained an enigma; impossible to figure out. Much of her behavior had been typical of a call girl, but she never asked for money from him. Had she been a woman emotionally lost, searching for the ideal lover or husband? Loved him as she had eventually claimed? Faithful to him between his visits? Not likely. She had shown without a hint of embarrassment she could jump from one bed into another in the space of hours.

He should be thinking only of Veronica and their love for each other. Why had thoughts of Apries come back, suddenly and after so many years? Only because of the singularly good sex she had provided so passionately and that he yearned to experience one more time? Or because of her carefree personality? Her strength in surviving adversity and her shockingly horrible youth?

He had not seen or heard from her in twenty years. Couldn't remember the last time he had even thought about her, and now, for the past few weeks, she had invaded his sub-consciousness and he could not banish her from his thoughts. He wondered what she was doing now. Whether she had ever re-married. Was still working as a translator. Still living in Beijing. What kind of life she had led since they had separated. Was still alive. He didn't know.

He gave up trying to read and went to bed, his recollections scrambling his brains.

*　　*　　*

It was late when he woke up. He had had a troubled, restless night, with thoughts of Apries continuing to pursue him as he tossed and turned.

She was history, he concluded, no more than a brief chapter of his checkered past. He was free now but rejected the crazy idea of making an effort to try and get in touch with her again.

He concentrated on the looming apartment decision he had to make. The 90 day clock was running inexorably. He would need time to liquidate some of his assets prudently in order to make the full payment. He had to determine which payment option was best.

Then there was still the issue of the background check. Try as he might, it continued to worry him, nagging at his inner peace. How exhaustive would the check be? Shad had no idea how far back they would go and he could not shake his apprehension.

Assuming nothing untoward would be uncovered, what else did he need to know that would help him make up his mind once and for all? He thought of his old army friend and former colleague, Neil Clifford, also retired and a few years his senior, and wondered how he was coping with idleness and whether he too had contemplated moving into a retirement community. His circumstances were not all that different.

He decided to give him a call to invite him for lunch to explore his thinking. He also had to see Sybil Delatour again; some additional questions had occurred to him. And then there were the Radfords, who had offered to show him their unit. He did want to see both of them and look at how they were living. It couldn't hurt to have some additional friends in the Towers and they might be able to provide different, valuable insights.

Thomas was on his mind as well. The memories of Apries and Beijing had triggered a nagging thought. It pertained to Thomas and Apries. He couldn't quite put his finger on it, but it had to do with the evening in Beijing when they had all gone back to the Sheraton. Something puzzling had been reverberating between the two; a latent tension or awkwardness. It had been out of place. He hadn't been able to understand it then, and still couldn't. He could not pinpoint what specifically kept bothering him, but he had to discuss it with Thomas. Maybe he would be willing to shed some light on what kept troubling Shad.

He called Sybil first and she gave him an appointment for the next day.

Neil was happy to hear from him and was delighted to meet him for a late lunch at Sammy's.

"Neil," he said, "how have you been?"

"Fantastic, Shad. And you?"

"Physically well but emotionally a mess. I am still trying to get used to being alone again and am debating whether or not to move into the Tranquil Towers. I can't seem to make up my mind."

"How come? You were always so decisive. This can't be all that difficult for you."

"It is though. Living alone can get pretty lonesome. I need to be among people again. I don't have that many close friends, you know. On the other hand, I love the comforts and familiarity of my place and I think I would miss it terribly if I were to give it up. And yet I also have to think ahead and I worry about what will happen when I can no longer look after myself."

"What makes you think you can not do that for many more years? Didn't you just tell me you were physically fit?"

"I did. But I went to see my doctor the other day for my annual physical, and he told me my cholesterol level was too high. I eat and drink too much. Based on my age and lifestyle he predicts I have an 18% chance of having a heart attack within ten years. As a result, he wants to put me on *Lipitor*. I argued with him; told him I did not want to have to take another drug every day. So he told me I could drop my daily Omega-3 capsule if I agreed to take Lipitor. Big deal! But I have to admit he succeeded in scaring me a little."

"That doesn't sound so bad. You should see the shitload of medicine I take every day! Besides, do the math. You have an 82% chance of *not* having one; not bad odds," Neil said.

"You always were the optimist. I also know that with the steady advances in medicine, a heart attack these days does not have to be fatal. I worry more about Alzheimer's, or cancer, or a stroke, or just an accident. Who would take care of me? Or even find me, if I were unable to call for help?"

"If you are that concerned, it should be easy for you to decide to move into the Towers."

"Have you been there? Do you know how depressing it is to see all those old people shuffling down the corridors on their walkers or in wheelchairs? The tubes from their oxygen tank going into their nose? Spittle drooling from their mouth?"

Neil had to laugh. "Don't worry about it. In a few years you will fit right in and won't notice it anymore."

"Thanks a lot. Easy enough for you to say. You have your Jennifer to look after you."

"Yes, I do. But don't think that makes life so much easier. She keeps me chained to her. She told me after 40 years of traveling and never being at home, it was her turn to have me. That my time now belonged to her exclusively, fulltime. I can not go anywhere or do anything by myself. Even when I play golf she comes with me, although she hates the bloody game."

"That's tough, Neil, but you don't look all that unhappy to me. Anyway, have you ever thought of moving into a retirement community?"

"I have, but as long as Jennifer and I are together and in reasonably good health, I don't see the point," Neil said, "and if one of us would get sick enough to require care, the other one would be there. Or we could afford to get a nurse."

"Yes, AmeriDerm has been very good to us, hasn't it?"

"You can say that again. It's just like I told you when you were wondering whether you should join the company."

"Well, it was an easy enough decision to make. I have always been grateful to you for having been so outspoken and unequivocal in telling me I should make the switch to AmeriDerm."

"It was the least I could do after having given your name to the headhunter," Neil said and smiled conspiratorially.

"What? It was you? I always wondered how he had targeted me."

Neil shrugged. "What can I say? I am just glad it worked out so well."

"Me too. Your advice was good and straight forward. If you were in my position today, would you move into the Towers?"

"You mean the so-called Terminal Towers?"

Shad had to laugh. "It is rather apt, isn't it?" he said.

"I was being facetious. I know nothing about the place except what I see when I walk by. But I do believe you would be better off in a retirement center where someone would find you if you keeled over. So, yes, I would move," he advised.

Neil hadn't changed, Shad thought. His advice remained unequivocal.

Shad nodded his thanks.

"Neil. I really appreciate it. It's so good to see you again. We need to get together more often."

"Anytime at all," Neil said. "Maybe you can invite Jennifer and me to dinner at the Towers once you have moved in. I would love to see the place—just in case we ever have to live there."

"If I do move," Shad said, "I would certainly love to have you come and visit, but as for dinner, I'd rather take you to a good restaurant. I see the dining room at the Towers—having eaten there once—as strictly for emergency use only."

"You are too spoiled, Shad. Anyway, give me a call when you want to have dinner. In the meantime, take care of yourself."

*   *   *

It was early afternoon when Shad kept his appointment with Sybil the next day. She greeted him like an old friend. His deposit had worked wonders.

"Are you ready to sign the final sales agreement, Mr. Cooper?"

"Not quite. I wanted to ask a couple of more questions and I have one request."

"Fine. Go ahead."

"First of all, I have a rather large house now, as you know, and when friends from out of town come to visit, I can put them up comfortably. That would change if I lived here. My unit only has two bedrooms. The guest bedroom will be converted into a library, so I could not accommodate guests."

"That's not a problem. You wouldn't be the only resident who wants to have friends or family visiting. We have one two bedrooms/two baths unit set aside for overnight visitors. It's in the original tower, but is quite nice and available on a first come/first serve basis, for a nominal fee. You have to make reservations as long as possible in advance. It comes with laundry service and you can subscribe to daily maid service at a moderate expense as well. The length of stay is limited to one week. It's been a very popular program. You might have to be a little flexible on dates."

"Great. Now my second question. One of the real selling points you have made is that by coming to live here, it would be the last move I would have to make."

"That's right. I think it's one of our major advantages."

"But it doesn't make sense to me. I understand the part where, if needed, you could provide part or even full time care."

"And which part don't you understand?" Sybil interjected.

"What would happen to me if nursing care in my own apartment would no longer suffice?"

"Well, I think that would depend on the cause. If you were terminally ill with cancer, you might have to go into a hospice. But other than that, I am not sure why nursing care, around the clock, would not suffice. If your situation became critical enough, you could even have a nurse staying with you in your guest bedroom."

"I wasn't thinking of cancer or some other terminal impairment. I was thinking of what would happen if I developed Alzheimer's or dementia."

"Is that a legitimate concern?"

"Yes, it is, based on my family history," he said, not knowing if this was true. He wanted to draw her out.

"In that case I can also put your mind at rest, because as I told you before, we have a special Alzheimer section."

"Into which I would have to move, if the time came."

"Well, yes, eventually. I am no doctor, but from what I have seen, Alzheimer's is not something that affects you overnight. It develops very slowly, and if, statistically, you could expect to have a twelve year survival rate, then during most of those years you could stay in your apartment. Once you reach the stage where you could no longer be trusted to stay by yourself and you would have to move into the Alzheimer section, I honestly don't believe you would still be aware enough of your surroundings to notice you have been transferred."

"A brutal assessment," Shad said, "but true enough, I suppose."

She nodded. "What else, Mr. Cooper?"

"My request. You remember me asking about your massage service."

"That's right," she said, sounding tentative.

"I was wondering whether it would be possible to get a sort of "trial" massage. To see what it would be like and to find out what kind is being offered."

"I suppose so. I would have to check. No one has ever asked me that before. The masseuse we have is not an employee of the Towers and is not here fulltime. She is an independent contractor. She comes based on appointments and charges customers directly. We get a token commission from her. Our only direct involvement is to provide the facility and handle appointments as requested."

"I understand," he said. "So could you please call and make an appointment for me?"

She nodded reluctantly and reached for her telephone directory. "When would you like your massage?" she asked while dialing.

"Whenever. I am free any time. Right now, if she has time."

"You are in luck," Sybil said. Her voice did not sound enthusiastic. "She is here and has time to see you right now. Do you know how to find the health club?"

"Yes, don't worry."

He thanked Sybil for her time as she ushered him out. "Don't hesitate to give me a call if you have any other questions," she said, smiling again, but he thought she was frowning on the inside, suspicious of his desire to get a massage. His many questions were surely a nuisance as well.

The health club was bright and airy and well equipped with state of the art exercise equipment selected especially to meet the requirements of geriatric users. The club was empty; must be afternoon nap time, Shad thought.

He found the masseuse waiting for him. He introduced himself and she reciprocated. "Hi, I am Ruth Merceda. What can I do for you?"

He tried not to be obvious about studying her. He liked what he saw. She seemed to be in her mid to late thirties. Of Mexican heritage, he thought. Not bad looking. Shiny black hair pinned back over her ears in a ponytail. Rather almond shaped black eyes. Smooth skin. Beautiful teeth. Small nose and full, sensuous lips. Good body; a little wide in the hips perhaps, but this suited her.

All this he took in at a glance while registering that she wore tight hip hugger jeans, a red polo shirt, and white sneakers. Her arms looked strong. She was not very tall and looked up to Shad while waiting for his response.

"I'd like to get a massage," he said. "I think Sybil spoke with you. I am thinking of buying an apartment in the Towers and wanted to see if this massage service she mentioned is as good as I hope."

"I am sure you will be more than satisfied," she assured him. "Did she tell you about my fees? I charge $75 for 45 minutes. You can give me cash or a check, but no credit card."

"That's fine," Shad said. "Do I pay you now or later?"

"Up to you. Afterwards is fine with me."

Shad nodded his agreement. "Where do we go?" he asked.

"There is a men's dressing room right over there," she said, pointing towards his right. "Please go and get undressed and put on one of the clean bathrobes you will see. When you are ready, just come over here to the massage table."

He did as instructed, and when he came back she had draped a large towel over the table. She asked him to take off his robe and lie face down on the table.

"You were not supposed to take off your shorts," she scolded him with a frown of exasperation when he discarded his robe and she saw he was completely naked.

"I am sorry," he said. "I guess I have gotten too many massages in Asia. I just did it automatically."

"Well, you are not in Asia now," she pointed out. "We have certain rules here, and no total nudity is one of them. But forget about it. It's not that big a deal for me. No one ever comes down here this time of the afternoon anyway. It makes no difference to me whether or not you have your shorts on, except that I don't want to risk jeopardizing the agreement I have with the Towers."

Did this sound promising or indifferent, he asked himself? He felt a slight twinge in his groin, whether from the masseuse's voice or her appearance or from memories of earlier massages, he wasn't sure.

When he stretched out on his belly he tried unobtrusively to make sure he was not lying with his cock under his belly. He wanted her to be able to see it if he spread his legs a little; wanted to test her reaction. If she took note of this, she ignored it completely.

What she could not overlook was the pattern of scars marring his back from where his stepfather's belt buckle had bitten into his flesh. He felt Ruth's fingertips exploring his shoulders delicately. He could literally sense her curiosity as to what had scarred him so indelibly.

"That must have hurt," she finally said, "when you were wounded enough to leave so many scars on your skin."

He shrugged as best he could. "I suppose. It was so long ago I have forgotten," he lied dismissively. In fact, he remembered the excruciating pain as if it had been yesterday, but he didn't want to dwell on those horrible memories.

She wouldn't leave it alone. "I saw scars like this once before," she said, "but on a woman. She had been whipped by her sadistic boyfriend."

"Well, I can assure you that's not how I came to mine."

She picked up that he did not want to discuss the subject and started working. He felt slightly disappointed when she took a towel to drape over his buttocks before proceeding to dribble some oil on his shoulders.

"Do you have any particular aches or pains you want me to address?" she asked.

"Not really. What kind of massage do you usually give?"

"For want of a better word, I would call it therapeutic. That's what my license says. It's probably not the kind you would have gotten in Asia."

"How would you know what I got in Asia?"

She shrugged her shoulders while kneading his back with strong fingers. "I may be only a licensed therapeutic massage therapist, but I am not an idiot. I have heard enough stories about what all goes on over there under the guise of a massage. And I have been working in my profession enough years to know that clients often expect much more from me than I am willing to provide."

He only grunted in response. He wanted to look at her face, but she was standing too far behind and above him. Her hands felt good. Sensuous. Cool and firm. Maybe it had been much too long since he had felt a woman's hands moving so intimately over his body. Veronica, with all her broad-mindedness, had not been into giving him massages, and he had not been in Asia in many years.

"Am I using too much pressure?" she asked after a while, "or not enough? You have to tell me how you like it."

He could not detect a hidden meaning in her request, but was tempted to tell her what he really liked. Common sense prevailed. He decided it was better to behave. "I like it just fine the way you are doing it."

Her hands kept moving lower down his back, until she reached the edge of the towel over his buttocks. Then she went back up and began massaging his arms, hands and fingers. She asked him to raise his head so she could knead it and his neck. He could feel the blood flowing through his scalp as she worked her fingers through his hair. He gave himself in to the pleasant sensation.

Finally she reached down and pulled the towel up from his buttocks and over his shoulders and arms. He felt her hands on his butt and automatically spread his legs.

"Hey, what do you think you are doing?" she said and slapped him lightly, he thought playfully, on his cheeks. She didn't sound angry or upset. He imagined she was smiling.

"Just giving you better access," he teased, trying to provoke her.

"I have all the access I need," she assured him, ignoring his implied invitation and massaging his thighs.

He knew she had to be able to see his cock, and she couldn't possibly overlook that it was stiffening. But his hope that she would say something, or better yet do something, remained unfulfilled.

"Talking about access," he finally said, "do you ever give massages in the apartments upstairs?"

"Occasionally. But I prefer doing it down here. I hate dragging a portable massage table around."

"Why do you need to take a table along? Why not simply have your customers lie on their bed?"

"Because most of them have at least queen or, more commonly, king size mattresses, and that means I can not reach them from both sides and the beds are too low. I also think giving a massage to someone on their bed can be too easily perceived as being too personal and would encourage more clients to try some hanky panky."

"Is that really an issue for you?" he said, rather astounded.

"You bet it is. Just look at yourself. Do you think I don't get your insinuations? You are not the only one who tries, you know. You'd be surprised at how many dubious offers I have to listen to," she said, and the disgust in her voice was unmistakable. "And from both men and women," she added.

"I guess I am not really all that surprised when I stop to think about it. A massage tends to be a rather intimate affair, and it's hard for a man to control his body's reaction when your hands go over it so sensuously," he said. He kept his voice neutral, conversational.

"It's not supposed to be sensuous. It should be relaxing. Relieve tight muscles. Ease aches and pains. I must be doing something wrong if you find it sensual. Maybe you are too hard up and I should use more pressure on you, make it hurt."

"No, please don't. It feels so good just the way you are doing it now," he said. He picked up on what she had said previously. "I don't really see the difficulty of massaging on a large bed. All you would have to do would be to kneel over your client's body."

"In your dreams!" she exclaimed.

"Why does it have to be a dream?" he said, his imagination starting to get away from him. "Haven't you ever thought about it? Maybe even fantasized about it?"

"I don't have to fantasize about it. I have a boyfriend who insists I massage him in bed."

"Lucky bastard," Shad observed. He thoroughly enjoyed this playful bantering with her. "An erotic one, I bet."

He thought again of all the things Veronica had done for him, alone and with Caitlin's involvement, but an erotic massage had not been one of them. He had missed it at times. Yearned for it, in fact, especially later in life, but whenever he had suggested it to her, she had told him to go to a massage institute. That he had not been inclined to do, knowing his expectations could not be met there.

"None of your business," she chided him, but when he felt her pummeling the back of his thighs with the edges of her hands, her fingers would periodically brush briefly against his now engorged shaft. As she reached between his legs to knead the muscles inside his upper thighs he wondered whether her fleeting touches of his sex were accidental or deliberate.

"Don't get any ideas," she warned, setting the record straight when she felt him squirming around.

"Too late. The ideas are already there," he confessed and smiled wickedly.

She laughed despite herself. "You are a hopeless case, you dirty old man," she said. "Get rid of them. I am not going to do anything."

He sighed dramatically. "I was afraid of that. I suppose you are right about me being a dirty old man, although your choice of terminology borders on disrespect for a customer, don't you think? But that's okay. Maybe, once I have moved in here and you come up to my apartment to give me a massage, you will become a little more accommodating. You only need to understand me better."

"I already understand you enough. I am not going to do anything for you other than give you the best therapeutic massage. I told you, I value my job."

"So how would anybody find out if you went beyond these conventions? You think I would be dumb enough to talk about it?" he asked, unable to stop pushing.

"How should I know? I know nothing about you at all. You don't even live here yet. Maybe you are someone who has to brag about what he has experienced."

"I understand your concern, but I can assure you I do not belong in that category. I guarantee you no one would ever find out from me," he said. "And besides, if you not knowing anything about me is the problem standing between us, we can quickly resolve it. All you have to do is get to know me. You could come have a cup of coffee with me when you get off work, and we could talk and I could tell you all about me."

He felt good. While believing what she had said and had dashed his immediate hopes, he also thought she had not completely closed the door on him. He just had to convince her that she could trust him to be discreet and that whatever she might be willing to do would remain their secret.

"You are damn persistent, aren't you," she sighed, sounding resigned. It was not a question. "But the answer is no. Maybe some other time."

"That's fine. I can be patient."

She snorted with derision. "That's not the impression I get."

"Well, I would love to prove it to you."

She asked him to turn around. His tool stood up embarrassingly straight. There was nothing he could do about it. She ignored it, even as she draped the towel over his erection and started massaging his chest.

"You seem to be starved for sex," she observed nonchalantly.

He grinned at her. "It's rather obvious," he said, "isn't it?"

She laughed. "For an old man, you still seem to be in pretty good shape."

"What can I say? You are right. I am an old man, although there is no call for you to keep reminding me. You should keep in mind that old men have advantages as well."

"Really? Like what?" she was curious enough to ask.

"They are more patient. They can make love longer because they are not so eager to come. Most importantly, they are not as egotistical as young men. Instead of focusing only on themselves and their own pleasure, they can concentrate on making the woman feel good. For an old man like me it's more important to make sure my partner's satisfaction comes before my own. If I can make you feel good, bring you to heights of ecstasy and spoil you in bed, I would be totally happy. Whether I would come in the process is not important. You are the only one that would count."

"Metaphorically speaking, I assume." She looked rather pensive, he thought, but then she said, "I think you are full of it. You are good at talking the talk, but I doubt you can walk it."

"Only one way for you to find out, isn't there?" he said. "You shouldn't ignore what your eyes are telling you. Believe me, my only sexual priority with you would be to make you feel better and more content and fulfilled than you have ever been."

He was speaking the truth, but didn't know if his words sounded arrogant or haughty.

She acknowledged his promise with silence. Maybe, he thought, she was seriously considering what he had said and was wondering if it could be true. She was still massaging his upper body, leaning over him. She looked as if he had made her thoughtful; that she was gazing at him with different eyes; seemed to be mentally evaluating him. He speculated her boyfriend had to be young and primarily interested in looking out for himself. That he did not pay enough attention to what she wanted or needed.

All too soon she told him his time was up. Nothing had happened beyond a soothing massage, but he felt good and completely relaxed. He found himself liking Ruth more than he should have. Were his feelings distorted by the fact he had had no sex at all since Veronica's passing? Was it simply the touch of a woman's hands on his body, or was it Ruth herself? He reminded himself he knew no more about her than she about him, other than her reference to having a boyfriend. But an unmistakable, he imagined mutual, attraction was palbable. True, she had not relented in her determination to remain professional and above reproach, but his persistent flirting had evidently not angered her.

He thought they were off to a promising start and was committed to getting another massage from her.

"Do you only work here, Ruth, or elsewhere as well?"

"Not only here. I would starve to death. There is not enough demand for massages among the residents. And besides, despite what you said about old men and their advantages in bed, they are not a lot of fun. You should see some of my clients here; I have to focus on ignoring what I see when I work on these walking dead. I would change professions if I only had to deal with people in retirement homes."

"I suppose you are right," he concurred. He only had to picture the procession of senile, flabby and wrinkled residents in their wheelchairs or walkers to understand what she was saying. "So where else do you work?"

"I share space with three other girls in an institute called Massage Mahal."

"Massage Mahal? What kind of a name is that?"

"The senior partner is from India," she said, "and I guess she was thinking of the Taj Mahal when she was searching for a name. I kind of like it, I must admit. It sort of awakens visions of splendor and the mysterious allure and ambience of the East. Come by any time you want another massage, but don't expect any more from me than you got here. It's only $50 when you come to our offices. Here, I have to give $25 to the Tower."

A lot more, for her, than the token fee Sybil had mentioned, he thought.

"How about coming to my house and giving me a massage there?"

She had to think about that for a minute. "You really are persistent, aren't you?" she finally repeated herself, avoiding answering his question. "Besides, what about your wife? Wouldn't she mind?"

"I don't have a wife anymore. I am a widower."

"Oh, I am sorry. Maybe that explains why you are trying so hard to get some extra attention from me," she said, a smile in her voice.

"Maybe. And why not? You give a very good massage, and it's fun talking to you while you are doing it. Besides, I like you. You treat me like a normal man, instead of the decrepit old geezer I am. You tolerate my flirting in good spirits and make me feel young and alive. How come you are reluctant to come to my place? Don't you have to provide outcalls these days in order to survive?"

"Sure, but very selectively and only for customers I know well. Too many people still believe a massage service is just a front for prostitution and are not willing to believe I am sincere in not responding to their overtures for sexual gratification."

"Are you serious? Is that really a problem for you? Here in La Jolla?" he said. He was quite astonished.

"La Jolla has nothing to do with it. It's just the way things are. I told you. You'd be surprised at the number of clients, both men and women, who literally beg me to do something. A hand job for the men. The women want me to massage their breasts and nipples and play with their pussy. Lots of times I have been offered big tips. And I have had more than one couple where one of the partners was begging to watch me satisfy the other one. They are very open about it; get upset when I say 'no'. So I have become extraordinarily cautious about accepting requests for outcalls and only go when I am convinced the customer wants nothing more than a legitimate, straight forward therapeutic massage."

He wouldn't give up. "So how can I convince you that is all I would want?"

"It wouldn't be easy, especially after your behavior and your comments here today, although I have to admit I enjoyed this time with you as well, despite your outrageous flirting."

Shad was glad to see she was smiling. "Maybe it's like I said, we just need to get to know each other a little better first," he ventured, smiling in return.

"That would definitely help. And you would have to be a lot less blatant about what you want from me than you were today."

"Oh, come on, Ruth," he implored. "You know I was only teasing. I was quite harmless, wasn't I? Always backing off immediately when I saw I was pushing you too hard. And now I am completely satisfied."

"Are you? I hope so."

"I am," he assured her. "You were great, and I feel fantastic. Can I call you to set up our next appointment? In my house this time? I promise I would behave. And if you want, my offer of coffee stands."

She studied his eyes carefully. "All right", she finally said. "Call me anytime. But I can't promise to come to you. I have to give that some thought; you may have to come to our offices. Or have it done here again, if you decide to move in. Or I might just take you up on that coffee invitation."

She gave him her business card and he paid her, adding a $25 tip. He thought showing generosity couldn't hurt. She tried to refuse the money at first, but then acceded.

"That's very kind of you," she said and bid him good-bye with a rather formal handshake.

11

Shad had not been pushing his China trip forward as aggressively as he could have. He had procrastinated, unsure of whether an early China market entry was the right thing to do. He had corresponded with potential distributors in Thailand and Korea, looking for safer alternatives to China, but nothing had come from these overtures. Actual trip arrangements had taken longer to finalize than anticipated, including obtaining the mandatory formal invitation from an officially sanctioned entity in support of his business visa application.

Dave Hardee had not been easy to convince Shad should go and a series of meetings had been required before the green light had been given. Consequently, it was early summer before a mutually convenient date had been agreed upon.

As the Boeing 747 carrying him made its final approach into Beijing International, Shad looked out the windows at the desolate surroundings. A heavy layer of smog blanketed the warren of buildings around the airport. What he saw looked eerily lifeless. There was no sign of traffic on the streets below him. He could not see a second runway.

When the aircraft touched down he was relieved. His interminably long flight on China Air out of San Francisco had been anything but a delight. While offering the lowest fare and the only non-stop flight and seats had been surprisingly expansive upstairs in the stubby version of the 747, the aircraft had been tacky and rumpled, looking soiled and dingy.

Entertainment had not been designed to elicit enthusiasm for what lay ahead. Films had been shown. Endless, boring series of propaganda films depicting farmers working their fields; food preparation for the airline industry; young children in cooperative rural schools, studying and playing; government officials exhorting the population to work harder and expounding the wonders, successes and miracles of communism. Fields of wheat, their stalks bending gently in the prevailing winds, had flimmered across the screen for hours. It had been so excruciatingly numbing that intermittently falling asleep had been unavoidable.

Meal service and the food had been terrible. Between meals, the flight attendants had stayed out of sight. Shad hoped the flight was not indicative of the country itself.

It was early evening by the time he disembarked and entered the terminal building. A long corridor led directly to the arrival hall. Dirty, rain streaked windows, their sills covered with soot and debris, allowed a glimpse of the visibly polluted air in the gathering twilight, hovering like a cloying layer of fog over the tarmac.

The corridor was poorly illuminated by harsh, flickering white neon lights, their fixtures dangling on rusty chains from the bare concrete ceiling. The linoleum floor was scuffed. Grime, filth and dust were everywhere. The prominently displayed *No Smoking* signs were being ignored. Impossibly young looking militias were keeping watchful eyes on the arriving passengers.

Their uniforms were ill fitting. A number of them wore sandals or sneakers, much the worse for wear. Armed with pistols and AK 47's, their demeanor was less than friendly as they watched with undisguised miens of distrust.

The lines at immigration were long and moved nearly imperceptibly. Shad became concerned when he noted the computer terminals at the officials' work stations, but when he saw the monitors were all blank—not turned on or not working—he relaxed. He realized his passport data would not have to pass computer screening. The immigration officer kept scrutinizing his visa and passport, time and again looking up from the photo in front of him to Shad's face, comparing images, searching for discrepancies before, with apparent reluctance, stamping his passport, immigration entry form and customs declaration.

The procedure looked designed to intimidate and make people nervous, and in Shad's case, it certainly worked. He was assailed by an unfathomable guilty conscience and he found himself drenched in sweat by the time he pocketed his documents again.

The baggage claim area had only two working carousels; baggage from the same flight came out on both belts. More than one suitcase tumbled to the dirty floor. The volume of baggage being disgorged was staggering. Cardboard boxes and sloppily tied together bundles and blankets vied for space on the carousels. Pushing and shoving was the norm.

How this facility could serve a city of 10 million people was hard to understand. It was cramped and dirty, with unpleasant, unfamiliar odors. Large, wall mounted fans stirred the stale air. Not enough light. Soldiers patrolling with vacant eyes, automatic weapons at the ready across their chests.

Customs control was a joke. No one was watching the X-Ray machines through which all baggage had to pass. Customs officials stood by impassively. Perhaps the machines were not even working, Shad thought. Occasionally a random passenger would be pulled out of line and furious haggling with a customs official would ensue. Then money changed hands and the passenger proceeded out of the building with his baggage.

Outside, it was hot and humid. Policemen made valiant if futile efforts to keep the traffic moving.

Shad was relieved to discover a man holding up a sign with the Pan-Asia Import/Export logo and his name. He was hustled into an Audi A4 and with incessant honking of the horn the driver forced his way into the slow moving traffic.

Traffic was light on the road into the city. It was narrow and tree lined and left little room for passing the overloaded trucks and decrepit old buses spewing noxious diesel fumes. A head-on collision looked unavoidable, but with continuous blaring of horns the vehicles would just scrape by unscathed.

It took more than an hour to reach the Sheraton Great Wall Hotel, not, as Shad had assumed from the name, anywhere close to the Great Wall. The streets looked oddly dark and quiet. Motorized traffic consisted primarily of buses, trucks, some military vehicles and a few taxis. Bicycles and freight pedicabs, on the other hand, were too numerous to count, and all of them, he noted, seemed to be without lights or at least reflectors. The size of the conveyance determined the rules of the road. The bigger the vehicle, the greater its right-of-way. Shad was surprised he did not see any accidents.

A sigh of relief escaped his lips when he finally entered the generously laid out lobby of the hotel. Apparently Thomas had been waiting for him, for he no sooner walked towards the registration desk than Thomas was at his side.

"Welcome to Beijing, Shad! I am glad you could make it," he said.

"Yeah, me too. It's good to see you again, Thomas. It was very nice of you to send a car for me. I don't know how I would have gotten to the hotel without your driver meeting me at the airport."

"Don't mention it. Come on, I have made arrangements for you to check in on the Executive Floor."

Shad was consternated to learn his passport would be retained until his presence had been registered with the local police, but Thomas assured him this was standard procedure and nothing to worry about. "Why don't you settle in and then come downstairs for a drink?" he said. "Or are you too tired?"

"No, no, I am fine. A drink would be great."

Shad was aching for one, in fact, and wasted no time in returning to the ground floor bar, searching for Thomas in the packed, noisy lounge. It was full of foreigners; no Chinese in sight except for the wait staff. He finally spotted Thomas sitting at a small corner table.

The drinks they ordered arrived quickly.

"So how was your flight?" Thomas said.

"The sooner I forget about it, the happier I will be."

Thomas laughed. "If you had asked me," he said, "I would have told you not to take China Air. They are terrible. State owned, so no one cares. They don't know how to spell service. You should have flown to Hong Kong with Cathay Pacific and then with DragonAir up to Beijing."

"Next time I will know better," Shad assured him.

Their small talk continued until Shad felt waves of weariness washing over him. Jet lag and the long flight had caught up with him; his eyes were drooping.

"I think I better let you go to bed, Shad. I can see you are falling asleep."

Shad glanced at his watch. Almost 10:00pm. He nodded.

"I want you to get a good night's sleep," Thomas said. "Our business meetings won't start until day after tomorrow, except for a dinner in the evening. I thought we could do a little sightseeing tomorrow. We'll take a quick drive out to the Great Wall, walk through the Forbidden City and across Tiananmen Square to see the Great Hall of the People, and if time permits, maybe look at the Temple of Heavenly Peace and the Summer Palace. And driving to these places will give you a little flavor of China. I suggest I come by and pick you up at 10:00."

"Excellent! I really appreciate you taking so much time for me, Thomas."

Once up in his room, and despite his exhaustion, he was so keyed up from the long flight and the unfamiliar, exotic surroundings that he needed a sleeping pill to find the rest his body craved.

*   *   *

The time difference kept him from sleeping as long as he would have liked. By 6:00am he was tossing and turning so restlessly he arose to go jogging. He slipped into a T-shirt and shorts and went towards the elevators.

When he stepped out of the hotel for his run the cloying stickiness of the air and the hazy, heavy pollution that greeted him were so bad he nearly turned around to go back to his room. Traffic was heavy on both the North Donghuang Road itself and its narrower parallel side streets, theoretically dedicated to bicycle traffic only. But taxis used them also and forced their way through the throngs of hapless cyclists.

He wasn't sure jogging in this environment was conducive to good health; running along the main thoroughfare with its chaotic traffic mix definitely did not seem advisable. He thought a side street behind the hotel would be better. He would run a mile or so out, a short block or two over to Donghuang Road, and then back.

He set out and had run for perhaps 10 minutes when he realized that the road gradually curved away from its parallel track to Donghuan Road. He made a right turn at the next intersection, thinking this would have to lead back to where he wanted to return. But no such luck. The road ended abruptly at a canal full of stagnant sludge. People were staring at him as he was forced to turn back.

He found another street leading in what he surmised would take him back to the hotel, but found this one quickly narrowing and starting to meander among slum like looking dwellings. He lost his sense of direction. He became concerned when he realized he was basically lost. He had no idea how to get back to the hotel. He had nothing on him except the clothes on his back. He had left his room key with its tag showing the name and address of the Sheraton at the reception desk. He had no money in his pockets. He did not know how to ask for directions. No foreigners who might have been able to help him were in sight. There were no taxis to be hailed.

He could not recognize any landmarks. He didn't know how to double back, not having paid much attention to where his feet were taking him. He became seriously worried. And he was exhausted; his usual jogging time of thirty minutes had long been surpassed.

He stopped, soaked in sweat, both from his running and his steadily increasing anxiety. He looked helplessly at the people streaming past him.

"I think you do not belong here," a woman suddenly said in good English, "you must be lost."

"Is it that obvious?" Shad said, while his eyes sought out the pleasant English speaking voice. A Chinese woman stood close to him, studying him with a slight smile playing around her lips. She was dressed in western business attire, with a dark blue skirt and red jacket and a light blue scarf knotted around her throat. Perhaps in her late twenties. His eyes were drawn to her mouth, where a thin scar bisected her upper lip. She must have been born with a hare lip, he thought, which had been expertly repaired. Rather than disfiguring her, it added to her attractiveness; gave her a distinctive and somewhat mysterious look that he found strangely appealing.

The skin of her face was as smooth and wrinkle free as that of a teenager, but the aura of maturity radiating from her made him think she could be not all that much younger than he was. Her long black hair hung straight down over her shoulders. Although rather tall for a Chinese, she was considerably shorter than his own lanky six feet two so that she had to crane her neck to look up to him.

Her eyes reflected amusement. Definitely a beguiling woman, Shad thought.

"Yes," she said, "not many foreigners enter these *Hutongs,* especially early in the morning. And certainly no one goes jogging around here."

"I should not have either," Shad said, "but I only arrived in Beijing last night and could not sleep. When I decided to go running the air looked so polluted I stayed off the main road and then found myself here, lost, without knowing how it happened, let alone knowing the way back."

"Perhaps I can help you," she said. "Where are you staying?"

"The Sheraton Great Wall. Do you happen to know where it is? I am afraid I don't have the address."

"Everybody knows it. It's not very far."

Shad liked the sound of her voice, and her English was nearly flawless. "That is so good to hear!" he said, and added: "Your English is excellent."

"Thank you. It has to be. I work as a free lance translator for some wholly owned foreign enterprises and as occasional tour guide for English speaking visitors."

"Would I recognize the names of the companies you are associated with?" he asked.

"Perhaps," she said and left it at that. Her accompanying smile looked mischievous.

Shad waited for her to continue, but she remained silent. The longer he looked into her black eyes, the prettier and more mysterious she seemed to become. But she quickly became noticeably uncomfortable under his probing gaze and he averted his eyes.

"Is there any way you can help me get back to my hotel?" he finally ventured to ask.

She nodded. "Yes," she said, "but I couldn't explain the way to you. It's best if I take you there. I was on my way to the bus stop to go to work anyway, so I can just get us a pedicab and have it drop you off at the hotel. Unless you want to get on the bus with me," she added and laughed, as if she had told a joke.

"I don't think so," he said. "Look at me, in T-shirt and running shorts and totally drenched in sweat. Besides, I don't have any money with me." He tried to hide his embarrassment over this confession.

"Well, the pedicab costs money as well, you know, but that's all right. Wait here." With that she turned and walked away, still looking amused, whether at him or his predicament he could not tell.

He did not have long to wait. A rickety tricycle with her sitting on the seat bench over the rear wheels pulled up next to him, and she beckoned him up next to her.

The pedicab started moving, the driver's legs pumping, straining with the weight of his two passengers.

"As I mentioned, I don't have any money with me," Shad said. "Can you wait for me at the hotel for a few minutes while I go up to my room to get some so I can repay you?"

"No. But don't be worried. Unless you have already changed money, you only have dollars anyway, and you are not allowed to pay with those. You can only use the Foreign Exchange Certificates—or FEC's, as we refer to them—that you get when you exchange dollars legally. Your hotel is on my way anyway and the fare is very low."

"You are too kind. You rescued me; saved me. I couldn't possibly accept you paying for the pedicab as well."

"I insist," she said, "and besides, I wouldn't want to be seen waiting for you outside the elegant Sheraton in this rusty pedicab, and then you coming back out and handing me money. Anyone who saw us would certainly get the wrong impression, if you know what I mean."

It took Shad a couple of seconds to figure out what she meant, but when he did, he apologized. "I am sorry. I did not think that through. I guess it could look suspicious when you arrive with a foreigner in the morning and he hands you money, although the way I look right now should set people straight."

"Or they would think I really did a good job!" she said and laughed loudly. He wasn't sure whether she was just enjoying herself at his expense or flirting with him. She was certainly outspoken. Or was this simply her nature, he wondered?

It was worth the risk to bet on the flirt, he decided, and smiled at her. "Well, I guess I don't know what to say. But wouldn't it be exciting to know whether I would actually look this bad if people's suspicions about us were true?"

"I suppose we will never find out," she said, but her choice of words and the grin on her face let him think it was not inconceivable. He wanted to see her again.

"Maybe I can get you to change your mind," he teased. "But in the meantime, I really want to thank you again for helping me out like this. I don't know what I would have done without you. Is there any other way I can make it up to you if you won't let me reimburse you? Maybe I could at least invite you for a cup of tea or a drink or something to eat?"

Despite the flirtatious bantering, Shad convinced himself he was merely eager to repay her kindness. He was sure Veronica would not mind such a courtesy.

She did not hesitate for long. "Yes, that would be fine." Her eyes were sparkling.

"Great! How can I get in touch with you?"

"Just call me any time in the evening. Here is my phone number," she said and reached into her purse to retrieve one of her business cards.

He held her card by its edges and studied it carefully. He tried to pronounce her name correctly. "Xie Hsu Fang?" he asked hesitantly.

"Yes, but please call me Apries. What is your name?"

"Oh, I am so sorry. I should have introduced myself a long time ago. It's Shad. Unfortunately I don't have a card with me."

"I didn't think you would," she laughed, and again he liked the sound of her uninhibited laughter. It was natural, the expression of a carefree, happy person. "Shad?" she repeated, "I don't think I have heard that name before."

"It's a nick name. I picked it up while I was in the army," he lied, not knowing why he did. "My real name is Roger Stevens," he went on before he could stop himself. What had come over him, made him so careless, to share this with her? He had not told a soul since becoming Shad Cooper, and here he had just blurted it out to a total stranger.

"But why 'Shad'?" she wanted to know.

"The name Roger caused confusion because it is the positive acknowledgement of a message received in military radio transmissions. You might have heard this being used in war movies. Someone sends a radio message and the recipient confirms receiving it by saying: 'Roger'.

But anyway, when we were on camouflage maneuvers, I discovered this ability to make myself virtually invisible. I was like a shadow, and from that someone came up with the nick name Shad, and it has stuck ever since."

He did not explain he had been living as a shadow of his true self for years.

"How funny! Almost like with me. Everyone calls me Apries, rather than Xie Hsu Fang."

"That's a unique name," Shad said. "Where did it come from?" He was glad she used an English name; he wasn't sure he could remember her Chinese name or know which of her three names to use when addressing her.

"I made it up myself. When I was a kid and had English. Our teacher could not remember most of his students' names. So he invited us to select English names for ourselves. I was born in the month of April, which, under the western zodiac signs, is Aries, so I simply combined the two to make Apries."

"That's a beautiful story, Apries. Isn't Aries the ram? I hope you are not as stubborn and hard-headed as that animal. And then combining it with April, an unpredictable, blustery month. Potentially an explosive contraction," he teased. Before she could react, he quickly added: "Please don't be upset. I was only giving you a hard time. Trying to be funny. It's a beautiful name. I often have problems with Chinese names, and for you to use an English name is very considerate. I feel rather stupid when I can't pronounce or remember Chinese names."

"Don't. We Chinese have the same problem with western names. And I don't think I can be compared to a ram, since I am a woman, but the unpredictability factor is something you should keep in mind," she warned playfully and again laughed as she said this, putting him at ease.

"I am sure you are right," he said. Keep in mind when, he asked himself?

The portiere of the Sheraton did not bat an eye when the pedicab pulled up at the entrance, with the barely dressed and sweat soaked Shad and the elegantly dressed Chinese lady. Shad realized his new acquaintance had been right in not wanting to receive any money from him within sight of the people milling around the entrance, ready to smirk at such a transaction.

Shad jumped off. "Thank you so very much again, Apries," he said, and was rewarded with a provocative smile. "I would like to shake your hand or—even better—give you a hug, but I don't think either one would be appropriate. I will call you."

"I look forward to it," she assured him, laughter accompanying her words. Shad turned away, a huge grin on his face. Her happiness had been contagious.

12

Beijing, 1986

The fortuitous encounter with the spirited Apries had thoroughly revitalized Shad. Forgotten were the short night and jet lag. While convinced the harmless flirting meant no more then having a cup of tea with her, a tinge of guilt remained because his thoughts lingered on their bantering. Finding her spontaneously attractive when he and Veronica were close to getting married didn't seem right. It wasn't Apries' looks that fascinated him. It was the perceptible sexuality she radiated. He sensed a danger in her for him. He owed her for what she had done for him, but shouldn't he stop fantasizing about what she might be like? What might happen between them if they met again? The signals she had sent his way seemed straight forward. He felt physically drawn to her. Veronica satisfied him completely, and yet the urge to find out more about Apries and what she projected was strong.

As he stood in front of the hotel, waiting for Thomas, his thoughts continued to linger on her. She was charming and unpretentious. Their meeting had been auspicious, and he was eager to talk to her again, and yet he sensed this was potentially dangerous. It could have unforeseeable consequences for his relationship with Veronica.

He wondered if he was letting his imagination run away from him. She was an unusual woman, he thought. A bit of a dichotomy. Obviously highly westernized and outgoing on one hand, but living in a *Hutong*, a lifestyle and an environment definitely traditional Chinese. Why had she seemingly come on strongly? Had she played with him, having fun at his expense? Or had a message been communicated? An implied promise she might be willing to take their chance meeting further? She had apparently behaved completely naturally; with openness and blatant sexuality. It could be fun to learn who and what she was, he concluded. He was not looking for a girl friend, but the prospect of spending an evening with her excited him.

He was still lost in these thoughts when Thomas' car pulled up.

"Lucky bastard," was all Thomas said after they had exchanged greetings and were sitting in the hire car and Shad had related his early morning adventure to him.

"That's for sure," Shad said. "Do you think she really meant it when she said I could call her? I don't want to do anything to offend Chinese sensibilities." He hadn't told Thomas about the flirtatious connotation of parts of their conversation and that he speculated it could have had a deeper meaning.

Thomas shrugged. "I wouldn't worry about it," he said. "If she gave you her phone number and said it was okay to call, I'm sure she meant it. But you might want to think about where this could lead, and what it might mean for your relationship with Veronica. You seem to be much too interested in this woman when you consider how you met her and that you know absolutely zero about her."

"I'm sorry I gave you that impression, Thomas. I was simply having a good time and thought it would be fun to have a drink with her."

"Could be, but I thought you said you were planning on marrying Veronica shortly, and if that's the case, you might want to be prudent and not call this woman. She appears to have captured your imagination. Chinese women can be surprisingly open and are not as hindered by convention as western women tend to be. They are more apt to be honest in what they want and don't worry about such concepts as sinning or faithlessness. If they are interested in having sex, they will let you know. No doubt about it."

"That sounds promising," Shad said, grinning.

"Yes. Well, as far as you are concerned, what would you like to see happen? An affair? A one night stand? Or that she would pretend not to remember? My only advice would be not to do anything to hurt Veronica. Think of the future."

Shad pondered what to say. Although highly presumptuous, the thought of sex with her had crossed his mind, but he had pushed it aside, remembering Veronica waiting for him in La Jolla. Maybe her spending the night with Caitlin but certainly not fantasizing about another man the way he was about Apries. He didn't believe she fell into the category of women Veronica had allowed him to see if he had an emergency.

"You are right. I know nothing about her," he admitted, "and besides, I would think someone her age would most likely be married."

"That wouldn't necessarily make a difference to her," Thomas said. "She could also be divorced; that is something you see more and more often in China these days. How old is she anyway?"

"I wish I knew. I am guessing late twenties, but I can never tell with Asians."

"You are not the only one. But rest assured, they have the same problem with us."

"What did you mean when you said her maybe being married would not necessarily make a difference?" Shad wanted to know.

Thomas shrugged. "What I said earlier about sin and convention. It goes back to our western concept of fidelity and the sin involved in being unfaithful. We are church raised to consider extramarital sex as a sin, right? But the Chinese do not have this concept of sin. It is not a part of their religion. Even the word itself does not exist in the Chinese language, as far as I know. They can not sin, in the sense that we do. They may be afraid of getting caught and the consequential loss of their all important 'face', and therefore regret what they did, or—more accurately—regret they got caught, but not of committing a sin. And if by definition they can not sin, they can not have a guilty conscience either."

"That's certainly an interesting cultural concept," Shad mused. "Very convenient too, I might add."

"Yes, it is, isn't it?"

Shad wondered if Thomas had ever taken advantage of these circumstances. Hard to believe after having met his wife Jade and seeing what she was like, but who could tell what temptations Thomas had been exposed to?

They lapsed into silence, Shad staring out the windows of the car, watching the city teeming with pedestrians and bicycles, overcrowded buses and trucks loaded with coal or cabbages go past. He had no idea where they were or in which direction they were going. The sun was a hazy, diffuse ball barely visible through the layers of smog blanketing the city.

It took them more than an hour to reach the Great Wall. They quickly set out to conquer the challenges of the ancient structure. The further they moved away from the tourist entry, the more difficult their hike became. Soon they had to start climbing up steep ramparts. Narrow surfaces and unevenly spaced steps leading up to the first of many towers were daunting. Shad felt as if they were climbing ancient pyramids, so steep and uneven were the rough hewn stone blocks.

It was awe inspiring. The Wall was a huge, incredible monument to perseverance, building skills and heroic labor. It was understandable that astronauts had been able to see it from outer space. Craggy ridges and mountains, overgrown with shrubs and trees, shimmered endlessly, far into the nebulous distance. No buildings or roads or other signs of habitation marred the view.

They went all the way to the end of where the Wall had been renovated. The subsequent sections were still in disarray. Both Thomas and Shad were sweating and breathing hard. The past hour had been physically more than demanding. In the distance, remnants of the Wall snaked along the mountain ridges, long stretches seemingly still complete, others more a pile of haphazardly thrown together stone blocks.

Shad kept marveling at the engineering feat and labor which had allowed it to be built nearly two thousand years ago in such an inhospitable environment. He recalled reading that more than a million slaves and prisoners of war had been forced to construct it and that many of the ones who had died of exhaustion and diseases had simply been mixed in with the rubble needed for the foundation for quick disposal and had thus forever become a part of the Wall. As a result, for hundreds of years it had been rather sarcastically referred to as the world's longest cemetery.

They arrived back at their car, knees wobbling with exhaustion, and perspiring. Shad was moved by the history and astounding magnificence of what he had seen and knew this sight and experience would stay with him for the rest of his life.

"Isn't it absolutely overwhelming?" Thomas said.

"It truly is. The photos I have seen of the Wall just do not do it justice. It reminds me—in one way—of the Grand Canyon, as different as they are. All the photos I had seen of the Grand Canyon also did not prepare me for the first time I saw it in person. Neither one can be adequately captured in photos. The perspectives and monumental size has to be seen in person to be fully appreciated. Or maybe a better comparison would be to the great pyramids in Egypt, since they must have been nearly equal challenges in construction."

By the time they had driven back into the city and had spent hours touring the huge Forbidden City and circumnavigated sprawling Tiananmen Square, where they had seen the Great Hall of the People and the Mao Tze Dung Mausoleum, it was too late to visit any other sights before their 6:00 o'clock dinner.

Over a quick drink in the lobby bar of the Sheraton, Thomas briefed Shad on what to expect at their dinner. "I doubt if there will be more than five or six others besides us two. It will be very formal, with no doubt a couple of speeches. Some of the food you might not like all that much and find a little strange, so be warned. Our host is a lady by the name of Ning Chang. She has a modest distribution company called Kang Ming and appears to be well connected. Her husband is a general in the People's Liberation Army. She tells me he is not involved in her business, but I don't really know. Things in China aren't always what they appear to be. She speaks excellent English and commutes between China and San Francisco, where she also has some kind of business interests. She is the principal for a couple of small to mid-sized US pharmaceutical/device companies. Currently, her focus in China is on Beijing and Shanghai only, but she wants to expand to Guangzhou, Hangzhou, Tianjin, and a couple of other large cities along the economically strong eastern coastal corridor."

"And you think she might be a suitable partner for us?"

"She is one option. Because her company is small, she would certainly give you her undivided attention and put all of her resources behind your product line. What I don't know is whether or not those are sufficient for your needs. You will have to take a close look at that when you visit her offices."

"Day after tomorrow you said, right?"

"Yes. She will thoroughly brief you on Kang Ming then," Thomas confirmed. "Tomorrow we will visit a couple of large local companies so you can make comparisons. The advantages of a big Chinese outfit are that they have good territory coverage, large support organizations and resources, know everybody, and have the all important connections to facilitate business. Their disadvantages are that for them, you would be a very small fish and would most likely not get the attention or the sales force time you want for your products, regardless of what they may promise. They will also almost certainly push you to agree on local contract manufacturing, which is not something you should do."

"Why not at least consider it?" Shad said.

"Because you lose control, and before you knew it, they would use your formulas and manufacturing know-how—and maybe even a slight variation of your trademarks—to produce their own version of your products. You would then be competing against your own products."

"Well, that's certainly good to know. I appreciate the input. What else is on the program for tomorrow?"

"A visit to the Ministry of Health; strictly a courtesy call. Tell them about AmeriDerm and your products and get their feedback on health registration issues. *Melavict* should be of interest to them. Since the ministry people either don't speak English or do not show how much they understand, I have made arrangements for a translator to join us. The ministry will have its official interpreter, of course, but if you don't have one of your own, you lose face."

"Is that why I always see two translators when the news shows a Head of States meeting?"

"Precisely. Both will always have their respective translator hovering behind their shoulders. Neither trusts the other side to translate accurately, especially nuances, idioms, or perhaps even slang. It's the same with you at the Ministry of Health. You might lose something in the translations."

"I see," Shad said. "So how does that actually work?"

"Their translator relates what the ministry people say, and yours puts your response into Chinese."

"Okay. And this meeting will be when?"

"3:30. In the morning, at 10:00, we meet with People's First Pharmaceutical Company; then a 12:30 luncheon with Great Wall Pioneering Research. I think the latter is a PLA owned company, but I am not sure. Transparency is always an issue in China."

"Does the ownership make any difference?"

"It could. It would certainly smooth the way with the ministries and would give you the inside track at the army hospitals, which are important from both a medical and accessibility to hard currency point of view. The PLA controls the arms business, so they generate a lot of revenue and are an economic powerhouse. The government gives the military top priority in everything in order to maintain their loyalty and a high level of morale. Of course the air force, the navy, and the police all have their own hospitals, and these do not necessarily want to buy from the army. It's an incredibly complex scenario. In any case, both of the companies we will visit are highly diversified and have been growing rapidly. Both have some dermatologicals in their product range, but I don't believe there would be a conflict with your products," Thomas said.

"What about the next day?"

"You will have to get along without me. I need to fly down to our factory in Hainan tomorrow evening, but I have spoken with Ning Chang and she has agreed to take you to the Army's Military Hospital #402 to meet some dermatologists. It's arguably the most important hospital in Beijing, and I am sure you can pick up a lot of useful information there."

*   *   *

Ms. Chang arrived to pick them up for their dinner and Thomas introduced them.

"Please call me Ning," she said. Her tone was brusque. She was in her early forties and looked rather plain and non-descript in her dark blue pants suit. Not very feminine and serious of mien; short in stature. With somewhat unkempt hair, she seemed not to put much importance on personal appearance. She was all business and immediately launched into a glowing description of her company and what she could do for AmeriDerm.

Shad would rather have liked to look out the window of the car as they sped towards the restaurant to familiarize himself more with the city but instead forced himself to listen to Ning's constant chatter. She was totally focused on convincing Shad on the wisdom of working with her company. He was not impressed. She talked too much. His jet lag had returned and he was tired; had problems concentrating. Thomas remained silent. Shad was relieved when the car disgorged them in front of the Peking Hotel and they took the elevator up to the Peking Duck restaurant on the fifth floor.

A bowing host led them into the private dining room Ning Chang had reserved. A muted décor greeted them, with Chinese scroll drawings hanging on the dark paneled walls and lacquer sideboards holding various serving dishes. A wide chandelier spread yellowish light over the round table with its lazy Susan. Five people were waiting for them. Ning introduced her staff members.

An exchange of business cards took place, with much bowing and studying of the cards. One chair remained empty when they had taken their seats, with Ning sitting between Shad and Thomas.

"I hope you don't mind," Ning said, "but I invited my husband to join us. I don't see very much of him, with me spending much of my time in San Francisco and he being in the army."

"Not at all," Shad assured her; Thomas merely nodded.

"What do you do when you are in San Francisco, Ning?" Shad asked.

"Oh, I have a small business there through which I maintain operating contacts with our US principals. It actually works out quite well. I divide my time roughly equally between San Francisco and China."

"I guess that doesn't leave much time to enjoy your marriage," Shad couldn't help but observe.

"It's all right. We understand each other, and this arrangement serves us both well."

Shad wondered what that meant. Her husband had a Number Two wife in Beijing and she a lover in San Francisco? He didn't know about her husband but found it hard to imagine from what he saw of her that she had one. To call her plain would be to pay her a compliment, Shad thought.

"We are having a Peking Duck dinner," Ning announced proudly, and when silence greeted this pronouncement, she continued. "Have you ever had one before?" she asked, turning to Shad.

"Not in China I haven't," he said.

"Then I think you will be in for a surprise. This restaurant has the best one in all of Beijing." She paused, as if waiting for applause, before asking, "What would you like to drink?"

Shad and Thomas both ordered beer; Ning and her employees remained faithful to their jasmine tea.

A brief conversation in rapid Chinese ensued between Ning Chang and her employees, but the speech Thomas had predicted failed to materialize.

"I am afraid my people are not so good with English," she finally said as she turned back towards Shad.

"Not to worry," he said, "it's got to be better than my Chinese."

His small audience laughed politely at his stale joke. "Perhaps you could tell me a little more about Kang Ming," Shad encouraged, "and your employees."

"I would be happy to, but we have prepared a formal presentation for you in our offices, so why don't we just enjoy dinner tonight? This restaurant is the standard in Beijing for Peking Duck," she repeated, making sure Shad and Thomas understood how privileged they were to have been invited here. It had to be expensive, Shad mused.

No sooner had she finished speaking than the first course of assorted cold appetizers was brought out. A large platter with morsels of barbequed pork, duck and chicken, together with various pickled vegetables was placed on the lazy Susan, and Ning invited Shad to take the first piece.

The soup arrived, and while the waiter divided it into eight small bowls at the serving sideboard, short thrift was still being made of the appetizers. Shad was fascinated by the skill with which the Chinese managed to spit out the pieces of bone—large and small—embedded in the bits of chicken and duck.

As the waiter distributed the soup, the door opened and what could only have been Ning's husband arrived. If he had not been wearing his brown uniform, he would not have been recognized as a high ranking PLA officer. His uniform was wrinkled; ill fitting. His hair was plastered to his head from the peaked cap he had been wearing. He was overweight with a protruding belly. The expression on his face was studied neutrality; no sign of pleasure at seeing his wife or her guests.

Introductions were made. Shad found it interesting that the general did not hand out business cards. An inadvertent oversight, or deliberate? Shad gave him one of his cards; even then he did not receive one in return. Instead, without further ado, he sat down and started eating.

Shad felt indefinably uncomfortable with a PLA general sitting next to him. He didn't know what to say or how to behave. Was he to be feared? He decided to ignore him, just as the others seemed to be doing, including his wife.

A large whole fish, a sea bream, came next, steamed and in soy sauce. It was unceremoniously hacked into chunks and distributed into small bowls. It was hard for Shad to find a bite without bones in the otherwise excellent tasting, delicate fish.

A plate of broccoli in oyster sauce quickly followed. Then came the chicken, also scissored into bite sized portions. Again none without bones. Shad did not care for the rubbery skin of the chicken.

Just as Shad was beginning to wonder why Ning Chang had called this a Peking duck dinner, a chef entered the room, wheeling in a cart with two glistening, roasted ducks. After appropriate expressions of admiration for the ducks on the part of the diners, the chef took his cleaver and began shaving off pieces of the crispy duck skin.

The waiter picked up the skin carvings with his long serving chop sticks and, after first putting some scallions and plum sauce on the thin crepes the chef had also brought, he would put a thin layer of skin on the crepes and with practiced dexterity and using only his chop sticks roll them, taco-like, into small rolls he then distributed among the guests.

It was a bit of a struggle for Shad to pick up a roll with his chop sticks; to keep it from unrolling or the meat from falling out. The others did not have the same problems he did.

The rolls were indeed a delight to savor; a delicious combination of the flavorful duck skin enhanced by the sweet plum sauce and tangy scallions. His real surprise was that only the duck's skin was being used. What about the meat? He was disappointed when he only received two of the excellent rolls.

Only when the next course—stir fried duck with bean sprouts—was served, did he understand what was done with the meat.

The sea slugs that came next were more than he could manage. He was determined, but could not swallow the small bite of the gelatinous, unappetizing looking thing smothered in some indefinable sauce, despite Ning's assurance that slugs were one of the greatest delicacies imaginable, only served at very special events. He felt honored, he assured her, but he could not eat them. His throat refused to open.

He glanced towards Thomas, who was chewing stoically, his face expressionless.

Shad had to consume copious amounts of steamed rice and several swallows of beer to get the obnoxious, sticky taste of the sea slug out of his mouth.

Dessert, in the form of sliced oranges, finally arrived, and Shad was glad. They cleaned his palate. He was disappointed that the highly anticipated Peking duck dinner had not consisted of more duck. Later, when he asked Thomas about this, he learned a Peking duck dinner was always like this; merely one or two of ten or more courses.

The table had hardly been cleared when the party broke up. "My people came here on their bicycles," Ning explained, "and they have a long way to go home."

Shad was not unhappy at this rapid conclusion of their dinner. It was only 8:00pm, but he was dead. He was ready to get back to the hotel and sleep.

"So what time will we go to your office day after tomorrow, Ning?"

"I will pick you up at 9:00am," she said.

"Will that give us enough time before going to the hospital 402?"

"I think so," Ning said. "Whether we get there at 12:00 or half an hour later makes no difference."

With that she led the way out of the restaurant and to the car waiting to take them back to the Sheraton. Her husband, after a perfunctory good bye, walked to the PLA jeep parked at the curb, his driver sound asleep behind the wheel. Shad found it strange that no words had been exchanged between Ning and her husband before they drove off in their respective directions. What a strange relationship, he thought.

*   *   *

"I am not sure I would like working with Ning Chang," Shad said as he settled down in the bar of the Sheraton with Thomas.

"Why is that?"

"I can't put my finger on it. She seems rather impersonal. Lacks warmth. There is something missing which would make me comfortable with her. She ignored not only her employees all evening long, but also her husband. But maybe I shouldn't jump to conclusions. It was only one dinner. She does not seem to care much about food."

"You noticed that, did you? Even though she was so full of praise for the duck and the sea slugs we had?"

"How could I not notice?"

"True enough," Thomas said. He was laughing quietly, having seen on numerous occasions how much Shad appreciated good food. "But I am not sure that has any relevance when considering a possible business relationship. After all, not everyone feels about food the way you do! When I met her a few years ago and we went out to lunch, she explained to me she only ate because her body needed nourishment. I think you could put anything in front of her without her paying the slightest attention to what she was having."

"Highly suspicious," Shad insisted. He did not want to belabor the point, but he felt strongly that to be successful, you had to be passionate, and if you were not passionate about food, how could you be so over your job or your business?

"Don't jump to conclusions," Thomas cautioned. "Give her a chance. Listen to her presentation. She is a tough businesswoman and knows what she is doing. She doesn't get distracted or stop working just because it's lunch or dinner time, and I don't think that's necessarily bad."

Shad grunted. He didn't agree but couldn't win. He changed subjects. "You are concerned about her means?"

"I don't know if concern is the right word, but as I mentioned, they could be an issue. I suspect she is not exactly over-capitalized. Perhaps she has a silent partner with pockets deep enough to not only keep her going, but allowing her to expand," Thomas said.

"Maybe her husband tapping into army slush funds?"

"Anything is possible in China, of course. The military, especially the PLA, is a conglomerate onto itself; a monster that owns more companies than anyone else. But having access to PLA money for private investments? I doubt he is high ranking enough for that, but I have no idea just what his function or sphere of influence is. You can assume that as a general he solicits under-the-table-money, and putting some of this illicit cash into his wife's business would be a good way of laundering it. He needs more money than his salary to maintain the mistress he no doubt has stashed away. But why don't you ask her? I mean about her sources of funding, not her husband's income or girlfriend. I think inquiring about all aspects of the origins of her capital are legitimate business questions."

Shad nodded. He was trying to keep an open mind. "Maybe I am being paranoid," he said, "but I also worry about what might happen in the future if we worked with Kang Ming."

"What do you mean?"

"Well, let's assume for a moment that we appoint her as our distributor," Shad said, "and then, five or six years later, our business has grown to the extent that we wish to set up our own organization. We would have to terminate our agreement with Ning Chang. Would we then not have to fear some kind of retribution through her husband?"

"You always have to worry about terminating a distributor," Thomas explained, "because when you do, you stand a good chance of getting sued. Almost inevitably, you will have to cough up some kind of severance pay, to compensate the distributor for the time and money he has put into developing your business. Believe me, I know."

"So her husband being military would just be one more potentially complicating factor?"

"Yes, although not a likely one," Thomas said. "If the general is channeling black market money into his wife's business, he would have a powerful incentive to maintain a low profile if acrimony were to arise between her and an international principal. Let's face it, the nature of a distributor's business is such that principals come and go. You sign one up, you go all out and are successful. Then he puts the squeeze on you to reduce your margin and eventually you get punished by losing the distribution rights *because* you have done such a good job that he has become big enough not to need you anymore. On the surface it's simple math: what do you have to pay the distributor versus what would it cost you to do the job yourself?"

"Remind me never to become a distributor!" Shad said.

Thomas shrugged philosophically. "Keep in mind that it is conceivable to set up your own sales and marketing entity without going into physical distribution yourself. Even if you establish a full-fledged subsidiary, you would not want to get into invoicing, credit collection and physical distribution to doctors and hospitals in China. You couldn't possibly handle the accounting for necessary facilitation payments, and your number of days outstanding and inventory carrying costs would kill you. Plus, as you know, off-the-books payments are illegal under the US Foreign Corrupt Practices Act, so you would not only risk your business getting shut down, but also significant fines for your company and prison for you personally."

"I hadn't thought about that," Shad admitted. The possibility of getting dragged into court—no matter how remote—reminded him of his past and scared the shit out of him. "I guess you are right," he went on. "I obviously still have a lot to learn. But I keep coming back to Kang Ming's unique situation. Not every distributor has Ning's personal relationship to the PLA. I would feel better if I knew just what her husband's function is in the army."

Thomas shrugged again. "Why don't you ask her? Who knows, she might even tell you the truth."

"That's pretty cynical, Thomas."

"So is China many times. Anyway, I think you are worrying too much at this point, not having heard what she plans on doing for AmeriDerm and before having met the other distributors. You should keep an open mind until you have a broader perspective."

Shad nodded in agreement. They called it a night.

*　　*　　*

Once Shad was up in his room, he glanced at his watch and debated with himself whether or not he could—or should—give Apries a call. It was already after 10:00pm. She could be sound asleep. Perhaps she had forgotten him. Most importantly, where would it lead if he did call her and she remembered her promise to meet him? Why couldn't he just dream of Veronica and forget about Apries? Why not avoid the temptation she represented? He should be calling Veronica, not Apries, but he knew she was at work and would not be able to talk.

If he did see Apries, could he keep from flirting with her? Maybe even trying to seduce her? What the hell would he be starting if he called her?

He stood and stared out the window, undecided. What could he say to her if she answered her phone?

He went to the mini bar of his room, poured himself a night cap and flopped down on the small couch by the window, within reach of his telephone. He stared down at the city from his 15th floor and was amazed at how few lights could be seen. He thought of how different this was from Hong Kong.

Another fifteen minutes passed before he quickly extracted Apries' business card from the stack he had in his shirt pocket and started dialing before he could change his mind. What did he have to lose? All he wanted to do was thank her for her kindness, he told himself.

"Hello?" she answered after so many rings Shad had almost hung up. Her voice was a hesitant croak, drugged with sleep. He felt bad about having interrupted her sleep.

"Hello, Apries? This is Shad Cooper. I am sorry I woke you up. I couldn't call any earlier and was hoping I would still catch you before you went to bed. I guess I was wrong."

"That's all right. People are always calling me at all hours. As soon as I hang up, I fall right back to sleep. How are you? Did you get lost some more?"

He heard her quiet chuckling over the phone. "No, I was well taken care of," he said. "I even had my first Peking duck dinner tonight."

"How did you like it?"

"It was good. In the Peking hotel. But I was a little surprised that there was so little duck and so much of everything else."

She laughed some more. "You should have called me. I could have warned you. But someone must really be trying to do a number on you, if they took you to the Peking Hotel. That place is expensive. The only Chinese businessmen who go there are on an expense account and want something from you."

"I suppose. But if there is a next time, I will be glad to call you," he said. "Anyway, how was your day?"

"Normal. Busy. I took some business visitors for whom I was translating out to the Great Wall. They wore me out, climbing up and down the ramparts, which is why I went to bed early."

"Too bad we didn't meet out there. I was at the Great Wall this morning as well."

"You were?" she said, surprise in her voice, and added: "Maybe you saw me but did not recognize me." Her teasing tone was back.

"No, I would have recognized you."

"Are you sure?"

"Absolutely. How could I have forgotten so quickly how you look?" he said. And it was true. Without even closing his eyes he could still see her standing in front of him, smiling so mischievously, her eyes sparkling, her long straight hair framing her face with its flawless skin. And the minute scar across her upper lip gave her an enticingly distinctive appearance in any case—not that he could have seen that from a distance.

"Because I think to you foreigners we Chinese all look the same."

"There may be some truth to that, like when I arrive at an airport in Asia and see a thousand people waiting and the women all have long straight black hair, are all the same height and have the same skin color and black eyes. But I would certainly recognize you. Besides, maybe *you* would not recognize *me* again."

"Perhaps," she said, but it was apparent from her voice she was only kidding. "On the other hand, you are a little more difficult to overlook with your light hair and being a head taller than anyone else."

"There is that," he admitted. "I suppose there is only one way to find out if we would recognize each other again," he said, pausing, waiting for her to fill the void. When she didn't say anything he continued, "But as much as I enjoyed being saved by you this morning, I don't want to get lost again."

"But I wouldn't mind rescuing you again," she assured him softly and added, "I think this was my lucky day." He thought her voice sounded promising.

"In that case, I will reconsider," he joked, "hoping I would run into you again. What do you think about meeting day after tomorrow so I can reciprocate your kindness? Would you be free in the evening? I am afraid I will be tied up all day tomorrow, probably including another official dinner." He ignored the fact he had only promised to invite her for a cup of tea or a drink.

"That suits me well," she said, "because I have an afternoon translation assignment tomorrow and I don't know how long that will take. Maybe you could call me when you are back and let me know when you will be free? I should be home by nine. It would be good to see you again before I forget what you look like."

"Thanks!" he said. He could hear she was teasing him. "I could play it safe and wear my old jogging outfit. Then you would surely know."

"Hmmm . . . good idea. Fewer clothes for you to take off," she laughed.

What was that all about? Shad wondered. He didn't know what to say. He felt himself breaking out in a sweat and was glad she could not see his nervous anticipation.

"Did I shock you, Shad? I am sorry. I have a lousy sense of humor. I was only kidding, you know."

"You were? Too bad. I was hoping you were serious," he said, recovering quickly.

"Well, you never know what might happen. But if we are going to have dinner together, it might be better for you to wear some regular clothes, even here in Beijing where everything is very casual."

"All right," he said. "Then I will call you. I am very much looking forward to seeing you again."

"Me too. But don't expect more from me than you can handle," she said.

"Huh?" he choked out.

"Just kidding, Shad. Good night."

"And a good night to you, Apries. Sleep well and dream about me."

It took him a long time to fall asleep. Not because of jet lag, but because of what she said. Was she just a tease? Was she seriously interested in him? And if she was indeed ready for an adventure after having just met him, what would that say about her? She puzzled him. He had no experience with Chinese women. He only knew and remembered what Thomas had told him. She had been so concerned about her reputation that she had refused to let him reimburse her for the pedicab fare in front of the hotel, and yet she was so outspoken and more than just flirtatious. He knew he was far from irresistible, so why was she willing to see him again and was deliberately turning him on? He could not figure it out.

He was thinking of Veronica and how she would feel if she knew he was picking up on Apries' double entendres. It would be much more prudent to avoid getting to know her better. What if she had been more than just flirting? What was driving her, and what were her intentions? He gave up torturing his brain.

13

Beijing, 1986

Thomas and Shad arrived at People's First Pharmaceutical Company for their meeting and were greeted in the foyer by an attractive young woman wearing a bright red business suit, well tailored. She introduced herself and business cards were exchanged.

Shad studied her card carefully, trying to memorize her name, Li Shu Ling. The title under her name identified her as Manager of Foreign Relations. He was tempted to ask her what this meant.

"If you will follow me, I will take you to the conference room," she said and flashed a brilliant smile before leading them down a narrow corridor.

"May I get you something to drink? Perhaps tea?" she asked when they were seated.

"Tea would be fine," both Thomas and Shad acknowledged.

She walked over to a sideboard, picked up the telephone and said something in Chinese.

Moments later a contingent of eight Chinese walked in. With formal bowing they presented their cards and received Shad's and Thomas' in return. Shad felt slightly overwhelmed by such a large group. He studied their cards and the English titles confused him as to who was actually in charge. He assumed it was the chairman. But there was also a Director General, a Director, a President, a Vice-Director, a CEO, a Marketing President and—strangest to Shad of all—one with the title 'Senior Engineer, Vice General Manager & Director of

Product Development Section'. Nothing like a huge bureaucracy, Shad thought.

There was no way he could have remembered who was who. He lined up the received cards in the order in which his hosts sat. Li Shu Ling, as interpreter, took a chair next to the chairman who proceeded to welcome them and thank them for their visit. Tea was served. Shad was surprised to see the whole senior management team wearing identical blue wind breakers, the name First People's Pharmaceutical Company and its logo embroidered over the left breast pocket.

A brief exchange of pleasantries ensued; a mix of Chinese and English with Li Shu Ling helping out as needed. As had been the case during the previous evening's dinner, where Ning Chang had dominated the conversation, so it was here, with the chairman doing the talking and his colleagues remaining largely silent.

An overhead presentation of the company's history and what they envisioned doing with AmeriDerm's product line was given by the marketing president. His English was not faultless, but all slides were in English and generally easily understood. Most of them, at least.

The growth of the company over the past ten years was indeed impressive, but Shad had difficulties understanding why the company had sales offices and distribution centers in so many cities, largely unfamiliar to him. He was puzzled by their justification, seeing them as unnecessary expenses.

He asked for an explanation. A flurry of discussion in Chinese resulted before the marketing president responded: "Perhaps you are not yet so familiar with China. Our country is huge and the infrastructure is still being improved upon. If we tried to ship our products from only two or three locations, our customers would often have to wait many days—perhaps weeks—before the goods arrived. But we want our customers to receive their orders within a few short days, so we need facilities all over the country. Also, our salesmen must have a place where they can store their samples and promotional materials, and from where they can call their doctors to make appointments or solicit orders. They must be closely monitored. This we can only do if they come to the office every morning before starting out on their sales calls. This structure reinforces to our people every day who they work for; they get their instructions on what they need to do that day; they track their sales, and, perhaps most importantly, the office environment allows them to become an integral part of a relatively small working unit—a family, if you will. This in turn creates greater loyalty and discipline."

This concept seemed awkward and expensive to Shad, but he nodded in understanding, aware he knew nothing about working conditions in China.

"You also have to realize, Mr. Cooper," continued Zhu Long, the marketing president, "that nothing is less expensive here in China than manpower. We use manual labor instead of machines wherever we can. We have thousands of people in production simply because it is less costly for us to have more employees than to invest in high capacity, expensive foreign machines, which would present us with problems of maintenance and service. Our reps have small territories and use public transportation, so we don't have to provide company cars. Most of them do not know how to drive anyway, and if they did, there would be no place for them to park, and we would have to deal with accidents and car thefts."

Shad had to accept this at face value. "Given your idea of creating a separate and new sales force just for our product line," he said, "you would be looking at significant up front expenditures, especially for inventories. You would have to stock our products in all 23 of your locations, based on what you said about the infrastructure problems. What are your thoughts on how many total units of each product you would have to carry initially?"

Ms. Li translated his question. Everyone was looking at the chairman, who was looking at the marketing president.

"I would have to say," the latter finally ventured, "that it is too soon to answer your question. We don't know what your strategies are, which products should have priority, how many free samples you would be willing to supply, how many clinical trials you would underwrite, how effective your products are or the prices at which you propose to sell to us. Until we have this information, we can not realistically calculate our inventory levels."

"I understand. I wish I could give you an easy answer, but you catch me by surprise. My idea was to start rather modestly, with a few important products and a couple of salesmen in perhaps no more than three key cities each, and then expand rapidly with additional products and sales reps, both in those cities and others as well. The aggressive scenario you envision requires me to give this some thought. It has a dimension I had not considered."

"We don't believe in doing things halfway," the chairman said. "You have to think big. You have to have vision and be willing to share risks. A long term relationship with AmeriDerm is only of interest to us if you are willing to make a major commitment, including the option of a contract manufacturing agreement. Without local production we would have no control over cost of goods and we would not generate the margins we need to make this relationship financially attractive."

"That would not be easy," Shad said. "Our manufacturing and quality control procedures are highly proprietary, and given the fact that China does not protect intellectual property rights, my concerns about releasing this know-how would have to be put to rest."

The chairman nodded his understanding. "I can assure you, Mr. Cooper," he said, "we are a highly ethical company. Our long term strategic goal is to become a global player in the pharmaceutical industry. For that, we need reliable international business partners, and these we can only win and maintain by sticking scrupulously to any agreements we sign. All of your technology would be absolutely safe with us."

"Perhaps," Shad suggested, "one of our senior technical people should come here and look at your factory to see what, if anything, would need to be done to bring you into compliance with our specifications."

"That would be perfectly acceptable to us. I think your people will be surprised when they see our high standards. We are already fully in compliance with Good Manufacturing Practices."

"Excellent! I will check to see when someone will be available. In the meantime, I will give some thought to your marketing proposal," he promised. "But I need your help on pricing. I recognize you do not know much about our products yet, but you know the market and the hospital environment, and if you could make some suggestions as to the price range at which you feel you could sell our products successfully, we could move forward."

It was Zhu Long who responded. "We would be happy to do so. If you could be kind enough to send us 48 samples of each of your products, we would test their acceptance, determine need and recommend prices."

Shad made notes of the action steps required of him and felt the meeting had gone as far as it could be taken. He thanked his hosts profusely for their time and courtesies and promised to get back to them expeditiously. He courteously declined the dinner invitation they extended.

"We look forward very much to seeing you again, Mr. Cooper," the chairman said. "Please accept this small token of our appreciation." He reached over to Ms. Li, took the gift wrapped box she was holding, and presented it to Shad.

He did not know whether or not to open it in their presence. He thanked him and asked, "May I open it?"

The chairman nodded. "Of course," he said and smiled.

A moment later Shad held a beautifully black lacquered box in his hands, inlaid with mother-of-pearl in the form of a dragon. He opened the small brass clasp and admired the intricate miniature tea set embedded in red velvet cushions.

"This is very beautiful," he said. "Thank you ever so much. I will cherish it and enjoy a good cup of tea when I am at home." He was chagrined that he could not offer them a present in return.

Ms. Li accompanied them back out of the building and bid them farewell when their car pulled up.

"I take it this is not their main facility," Shad said to Thomas when the car pulled away.

"Yes and no. This is their administrative headquarters. Their main manufacturing plant, research and development, and central warehouse are all in Tianjin."

"You were right about the contract manufacturing."

"Yes," Thomas said, "no surprise there. But I never expected them to be willing to set up a dedicated sales organization for you and to immediately go country-wide."

"It scares me, not knowing the market and pricing. The very thought of putting inventory into 23 locations is intimidating. I can just see Dave Hardee's reaction when I tell him about this plan. It will be difficult enough just to get him to agree to have our experts evaluate their factory."

"Well, like the chairman said: they don't believe in doing things half way, and their success seems to bear them out."

Shad nodded, thinking about whether such an ambitious plan had any realistic chance of success. He had to admit he liked the idea of immediately making a big splash. The sales results could be astronomical, but so were the risks. Was AmeriDerm large and its products promising enough to justify the risks? He was far from convinced, and if he had doubts, how could he convince his boss?

*   *   *

Thirty minutes later they were at Great Wall Pioneering Research Company. Their offices were located in a modest high rise. Shad had expected more representation, but when they walked into the building and found the listing of occupants, he understood. This was their Beijing Sales Office; not corporate headquarters.

Shad and Thomas went up to the fifth floor where a friendly receptionist greeted them. Moments after she had announced their arrival, another woman appeared and showed them to a conference room.

It was a repeat of their previous meeting. Names and cards were exchanged. Again it was a large group around the table. It occurred to Shad that being outnumbered like this could be a deliberate part of a psychological campaign to intimidate him, or to create the impression the company was larger than it actually was.

After the mandatory pleasantries had been exchanged over some tea, they were invited to go downstairs for a quick lunch before a presentation would be made.

Shad had some trepidation about dining in a local restaurant but these were dispelled when he saw serving carts piled high with Dim Sum being wheeled around.

Within minutes piles of steaming bamboo baskets were placed on the lazy Suzan of their table; shrimp dumplings, pork buns, deep fried crab balls, morsel sized beef short ribs, spring rolls, the ubiquitous chicken feet and other delicacies. No sooner were the baskets emptied then a huge platter of fried rice was served.

Less than an hour later they were back in the conference room and Shad listened patiently while one of the managers presented a profile of his company. It became quickly apparent this enterprise was not on the same level as People's First. While extolling at length how good they were and how they would excel in distributing AmeriDerm's products, they did not present a credible plan as to how they proposed to accomplish this.

When the lack of specific plans dawned on Shad, he decided Great Wall would not be the right partner and consequently asked no more questions than simple courtesy demanded. The meeting was concluded with a mutual agreement that it had been enlightening and productive, and that they would stay in touch.

*   *   *

There was no time to freshen up in the hotel before their appointment at the Ministry of Public Health.

Their meeting was scheduled with the International Center for Medical and Health Exchange. Shad had no idea what this meant. He assumed Thomas did. He led them through the warren of corridors to the correct section.

The blue uniformed receptionist behind the desk of the waiting area greeted them deferentially in English. "The Secretary General is ready to see you," she said and reached for her telephone to announce their arrival.

"Our translator was to have met us here," Thomas said to her when she had hung up.

"Yes, she is here and is waiting for you in the conference room. I will take you there now," she said and smiled cheerfully.

The surprise waiting for them could not have been greater for Shad if it had been the President of China. He was momentarily speechless when he stepped into the room and saw Apries looking up at him from her chair. She was obviously equally surprised as she rose to greet him.

"What are you doing here?" they both said, and then had to laugh.

"I take it you know each other," Thomas said.

"Yes, we met early yesterday morning, under somewhat different circumstances. What a coincidence!" she said.

"You remember me telling you about how I got lost, jogging, and was rescued by this charming lady," Shad explained to the puzzled looking Thomas. "That was Apries. You know each other as well?"

"Yes," Thomas admitted, seemingly with some reluctance, and turned to her, offering his hand in greeting.

"Hello, Apries. It's good to see you again."

"Thank you," she responded. "I am happy to see you too."

"I don't really *know* Apries," Thomas went on. "I have only utilized her for translation purposes."

Shad thought he detected some discomfort in Thomas at this bland, unsolicited explanation.

Before they could continue, the Ministry retinue entered the room while Shad studied his surroundings. He had been so surprised by the sight of Apries he had not looked at the set-up of the room.

Ten easy chairs, upholstered with red velour, their arm rests a dark lacquered wood with white doilies gracing them, were arranged U-shaped with two of them as its head. Small, low, rectangular side tables, their wood matching the arm rests of the chairs, separated them. Fresh cut flowers were on the table between the chairs at the head of the U, and two high stools with short back rests were placed behind and slightly off to the side of these chairs. Chinese scrolls of brush drawings hung from the wood paneled walls. Tall traditional Chinese vases, on high stands, completed the adornments.

A ministry translator hovered by the side of the delegation leader, the Secretary General. When cards had been exchanged, Shad was happy to note that the Deputy Chief of the Division of Drug Registrations and Standards was among the group, as were the Deputy General Director of the ministry, a Deputy Chief, a Program Officer, and two further "Chiefs".

He was politely invited to sit in one of the two head chairs, with the Secretary General sitting next to him. The others took their place along the sides. The ministry translator, Margaret Hsu, and Apries sat down on the stools.

They were officially welcomed by the Secretary General and Shad thanked him and his group for their time and their willingness to meet with him. He spoke briefly about AmeriDerm and his own function in the company, with Apries translating his remarks, before handing everyone a short brochure he had brought along about AmeriDerm's history and product line.

"What brings you here today, Mr. Cooper?" Ms. Hsu translated.

"A courtesy visit, Mr. Secretary General. We are exploring the possibility of launching our products in the People's Republic of China and are searching for a suitable partner to help us with the health registrations, importation and distribution."

"I am afraid the Ministry can not help you with the latter, but I can assure you that the Division of Drug Registrations and Standards will not place undue burdens on you. I assume all necessary clinical trials have been done and your FDA has approved the products?"

"Most assuredly. And we would like to expand the scope of these clinical trials by implementing a number of additional ones here in China."

"We would welcome such an approach. Good local studies, in reputable hospitals, would no doubt facilitate product approvals. We would be glad to give you a list of those hospitals most suitable. We would encourage you to involve some sites in other major cities, not just Beijing."

"A point well taken. This is precisely why we need a good, dependable local partner."

"Have you made any progress yet in identifying one?"

Shad told them about the three companies with whom he was in discussions.

"I don't know this Kang Ming company, but both People's First Pharmaceuticals and Great Wall Pioneering Research are well recognized."

With the time the translations consumed, the meeting went longer than Shad had anticipated. An hour had passed before he was able to talk about *Melavict* and its reliability in treating melanoma, a serious problem in China, he pointed out.

"Such an oncology drug would definitely be welcome here, especially if it were priced at a level the average patient could afford."

"That would also be our desire," Shad said.

"To keep the costs down, I would strongly encourage you to have it manufactured locally. The government is highly desirous of bringing more manufacturing technology into the country and rewards this with attractive tax and price advantages."

"I will definitely keep that in mind," Shad said.

He saw the Secretary General glance at the wall clock in front of them and was not surprised when he stood up and started saying good-bye. "We appreciate you coming to see us," he said. "By visiting us first, before making any decisions, you have shown you are taking the right approach."

He walked out the door and his delegation followed him.

The receptionist appeared moments later and escorted them out. Shad felt drained. He hoped the meeting had gone well.

"Can we give you a lift back to the hotel, Apries?" he asked while they waited for their car.

"Are you sure you wouldn't mind?" she asked, looking from Shad to Thomas and back again.

"Not at all," Thomas said, "we would be delighted." He sounded less than enthusiastic, his voice devoid of emotion.

Shad thought she had asked him, but when he looked in her eyes, he was sure she had wanted to clear it with Thomas. He wondered why.

14

Beijing, 1986

Hazy, diffuse polluted light still hung over the city upon their return to the Sheraton.

"How about having a drink with us, Apries?" Shad asked as they were milling around undecidedly in front of the hotel. The air was sticky and hot.

She glanced at her watch. "I suppose so," she said after a moment's hesitation. Shad saw her looking at Thomas, as if to make sure it was all right with him. Thomas nodded almost imperceptibly and they walked into the lobby and went up to the executive lounge.

"What would you like to have?" Shad asked her.

"A scotch, please, with lots of ice."

"And you, Thomas?"

"I'll have the same, thanks. No ice. Just a drop of water."

Shad walked over to the bar counter where a selection of bottles had been arrayed. He made the drinks, poured himself a glass of Dragon Seal chardonnay and brought the drinks to their table. Apries immediately took a big gulp of her scotch. She seemed nervous. Thomas and Shad clinked glasses and sipped their drinks.

"Did you have any problems with the translations, Apries?" Shad asked.

"Not really. I was a little concerned when I was given the assignment because I thought there might be a lot of unfamiliar medical terms, but it all seemed rather straight forward."

"Well, I am certainly glad you were there," Shad said. "Where did you learn to speak such excellent English anyway?"

"At the university."

Shad saw Thomas' eyes opening wide but he remained taciturn. He had been, since their ministry meeting. Shad thought this odd, but he let it go.

"What time do you have to leave, Thomas?" Shad asked, remembering that his friend was to fly to Hainan.

"Well, I had planned on leaving tonight, but it's a three hour flight and I didn't know how long we would be tied up, so I changed to an early morning flight tomorrow. That also gives me the chance to visit an old friend here tonight. The downside is that I will have to be on my way by 6:00am. Traffic out to the airport can be a killer. If I hadn't promised my friend to stop by, I would probably be in bed by nine."

"What time is he expecting you?"

"Around 7:00 o'clock. In fact, I should go to my room in a few minutes and freshen up a bit."

They spent another thirty minutes in idle conversation, but it never developed into one in which all three partook. Shad would talk with Thomas, or with Apries, but nothing was said between the latter two. Rather strange behavior, Shad thought, and made no attempt to keep Thomas when he got up to leave.

"Please excuse me a minute, Shad," Apries said, standing up when Thomas had said his good-byes, "I need to make a quick phone call."

"No problem. Can I get you another drink in the meantime?"

"Better not, if you still want us to have dinner together. I need to find out how much time I have," she explained.

He couldn't remember having invited her for dinner, but it was fine with him. He was still more than curious to find out whether she had only flirted harmlessly with him, or had sent him a message. While Veronica intruded on his thinking, it was Apries who was here and now, and Veronica the one who was far away. There was no doubt in his mind whatsoever that Veronica was the woman with whom he wanted to spend the rest of his life, but this did not mean he could not find someone else attractive and desirable. After all, Veronica was totally committed to him, but did she not also seek physical pleasure elsewhere, with Caitlin? Had she not told him she would understand if he developed an emergency and did something about it? Studying

Apries, he felt such a situation developing. She was irresistibly appealing, with a sexuality to which his body responded automatically, uncontrollably.

"Is everything all right?" he asked when she returned. She did not look very happy, he thought; rather distracted.

"Yes, but I don't have that much time. I am going to be picked up at 9:00. Is it okay with you if we eat here in the hotel?"

"Sure. Fine with me. Should I call for a reservation?"

She shook her head. "We can go anytime you want."

"Give me a minute to finish my drink," he said. "I don't mean to pry, but you don't look very happy. Did you get some bad news?"

"Not really. In fact, I should be elated."

"Then why aren't you? I don't understand."

"I don't know if I should tell you. Maybe later," she said with a toss of her hair.

He was mystified. The expression on her face made it obvious she didn't want any more questions. He looked at his watch. Just past 6:30. If she had to be down in the lobby by 9:00, they didn't have much time. He liked being with her and enjoyed looking at her and wished she could stay longer. He hoped to find out if he had read her signals correctly.

She put her hand on his arm and gave a slight squeeze. Her slim fingers felt delightfully cool on his skin and she let her hand linger while she asked, "Are you about ready?"

He nodded, drained the last of his wine and stood up. He took her by the arm to walk to the elevators. She looked up at him, a mysterious, promising smile on her lips. Her unhappiness had apparently been forgotten. Her eyes sparkled. In the elevator she snuggled up against him and put her arms around his waist. "I am glad we are going to have dinner together," she said. "I like you."

He hugged her as answer.

They were shown to a quiet corner table. She took charge of the menu.

"Is there anything you particularly like or absolutely don't like?" she asked.

"I don't think so. I wouldn't want to have dog or snake, but other than that, I trust your judgment. Order whatever appeals to you. I enjoy trying local favorites."

"In that case, how about some deep fried scorpions?" she asked, challenging him with a broad smile.

"Maybe another day," he replied, keeping a straight face.

"Okay."

She beckoned the waiter over and started a lively discussion with him. What was there to negotiate when she had the menu in front of her, Shad wondered? He was ravenously hungry.

He did not have long to wait once the selections had been made. Within minutes, it seemed, steaming hot, thinly sliced pork in garlic sauce was brought, followed quickly by string beans fried with finely ground spicy pork. Then came what looked like rather thick pancakes, pan fried to a crispy brown texture. A big bowl of steamed rice was placed on the table. It was all delicious, but too much. He couldn't pace himself and ate too fast and was consequently full all too quickly.

Apries took her time, obviously immensely enjoying the excellent food. Between bites, he found her staring into his eyes. He was mesmerized by the sight of the tip of her tongue passing languorously over her sensuous lips and slightly parted mouth. It was, he thought, deliberately, provocatively erotic, sensual, sending a message he hoped was not just a tease. He swallowed reflexively. What was she trying to do to him?

She could tell she was getting through to him, the light in her eyes dimming. "I am just playing with you, Shad," she said and laughed. He blushed at having been caught.

"What will you be doing tomorrow?" she asked between bites.

"I am going to be in the offices of Kang Ming, one of the distributors I am looking at, first thing in the morning. Then, around noon, the lady who owns the company, Ning Chang, will take me to the Military Hospital 402. I don't know what will happen after that. Maybe another hospital. I guess it will depend on how much time we will have. I want to learn as much as I can about the market for our products. How about you, Apries? Will you have time to meet me again tomorrow evening?"

She shook her head. "I am afraid not," she said. "I am going to be tied up. What about the day after tomorrow?"

"I've got an early afternoon flight to Hong Kong," he said, more disappointed than he was ready to admit.

She did not look happy either. "You are leaving so soon? When will you be coming back?"

"I don't know yet. It all depends on how far my current negotiations take me. It could be as soon as two or three months, but—worst case—much longer if I have to conclude entering the China market is premature."

"That's bad," she sighed, "but I appreciate your honesty." She thought for a moment before adding, "Maybe we could at least have breakfast together before you leave."

It was not his favorite time of day, but he would take whatever he could. "That would be great. What time could you be here?"

"How about 8:00 o'clock? That would give us at least a few hours alone."

Alone, Shad thought? What did that imply? "Eight would be fine," he assured her. "I will wait for you downstairs so that security does not give you a hard time. Then we can have breakfast up in the lounge where we will have more privacy than we would have in the restaurant."

"Do you think we will need that?" she asked with an unfathomable look in her eyes.

"I hope so!" he said and grinned at her. "Besides, the lounge is not far from my room."

"Really?" she said with mock innocence. "And why is that important?"

He shrugged. "Because you said we would have time to be alone, and where could we be more so than in my room?" He was afraid he had gone too far, but she didn't seem to mind.

She put her hand on his arm again. "Thank you so much for a wonderful meal," she said, "I really appreciate it." She paused; switched subjects. "Tell me, Shad, are you married?"

"No. Divorced. For nearly 20 years already. I do have a steady girlfriend, however," he admitted. "How about you?"

"Also divorced for a long time, with an eight year old daughter." She didn't say anything about a boyfriend and did not seem concerned about his having a girlfriend.

"Do you live in that *Hutong*?"

"Yes, with my mother and a sister and her husband. And my daughter, of course. I can't afford to rent an apartment."

"Does translating pay that poorly here?" he asked.

"It's not that," she said. "I mean, I don't make all that much money, but I have to support not only my daughter and myself, but also my mother and another brother, and another sister of mine who lives in the UK but owns a house here for which she can not make the payments unless I give her some money. That's where my other brother lives. If I don't help out he will not have a place to live."

"What about your father?"

"I don't want to talk about him. He passed away many years ago."

"And the brother who lives in your sister's house? Doesn't he earn enough money? And if your sister can not meet the mortgage obligations on her house, why doesn't she simply sell it?"

"It's not that easy. If she sold the house, my brother would be homeless. He doesn't have a steady job," she explained. She made it clear she did not want to talk about this brother.

He realized he had a lot to learn. The much vaunted family ties he had heard about obviously created problems he could only imagine. But he was also a little suspicious. She was so friendly with him; coming on to him. Her hand on his arm expressed warmth, maybe promise. Her words yesterday and during dinner had been so suggestive. Did she have an ulterior motive? Was she looking for money? Did she think he was rich? He couldn't quite get these cynical thoughts out of his mind.

"I guess that doesn't give you much freedom," he finally managed to say.

"I can come and go as I please," she said, "because my mother looks after my daughter. But I would love to have my own apartment."

"I am sure it will work out one day."

If she was disappointed that he did not offer to help her, she hid it well. "Excuse me," she said, "I have to go to the bathroom."

"You are welcome to use the one in my room," he offered, tongue in cheek, before he could stop himself.

"No doubt. Maybe later. I will be right back," she said with another dazzling smile, giving him to understand she knew what he wanted and showing him she was not offended. He stared longingly at her shapely legs and body as she walked away, hips swaying.

A highly desirable woman, Shad thought not for the first time. He pushed his thoughts of Veronica to the back of his mind.

* * *

He stood up when she returned and pulled her chair out for her. It earned him another dazzling smile as she sat down.

"You have beautiful eyes," he told her. She ignored the compliment. He was sure she had heard it many times before.

The waiter came with the bill. Shad signed it and helped Apries get up. They exited the restaurant wordlessly and only stopped when they came to the bank of elevators. He pressed the button for up. The doors hissed open and she did not resist when he gently propelled her inside. They rode up in silence.

Maybe she thought they were merely going back up to the lounge, he speculated, since she was coming along without prompting, but he went right by the door to the lounge and continued down the hallway. She did not resist.

His pace slowed as the imaginary shadow of Veronica suddenly loomed over him and he asked himself, "What the hell am I doing?" Granted, she had given him her reluctant blessing to take a prostitute if he was really horny, which he most definitively was by now, but did Apries fall under this permissiveness? She was following him so easily, voluntarily, carefree, that it occurred to him she could well be working as a call girl. She had made it clear enough she needed more money. Was she freelancing at night? He didn't want to think so, but was it even remotely possible anything other than money could motivate her enough to come to his room with him? He recognized he should stop before it was too late, but his physical needs overruled his common sense.

A few steps from his door she halted and turned towards him, looking up into his face. She appeared to be suddenly unsure of herself. He glanced around but the floor was blessedly deserted. He pulled her against him and she leaned her head against his chest.

"You don't have to be afraid," he murmured and turned her gently in the direction of his room. When he did, her hesitation disappeared.

He unlocked his door and walked in, neither one of them saying a word.

They stopped next to his bed. He was unsure what to do; felt nervous. She put her arms around him, hugging him tightly. He shivered, either because the room was so cold or because of his anxiety. Was this really happening? A beautiful girl in his room, not even having been asked? It was a first for him. Again he wondered fleetingly if she was working or just wanted him. It did not matter. What was there to understand? She was with him and patently ready and he wanted her. Badly.

She turned her mouth up to be kissed. Not softly, hesitatingly, experimentally. No, there was an immediate fierceness, a hunger, a desperate passion that gave their tongues a life of their own. It defined the term oral sex in a way he had not known.

Before he could dwell any longer on what was happening, he felt her hands on his trousers, unzipping him. She reached inside and pulled him out and caressed his erection with both hands. Then she lifted her tight dress up around her waist and squatted in front of him with spread legs in that typical Asian fashion—both heels flat on the floor, buttocks almost touching it, knees up and wide apart.

She had her left hand on his butt, pulling him towards her, while her right hand was wrapped around him, stroking him. She took him in her mouth. He couldn't believe this was happening. She was deep-throating him and he gave in to the ecstasy.

It dazed him. He had never known a woman so openly showing what she wanted, without pretenses or modesty. It was as if she was doing it more for herself than for him. There could be no doubt she had lots of practice; her skills had to have been acquired over years.

It was too much for him and when he came, all too soon, she swallowed and licked her lips in delight.

"Hmmm . . . delicious," she murmured and gazed up at him. "That was good, but you were too fast! I was just getting started."

"You caught me by surprise," he managed to say.

She grinned and swiped the back of her hand lasciviously across her mouth. "Good. I wanted you to like it as much as I did," she said and stood up and started getting undressed. He helped her. She had an incredible body. Slim and well proportioned with strong legs. Tawny, flawless skin. Her breasts were small, with prominent nipples, and when he kissed them, they became hard immediately. She pushed her perfect little cones deeper into his mouth, her nipples wondrously long and hard.

"Bite me!" she said, almost shouted, and when he did, she wanted more. "Harder!" she demanded hoarsely, until he was afraid he would hurt her. She groaned. She flopped down on the bed.

"Get undressed," she ordered. "I need you!"

He got on top of her and she became an animal; totally out of control. She shouted at him, telling him what to do and where and how. She screamed; bit her lips and the pillow and her eyeballs rolled up. She was making so much noise he was dimly afraid security would be knocking on their door at any moment.

She rolled out from under him and straddled his body, riding him with wild abandon. Her head tossed wildly, her hair flying. Her mouth was wide open and only the white of her eyes could be seen.

He let her do what she wanted and only reacted. It was over much too soon. He lay there, panting, sweat rolling down his body.

"Not bad," she said rather haughtily, "but you were too fast again. I only came five times."

"I am sorry. I guess it's been too long for me," he apologized automatically.

"Don't be silly," she said and kissed him deeply. "I was only teasing."

"Did you really come five times?" he asked in wonderment. It didn't seem possible to him.

"Of course. Why not? I can come very quickly and keep on coming every couple of minutes, twenty or thirty times. Easy!" she claimed very matter of fact. For some reason he did not doubt her.

"You are unbelievable," he finally managed to gasp as his breathing began normalizing.

His thoughts whirled around madly. He didn't know what to think. How did she get to be so good, he asked himself? And so aggressive and uninhibited! She was his wildest sexual fantasies come true. *Better* than any fantasy. Perhaps she was a nymphomaniac, insatiable? But he seemed to remember reading that nymphos usually didn't come at all. So what did Apries' multiple orgasms indicate?

The more rational part of him said she had to be a professional. No one else would just come up to his room with him and do what she had done, with hardly a word having been exchanged. He also needed to believe this to assuage his conscience regarding Veronica. No matter who or what Apries was, he felt she had gone far beyond what sex with a prostitute could possibly be like, and he was sure Veronica would not have approved or understood.

Should he offer Apries some money? Tell her it was for the taxi fare home? Buy her a nice present for their planned breakfast meeting? He deliberated silently and decided not to do anything until he knew more. It could be too easily misunderstood.

He didn't know who this woman was. If a professional, what had made her omit to ask for money? Perhaps that was the Chinese way; perhaps she was waiting to be tipped voluntarily. He had certainly never heard of, or met a professional working free of charge.

Her claim of having had multiple orgasms was equally puzzling and contradicted the reaction of a professional. It was inconceivable to him a pro would have multiple orgasms with a customer. Not totally impossible if she enjoyed her job so much that she was able to let go, but what were the chances? More likely she had lied. He was back to square one: her immediate willingness indicated professionalism; her sexual aggressiveness and passion were those of a woman desperately in need of sex. He was at a complete loss.

He tried not to think of Veronica, but when he did, he imagined her spending the night with Caitlin, which assuaged his guilt somewhat. Besides, it wasn't as if he had already taken his vows of eternal faithfulness. The thought of Veronica and Caitlin making love reminded him of how it had been when he had been with the two women just before his trip, the three of them naked, kissing and hugging and fondling each other passionately. He had found himself literally caught in the middle and wondered how Apries would react if she were invited to such an event. He was sure she would be more than willing.

"Oh, shit!" he heard Apries exclaim, "I have to leave. I promised my boyfriend to meet him in the lobby no later than 9:00. I need to take a quick shower. May I?"

Not waiting for an answer she was off the bed and in the bathroom, squatting on the toilet to relieve herself. She was not in the least bit shy about Shad seeing her.

"Can't you stay a little longer?" he asked, standing in the door, watching her. "I promise the next time won't be as fast."

"I will hold you to that promise," she said, "but I really have to go. My boyfriend will be furious if I don't show up on time."

The second time she mentioned this boyfriend it finally registered with Shad. She was in the shower and had the water running. He ignored what she had revealed and was elated there would be a next time.

"Can you please hand me my purse?" she asked as she was drying off, standing in front of the mirror. He took it to her, returned to the bedroom and started getting dressed. He thought he would shower after she had gone so he could accompany her downstairs to make sure she did not run into problems with hotel security.

When she came out of the bathroom, she looked as fresh as a new cut flower in full bloom. She had put on some make-up and smelled wonderfully. He admired her as she hastily dressed, and only with a great deal of self control did he keep from touching her. He saw she was in a hurry.

"I'll go down with you," he said when she was finished.

She did not argue with him and rushed out the door. He tried to look serious and nonchalant and wondered if anyone meeting them would be able to tell what they had just done. Maybe he should have taken a quick shower after all. He worried that the smell of sex clung to him.

If she was equally worried, she did not let on. With long purposeful strides, her heels clicking on the marble floor, she marched ahead of him out of the elevator, slightly off to his side, her purse slung carelessly over her left shoulder.

A man, a western foreigner, was pacing restlessly in the lobby, his eyes darting back and forth until he espied Apries. Her boyfriend, Shad concluded quickly. For some reason he had assumed he would be Chinese.

The man rushed over to her. "Where the hell have you been, Apries?" he demanded to know, his voice a threatening hiss.

A strange greeting, Shad thought, but if she was offended, she did not show it, although the tight little smile around her lips looked rigid.

Shad didn't know how to behave or what to say to this man whose fiancé had just climbed out of his bed. He was acutely embarrassed. Chagrined. How could she have allowed this impossible meeting? Did she have no shame? Could she really jump out of his bed and then go home, or wherever, with her fiancé? Why hadn't she said anything to him about being engaged? About her fiancé being in Beijing and coming to the hotel to pick her up? If he had known she was engaged, would it have stopped him? It certainly had not slowed her down. She had not exactly needed a lot of persuasion to come up to his room, and she had then immediately seized the initiative and left him with no choice.

He could only watch silently and abhorred as Alan and Apries left the hotel, arm in arm.

Seeing the two of them wandering off made him wonder what thoughts were running through her mind. If simple lust had brought her into his bed, why could that not have been taken care of by Alan? Or was she insatiable? Wanted more variety? Only a professional, full or part time, current or former, he felt, could sexually handle two different men in such a short time span, and yet he was sure it had been something else motivating her.

He was alone with his thoughts. He returned to his room, showered, went to bed, trying—not too successfully—to shut thoughts of both Veronica and Apries out of his mind.

15

I was nervous when I stepped out of the elevator with Shad. Although I tried to act composed, as if nothing out of the ordinary had happened, I felt suddenly exposed when I saw Alan. It was as if I was standing there naked. That the entire world could detect I had just been fucking. Alan spotted me and rushed over. He did not appear to be happy. His tone was curt, almost vicious, when he demanded to know: "Where the hell have you been, Apries?"

My immediate inclination was to tell him it was none of his fucking business, but I swallowed this antagonistic response. I had too much to hide. I did not want to upset him further. I thought I could be a pretty good actress, but this role of playing the innocent would put my acting skills to the test. I felt pretty confident I could pull it off; looking and behaving as if I had done absolutely nothing wrong. I was ready to explain in some credible detail what I had been working on with Shad in the lounge. I had to be careful with Alan in such a foul mood.

I kept quiet, thinking hard. I knew how much simpler life would be if I learned to constrain my hormones and listened to my brain instead. Why was I always so horny, needing sex as much as a heavy smoker his cigarette? No matter how much I had, I always craved more. It had become an addiction, one I could neither shake nor rein in. Over the years, one well intentioned resolution after another to free myself of this dangerous habit had come to naught. The constant hunger I felt between my legs determined my behavior. My throat felt perpetually parched and demanded to be quenched by a lover's juices. As time went by I needed ever more frequent and wilder bouts of sex. I liked experimenting to see how I could achieve new, unknown heights. I was in a self-imposed contest to see how many times I could come during a single session. My record was thirty five. I knew I could have done better but my lover had capitulated.

I had identified this as a real problem long ago, but recognizing it and coming up with a cure was something else. I was powerless to do anything about it. It was why I had accompanied Shad to his room with little prompting. My body's demands had determined my behavior. Admittedly, I had also found him sexually attractive when I first saw him, so obviously lost, wearing those sweat soaked shorts and T-shirt, and I had taken an immediate liking to his sexy legs. But I had certainly had no intention whatsoever of fucking him—ever—let alone the very first time we had the opportunity. I knew I had led him on, sending those flirtatious messages his way and inviting him with my eyes, not really doing it deliberately but unable to constrain the impulses that had made me do it. I had played with fire and had gotten burned. Not for the first time, either. I knew this was par for the course—flirting—but I had fallaciously deluded myself into believing it would remain just that: a harmless flirt. But I had been wrong once again.

I had completely ignored my common sense. Had not anticipated becoming so incredibly horny during dinner, my pussy itching, and had not considered the ramifications of fighting with Alan that morning after his arrival the evening before. As usual it had been over his questioning my faithfulness. He was *always* suspecting me of going out with other men, and it had finally dawned on me that as long as I was inevitably under suspicion anyway and was never believed, I might as well go ahead and do what I wanted.

Recalling this fight and having then been alone with Shad and seeing how much he wanted me, I had not been able to resist. Attacked from the inside by my hormones and from the outside by Shad's eyes, going to bed with him had become a foregone conclusion.

I did not want to admit to myself this was poor rationalization for something I absolutely should not have done. I only hoped Alan would not notice how weak my legs felt and how unsteadily I must have been walking. I was afraid he would detect that post-coital dreaminess enveloping me. I found it impossible to suppress with the man responsible for it standing next to me.

"I was working on some documentation with Mr. Cooper," I finally answered his question as to where I had been. My tone was as brusque as his had been. The expression on my face must have been defiant. I did not care. He did not own me, even though he tended to behave as if he did. I did not like the way he was looking at me now; the probing way his eyes roved over my body. I felt exposed. Vulnerable. His gaze lingered on my arms, I noticed, and felt more than saw the slight bruising Shad's hands must have left on them. I *had* to assume bruises were visible, just as I was sure Shad had bite marks on his shoulders.

"Maybe you could introduce us, Apries," Alan suggested.

"Alan, this is Shad Cooper. Shad, this is my boyfriend, Alan Sykes," I said and watched the two men mustering each other warily. I thought I detected an instant animosity between them.

"She is actually my fiancé," Alan corrected me. "Aren't you, darling?"

I tried to cover my discomfort with silence. I should have warned Shad. I took for granted he was embarrassed to be there, standing in front of my boyfriend, when hardly more than half an hour ago we had still been in bed together. He had to be consternated to learn I was engaged.

He was a good six inches taller than Alan, I noticed, and had an almost military, straight posture, whereas Alan seemed more slouched over. His clothing was rumpled, not like Shad's suit jacket, which fell smoothly from his shoulders. Shad looked more relaxed and in control of himself than did Alan, perhaps because of the latter's physical handicap, which made him lack self confidence.

I couldn't make up my mind which one of them was more handsome. I found them equally attractive, but at this moment was drawn inexplicably more to Shad, in whom I thought I had detected a selflessness, a kindness and an understanding lacking in Alan and which I longed for. The stinginess I had often observed with Alan, and which had made me mad so many times, stood in marked contrast to the generosity I had sensed in Shad. But it was his personality, I concluded, more than anything else that had drawn me to him so unstoppably.

The two men had to see each other as competitors for my affection. It had not been very smart of me to have them meet like this, in the lobby of Shad's hotel. Alan knew I had been alone with Shad and given his suspicious nature, he was surely convinced more than working together had taken up our time.

I could tell how shocked and embarrassed Shad was when he wanted to shake Alan's hand and discovered his hooks and was proud of Alan for the way he handled it. To his credit, Shad had recovered quickly as well, even going so far as to ask how Alan had lost his hands. He nodded when Alan talked about the industrial accident in his late teens that had led to the loss of his two extremities. He did not show pity, which I knew Alan would have detested.

"So how long have you two been engaged?" Shad wanted to know.

"Almost a year," Alan said. "As soon as Apries comes to England with me, we are going to get married."

This assertion angered me and I frowned. We had no such agreement. He had pushed me repeatedly, but I had never accepted. I did not consider us being formally engaged. Only because I didn't have the courage to turn him down outright did he assume I was going to become his wife. He had slipped into the habit of referring to me as his fiancé. I never liked it but had to admit I occasionally used it as an excuse if I wanted to refuse advances of men. I thought he was being presumptuous. His claim did make me look respectable and unavailable, and given my earlier employment, I did not fight it as vigorously as I should have.

I had initially remained more or less faithful to him. I say more or less because I had intercourse with very few other men, and when I did, it was a straightforward physical thing—no love or emotion involved. Taking someone in my mouth, I thought, did not really count, no matter how often I enjoyed that pastime.

I had fallen in love with Alan during my first visit to Manchester to see my sister. I had even considered marrying him at one time. But when I accepted his subsequent invitation to visit him in the UK some months later, and had spent those two weeks with him in his house, it had been made dramatically clear there were too many obstacles between us. The fights and disagreements we had had over how we viewed life and the irreconcilable differences between us had made me realize we could never be happy together permanently. While on my return flight to China a year ago I had pretty much concluded it would only be a matter of time before we would break up. If I had not been so reluctant to hurt him, and if I hadn't liked the sex with him so much, I would not be standing here in the hotel lobby now.

"And when will that be?" Shad asked, following up on Alan's assertion.

Alan shook his head. "We still have to resolve a few issues, Apries, don't we?" he said, and put his arm around me.

I squirmed uncomfortably. I resented his familiarity; his trying to demonstrate a sense of ownership in front of Shad. I could see jealousy clouding Shad's eyes and tried to extricate myself from Alan's embrace, but he would not let me go.

"How do you feel about possibly living in the UK?" Shad asked me.

"That's precisely one of the things we still need to resolve," Alan answered on my behalf, as if I should not have an opinion. I resented Alan responding. "She has some reservations, of course," he continued, ignoring me, "but I know she will be fine once she has settled down with me and we have a couple of kids."

"And that's why you are not marrying here in China?"

"Yes and no," Alan said. "I would marry Apries immediately, here or anywhere else, but she doesn't feel comfortable with marriage yet. She wants to live in the UK for a few months first and see how her daughter gets along before considering tying the knot. Alternatively, she is thinking of maybe coming over without bringing her daughter along immediately, and then having Rena follow at the end of the school year. Frankly, I think she worries too much, probably because her first marriage was such a bloody disaster."

I forced myself to be a good Chinese girl and not contradict my boyfriend in front of a stranger.

"Well," Shad opined, "I am not sure I blame her. I know that relocating internationally is extremely difficult. It puts tremendous pressure on personal relationships. To go from this Chinese culture and environment to an England, where everything is different, would be highly challenging."

"And don't forget my daughter," I finally pointed out.

"She will be fine," Alan insisted. "You will see how quickly she will make friends in school. And all you need, Apries, is to get a decent job. Once you have that—which shouldn't be difficult—you will love it there as well, I am sure." He had apparently forgotten he had originally offered me a job in his own company.

"Do you really think it would be that easy for Apries to find a job? Her English is fantastic, of course, but would she not need a visa and work permit?"

"Of course she would, but finding a job? Not a problem," Alan stated. "She has a university degree in . . . hmmm . . . what do you call it again, Apries? The study of bugs?"

I was furious. Livid. He was deliberately making fun of me and my degree in entomology. How could he be so insensitive?

He wouldn't let go; nudged me with his hook and said, "Why don't you say something, darling? You can be proud of what you have studied."

"You mean entomology?" Shad interjected, helping me out. Even to a foreigner such as Shad my loss of face must have been all too obvious.

"That's it," Alan said. "Entomology. An important science degree. She is smart. Her English is outstanding, even if not British English. She has almost ten years experience as a translator and works hard. Companies would be vying with each other to hire her."

"Assuming they have need for a Chinese/English translator," Shad observed drily.

I could see this conversation was not going anywhere. "I think we should go, Alan. Rena is waiting for us to pick her up. We promised to take her to a movie, remember? My daughter Rena loves movies," I added, turning to Shad.

Alan balked but relented. "Okay, then," he said.

I regretted Shad and I had to part like this. I wanted to spend more time with him. I yearned to continue talking to him; wanted reassurance from him that he felt as good as I did about what he had experienced. But I could not get away from Alan. He hooked my arm under his and after a brusque good-bye led me out of the hotel. I didn't dare look back.

I was mad at Alan for demeaning me in front of Shad. I was mad at myself because when I had returned to the hotel with Thomas and Shad, I had had absolutely no intention whatsoever of bedding Shad, but then I had. I didn't know what Thomas might have told him about *our* history. I was disappointed with myself for having given in to my overpowering desires. Why had I let it happen? I could not understand it. What had made me forget all my good intentions? It had to be this addiction of mine. I felt physically so good after having been with Shad, but my close call at almost having been caught shook me up.

Out of the corner of my eye I saw Alan studying me as we walked towards the car he had hired. I could tell he was fuming.

"Go ahead and say what you think," I said. My expression should have warned him, but he was too upset to exercise caution.

"All right, I will. You fucked him, didn't you?" he hissed.

I looked defiantly at him. This was not the right thing to have said if he understood me at all, and not the most elegant way of putting it either.

"Fuck you!" I spit at him. "None of your fucking business!" I wondered what my translation customers would think of me if they heard me talking like this, spewing profanities like some whore. It almost made me chuckle.

We got into the car, and as the driver pulled away, Alan said, "Look at your arms and the bruises you have there and then tell me you didn't fuck him, you horny little slut." A mean, vicious grin distorted his mouth.

Before I could stop myself I found myself studying my arms. I could see some discolorations where Shad had apparently grasped me too hard in the throes of passion. I didn't think these bruises were enough to prove my infidelity. Alan was just guessing, I thought; bluffing, trying to trap me.

"You call me a slut?" I shouted disbelievingly. "Thank you very much, Mr. Sykes. I guess that tells me what you really think of me." My voice was dripping with sarcasm. "That's certainly not what you thought the day we met and I let you fuck me. You have no right to call me names." I could feel tears coming to my eyes.

"Don't try to deny it," he admonished fiercely. "I can see the proof on your arms. I can smell it in your hair. Your eyes tell me. Your face reflects it, and your evasiveness confirms it."

"And you, Alan? Can you swear you have not fucked anyone else since you met me?"

"Of course I haven't," he said, but his answer was too glib.

"Bullshit! I know for a fact," I bluffed, "you were fucking your old girlfriend behind my back while I was helping my sister out in her restaurant."

"Who told you that?" he asked. I found it interesting he did not try to deny it. Instead he frowned with consternation.

"You think I am stupid? You think I couldn't smell you had just had sex when I came into your house? A woman can always tell."

"Oh really? Well, I have news for you. Maybe a man can smell it as well, like I smell it on you right this minute."

"No, you can't," I argued. "You just believe what you want to believe, and then you look for proof to support your theory. You don't trust me because I was too honest with you about my past. And since you are unable to resist any little slut willing to fuck you, you assume I am the same way. Every time you see me flirting harmlessly, you are convinced I will fuck the guy. That's bullshit, and I am sick and tired of your constant distrust. You are going to have to decide whether to believe in me or not, once and for all. There is no point in me staying faithful to you if you keep on thinking I am an easy lay. I can't deal with your doubts when I don't deserve them."

I hoped I sounded appropriately righteous. I was fed up with these arguments and accusations and thought attacking was my best defense.

"I wish I *could* trust you, Apries, but I know how horny you are, and how often and how desperately you need sex; that you can never seem to get enough."

"That doesn't mean I have to fuck. You know yourself I can take care of myself perfectly well. You have watched me often enough when I played with myself. I can get off easily enough. I don't need a man all the time."

"You make it sound simple," Alan said, "but I also know masturbating a few times makes you crave a good fuck even more. The moment you meet someone you like, who has two hands and more money than I do, you are ready to jump into his bed."

I was far from ready to acknowledge the truth of what he said. Not about the two hands and money, but how I had just taken Shad did prove Alan's point.

"Is that what you really think of me, Alan? Well then, fuck you!" I spat at him, so mad my head hurt. Shad had been an exception. It had merely been physical; no emotional involvement, I tried telling myself. I had given up so much for Alan. Had tried so hard to be good. Had looked after him. Had wiped his ass for him. Had spent my money on him when he was too cheap to spend his. And this was how he was thanking me? I couldn't believe it.

I came to the realization that my relationship with Alan was all but finished. He could not accept me the way I was. Kept wanting to change me. Ignored that I loved him. But I could not get over his mistrust. I was sure the differences between us had become insurmountable. Maybe if I hadn't spent the evening with Shad and felt so good about it, it might have taken me longer to recognize I had to break up with Alan, but it would have been inevitable regardless.

My decision was suddenly in clear focus but I was not ready to tell Alan just then. The utter contentment I had reached with Shad still coursed through my body. I was physically weak from our furious coupling; emotionally drained from the awkward meeting in the hotel lobby and now this argument with Alan. And I had Rena waiting for me at home, with my mother and sister and her husband no doubt standing around, scrutinizing Alan and me and how we behaved towards each other. They had never been crazy about him, perhaps sensing something in his character to which I had been oblivious. They had been vociferous in their prediction of an early and messy end to our relationship.

Rena was happy to see me, as always. I couldn't wait for her to be a few years older so I could have her fitted with the braces she would need, and maybe get her contact lenses instead of the rather ugly glasses on which she now had to rely. I was sure she would become a beautiful girl, but hopefully not too soon. I did not want her to grow up too quickly and risk exposing her to the kind of horrible childhood I had had. I had seen my brother-in-law looking at Rena when his wife was not there, and I did not like what I had seen in his eyes. I had been Rena's age when one of my father's brothers had raped me, and I was absolutely determined to protect my daughter from the same fate.

I pushed these painful memories to the back of my mind. There were too many bad ones. Taking Rena to the movies was a good remedy against encroaching depressions and I was ready to surrender to the distractions the wide screen offered. Alan was willing to go along. He had never liked my family much. Going to the movies was a welcome excuse to get away from them.

Rena was at an age where she wanted to see a film every day. She was driving me crazy with her incessant clamoring to go to the movies.

It was quality time for her and me, of which we never seemed to have enough. My working hours frequently prevented me from being home before bedtime. I had spent too many weekends away from home, thinking I had found the perfect lover. It had been more my mother than me with whom Rena had grown up. I knew I had not been a good mother. I loved her desperately and wanted her to be happy and was willing to do anything for her, but it never sufficed, I felt. And I knew for sure Rena would never be happy in England and with Alan as her stepfather.

I had not offered to get us our usual Emperor's seats when I bought our movie tickets. I was in no mood to sit in these plush easy chairs that offered privacy and virtually encouraged petting. I did not want Alan to think I would let him grope me with Rena sitting next to us. Not that it had not happened in the past.

I thought of Shad and dreamed he was sitting next to me, his fingers slipping under my skirt, fondling me. I felt myself getting wet and squeezed my legs together, hard.

My horniness escalated and I concentrated on what I imagined Shad was doing, but I was interrupted. Alan surprised me by leaning over and shoving his tongue down my throat, but in my mind's eye it was Shad. With Rena sitting next to me, the movie flickering across the screen, Alan fucking my throat with his tongue and Shad on my mind, I was torn between lust and common sense.

From the lust side, I was more than ready. From the practical side, I had to remind myself I was determined to break up with Alan and I certainly did not want Rena to be a party to what Alan was trying to do, regardless of how it turned me on.

It got me thinking. Having remained emotionally faithful to Alan had not been easy for me. Many temptations had come my way. In the past I had seldom been able to say no. Had not wanted to, and it had sometimes bothered me, especially the next morning. But my relationship with Alan had motivated me to give abstinence a try. I had not completely succeeded, but in my own mind my lack of emotional involvement and relative infrequency of the act itself had made me as faithful as I could hope for. Why I had thrown this achievement overboard by getting emotionally involved with Shad was impossible to explain. He had immediately recognized I was ready and acted accordingly. My reaction should have been predictable.

I had often asked myself why I was inevitably identified—even by complete strangers—as an easy lay. I knew it wasn't my beauty. My eyes are too far apart; the scar through my lip ugly; my lips too fat. It wasn't my body because I have small tits and don't have the nice round butt most westerners seem to prefer. My figure looks sort of boyish. So why was it a man—at the airport, a store, in a hotel, while working or in the subway—would look me in the eyes and know I was easy? Or was it the other way around, that I had the good luck or misfortune to run into men who had the talent of diagnosing my promiscuous character with one glance? Like Shad. We met, and he knew I could be his.

While with him, I had not thought about Alan. Then I had concluded I was finished with Alan. I was still determined but knew my flesh remained weak. The vociferous arguments with him had crystallized my decision to break up with him. Reminding myself of this gave me the strength to fight off his persistent advances. He finally gave up and pouted. I was proud of myself. I had been strong, but was still wet. I couldn't help it.

I would rather not have taken Alan home with me after the show, but I did not want a scene with him in front of my daughter.

Back at the house, noisy discussions raged, typical for after dinner hours.

No one else in my family could speak decent English, and Alan's Chinese was limited to a few simple words. As a result I had the impression he thought we were talking about him; he looked tense.

"Come on, let's go to your room," he said as soon as he saw an opening.

I did not feel like getting into an argument and went with him. The disapproving eyes of my family followed us.

There was no place in my small room to sit down other than on the bed I shared with Rena. The television on my credenza ran continuously for Rena's benefit, but with her still in the family room, I turned to switch it off. Alan stopped me before my hand reached the control knob.

"Leave it on," he said, "and lock the door."

"Are you kidding? Shit! You know we can't do anything now." I knew full well why he wanted me to lock the door and maintain the noise level of the TV. But I was not in the mood. I did not want him. Not here. Not now.

"Lock the door!" he repeated. It was a command instantly setting me on edge. "I don't want Rena to come in here and see me fucking you."

"We are not fucking tonight, Alan, or any other night. Forget about it. Don't you realize it's over? Rena can come in any time she wants to."

"Oh, come on, Apries," he pleaded. "Don't be like that. You know how much I need you and love you. You can't just let me hang out to dry like this!" And with that his hook guided my hand to his already erect cock.

I resisted, but it was hopeless. I couldn't keep myself in check. He had pushed his pants down and when I felt his familiar skin all my resolutions were forgotten. I started slowly stroking him. I didn't really want to, but my hand seemed to have a mind of its own. I felt myself getting wet. I had zero control over my body. I was getting horny despite my determination not to relent.

He kept encouraging me. He knew I could not resist. He began playing with my breasts. He had slipped his prosthesis off and was rubbing my nipples with his stumps while trying to suck on them through my thin bra. He knew how sensitive they were and how my body would react. I felt my resolve weakening. He knew exactly what to do to overcome my resistance. Not that I had ever resisted him before, but he played to my weakness and knew what turned me on. It wasn't fair. He was taking advantage of my nature.

He pushed me down on the bed and kissed me and squeezed my tits out of my bra. It felt good! I didn't want it to, but it did.

"No, Alan, I don't want to," I protested weakly, but even I could tell my voice lacked conviction.

He did not believe me. Or did not care. He left me no choice other than to take him in my mouth while he kept rubbing my exposed nipples. I tried to pretend I was not interested but in fact I was, as Alan knew very well.

By then it was almost too late. I could not have stopped if I had not heard the doorknob rattling. When I did, I still had the presence of mind to lift my head and quickly pull the sheet over Alan's lower body. I pulled my blouse together.

For a moment no one knew what to say. Rena, eight years old and completely innocent, stepped into the room and must have sensed she had interrupted something she shouldn't witness. Instead of contrite, however, she looked defiant. Alan was thoroughly pissed off, ready to strangle poor Rena. And I? I was acutely embarrassed and only hoped Rena had not been able to see anything she shouldn't have or suspected what we had been doing.

"Why don't you leave us alone for a while, Rena?" Alan said, his voice hoarse. "Your mother and I need to talk."

I did not translate. I didn't trust myself to speak. I wasn't sure my daughter had understood Alan's request. After a few seconds I asked Rena in Chinese what she wanted.

"I just want to be with you, Mom," she answered, also in Chinese, "because you are always gone. Besides, I don't like that man. He makes me afraid of him."

"Why? He hasn't done anything to you."

"But I have seen him looking at me . . . so strange . . . funny. It gives me creepy feelings."

"What's she saying?" Alan wanted to know.

"That she is happy we took her to the movies today," I lied without hesitation.

He grunted, frowning. "Is she going to leave us alone or what?"

I wanted her to stay. She could help protect me from my weakness. I did not say anything when she settled down at the foot of the bed to watch TV. Her reaction was answer enough to Alan's question, as was my silence.

Rena could not see Alan and me lying behind her on the bed. We were both staring vacantly at the TV. Alan's stumps kept rubbing my tits under the sheet I had pulled over us. Several buttons of my blouse had become undone. I tried to stop him. Not because it didn't feel good—which it did—but because I did not want my horniness stoked even further and was afraid Rena would turn around and see us.

I wanted to be alone with my thoughts and mentally relive the evening hours with Shad. I wanted to prove to myself I could resist Alan. I did not think I could handle two boyfriends and be intimate with both. I had already tried it a couple of times and it had not worked out well. I had no idea and could not picture what the future might bring me with Shad.

As late as our dinner, I had not even consciously considered going to bed with Shad. I had deluded myself into believing my flirtatious comments had been exactly that—a flirt. Going up to his room with him had been automatic. The time with him had turned out to be perfect and deeply satisfying. We had connected. It had made me realize Alan was not the man with whom I wanted to spend the rest of my life.

I was getting drowsy. Alan made no move to get up and leave. It was late and Rena had school the next day. I would have to work and was exhausted. I told Rena to get ready for bed, and when she was and climbed into the bed we shared, away from Alan's side, we cuddled.

The sleep I yearned for kept eluding me. I wanted to turn over on my side but found myself wedged in between Rena and Alan. I could tell Alan was not sleeping yet either. Somewhere in the house a TV was still blaring, its sound penetrating our thin walls. I shut my eyes and ears against the ambient light and noise and did not move and waited for sleep to come, but it did not.

I knew Alan. He had stripped down to his T-shirt and boxer shorts while Rena was in the bathroom. I knew he would not leave me alone, given the slightest opportunity. I didn't want to have to fight off further advances. I was in an emotional uproar and simply wished he would go away, to magically disappear from my life. I wanted peace and solitude; to think. A milestone had been set when I had gone to bed with Shad and had become emotionally involved while ostensibly engaged to Alan. I would need strength and willpower to implement my decision to finish with Alan, and I wasn't sure I had either. All too often in my life, starting as a young girl, I had gone the way of least resistance, and the consequences this had led to now characterized my behavior. It had made me the person I had become. I wasn't sure I liked myself.

My ruminations were interrupted by Alan forcing an arm between my legs. Opening them to allow easier access was automatic, a reflex. I remained on my back, not moving, trying to ignore the pleasant tingling I felt when his stump glided slowly over my clitoris. I felt trapped. Despite my nervousness about Rena lying next to me, asleep and nestled against my side and my determination not to have anything to do with Alan anymore, I felt my physical senses betraying me. I tried concentrating on something else entirely, to distract me from the familiar stimulation, but all I could think about was what Shad had done to me, and that only made me weaker.

Alan noticed this and it emboldened him. At first, when he tried to nudge me over on my side, I resisted and attempted to move further away from him, but I was caught helplessly between two bodies and the uncontrollable yearning of my body. I was still determined not to give in, but that was my mind speaking while my body listened to another language. It craved relief. He had succeeded in making me so horny I thought I would explode if I couldn't come. But I wanted to remain strong.

I told myself I was sending a message of refusal to him by turning away from him, over on my side, facing Rena. I tucked my legs up against my chest. I thought this might discourage him, but no. I felt his cock searching for the entry to my pussy and it was so wet he slipped in effortlessly, deeply, without my having to guide him. It felt so good, and yet I fought not to enjoy it. But I did, despite being deathly afraid Rena might wake up. Maybe it was so delicious because I imagined it was Shad who was in me.

I realized my body was beyond restraint. The darkness, the silence we had to maintain, and the fact we were not alone and could hardly move combined to make our coupling singularly erotic. It was tantalizingly illicit, something I had always found to be a particular turn on.

Alan must have felt the same way because he suddenly thrust hard and came, without warning, catching me by surprise. I had been on the verge, but he was too fast and now it was too late, and I hated his egotistical behavior. He started snoring almost at once, still glued to my back.

*　　*　　*

'What the hell have I done?' was my first thought the next morning, and my dismay stayed with me throughout the day. It was not a proud moment for me. I had had sex with Shad while being more or less engaged to Alan, and had enjoyed it tremendously. Then I had let Alan fuck me after I had decided it was over between us. And I had permitted it to happen with my daughter lying next to me. What sort of woman could do that, I asked myself? What kind of messed up personality did it take, I wondered, that made me behave like this and within the span of a few hours? Could I really blame my behavior on the disconnect between my common sense and physical weakness? Hardly. But I am how I am, and I don't know how to change.

I know I am a psychological disaster. Is my history of getting raped repeatedly responsible for how I live my life? Makes me the way I am? Or was I the victim of multiple rapes because of the way I am? Had my violators simply been unwilling to believe I had meant it when I said 'no', seeing something in me that had convinced them I actually wanted it, despite my entreaties? Could I hold my parents responsible because they had sent me at age ten to work as a gofer in a whorehouse to help support the family? Had this early exposure to the sex business, where I had witnessed depravity but the girls working there had befriended me, programmed me to become the way I am? Had it been my uncle, who had forced me to have oral sex with him when I was only thirteen and he had assumed I was experienced just because of where I worked?

Oddly enough I had subsequently developed a real passion for it when I started working in the bar a few years later and it became an unofficial—voluntary—part of my duties. Now I could not do without it. Had my environment formed me, or had my inherent nature pushed me into the environment? What had gotten me into the habit of masturbating, starting with a broom handle the first time, when I was only fourteen? And then found my first steady boyfriend at fifteen, whom I married three years later when I became pregnant?

I could not decide what had been cause and what had been effect in how my life had been shaped. Maybe it was time for me to consult a psychiatrist, someone who could help me change, but here in China? No way. Besides, if I was really honest with myself, did I actually want to change? After all, it was only my sex addiction that differentiated me from other women, and this I enjoyed so much I wasn't at all sure I wanted to be healed. What could take its place? How would I fill the void? What could possibly be better, more gratifying and satisfying than good, frequent sex? I could not think of anything.

I fought off my tears. I did not want to feel sorry for myself. That time had passed long ago. So many questions; so few answers. A number of boyfriends had tried to analyze me and how and why I behaved the way I did, but all had eventually given up in frustration. Some few had tried to accept me the way I am, but the majority had found my personality too complex and had abruptly given up. They couldn't handle my lack of faithfulness and my insatiable sexual appetite, and

I couldn't stop. Good riddance, I had thought. I was always hesitant in investing emotion in my lovers. As a result, I had no problem with fucking without loving. I loved the sex; not them.

Alan was noticeably, uncharacteristically kinder and gentler with me when we parted for the day, and between his declarations of affection and the high risk sex during the night, I suddenly found myself having second thoughts about what I wanted to do with him. Maybe quitting Alan was premature? We had known each other for almost two years, and had had great times. I knew how he was and what he wasn't. A known entity I could maybe still learn to deal with. His long absences gave me the freedom I needed, and what if he wasn't exclusively true to me any more than I was to him? How much difference would that actually make? I am not a jealous person, and as long as he kept coming back to me, what would be the harm?

Keeping him for the time being, stringing him along, was an option. Meanwhile I could explore a longer term sexual relationship with Shad. After all, I knew nothing about him other than that he was great in bed. And that—apart from our breakfast—I would not see him again for at least several months, assuming he would return to China at all. Was he a practical alternative to Alan? It seemed to me the two men were almost interchangeable, both gone for long stretches, sex with them wild and fantastic. There was no immediate need to finish with either one. They wouldn't have to find out what I was doing. I thought I could pull it off. It would be playing with fire, I knew, but wasn't this what my life had been all about anyway? I had rarely gotten burned, like the time my Mama-san had caught me upstairs, naked, on my knees, doing it doggie style with her husband. I had gotten the blame, understandably enough and it had cost me my job, but the Mama-san had been forgiving and we had remained friends to this day. Perhaps she had known her husband had not been totally innocent.

The risk I would incur by two timing my two lovers would be to lose both of them, and this seemed acceptable to me. It wasn't like I couldn't find someone else and since I basically wanted to finish with Alan anyway and hardly knew Shad yet, what would be the problem?

I felt a lot better after having rationalized my way through these thought processes. I had time. Alan was still in love with me and would stay with me even if he suspected I had another lover. Shad I needed to get to know better and see what might develop. I could compare the two without them knowing they were competing with each other, and I was sure I was good enough to carry it off. I looked forward to seeing Shad again while giving Alan what he wanted. I had the best of both worlds.

16

Beijing, 1986

Dawn arrived early this time of the year, waking up Shad. He thought briefly about going for a run, but one look out his window killed his good intentions. Dense smog marred his view. This, together with his all too vivid memory of getting lost and fearing it could happen again kept him in the hotel.

He was still exuberant from his time with Apries the previous evening, but in the cold sobriety of the morning, thoughts of Veronica intruded. He was ashamed he had succumbed to his first sexual temptation since meeting and falling in love with her. Could he justify his tryst with Apries as something Veronica had sanctioned, a purely physical thing with no emotional involvement? He was not at all sure. Apries was a puzzle. Her behavior had been totally beyond his previous experience with women.

He told himself to simply accept what had happened. It had been so good and completely unexpected. He remembered her promise to have breakfast with him the next morning and looked forward eagerly to seeing her again. And yet he could neither erase the picture of her fiancé waiting for *her,* nor ignore Veronica waiting for *him.* He did not want to dwell on how Apries might have spent the night. He refused to think about how she could have made wild, passionate love with him one minute, and then leave to spend the night with her fiancé. Where were her morals? No conscience?

He found it difficult to concentrate on his newspaper during breakfast. Rambling thoughts went in directions he could not control.

He became unreasonably jealous when he thought of Apries being with Alan. He suspected strongly she would not hesitate to give Alan what she had given him, and it drove him crazy. He knew he had no claims on her; it was her choice and her fiancé. And yet . . . was there a difference between how Apries cheated on Alan and he, Shad, had cheated on Veronica? Could two wrongs be construed to make one right?

He finally reminded himself he was in town to work and started thinking about his day's schedule. Ning Chang would be picking him up shortly and he went back to his room to organize his materials for the upcoming meeting. He still thought she would be problematical to work with and he agonized about what he should do. He wanted a long term partner with whom he felt comfortable and was unsure Kang Ming fit the bill.

Ning Chang was waiting impatiently for him when he exited the elevator. Her demeanor was as severe as it had been during their dinner. No small talk apart from a cursory good morning and how are you. She was already in full business mode.

"Larry Zhang, our office manager, will make a presentation on our company," she said as soon as they were in their taxi. "After that," she went on, "our marketing manager, Christina Yang, will present our plans for AmeriDerm. I think you will like what she will propose."

Shad nodded in agreement. His concern at the moment was his ability to focus on business issues.

The team from their dinner was assembled in the rather small Kang Ming conference room. He recognized their faces, if not their names. A small sign on an easel said "Welcome Mr. Shad Cooper" and stood next to the doorway into Ning Chang's offices. These were not impressive, neither in size nor décor. Utilitarian at best, with drab walls and even drabber furnishings. The windows could have been cleaner, but this would not have improved the sight of the stark brick wall only feet away. The floor was bare concrete. Fluorescent lights bathed the room in harsh white light. The whole environment stood in stark contrast to what he had seen at the two local companies he had visited. Ning Chang obviously did not believe in—or could not afford—spending money on surroundings. He wasn't sure what this indicated.

He was invited to sit at the end of the table, opposite the screen which had been put up. Tea was served.

"May I begin, Mr. Cooper?" Larry Zhang asked. He had his first acetate in hand, and when Shad acknowledged his readiness, Larry turned the projector on and began.

His presentation was mercifully short. The company had been in existence for almost ten years. Their primary principal was a US manufacturer of catheters and disposable surgical accessories. They were active only in Beijing and Shanghai but had plans to expand as the business continued to grow. No data were provided on in-market sales or profitability. They worked with a reliable import company. No separate warehouse facilities existed; their product inventory was on site in an unused office. Delivery to the customers was handled through the sales force, as was credit collection. Truly a shoestring operation, Shad thought. He tried to keep an open mind regarding their ability to launch a new product line.

Christina Yang came next. She was a pleasant looking young lady, somewhere in her twenties. She spoke much better English than he had been led to believe during their dinner. She was an MD; a gynecologist. When she mentioned this, Shad could hardly believe someone so young was already a MD, let alone having qualified as a specialist. But this was China, he reminded himself.

She had started out as sales representative and had recently been promoted. She was obviously bright and enthusiastic, but Shad wondered as much about her qualifications in marketing as in gynecology.

The gist of her presentation outlined their intention of hiring a new three member sales team for Beijing and two reps for Shanghai. The latter two would work out of their office there. AmeriDerm would have to provide the necessary training, which should be easy enough since they would only hire MD's. China appeared to have an abundance of these, all eager to get a job with a foreign company which would keep them out of the government hospitals and offered better pay and working conditions. Distribution would be handled in tandem with their other product lines since their customer base overlapped. If they needed more space to store product inventories, they could rent additional rooms in their office building.

They proposed to develop loose leaf sales aids in ring binder format so updates and additions could be inserted as new products were introduced. Based on the advance data Shad had provided their registration pharmacist thought first approvals could be obtained within three to six months, given Kang Ming's purported connections.

A longer discussion ensued when it came to pricing. The Kang Ming group was unanimous in their conviction that the proposed CIF prices Shad shared with them were too high for China. He asked them to provide him with a rationale for lower prices, and what these should be. This, they said, they could only do once they had received some samples and tested the market.

"How do you propose to do that?" Shad wanted to know. "Through your existing surgical team?"

"No," Ning Chang said, "we would only do this once we have hired and trained a dedicated sales force. We would begin this process as soon as we have an agreement."

"And what would you do with the team between the time we signed a contract and the first products are approved?"

"We would have them prepare lists of doctors needed to be seen and then establish personal relationships with them. You know, here in China, you can only sell successfully based on relationships. Without those you can not succeed."

"Isn't that rather risky?" Shad asked. "Salesmen in Asia don't always show the greatest loyalty to their company, I have found. Someone offers them a higher salary and they are gone. Wouldn't the safer approach be to sell our products on their merits—their features, advantages and benefits?"

"That plays a role as well, of course," Ning Chang agreed, "but before you can get to that point, you need to cultivate connections."

Shad decided he could not win this argument. He switched subjects. "When do you think you will be able to develop a preliminary sales forecast?"

"As soon as we have your samples, have done the necessary research, and have agreed on pricing."

"That creates a bit of a problem. Without having a price structure and a sales forecast we can not finalize a contract, and without a contract, you would not want to hire the necessary people. Both the CIF prices and minimum agreed upon sales targets are needed for an agreement."

Ning pondered this dilemma. Finally she came to a decision. "We are very interested in working with you. To that end, I would be willing to hire the three Beijing sales people based on my hope that we will come to an equitable agreement. Worst case, I would switch these three people to our existing product lines, or would let them go, depending on how they would work out."

"Fair enough. I can live with that."

Ning Chang and Shad retired from the conference room to her office to go through the draft agreement he had brought along and they were able to resolve most issues.

"Looking at the size of your business, Ning, I am a little concerned about your capitalization. Entering a new business segment is going to cost you money: in personnel, inventory carrying costs, purchase of goods and receivables. How do you propose to cover these expenditures?"

"Not to worry. I am aware of what it will take, and I can assure you, I am financially well prepared to handle this."

"Could you open an irrevocable letter of credit, drawn on a western bank, for an initial six months supply of our products?"

"Yes, but I would not want to do that. Here in China, you see, when you open such a letter, you have to deposit the full amount with the bank, so for me it would be the same as paying you up front, and that I would not be willing to do. *You* have to assume some risks; not just Kang Ming. I would need at least 150 days payment terms on open account, because our customers here are very slow in paying."

Shad swallowed hard. This would be a tough sell back home. Maybe he could negotiate her down to 90 or 120 days, if he started out with an offer of 60 days. "Let me get back to you on that," he said.

A look at his watch showed him it was getting close to lunch time and their appointment at the Military Hospital #402. "What time should we leave, Ning?"

"I suppose we better go. It will take us at least thirty minutes to get there and we have probably done as much as we can here for now."

*   *   *

The sight greeting them in front of the hospital was an eye opener. Dozens of people were milling around; whether they were patients trying to get in or relatives waiting, Shad could not tell. He studied the crowd. Uniforms could be seen but the majority wore civilian clothing reflecting obvious poverty.

A young man was struggling towards the entrance, carrying his grandfather on his back, like one might carry a young child. The old man, who couldn't have weighed more than a hundred pounds, was wearing striped pajamas and a pair of badly worn out flip flops on dirt encrusted, calloused feet. Shad couldn't tell what was wrong with the old man.

A freight pedicab, with a scarred wooden platform over its rear axle, was fighting its way through the gathering. On it, the driver was transporting another old man, lying flat on his back. A Chinese ambulance, it occurred to Shad.

He felt sorry for these patients. The sight was depressing, and he found it hard to believe he was in China's capital city with modern office towers rising towards the sky only a short distance away. If this was the situation here in Beijing, what would it be like in the smaller cities? And in hospitals like this he hoped to sell AmeriDerm's products? How could any of these patients afford them? Surely they had more serious health problems to deal with than skin ailments.

He resisted the impulse to turn around and walk away. He was ready to fly back home, but Ning Chang was unperturbed. She steered them through the crowd, resolutely ignoring what Shad found so depressing, and led the way into the hospital.

The lobby was Dante's inferno. Rickety plastic chairs were arrayed in long rows for the waiting patients. Not a seat was empty. Dozens of people were standing around, sitting on the floor or listlessly searching for a place to sit. Hopelessness and despair characterized people's faces, especially the older ones. Babies and young children were sitting on laps, squalling. The seated adults seemed reconciled to a long wait and had brought food along, wrapped in old newspapers or in plastic containers, and were chewing methodically. Long lines were in front of the registration windows, with people shouting and gesturing wildly to get attention. It was beyond Shad's comprehension how the organization worked and how any of the people waiting would ever get to see a doctor, let alone establish the right sequence in which they were to be called up, or whether there was some kind of triage in place to set priorities.

Ning Chang paid no attention to the mass of people and pushed through the lobby, up a stairway and down a long corridor. Stretchers and primitive hospital beds with grubby sheets were lined up along both sides of the hallway. Shad avoided looking at the pitiful patients lying there, seemingly forgotten or waiting for space in a ward.

"I am surprised at the number of women and children down in the waiting area," he said to Ning. "I thought this was a military hospital."

"It is, but it is not just for the veterans themselves. Family members are treated here as well. And you have to remember this hospital handles everything. Dermatology is just one small segment of their patient base. Military personnel on active duty are seen in hospitals located on their respective bases."

"Is your husband by chance involved in the healthcare aspect of the People's Army?" Shad asked, remembering he wanted to have more information on him and his role.

"No," she said, and offered no explanations.

Before Shad had a chance to probe further, she knocked on a door and upon a shouted response opened it and preceded him into a large room, apparently used as a lounge for the hospital staff's breaks. A long table dominated the center, with hard chairs along both sides. People were eating or drinking tea and having lively discussions.

Shad and Ning were greeted by a man standing by a door leading into a small office.

Ning and the doctor exchanged a few phrases in Chinese before she introduced Shad to Dr. Wu in English. His business card identified him as the director of the dermatology department. His age was difficult to guess. His boyish face could have placed him in his late thirties, but his position led Shad to believe he might well be ten years older. He had a wild shock of thick black hair which looked like it had not been combed for a while. His demeanor was friendly and open.

"Welcome to Beijing, Mr. Cooper," he said. "I am happy to see you. I think very highly of your company and have had some exposure to your products through my visits to the USA and international congresses."

"Thank you very much for meeting with us, Dr. Wu. It's very kind of you to spend some time with us. Were you in San Diego last year by chance for the world congress?"

"Why yes, I was. You were there as well?"

"I was. I had just started working for AmeriDerm. I am sorry we did not meet," Shad said.

"That is not so surprising when you consider the number of attendees." He paused a moment before continuing, "Perhaps you would be interested in taking a quick tour through the dermatology department before we sit down and talk?"

"If it's not too much trouble, I would certainly appreciate it."

He and Ning Chang followed Dr. Wu as he led the way out of the room, down the hallway, and up another flight of stairs.

"We have only 25 beds for in-patients," he explained, "because our melanoma patients are usually treated in the cancer ward. Our big business here takes place on an out-patient basis, where we normally see several hundred cases a day."

Shad was appalled at the condition of the patient rooms he was shown. With six beds each, three per side, not only could he see the patients in simple metal beds—more like cots—but also numerous visitors per patient. These were in the process of preparing and distributing the food they had brought along. Shad wondered whether the hospital provided no meal service, or the food was so bad patients refused to eat it.

The floor was unkempt. Food wrappers, old newspapers, remnants of bandaging material, bloody Q-tips and cotton balls and other detritus was lying around. He had a hard time meeting the eyes of the patients staring at him, openly curious about this foreigner in their midst.

It was not a pretty sight, and he was glad when they left the ward. He mentally thanked his company for having taken out a Medivac insurance policy for him.

Back in Dr. Wu's office, they talked about AmeriDerm and the hospital's requirements for new products. Dr. Wu thought opportunities existed and expressed support for Shad's plans to enter the market. He and his six dermatologists would be eager to begin using some of the products. He suggested they visit the cancer ward to talk to the oncologists treating melanoma and set up an appointment for them with a Dr. Hong for later that afternoon.

With the promise to send Dr. Wu some samples, Ning Chang and Shad said their good byes and left.

He found he had nothing to say as Ning flagged down a taxi and they sped away. He could not shake his discouragement. The lack of hygiene, the environment, the poverty of the patients, their treatment and accommodations were thoroughly depressing. How could AmeriDerm sell sophisticated and expensive products under these circumstances?

"Where are we going?" he finally asked, not sure he cared.

"We are running behind schedule. I hadn't counted on Dr. Wu showing you his department, and now, with the additional appointment in the cancer ward still ahead of us, we have to hurry to see Dr. Hu in the Peking Union Medical College."

"This means no lunch, I take it?"

"We don't have time," she said curtly. It was obvious the thought of lunch had never occurred to her. Shad was not particularly upset; what he had witnessed had dampened his appetite.

Dr. Hu was an elderly, dignified dermatologist nearing what Shad assumed had to be retirement age. His hair was white; meticulously combed, and his kindly face rich in deep wrinkles. Blue veins were prominent on his hands. Age spots dotted his skin. His English was impeccable.

"I spent three years at John Hopkins," he explained when Shad complimented him on his language skills. "Of course that was a long time ago, but I have managed to keep up with the language. It seems that without English, you can not remain current on medical advances these days."

Shad talked about AmeriDerm's products and his intention to launch them in China. Dr. Hu's feedback was positive and encouraging. He would be happy to provide Kang Ming's sales staff access to his team of physicians. He cautioned them not to be greedy on pricing, since such a strategy would certainly be counter-productive.

Dr. Hu saw them to the exit when they had concluded their discussion and expressed the hope he would see Shad again in the near future. Shad, after having seen the military hospital, was impressed with how clean, orderly and well maintained the Medical College appeared, even though here too many patients were waiting in the spacious lobby to be seen by a doctor.

By the time they arrived back at the 402 and had found Dr. Hong, Shad's stomach was growling. He was thankful for the tea and cookies a nurse brought as they talked about melanoma and *Melavict* with Dr. Hong. He was positive and encouraging. Melanoma was a major problem for them, and a new treatment regimen was highly desirable. Again the issue of pricing came up.

"It is obviously important for us—indeed it is our mandate—to save lives, or to prolong them," Dr. Hong said, "but at the same time, the cost/benefit aspect needs to be considered. Harsh as it sounds, most melanoma patients are old and extending their life by a few months—in which they would be miserable and in quite a bit of pain anyway—can only be justified if costs are reasonable."

"You mean it would be more cost effective for the government to simply let those patients die?"

"Yes, of course, but it's not that simple, I can assure you. We owe these patients for what they have done for their country, and we will do everything within our power to help them. To alleviate their suffering and to prolong their lives with some quality. Unfortunately, costs do come into it, so if you want to have broad use made of *Melavict*, and assuming it is as effective as you outline, I would strongly encourage you to price it at a level where it becomes a viable treatment option."

Shad wondered how they calculated how much an additional month of fair quality of life cost. He asked Dr. Hong if he could tell him what he paid for products currently being used, but this he declined adamantly. It occurred to Shad Dr. Hong was afraid of inadvertently revealing how he benefitted personally from his pricing arrangements with other suppliers.

There was nothing more to be accomplished that afternoon and they thanked Dr. Hong for his time and insights and promised to keep his recommendations in mind.

Although the crowd in the foyer of the hospital had thinned out considerably, Ning Chang and he still had to push and shove their way through the people to get out of the building. The long Beijing twilight had already started to settle over the city, and by the time their taxi reached the Sheraton, it was nearly dark.

"Do you have a few more minutes, Shad?" Ning asked as he started to get out of the cab.

He was tired and hungry. He had seen and heard so much during the day that all he wanted was a drink, an early dinner, some time to mull over what the day had shown, and then to go to bed. He was afraid once Ning Chang started talking, she would not stop. Nevertheless, after a moment's hesitation, he invited her to come into the hotel with him.

He took her to the lobby lounge.

"Do you think it might be possible for you to find out what Dr. Hong currently pays for melanoma treatment products, Ning?" Shad asked. "He might not want to tell me, but perhaps you could find a way? The information would be invaluable for us."

"I can try, but it will be difficult. You really need those personal relationships I mentioned before a Dr. Hong would feel comfortable enough to share such sensitive data. There is so much under the table money involved. Strictly illegal and dangerous. Only when we try to sell him our products will he make specific demands, and then we can calculate our actual net realization, rather than the official price to the hospital," she explained. "You have to remember the government periodically cracks down on bribes and sets examples. If Dr. Hong were to get caught, it would certainly mean jail for him, and perhaps even the death penalty. Everyone knows corruption is endemic, but it can still be extremely dangerous."

"I understand. But please try to find out anyway, would you?"

She promised she would, before changing subjects. "You are leaving tomorrow, right?"

"Yes, in the early afternoon."

"Can I take you to the airport?"

"Thank you, that's very kind, but I have already made arrangements for a hotel car."

"So what do you think?"

"I don't really know yet," he admitted frankly. "I saw and heard a lot today and need some time to think it through. What specifically are you curious about?"

"Your thoughts on appointing Kang Ming as your distributor."

He reflected a moment on what to tell her. "A lot of what I saw today was very positive. I liked the presentations your people made, and I am impressed with the commitment you are willing to make. My main concerns at this moment are your capitalization, and the size of your organization and lack of experience in dermatology."

She nodded. "We would need some time not only for you and I to get better acquainted, but for Kang Ming to beef up the company and become familiar with dermatology. But I can assure you I would do this, starting the day we have an agreement."

"Tell me, what happens at Kang Ming when you are out of the country? I couldn't see a general manager who looks after the business, and you said you spend about half your time in San Francisco."

"I have to admit it's problematical. We have done quite well with the staff I have. They know what they are doing and I talk to them on the phone every day. What I am thinking is that if we get your distribution rights, I would either have to spend a lot more time here myself, or hire a general manager," she admitted.

"And either option would be possible?"

"Yes, although I would need some time to reorganize things if I were to cut down on my time in San Francisco."

"Fair enough," Shad said. "So why don't we summarize where we stand today and then go from there?"

They did, with little disagreement, and to his relief, Ning Chang stood up and bid him good-bye. He breathed a sigh of relief as he sat down again and had a drink before going to his room.

*   *   *

He was restless. The day had drained him; worn him out. He paced back and forth, facing an empty evening. His room felt too small. He was hungry but did not feel like going to dinner. He should be writing his trip report while the day's events and discussions were still fresh in his mind, but he was unable to concentrate on working. Now that he was alone, thoughts of Apries and Veronica bounced around his mind, distracting him.

He stood at the window, staring out into the night, lost in thought. Eventually he forced himself to walk to the executive lounge to draft his report. It occurred to him he could drink and snack there in lieu of going out to eat.

The lounge was mercifully empty. He found a small table by a window where he spread out his notes. He got a glass of wine and a plate with snacks. He wasn't really hungry anymore and the little tidbits were enough. His work beckoned, but so did his anticipation of Apries' visit and the breakfast they would have the next morning. Apries won. Not thinking about Veronica took an effort.

Apries dominated his thoughts. She shouldn't have after only one evening. Yes, the sex with her had been incredible; so outrageously good and unexpected he could hardly believe it. Comparisons with Veronica encroached on his thinking. She was great and always willing to try something new or different. But what Veronica didn't have—now that he was involuntarily comparing—and Apries did, was unbridled, raw sexual aggressiveness. A wild abandon; not hesitating to loudly, unmistakably demand what she craved. She was completely uninhibited, self confident in her sexuality. Her passion was contagious and irresistible. It occurred to him that if Nellie had had as little as ten percent of Apries' sexual appetite, he might still be married to *her.*

He had not set out to seduce Apries, he consoled himself when he thought of Veronica. He had not known Apries was engaged. He had not fallen in love with her. He was flabbergasted she had come to his room when she knew her fiancé would be waiting for her downstairs. He felt bad about Alan's severe handicap and had no intention of taking her away from him, but this did not prevent pangs of jealousy from consuming him when he pictured her having sex with him. Would she make comparisons as well? How could she make love to two different men within a couple of hours? It was unreal. He should stop thinking about her, but couldn't.

He knew it would not be prudent to meet her for breakfast. Sex with her one evening was one thing; could conceivably fall under what Veronica permitted. But a second time? Hard to rationalize, and yet he sensed it was inevitable. And how would he feel when she came after just having spent the night with Alan? Could he ignore it?

He concluded he should stop analyzing what should be seen simply as a unique, singularly exhilarating sexual experience. He would take from her what she was willing to give. Why should he reject her all consuming sex drive? If she wanted him, why not let him satisfy her urges? He was not at all convinced she was truly committed to Alan. He did not believe Apries could imperil his engagement to Veronica. He would let events unfold and see where they took him.

*   *   *

His sleep had been one of exhaustion, deep and unencumbered. His apprehension only returned after he had showered and gone down to the lobby to look for her, not quite knowing what to expect. Still not even sure, in fact, whether she would actually show up.

He paced nervously up and down the lobby until he saw her strolling into the hotel, her eyes searching for him. They lit up when she saw him. Her face broke into a broad smile. They shook hands formally. She looked ravishing, wearing a tight, dark gray skirt that ended well above her knees and a red blouse, unbuttoned enough to reveal a black bra. No stockings, he noted. She was not wearing those high heeled pumps saying 'fuck me', but she might as well have. Her hair was tied in a ponytail that looked good on her. Just a touch of make-up graced her face. No lipstick. Her eyes looked clear, soft, with no trace of weariness or guilt.

"Good morning, Apries," he said. "You look beautiful!"

"Really?" she asked. She wasn't being coy, he thought.

"Absolutely! How have you been?" And without waiting for an answer, added, "Where would you like to have breakfast? The lounge upstairs or the restaurant?"

"I already had some congee. Why don't we go to your room and you can order something from room service?"

"Sounds like a plan," he acknowledged, not too surprised at her forthrightness. He steered her towards the elevators.

No sooner had the door closed behind them then she snuggled up to him, all formality gone. "I missed you," she whispered, and kissed him deeply.

He felt himself responding and wrapped his arms around her. "I am glad you came," he said.

"I haven't come yet," she said and laughed, "but if you keep kissing me like that, I may."

He turned to bolt the door after hanging the *Do Not Disturb* sign outside. He searched for the room service menu. "Are you sure you don't want anything, Apries?" he asked.

"I want something, but it's not on the menu. I need you. I can't wait," she told him, without a hint of embarrassment or hesitation. He wasn't sure whether she needed him or only what he could do for her.

He watched, open mouthed, as she sidled up to his bed, pulled her skirt up around her hips and kneed, legs slightly apart, on the edge of the bed, inviting him with her beckoning butt. She pulled her red thong aside to give him an enticing view of what she had waiting impatiently for him. It was another fantasy come true: A woman asking, no, demanding to be taken doggy-style with her clothes pulled up just far enough to allow easy access; still wearing her shoes; no foreplay; totally uninhibited; visibly wet already and unable to delay. He wished he had a camera to forever preserve this unbelievable image.

She was better than he could possibly have anticipated. He lost track of time and his surroundings, only vaguely registered her ecstatic shouting.

A loud knocking on their door interrupted their post-coital bliss. He wanted to ignore it, but it became more insistent. He became mad at his *Do Not Disturb* sign being ignored. He reluctantly untangled himself from Apries and slipped into a bathrobe. She quickly scooted into the bathroom and pulled the door shut.

Two uniformed men greeted him when he opened the door. He felt intimidated; more worried than scared.

"Yes?" he said.

"Sorry to bother you, Mr. Cooper. Hotel security. We have a complaint about a disturbance. Neighbors think someone is being hurt. Maybe getting beat up. Loud screams were heard. May we please come in and reassure us everything is all right."

It was not a question. Shad felt himself blushing. He had only a dim recollection of Apries having screamed. His embarrassment was acute, as was his apprehension, knowing Apries should not be in his room.

He admitted them; saw them scrutinizing the interior.

"Perhaps you have a visitor?" the more senior guard asked politely.

Shad thought briefly about denial but had no hope of getting away with it. And why should he? He did not think he had committed a crime.

He nodded and stepped to the bathroom door. "Apries? Could you come out a minute?"

She did a moment later and he hardly recognized her with all the cold cream smeared on her face and the collar of her bathrobe turned up high, hiding her long black hair. At first glance, it was hard to tell whether she was Asian or Caucasian. He saw the puzzled frowns on the guards' faces.

"What's the matter?" she said in English when she saw the security guards staring at her.

"These gentlemen wanted to make sure everything is as it should be. Someone complained about screams coming from our room," Shad explained.

"I warned you not to shout at me," she reminded him calmly. Then she turned to the guards and went on: "It was nothing. My fiancé and I got into an argument and it got out of hand. We became a little noisy. I am sorry. Everything is all right. We will be more considerate in the future."

She turned around and walked back to the bathroom. The guards were left standing undecidedly, staring after her retreating back. Still frowning, not knowing what else to do, they left. Shad was shaking. The uniformed confrontation was not something he had needed.

When Apries came back into the room, her cold cream and robe gone, they suddenly couldn't stop laughing. What a close call.

"That was a great acting job, Apries."

"It was all I could think of. If I had been recognized, I would have lost my translation assignments, at a minimum, and maybe gone to jail. It is strictly forbidden for Chinese women to visit guests in their rooms. I would have been apprehended as a prostitute."

"I guess we have to be a little more careful."

She only nodded. "Would you like some breakfast now?" she finally asked when they had recovered from their shock.

"You were the best breakfast I could have had," he assured her, smiling happily, foolishly. "But I didn't need the interruption. That was scary!"

"Same for me. Idiots! But I was thinking you must be hungry for some food by now. Why don't you go ahead and place an order?"

He was indeed hungry, he realized. He watched her straightening her skirt and blouse while he was on the phone with room service.

"How long will you have to wait for your breakfast?" she asked.

"About thirty minutes, they said."

"So what do you suggest we do until then?" she asked, smiling wickedly and giving him to understand what she wanted.

He smiled at her. "Give me a break, Apries. I need a few minutes to recover from the shock of those uniforms."

She pouted. "Poor me," she teased. "Maybe I have to play with myself if you neglect me."

"Go ahead. I would love to watch you," he encouraged her.

But she did not respond. Instead, she walked over to one of the easy chairs by the window and sat down. "What did you think of Alan?" she asked unexpectedly.

"What is there to think? Are you really engaged to him?"

"I suppose. As you heard, he certainly believes so. He has been after me to marry him for some time and is convinced I will do it. But I don't recall ever having agreed. I think he is just taking marrying me for granted, which pisses me off. On the other hand he needs me, as you can imagine, and he is not bad in bed."

That wasn't really something Shad wanted to hear. A cloud passed over his face. "How long have you known him?"

"Nearly two years. I met him when I was visiting my sister in Manchester and was helping her out by waiting on tables. He came for dinner in her restaurant and we got to talking and then one thing led to another and he fell in love with me. I don't see all that much of him. I have only been back to England once since I met him and he merely comes here every three months or so. He is pushing me to move to the UK with him."

"And what's stopping you?"

"A lot of things. My family needs me here. My daughter does not want to move to the UK. I am not sure *I* could be happy there. I love China and Beijing and my work. I am not sure how much I really love Alan."

"What do you mean, how much? I would think you either love him or you don't."

She shrugged dismissively. "Maybe. I guess I should have said I don't know whether or not I love him."

"Probably not, I would think, or you wouldn't be here with me."

"Don't assume that. I can't stand it when people make assumptions about me. I like you and what we do, but I don't love you. I enjoy fucking you. You make me feel good and know how to make me come like mad and fulfill my needs."

"Did Alan guess what we did the other night when he picked you up?"

"He didn't guess. He told me he knew, and he was thoroughly pissed. I denied it at first, of course, but when he continued to persist with his accusations I became so mad I told him that yes, we had fucked like crazy and you were much better than he. After that, he didn't know what to believe any more. He sulked for a long time and we argued."

"I am sorry. I shouldn't have compromised you like that."

"You did nothing wrong. You couldn't have known about Alan."

"True," he said, "just like you don't know anything about Veronica."

"Your girlfriend?"

"Yes. I didn't tell you we are basically engaged. We have talked about getting married next spring."

"So what?" she queried. "I don't care. I like fucking you and you don't have to tell her about me. And if she by chance should find out about us, you can tell her I am just some prostitute, which you probably think anyway. In fact, I like acting like one when you fuck me. I like when you talk dirty to me and call me bad names. It turns me on."

"Same here, but I certainly don't think that of you at all. I think you are incredible; a world champion lover."

"Would she mind if you fucked some whore?"

He could not get used to her bluntness; her profanities.

"No. In fact she allowed me to do it. She understands how necessary it can become. She just does not want me to tell her about it."

"Too bad," Apries sighed. "If I were her, I would love for you to tell me all about it. What you did and how it was. You could describe details while I put my finger in my pussy. It would make me very horny to listen to you telling me how you fucked. Why don't you tell me what you do with her?"

Her voice had gotten lower and huskier as she played this fantasy out for him. Her eyelids were drooping and she had her hand under her skirt; no doubt she was wet again.

"I couldn't do that," he admitted. "It wouldn't feel right."

"Then at least tell me about her."

He did. Talked about how they had met and what she looked like and what kind of a person she was. He did not mention her sexual proclivities.

A renewed, discreet knocking on the door made Apries jump up and dash into the bathroom. A waiter came into the room and set up Shad's breakfast tray. She only came back out when she had heard the waiter closing the door behind him.

"Are you sure you don't want to have some of this stuff?" he asked, pointing at his breakfast.

"I guess I wouldn't mind a cup of coffee."

"I wish I didn't have to leave this afternoon," he said after a while. "I really like being with you."

"Same here. It's a good thing we have enough time for another quick fuck," she pointed out unabashedly, "but as far as you staying longer is concerned, it would be a little awkward for me right now anyway with Alan here and making me account for every minute of my time."

"How long will he be staying?"

"He doesn't know. Maybe a month. It depends on his business in the UK."

"I have an idea," Shad said on the spur of the moment, without having thought it through or what it would mean. "I am tentatively planning on coming back in three or four months, as I mentioned, and hope to see you then. If you are interested I would love to take you to Hong Kong with me, which is where I would have to go from here. I could take the weekend off and show you around. Maybe take a ferry to Macau or whatever."

"I'd love to!" she said, immediately enthusiastic.

"Then it's a deal. As soon as I have specific dates, I will let you know. Meanwhile, maybe you should apply for a Hong Kong visa."

"I don't need to. I have been there before. My visa is still valid." Then she suddenly became thoughtful before asking, "Will we have to see Thomas while there?"

"We? No. I will have to spend maybe a day or so with him on various business issues, but you can go shopping or sightseeing. Why do you ask?"

"I don't know," she said. "I guess I don't feel totally comfortable with him when I am not translating for him." She sounded evasive, Shad thought.

"That surprises me. He is such an easy going guy. But anyway, don't worry. You don't have to see him if you don't want to." He glanced at his watch. "How much time do you have left?" he asked.

"I already told you: enough," she replied and grinned wickedly.

She was right. It was almost 11:00 o'clock when he finally took her back downstairs and very reluctantly said good-bye. She had worn him out. He couldn't wait to see her again.

17

La Jolla, 1986

Veronica surprised Shad by taking the day off to greet him at the San Diego airport. The two week trip to China and Hong Kong had been a long time to be apart and she had sorely missed him.

His thoughts were still on Apries during his return flight and the incredible time they had spent together. He worried about seeing Veronica again. Would she detect a change in him?

His arrival at Lindbergh Field was earlier than his departure from Hong Kong, based on local times, and while he had slept for long stretches of the flight, it felt strange to see it was only 11:00am in San Diego of the same day on which he had left Hong Kong at 10:00pm. He felt rather discombobulated, a little out-of-body, as though he were standing next to himself as he disembarked. He tried to re-establish his equilibrium on the short walk to the arrival hall from the turbo prop that had brought him from Los Angeles to San Diego.

He was not looking for Veronica as he approached the building. Did not know she was waiting for him; had assumed she was working. He could not have seen her in any case. The bright sun reflected blindingly off the tall, heavily tinted windows, prevented seeing anything inside.

"Shad!" he heard as he walked through the door, and then she was in his arms, kissing him hungrily. He wrapped his arms around her tightly and felt her breasts thrusting against his chest and he was so happy to be with her and hold her again.

Ever since leaving Beijing he had wondered how he would feel when he saw Veronica. Having been with Apries would be hard to block out.

Now he knew. Guilty. Awkward. A little afraid. While with Apries, he had conveniently ignored how much he loved Veronica and how beautiful she was and what she meant to him. Now he asked himself why he had not been able to resist Apries when Veronica was his, and he resolved he would not see Apries again.

They stayed embraced, their happiness at being together again striking them momentarily mute.

"I better get my suitcase," he finally said and gently disengaged himself. They held hands as they walked to the baggage carousel and he pulled his bag off the belt.

"So how have you been, Veronica?" he asked after he had stowed his suitcase in her car and she was driving off the parking lot. "Did you miss me as much as I missed you?"

"Even more. I was very lonely. I didn't think I would miss you as much as I did. Other than that, I've been fine. How was your trip? Did you have a good flight?"

"Yes to both of your questions. A smooth flight and I think my meetings went well. I got a lot of things done and feel more optimistic about China, and the business in Hong Kong is really going well. Thomas has been doing an outstanding job on our behalf."

"You have to tell me about Beijing."

"I will. Just give me a chance to figure out where I am first. I can't tell you how strange it feels reconciling the sheer endless flight with the time difference. Trying to tell you about my taxi ride to the airport, for example, late *this* evening. But it doesn't make sense, does it, to talk about Hong Kong more than twenty hours ago this evening when it's still morning of the same day here. Do you see how confusing it gets when I left this evening and arrived this morning? How do you deal with this grammatically?"

"I can't begin to imagine. Why don't you forget about the past twenty four hours and tell me about China instead?"

"You are right, and I will, as I said." He certainly did not want to say much about Beijing at that moment. He knew he lacked concentration and might inadvertently mention something about Apries. He worried Veronica would not be as understanding as she had professed before his trip. Sitting here now, next to her, he felt the memories of Apries mercifully receding.

He reached over and squeezed Veronica's bare thigh where her skirt had ridden up. He wanted her and couldn't wait to get her home.

She glanced over to him quickly. "You better stop that," she smilingly admonished him. "I'm trying to drive, you know."

He stopped squeezing but left his hand where it was. Her thigh felt good. He let her talk and listened as she told him about the past two weeks and shared with him some ideas she had for the house.

"I am so glad you bought that house, Shad. I just love it, even if I feel a little lost at times. It's so big. It can get spooky, especially at night when I am alone. I woke up a bunch of times from some strange noises and became so scared I had to wait for my heart to beat normally again before I could get back to sleep."

"Probably just the wood working," Shad speculated. "I am sure you will get used to it."

"Maybe. But not to you being gone."

"You didn't invite Caitlin over to keep you company?" He smiled with raised eyebrows, encouraging her to continue talking.

"No. I thought about it but wanted to wait until you got back."

Her tone made Shad suspect there was more to the story. "Have you spoken with her?"

"Oh, sure, almost every day. I needed someone with whom I could share my loneliness, and she is a very good listener."

"And?" he prompted.

"And she is eager to repeat what we did together. She had a lot of fun and thought you were admirable—the best sex she has had in years, she claims."

"Do you feel the same way?" he asked. They hadn't talked much about their feelings concerning their threesomes. Perhaps they had both been too embarrassed to dwell on them. Just recalling the memory now, however, made Shad hard. He had immediately liked Caitlin, with her waif like body and big eyes and breasts sized out of proportion to the rest of her. He wasn't sure he could continue to keep from having sex with her if Veronica encouraged him again.

"I sure do!" she responded vehemently. "To have the two of you at the same time was a huge turn on for me. I had a hard time deciding what I liked best: watching or doing or being done to. Combining the three was just unbelievable."

Shad was a little discomfited at discussing this so factually, but Veronica seemed at ease. "It's out of the world exciting for me too," he confessed dreamily. "I was nervous at first. Didn't know what was expected of me or the role I should assume. Wasn't at all sure I would be up to the demands you two might make of me. I used to fantasize occasionally about doing it with two women at the same time, but then being faced with the reality was something else entirely."

"You seemed to take to it naturally," she observed drily.

"Did I? Well, if I did, then it was only because you made it easy for me by showing me what you wanted me to do and letting me improvise," he admitted. "It also didn't hurt that Caitlin is so easy going and good looking and willing to do anything."

"You think you know that already? There are a lot of things we haven't tried and could do, assuming you would be able to perform."

"Ha, ha!" he managed to croak. Veronica's musings sounded highly promising. "Did you see her at all while I was gone?" he asked, following a hunch. After all, she had only stated Caitlin had not visited her.

Veronica hesitated noticeably before answering. "I told you I wanted to wait for your return before inviting her over, but last weekend I suddenly couldn't stand being alone anymore. I more than missed you and was horny beyond description. When she called me Saturday and we had talked for a while, she invited me to come over. I went, and then we wound up spending the night together."

He was pleased she was so open about it, and it assuaged his own guilty conscience considerably. "And how was it?" he wanted to know.

"Not as good as when the three of us were together." She was grinning wickedly. "I think you spoiled both Caitlin and me by joining us. Anyway, it was still very good and took care of my immediate problem. Until this moment, at least," she added and took her eyes off the road to glance at him. The message she sent was unmistakable.

It made him ask, "Can't you drive any faster?"

"No. Don't forget anticipation can be a greatest source of pleasure," she consoled him.

"But it's not an adequate substitute for me."

When they were home and their most urgent needs had been quickly and satisfactorily taken care of, they stayed in bed and napped. A long shower and a light brunch later and Shad felt almost human again. They walked through the house so she could show him what changes she wanted to make and where she proposed to put the additional furniture she thought they needed.

The larger of the two guest bedrooms was sized generously, with its own full size bath, on the opposite side of the house from their master bedroom. Veronica brought him to a halt when they got to the room.

"The other day when I was with Caitlin I was thinking of this set-up," she said. "We don't really need this room, Shad. I had a crazy idea. What would you think of inviting Caitlin to stay here with us?"

"Stay with us?" he echoed inanely. "You mean have her move in? Have her give up her own apartment?"

"Yes. Don't you think it would be fabulous? It wouldn't cost us anything, and she would save a lot of money. Think of how much fun we could have if we lived together. But be honest. I don't want to mention this to her if you don't agree or it would make you uncomfortable."

He did not have to think for long. "You should forget about it, Veronica. I mean, she can come visit us as often as she or we would like, but I want to marry *you*, and only you, and start a family. Caitlin is fantastic, but I don't love her. I don't see us having sex with her routinely; it should remain an occasional enrichment for us. If she moved in, I think all three of us would feel constant pressure to get together every night, and that's not something I would feel comfortable with. And I would hope you would not want to always share me with Caitlin either."

"No, I wouldn't. I hadn't thought of it that way."

"Well, I absolutely would not want to share *you* all the time. Besides, what if we got tired of the arrangement after a while? What then? We would kick her out? What is now a beautiful friendship would almost certainly be ruined, and that would be a shame."

"Okay. I got the message, and you are probably right," she admitted. She did not sound totally convinced.

In bed that night, in the midst of making love, Shad suddenly caught himself thinking of Apries. Veronica was so good to him; so eager to please him and make him happy, and yet he missed the sexual aggressiveness of Apries. Of how she had taken charge and been so direct. Try as he might, he could not banish her from his thoughts. He wanted her. Her lewd, almost perverse and definitely creative acrobatics met his basest instincts. He did not love her, but he loved her eroticism and what she did with him and that she was insatiable and never hesitated being the initiator.

Veronica was different. Her personality precluded her from being as wantonly direct as Apries unless Caitlin was present as well, but she was always an excellent and highly satisfying partner. What he could not understand was why she became a different woman when they were with Caitlin. The moment Caitlin was part of their sex life, Veronica changed personalities. She became the aggressor, showing and telling Caitlin and him what she wanted done, enticing him to do things that had never occurred to him. It was this side of her he sometimes missed when they were alone. It occurred to him this could be explained by her bi-sexuality. Still, he worried it was his fault; that he alone was unable to completely unleash the beast in her. Being married to Veronica was not going to be easy, he realized.

* * *

Dave Hardee called Shad into his office. "Looks like you kept busy, Shad," he said. "I enjoyed reading your trip notes."

"So what do you think? Would you endorse going into China?"

"I think it would be premature to decide right now. As you rightly point out, you need feedback on market size and pricing from the potential distributors, and if that information paints a promising picture, we need to see the contractual terms you can negotiate," Dave said.

"How do you feel about local manufacturing?"

"I don't like it," Dave said bluntly. "We are not set up for it, neither organizationally nor technologically. Even if we were, I would worry about losing control; being able to warrant the high standards we have established and our customers rightfully expect from us."

"I feel the same way basically," Shad acknowledged, "but the aggressive marketing proposal People's First Pharmaceutical Company made appeals to me. It's a very impressive outfit, and I was thinking if we went with them we might be able to stall the production issue for years by insisting on impossibly high standards. Sending our experts there for an audit could be dragged out for a long time."

"But that would cost us," Dave pointed out, "and if their facilities unexpectedly came up to our parameters, where would that leave us? It would seem to me this approach would increase our risks to an unacceptable level. Then add the marketing chances we would have to take by letting them go nation wide with the full range of products. It doesn't fit into our strategic growth approach which has served us well."

"I suppose you are right," Shad said, "but I would suggest we at least send them the samples they requested and see what kind of sales forecast and price structure they come up with. Our expenditures would be minimal."

Dave agreed and asked about Shad's thoughts on working with Kang Ming. Shad reiterated what he considered to be the pros and cons.

"So if I understood you correctly," Dave summarized, "your biggest concerns are Ning being married to a PLA general and her capitalization?"

"Yes, plus the fact she insists on buying inventory on open account."

"I wouldn't be too concerned about that," Dave said to Shad's surprise. "Initial unit numbers would probably not be all that great; the number of products limited, and if she didn't pay we would only be out our cost of goods. We could accrue reserves to cover that contingency. I am willing to accept that if we are going to enter the market at all, which, I gather, you would like to do."

"Yes, I would. I really like and have learned to trust Thomas Grady. He has kept all of his promises, and his advice has been consistently spot on. He is convinced we would seriously regret not getting into China now and I have become convinced he is right."

"What about the corruption issue to which you alluded?"

"It's definitely a bitch. Apparently no sales occur without under-the-table money."

"I see. You do realize we can not be a party to that, don't you?" Dave pointed out. "Apart from the moral issues involved, the Foreign Corrupt Practices Act would bring the government down on us, and I don't relish the thought of going to jail."

"I don't either," Shad said and almost added: I have been there and know what it's like. "We would stay out of it," he said instead. "We would merely have to grant our distributor a higher margin."

"I don't believe I want to know about those arrangements."

"Don't worry," Shad grinned, "I will keep you in the dark."

"Which distributor does Thomas think we should go with?"

"Admittedly, he is a little ambivalent," Shad explained. "He doesn't know what propensity for risk we have, and how much money we are willing to invest. If it came out of his own pocket, he would go with Kang Ming. Low risk, low investments, moderate but steady sales development. If he had a corporation with relatively deep pockets behind him, he would take the aggressive approach and go with People's First."

"In other words, he is putting the monkey squarely on your back."

"Yes, if you mean by *my* back, AmeriDerm's."

"Well," Dave ventured, "I trust you to make the right decision, Shad. Once you have sent the samples out and received the information you need, I want you to work up a formal proposal, including a cost/benefit analysis, time line, and best guesstimate long range sales forecast."

"That's going to be tough to come up with, Dave."

"I understand that, but I am sure you can do it. We all know it's bound to be wrong, but we need to establish pertinent bench marks against which we can measure our progress once we face the decision to continue, scale back, or invest more."

Shad had no problem with this philosophically, but he groaned inwardly at the sheer impossibility of the task. How could he possibly generate a long range sales forecast? He knew next to nothing about the market and AmeriDerm's first products had not even been health registered, let alone the first units having been sold. He would have to pressure the distributors to get reliable information and clearly spell out the assumptions underlying his plan.

He made arrangements to have the promised samples sent to Kang Ming and People's First. Then he drafted follow-up letters to them, the dermatologists he had met, to Thomas, Great Wall Pioneering Company and the MOH group.

Thomas called some days later. "I take it you made it back all right," he said after they had exchanged greetings.

"I did indeed. What a delight it was to fly Cathay rather than China Air. And I really want to thank you again for all your help and support, and especially for coming up to Beijing and introducing me to those companies. And the sightseeing as well, of course."

"Good," Thomas said. "I am glad you had a good visit." Shad thought his voice sounded strangely subdued. "Have you had a chance to discuss your findings with Dave Hardee yet?" Thomas added.

"I sure did. I think he views a China entry positively. He wants me to submit a formal proposal. I would like to run the draft by you before finalizing it, if you would be willing to whet it."

"No problem. I would be happy to. I expect you will need a couple of months, *after* you receive the promised feedback."

Shad sighed. "I am afraid you may be right. The speed with which they get back to me could be an indicator of how dependable a partner they could become. Anyway, what's happening on your side, Thomas?"

"That's actually the main purpose of my call, Shad. I wanted to share two things with you. I have been summoned to our head office in New York to discuss reorganization, whatever this might mean. I thought since I have to fly through Los Angeles, why don't I pop down to San Diego for a day or two and visit with you. I have never seen the city and have heard so many good things about it. Then I could also take a look at AmeriDerm and get to know more about your company; manufacturing and the senior management team in particular. Would that suit you?"

"Very well. I would be delighted to welcome you here. Just give me your itinerary as soon as possible and I will set up a program. I hope you will stay with us. Schedule your visit so you will be here over a weekend."

"Fantastic. It would be great if you could put me up. I'd love to have a weekend in La Jolla."

"I will show you around and give you a flavor of the area. There are tons of interesting and beautiful things to see. Anyway, you said there were two issues you wanted to discuss."

"Yes, well, the second one is a personal problem," Thomas said. His voice had become quiet; he spoke slowly, choosing his words carefully. "I am afraid I have received some rather bad news. Jade has been diagnosed with a highly aggressive form of ovarian cancer, and her prognosis is not good at all." His voice sounded tightly controlled. Shad could hardly imagine what it took for Thomas to remain stoic.

"Oh, no, Thomas. I am so sorry to hear that. That's absolutely terrible. I can hardly believe it. She seemed in such perfect shape when we had dinner together. I would have thought Jade would be much too young for that sort of thing." The words, sounding ridiculously inadequate, echoed in Shad's sub-consciousness.

"You would think so," Thomas agreed. "She is only thirty five, but I have been told by her doctors that age has little to do with it. She has to have surgery, immediately followed by both radiation and chemo, so this trip of mine to New York really couldn't come at a worse time."

"Has her surgery been scheduled already?"

"Yes. Day after tomorrow. The doctors insist a delay would be irresponsible."

"Oh, my God. So soon! What are you going to do about New York? Can you even think about going there under these circumstances?"

"It depends primarily on how the surgery goes. It's extremely risky, I have been told. As things stand, I have gotten New York to delay my visit for a month, but that's all they can do."

Shad was devastated. Jade was a vibrant, ebullient and vivacious Chinese, charming and filled with laughter. While she served pre-dinner drinks at home, he had admired her beauty and she had been a gracious hostess, obviously as much in love with Thomas as he was with her. They had been married for some ten years. Shad had learned that it was the second marriage for both of them and they were very close. What a blow for Thomas. He didn't stop to think of how much more terrible it was for Jade. He wanted to ask Thomas what her chances of survival were; what her doctors predicted regarding her post surgical quality of life, but he felt too embarrassed to voice these questions.

"If you are going to New York anyway, Thomas, have you thought of taking Jade to the Sloan-Kettering Institute? I understand it's far and away the best oncology center in the world, with access to the latest experimental drug regimens."

"Yes, we discussed it. Obviously both Jade's oncologists and I know Sloan-Kettering's reputation, but the consensus of opinion is that at this point they can do just as much for her in Hong Kong. The delay in surgery, together with the stress of such a long trip, would be counterproductive. Timing is critical, so I can't really argue with the experts. I feel she is in very capable hands here, plus, it is extremely important to have her extended family around in this crisis."

Shad didn't know what he could tell his friend that might comfort him. What was there to say in such a horrible situation?

"Thomas," he finally managed, "I can't tell you how sorry I am to hear this. My heart goes out to Jade and to you. I know it must sound trite, but I wish there was something, anything, I could do for her or for you. I am thinking of you and praying for Jade. Please call me the moment you have more news."

"I will certainly do that, Shad, and I appreciate your thoughts and prayers."

Shad couldn't get Thomas' and Jade's ordeal out of his mind. He was thoroughly depressed. Even discussing it with Veronica that evening did not help. He wondered how he would feel if Veronica had suddenly been diagnosed with cancer, but it was inconceivable to picture. The thought alone was too horrible to contemplate.

Every time his phone rang in the office, he was afraid it might be Thomas with bad news. He found it difficult to concentrate on his work. He was tempted to call Thomas but kept telling himself he would only be intruding—maybe at the worst of times.

Three agonizing days passed without news out of Hong Kong. Shad couldn't stand it any longer. He called Thomas at home; no answer. He called his office. Thomas' secretary, Janet Chiu, answered in a very subdued voice, and after he had identified himself, she confirmed his worst fears.

"I am so sorry to have to tell you, Mr. Cooper, but Mr. Grady's wife did not survive the surgery," she said. "She never woke up again. Mr. Grady is currently out making funeral arrangements."

Shad tried to keep his emotions under control. He felt tears coming to his eyes. "Do you already know when she will be buried?"

"Well, I don't know how familiar you are with Chinese customs, but there is not going to be a funeral as you might know it. Since Mrs. Grady and her whole family are Chinese Buddhists, her body will lie in state in the funeral home all day tomorrow so friends and relatives can say good bye and pay their respects. Drinks and snacks will be served and family members will stay all day, while friends might come for only a few hours. Mr. Grady will be there the whole time, of course. The cremation will take place the next morning. I don't know what disposition Mr. Grady will make regarding her ashes. Most people take them home and put them on their ancestor shrine."

Shad couldn't quite picture what Janet had described. It sounded altogether foreign, almost grotesque to him. He had thought of flying to Hong Kong for the funeral, but this had now become patently futile. Between the time difference and the long flight, it would take him two days to get to Hong Kong and by then it would all be over. He thought of Thomas and how painful it would be for him to be in the funeral home all day long, greeting relatives and friends and accepting their condolences. And he thought of poor Jade. So young. Her life ending so abruptly and prematurely.

He asked Janet to tell Thomas he had called, and to have her send two wreaths, one from him personally and one on behalf of AmeriDerm. He promised to reimburse her upon his next visit to Hong Kong. Then he drafted a letter of condolence to Thomas. He found it almost impossible to formulate something appropriate and spent several hours trying to come up with the right words. Eventually, although still unhappy with the inadequacies of what he had put to paper, he mailed his letter.

18

A month after Jade's death Thomas arrived. Shad picked him up. He was shocked how visibly his friend had aged. Thomas had gone to New York first and then come to San Diego, wanting to know what the planned reorganization of Pan-Asia would mean for him. It would allow a more relaxed time with Shad.

They had spoken only briefly on the phone during Thomas' mourning and had a lot to catch up on. Shad did not want to raise the subject of Jade and waited for Thomas to tell him as much or as little as he wanted. It was not very much.

"You know, Shad," he said, "I think in retrospect it was good I had to fly to New York. It forced me to think about issues other than Jade being gone, and I don't know how I would have coped without that distraction. I kept speculating about what Charles Lee wanted to see me about. He hadn't given me so much as a hint, and even though I felt pretty sure he wasn't about to axe me, I couldn't totally rule it out. Charles is a pretty hard nosed individual, and Pan-Asia has had its share of problems recently. We lost a couple of big principals and are still looking for suitable replacements. I had no clue what to expect. I certainly didn't think it would be advantageous for me personally."

"But it was?" Shad prompted as they were driving towards La Jolla.

"Definitely, in a way. We are re-organizing by business lines and Charles wants me to manage our pharmaceutical distribution segment throughout Asia."

"Hey, congratulations! That's great, Thomas. I am very happy for you and I know you will do a bang up job!" Shad thought this was fantastic news for both Thomas and AmeriDerm, and could well facilitate their entry into additional markets. Having only one senior manager to deal with should make his life much simpler.

"Thank you," Thomas acknowledged. "But there is a price to pay for this promotion. I would be based in New York, and that's probably the last place where I would like to live. And I would have to travel constantly."

"Wow," Shad commiserated. "That *is* tough. Resettling from Hong Kong to New York is going to be a major disruption. From what I have seen of New York and what I know about Hong Kong, it's hard to imagine two cities being as different from each other as these two are. I must say I don't envy you. Have you accepted the promotion yet?"

"No, not yet, but I don't have a lot of time. Keep in mind that Charles already wanted to do this a month ago. He has given me a week to decide."

"And did he tell you what would happen if you turned him down?"

"Not in so many words. I assume I would stay in charge of our Hong Kong and China operations, but I would definitely get a new boss, and that could well be some hotshot Caucasian manager who knows nothing about Asia."

"Not a very appealing scenario," Shad opined, "but I have a hard time believing Charles would do that. From what I have seen, you are a totally Chinese dominated organization, and I can't see Charles bringing in a non-Asian for such a critical position."

"Maybe, but no matter who the new guy would be, we might not get along and I could be out of a job."

"Sounds to me like you don't have all that much of a choice."

"That's what I have been thinking as well," Thomas said and lapsed into silence.

Shad left him to his thoughts for a while before he said, "Well, I think it's fortuitous you came here for a few days. It gives you a much needed change of scenery. You'll see a part of the States you are not familiar with and gives you time to think more dispassionately while you are away from the familiarity of Hong Kong."

"I hope you are right, Shad." He sounded morose and did not appear to be in a talking mood. Shad saw him looking around at the beautiful scenery, and decided to drive through Pacific Beach and up Soledad Mountain Road rather than following the freeway to La Jolla.

Bougainvillea, jacaranda, rhododendrons and brightly colored birds of paradise were everywhere, with palm trees, tall Torrey pines and eucalyptus trees catching the eye. The neat houses with their lush green lawns and landscaped yards were delightful, and when they crested Mount Soledad and turned into Nautilus Street, the endless, bright blue ocean met their gaze.

Shad rolled down the windows of the car, letting in the invigorating fresh air. The climate was perfect: not too warm, not too cold, and no pollution. In the distance an imposing Navy ship was outlined against the clear horizon. Tall palms dotted the skyline. The city was showing itself from its most beautiful side, and Shad was grateful for this welcome it provided.

He turned into his street and Thomas was suitably impressed when they walked into the house. Shad helped him carry his luggage into the guest quarters and showed him around. Following a quick tour of the dwelling he asked, "What would you like to do, Thomas? You could freshen up and take a little nap, or we could drive into town and go for a walk along the beach, or we could sit on the terrace and have a cup of coffee or a drink and just watch the sun set and talk. Take your pick. Veronica won't be home for another hour or so, I suspect, and our dinner reservation is only for 8:00, so we have time."

"I don't know what to say," Thomas confessed as he stood by the windows looking out over the ocean. "I am rather overwhelmed by what I see and how magnificent and peaceful it is up here. I never imagined you living so quietly, beautifully. What an absolutely glorious panorama!"

"It is, isn't it? You can see why I fell in love with this place when I came here for my interviews. It really helped me decide to join AmeriDerm."

"Easy enough to understand. Too bad Pan-Asia doesn't have its headquarters here. I would accept the new job in a heart beat."

Thomas seemed mesmerized by the view. Just as Shad had found time and again, simply staring out over the ocean made one lose track of time. The constantly changing colors of the water, the small waves rippling the surface and reflecting or breaking the sun's rays, were a source of endless fascination. Hypnotizing, Shad had learned.

The lower curvature of the descending sun was close to touching the water when a sliver of horizontal cloud split its bright yellow ball.

"Look," Thomas said, pointing at the unusual phenomenon, "it looks like a bloody hamburger!"

It didn't take much imagination to see what Thomas meant. Through an aberration of the distant cloud, it dissected the sun horizontally into two equal parts. The light gray sliver looked like a hamburger patty nestled between two halves of a golden bun. Even Shad, who had virtually watched hundreds of beautiful and unusual sunsets, had never observed such a strange constellation of cloud and sun. He rushed inside to get his camera, but when he returned, clouds and sun had merged and had lost their fascinating arrangement.

The last of the sun took a sudden dip and disappeared behind the horizon, leaving a radiating, glowing halo streaking towards the darkening sky.

They were still standing there watching dusk settling in when Veronica came home. Introductions were made and they moved into the comfortable chairs arrayed in front of the windows. Shad poured wine for them and Veronica expressed her condolences to Thomas over his recent loss of Jade.

"Yes," Thomas said, "I am having a bit of a rather hard time. I do think my having been raised in the Chinese culture helps. They accept death as a more natural event than we do. Her passing away was inevitable, Karma. It was preordained and could not have been prevented, and now the deceased will be re-incarnated and have a good afterlife, so let's get over it. What puzzles me is whether the suddenness of it all makes it easier or more difficult to accept."

"You have a son, don't you?" Veronica asked. "How is he taking it?"

"Stepson, actually. He seems to be okay. He is Jade's son from her first marriage, and is in boarding school in the UK. I suspect he doesn't have all that much time to grieve. I believe that in many ways leaving home and Hong Kong and his friends a couple of years ago was probably nearly as traumatic for him as losing his mother. I don't know. He is at an age where he doesn't talk much about his emotions," he finished somewhat ruefully.

"How old is he?" she asked.

"Fourteen."

She nodded as she thought about how a young teenager, away from home in a no doubt stressful boarding school would cope, and what kind of relationship he had with his stepfather. She was doubly glad a child had not been around to complicate her divorce.

Listening to this exchange, Shad was reminded of his own situation as a teenager with his brutal, abusive stepfather and how gruesomely that had ended. He had largely succeeded in relegating those dark memories to the furthest corner of his mind, but he could never completely forget.

"Well," Shad said, rather distracted, and looked discreetly at his watch, "I don't know about you, but I am getting hungry. What do you say we break up and go eat?"

Thomas nodded, and Veronica said, "Please give me a couple of minutes to freshen up. I'll be right with you."

Indeed it did not take her long, and they were soon seated in the Marine Room, fronting the Shores beach, watching the surf crashing against the retaining wall and heavy plate glass windows protecting the restaurant.

Shad was glad Veronica had come with them. She engaged Thomas in long conversations about Hong Kong and his life there and his visits to China. It was the perfect antidote for Thomas' blues, and it was obvious that the two enjoyed talking to each other. Shad was pleased at the intelligence underlying her questions to Thomas. It was one of her characteristics that Shad found so attractive.

Thomas was tired after his momentous days in New York and the trip to San Diego, and after they were back home and had digested their sumptuous meal with a cognac, he excused himself to go to bed. Neither Shad nor Veronica minded the rather early evening.

"He is a great guy, isn't he?" Shad asked when they were in their bedroom.

"He sure is. I like him a lot, and I enjoyed talking with him. He knows so much and is so experienced. I think I could listen to him all night. Can I go with you tomorrow when you show him around?"

"Absolutely. It would be great. I wouldn't have to worry about what to talk to him about."

"That wouldn't really be a problem, would it?" She sounded rather incredulous.

"I suppose not, but we would inevitably discuss business all the time, whereas I would like to get his mind off his future. The decision he has to make and the thought of having to move to New York weighs heavily on him," he said, and brought Veronica up to date on what Thomas had told him.

*   *   *

Shad had thought about what to show Thomas and had concluded the world famous San Diego Zoo and Sea World, fascinating as they were, would probably not be as interesting to him as some other sights. Consequently, he drove along the coast to Point Loma, with its incredible overlook of downtown San Diego, North Island Naval Air Station, Harbor and Shelter Islands, the Coronado Bay Bridge, and the harbor. The awe inspiring view silenced them, as did the rare sight of an aircraft carrier slowly making its way out to sea. It was so mesmerizing they stayed rooted much longer than Shad had intended. He had to hurry them up to the original old light house for a final look around before leaving.

Detouring past picturesque Shelter and Harbor Islands, Shad followed Harbor Drive past the India Star of the Sea, an old, massive, four mast iron hulled sailing vessel. He continued on to cross the harbor on the soaring Coronado Bay Bridge to show Thomas the enchanting little island with its red roofed Hotel Coronado and its unique, distinctive architecture. They stopped at the hotel for a light lunch on its seaside terrace. Beautiful sunshine and a cloudless sky with moderate temperatures made them never want to leave.

Eventually they drove down the Silver Strand and saw the Navy's mothball fleet. After a hasty look at the border crossing to Tijuana, they went back up north until they reached Balboa Park where they parked and walked along the Prado, admiring the old museums and the abundance of flowers and gardens.

Shad ended his tour by driving through the best residential areas of La Jolla itself. Thomas sat in the car, literally open mouthed at the sight of so many opulent houses, one more magnificent than the other, with huge gardens meticulously maintained and ornate wrought iron fencing.

One could easily get the impression *everyone* in La Jolla had to be rich. Thomas asked Shad if he knew the source of income that allowed so many people to live so luxuriously.

"I really don't," he said. "Certainly these folks up here would not earn enough through normal employment in La Jolla. An awful lot are rich retirees. The medical profession is well represented, with presumably high incomes. Any number of entrepreneurs and investors—venture capitalists—call this home, and then you have the old money. Real estate has made many people wealthy. The only thing I know for sure is that we have one of the highest proportions of millionaires, on a per capita basis, living here."

"It's really quite astounding," Thomas observed.

Shad couldn't help but agree.

As they drove through the village back home, Thomas commented on how many luxury vehicles he saw. It was true. At times it seemed there were as many Mercedes and BMW's and Jaguars to be seen as there were Chevrolets or Fords or Chryslers. Rolls Royce, Bentleys, Ferraris, Maseratis and Lamborghinis were not an unusual sight.

"Yes," Shad picked up on Thomas' observation, "I think it's indicative that the only two new car dealers we have are for Ferraris and Maseratis, and then we have a luxury dealer where you can spend more than a million dollars for a sports car, apart from the Rolls-Royce and Bentleys, both new and used, they sell."

Thomas only shook his head and marveled.

They had a drink outside on the terrace before dinner. Veronica offered to cook for them, but Thomas insisted on inviting them out.

"You know, Thomas," Veronica said after they had returned from dinner and were talking about what they had seen that day, "you ought to consider buying a condo here. If you accept that job in New York, you are going to be doing a lot of traveling, and will probably go through Los Angeles regularly. With the time difference, you could plan to arrive in San Diego on a Friday morning and then take the red eye to New York late Sunday evening. Or the other way around—fly here from New York Friday morning and then from Los Angeles to Asia Sunday evening. It would give you a three day weekend either way."

"Interesting thought," Thomas admitted.

"Who knows?" Shad added, "Maybe one day you will want to—or could—move here, and then you could sell your condo and use the proceeds as a down payment for a house. The way the market has been going for more than 20 years, I don't see how you could go wrong."

"You are saying it would be a good investment for me regardless of whether or not I would ever move here."

"Precisely. In fact, you could well buy a condo to lease out for enough to cover your mortgage payments, home owner's fees, upkeep and insurance."

"I have an idea," Veronica interjected. "Why don't we spend a little time tomorrow afternoon to look at some Open Houses? You could see what's currently available and get a feel for prices and what you like."

They quickly agreed and Sunday morning studied the list of Open Houses while they brunched at Harry's Coffee Shop.

By the time they had gone through four condos, Thomas had developed so much enthusiasm he seemed ready to buy something immediately. Shad wasn't all that surprised. How could one not get excited at the prospect of owning real estate in this paradise? Still, before buying, additional aspects should be considered, Shad advised Thomas, especially specific locations and whether he wanted to buy for his own use or merely as an investment.

"If you are really serious, Thomas, just give us your price range and Veronica and I will keep our eyes peeled for something suitable. We can also fax you copies of ads and suggest desirable locations. Then you can proceed the next time you come."

*   *   *

Monday was busy with a plant and facility tour of AmeriDerm in the newly developing area along Sorrento Valley Road. Several hours were spent with the company's senior management team to review business opportunities in Asia. It was obvious to Shad that Thomas made a good impression, and that everyone felt comfortable in working with him. The one question to which Thomas could not provide an answer concerned the impact his promotion could have, but Shad felt it could only be positive.

They had some time left before Shad had to take Thomas to the airport, and they went to his office.

"Hi, Mr. Grady. I am Pam Foster, Mr. Cooper's secretary. May I bring you some coffee or tea?"

"Tea would be lovely," Thomas said, not taking his eyes off Pam.

Shad had not hired her for her looks, but rather for her proven competency and efficiency, but she was very attractive and she knew it. She was no doubt aware of Thomas studying her and returned his probing look frankly. As always, she was impeccably dressed in a smart suit, dark blue with wide lapels, and her white blouse revealed a hint of cleavage. Her chestnut hair was trimmed short, almost boyish, and highlighted her long, graceful neck. She had an enticingly voluptuous figure. A subtle fragrance radiated from her.

It amused Shad that Thomas was noticeably enchanted. He was glad Thomas was taking an interest in life again. Watching him looking longingly at Pam was the best thing that could have happened, he thought, and he gave Thomas time to linger in the reception area.

They stayed and watched Pam prepare the tea. When it was ready she smiled warmly at Thomas before carrying it into Shad's office, and they followed her inside.

"What a lovely woman," Thomas sighed after she had left and closed the door.

"Isn't she? Not only that, but she is very good at her job. I was very lucky to have found her," Shad said. "In a way," he grinned, "it's too bad she works for me. I could easily have become interested in her if she didn't, and if I hadn't found Veronica just about the time I hired her."

"Well, she doesn't work for me," Thomas stated the obvious, "so I guess it's okay for me to show some interest. Is she married?"

"No. *That* much I know from her personnel file, but beyond that, I know very little about her. We don't really chat about our private lives. For all I know she may be divorced. No kids to the best of my knowledge. I did hear through the grapevine the other day that she recently broke up with her boyfriend."

"Do you think it would be all right for me to stay in touch with her?" Thomas asked.

"I think you would have to ask *her* that. I can not speak for her. If you want, I can run a quick errand and you can go out and talk to her. See what she says. Maybe she'll give you her address or phone number."

Without waiting for an answer, Shad got up and walked down the hallway to visit a colleague. He liked the idea of Thomas being interested in a woman.

Thirty minutes later, when Shad returned, he found Thomas and Pam in deep conversation. They nearly jumped when they suddenly felt Shad standing next to them.

"I apologize for being gone so long," Shad said, keeping a serious face despite his deliberate matchmaking effort.

"That's all right," Thomas assured him. "I enjoyed talking to Pam." He was smiling at her, and Shad saw a slow flush creeping over her face. He wondered what they had discussed.

"Well, Thomas, I think it's about time we took you to the airport."

As he announced this, he had a sudden inspiration. "I have another meeting coming up and I wonder whether you would mind an awful lot if Pam were to drive you to the airport? Pam, if you have time and are willing to do that for me, you could use my car."

"No problem at all," they answered nearly simultaneously, trying not to show how happy this request made them. Shad gave Pam his keys and walked them to the parking lot and bid Thomas good bye. Thomas reciprocated, asked Shad to convey his best wishes and thanks to Veronica and to be advised soonest of Shad's next visit to Hong Kong.

*   *   *

Shad was on the verge of leaving his office later that afternoon when his phone rang. When he picked up, there was a slight delay before he could hear and recognize Apries' voice.

"Apries?" he said. His heart started racing wildly at the husky sound of her voice.

"Is that you, Shad?"

"Yes. How are you doing, Apries?"

"I'm okay. I am sorry to bother you at work, but I just had to hear your voice. I hope you don't mind. I miss you so much!"

He heard her voice catching in her throat. Could she be crying? "I miss you too, Apries," he assured her. And he did. Just hearing her made him yearn to hold her in his arms and make love to her. "You must have gotten up early to call me. It's only 5:00am in Beijing, isn't it?"

"Yes, but I have to meet a tourist group at 6:30, so I had to get up early anyway. When are you coming back to see me?"

"Not much longer, but I am still waiting for some responses from the companies I visited before finalizing my next trip. I expect to be there in about a month."

"So long? How can I stand it?"

"Oh, Apries, I wish I could make it sooner, but I don't want to promise something and then disappoint you if I have to delay my trip."

"Maybe you are not that eager to see me again," she ventured, sounding petulant.

"No, you are wrong, Apries. Believe me, if I could, I would fly right through the telephone line this very second to be with you."

"Yes, yes, do it!" she said, and he had to laugh.

He was happy to find out she missed him so much. Forgotten was his determination not to see her again.

"You promise to come as soon as you can?"

"I promise," he solemnly said.

"I will pick you up at the airport, so please don't order a hotel car, okay?"

Shad hesitated. He wasn't sure how he felt about her offer. He knew already that after such a long overnight flight, he wanted nothing more than to get to his hotel and sleep. If she picked him up, it was inevitable what would happen. She might not even wait until they got to the hotel before doing something embarrassing. But there was also no denying his hunger to see her again, and so he agreed.

"I hope you won't arrive at a bad time," she said.

"What do you mean by bad time?"

"Because if I am on time, as I usually am, I will have started my period on the 25th, so you would only be able to fuck me in the ass," she whispered. He heard her words, but he could hardly believe them. Even for the incredibly outspoken Apries, this sounded like too much.

"Are you kidding me?" he managed to say.

"No. Why not? Would you mind?"

"I don't know. I have never tried it."

"Then maybe you should. You might like it. I do, but not always," she confessed with a giggle.

He couldn't take anymore. The lewd . . . explanation? Threat? Promise?—he couldn't decide what it had been—had made him so horny he couldn't concentrate anymore and brought the phone call quickly to an end.

As soon as he hung up, he called Veronica.

"Listen, Honey, what do you think about getting in touch with Caitlin to see if she might be free tonight?"

"Oh, oh. It's that bad, is it?"

"Well, we didn't really have much of an opportunity while Thomas was here, did we?"

"I didn't think you were going to blame Thomas. I thought you had just been too tired. Or didn't need me any more."

"Ha, ha! Very funny! Of course I do. But we haven't seen Caitlin for a while and I thought it would be great to spend a little time together."

"Let me think about it. I might want you all to myself tonight, after you let me starve to death this weekend."

"Okay. But don't take too long, or she might make other plans," he cautioned.

"Boy oh boy, you really are in bad shape, aren't you?" she said. "Maybe we can compromise. I will take you alone for an hour, and then we can have Caitlin join us."

"Beautiful!" he assured her. "I am on my way."

He was more than eager to get home. Apries' words lingered in his ear and he couldn't wait to have Veronica. He wondered if Caitlin would be available.

19

Jade's death hit me surprisingly hard, considering we had never met. Thomas' visit had brought us close together and I had seen how Shad had grieved for his friend's loss. When Shad had told me about Thomas' interest in Pam, I was glad. He was still too young to be alone and the prospect of having to relocate to New York, leaving his beloved Hong Kong with all his many friends behind seemed terrible to me. How quickly one's life could take drastic turns, I realized.

These thoughts brought me up short; made me think about my future with Shad. We had been living together for a year and while we had intermittently talked about marriage, we had been dragging our feet on a specific date. Neither one of us felt a sense of urgency. Maybe the fact we were both divorced made us cautious. There was no novelty involved for us in getting married. We knew what was at stake and it had kept us from rushing into formalizing our relationship. But Jade's sudden and totally unexpected demise put things into a different, more urgent perspective.

When I stopped to think about it I was admittedly somewhat concerned about Shad's frequent and extended absences. I have enough self confidence and am neither narrow minded nor jealous. I had meant it when I told him he could take care of his sexual emergencies with a prostitute while he was traveling. So why did it bother me when he reluctantly confessed after his most recent return he had been with one in China? He had only admitted it after considerable probing from my side, which I had done against my better judgment. And had it truly been only a physical thing for him, as he had claimed?

Try as I might I had not been able to get details out of him. One look at his face told me he would not be willing to share specifics of how or with whom he had resolved his sexual emergency, and I was left wondering. I would have to come back to the issue at a more appropriate time because I needed to know if emotions had been involved. I wasn't sure. He had seemed ever so slightly different upon his return. A little less focused and considerate in making love to me, as if absent minded or maybe thinking of how it had been with someone else. Almost as if he had just been going through the motions without any particular effort to make me feel good, striving only for his own release.

He had taken my night with Caitlin in stride. Originally I had been so afraid of telling him about Caitlin and our relationship, knowing from past experience it could well mean ending our friendship before it had really gotten started. But he had accepted me and the way I am. He didn't just say so; he showed me he truly did. Of course it probably helped that Caitlin and I had invited him to join us when we got together. He had not even tried to pretend it wasn't an incredible turn-on for him, and I was only surprised—and secretly pleased—he had refused to fuck her. Although I had encouraged him, thinking this would please him immeasurably, I am not sure how I would have felt if he had acceded and I would have had to watch him doing it. I suppose I was oddly grateful he had been so conservative.

And yet a question remained in my mind. How could he hire a prostitute, a total stranger, and be willing to pay for sex while turning down what he could get for free from Caitlin? Was it only the thought of me watching him do it? Was he afraid I would get upset or hold it against him?

I wasn't quite sure he had merely resolved an acute sexual emergency in China. Something seemed out of place, but I couldn't put my finger on what it was.

Perhaps he had picked up on the fact that when I was alone with him, I could not be as totally uninhibited as I was when Caitlin joined the party. If he had noted—and it wouldn't surprise me if he had—he had never mentioned it. In a way I was glad because I didn't know if I could have explained.

I know I am less inhibited with another woman than with a man. Even with Shad after living with him for a year. I have wondered why this is so. Could it be because anatomically women are the same? Or was it only my bi-sexuality? How else to account for the difference in my behavior? That to this day I have to work at overcoming certain inhibitions before I can run through the house naked when Shad is around and is watching me? It turns him on, I know, but I can never shake vestiges of embarrassment. Just like showering with him; I love it in a way, but I have to admit I can not completely overcome a degree of discomfort when I see Shad watching me doing what should be done in private. Almost like having a guilty conscience, afraid I might get caught. Silly, I know, but true.

What a complicated beast I am! Sometimes I envy Caitlin for her simplistic approach to sex. She can only love another woman. Men she tolerates. She has never expressed a desire to be fucked by a man—by Shad or anyone else. I know she does not need a hard penis in her, and yet, paradoxically, she could not do without a dildo. It's a dichotomy to me that I can not understand. The best, the most realistic dildo could never replace Shad's cock as far as I am concerned, and if Caitlin is going to allow—or want—any penetration, why not with the real thing instead of a lifeless substitute?

I wish I could understand why I feel freer with Caitlin, or when Caitlin, Shad and I are together, than with Shad alone. I have wondered whether this could be explained by how I was brought up: there were no restrictions on what I could do with my girl friends; no close supervision. But the moment boys entered the picture, it was a different story. Warnings to behave; not to let them do anything. The mystery of what they shielded in their pants. The scary size and hardness of their sex. The fear of pregnancy. The reputation to be protected. None of these factors applied to associating with girls, and I thought this could possibly explain why I was so completely natural with another woman while always holding back just a touch with a man.

I need sex. The fact that I need it heterosexually as well as gay stopped bothering me a long time ago. I feel comfortable with how I am. I don't think I am bad; just different from most other women. At times I have wondered whether I was born with a latent gay gene which drove me to those first experimental lesbian encounters with my teenage room mate in Guam or whether what the two of us did made me how I am today. I have read somewhere that researchers claim to have found a difference in the brain structure of homosexual males as opposed to straight men, but I don't recall ever reading about similar studies or results relating to women. I know strict lesbians are born that way and have zero control over how they are, but I wonder if this also applies to the kind of moderate bi-sexuality I have. Do none of the three different orientations—straight, gay, and bi—have any control over themselves? I don't pretend to know and simply accept myself the way I am and expect my partner to do the same. How lucky I am to have found Shad!

I feel okay about my particular sexuality. Always have, despite this little issue of being less inhibited with a woman than with a man. I have never thought of myself as perverse or depraved just because I like a threesome with Caitlin and Shad. I accept I may be different from most women in that I don't just fantasize about making love to a same sex partner, but actually do it and enjoy it tremendously. Not because it is better than with a man, but because it's different. Incomparable.

Whenever I have these periodic phases of in depth self analysis—which I have maybe every couple of months—it occurs to me I should discuss this with Shad. Maybe I could make him understand why I am the way I am, and allay any questions he might have as to why I seem somewhat more inhibited when I am with him than I am when Caitlin is with us. I don't want him to observe this and begin to wonder or start becoming frustrated with me or to look for another woman; one completely uninhibited.

I suspect strongly that would be his type, although he has never expressed the slightest dissatisfaction with me. From my perspective, our sex life is great. These little vestiges of ridiculous modesty I carry around with me don't infringe on the utter satisfaction Shad gives me. He is so forceful and yet romantic and I go out of my way to please him and share with him whatever he wants to do. I am always willing and ready for him. That I am sometimes not as aggressive in bed as he might like is a different story. Maybe he hasn't noticed. As I said, he has never complained, so I have to assume he is as happy with me as I am with him. If he has any reservations about my bi-sexuality, he has never voiced them, and I think he would have if he had.

Nevertheless it occurs to me that if Shad and I are going to get married, which we both want, we had better clear the air before doing so—if there is any to clear, and it is not just my imagination. Both of our previous marriages broke up primarily because of sex, and that is definitely not something I would want to happen to the two of us. Maybe it's only a question of time before I feel as free and uninhibited and sexually aggressive with Shad as I am with Caitlin, but can I afford to wait? I think it would be better to address the subject now. I am determined to try. I don't want to take the chance that he would find someone on one of his trips who would fulfill all of his fantasies. That would be the end for us and scares the hell out of me. Much as I love Caitlin, it is Shad I want to marry and his children I want to have.

Airing these nagging worries was high time, I concluded, and although I was hesitant about broaching the subject, one evening after we had made love I finally found the courage to confront him with my concerns. We were still in that post coital mellowness, and I thought this was the right moment.

"Shad, do I completely satisfy you in bed? Fulfill all your fantasies?"

That got his attention. "What are you talking about?" he asked, raising himself up on an elbow and looking me in the eyes. The light was on because he liked looking at what he was doing to me.

"Exactly what I asked. If I have to compete with some professional, I want to make sure I satisfy you as much or more than she does. That I meet all of your expectations and that you can do with *me* whatever *she* would let you do, and it would be better for you with me than with her."

"Oh, Veronica, of course you do. Nobody is competing with you. You have nothing to worry about. I love only you."

"I am not talking about love. I am only talking about sex; the physical thing." It sounded to me like he had been equivocating a little. I hadn't questioned his love. "I know you love me, Shad, just like I love you. I was wondering if maybe you had sexual fantasies or desires I don't completely fulfill, or that you are hesitant to ask of me but some whore in Asia is more than happy to take care of."

"I don't have any unfulfilled fantasies anymore. You make me very happy."

"But? I somehow sense there is something else, Shad."

I could see him hesitating, debating with himself. "Not really," he said after a while. "No but, as you call it. I guess what you detected was the feeling I sometimes get that you are not as liberated with me as you are with Caitlin, for example. As if you never feel as totally uninhibited with me as with her. Or am I just imagining that? I wouldn't mind if you were to be a little more aggressive with me at times, show more initiative and not wait for me to start things, but I can assure you I am not in the least dissatisfied."

His words hurt me, but he hadn't said anything I didn't already suspect. I was glad I had raised the subject; that I had brought it out into the open. "It's true," I said. "I can't deny it, even if I feel it's almost impossible to explain or to understand."

"Why don't you at least try?" he asked gently.

"You mean try to explain or try to be different?" I said, stalling for time.

"To explain," he said, making it easy for me.

And so I did, sharing with him in great detail what I had been ruminating about earlier. He listened patiently, not interrupting, occasionally nodding in understanding. "So that's how it is," I finished. "or should I say that's how I am?"

"I don't really see it as a problem. First of all, I was telling the truth when I said I am very happy with you. You satisfy all my needs. Secondly, as to this aggressiveness I occasionally miss a little, I think that's just a question of time. Maybe I should not make love to you for a while, until you get so horny you can't wait any longer and seize the initiative and rape me."

I could see the smile on his face and had to grin. "And if you get horny before I do? Or it doesn't happen to me before you leave on another trip?"

"Then you have to force yourself. You have to fuck me so long and so hard that I will be completely drained for as long as I will be gone. Or you have to get Caitlin to help you."

"That's always an option, I suppose. I told you, I really do not understand why I can be so completely wild with her and then become a little shy with you."

"Well, you are not exactly shy with me," he assuaged her. But I knew I was. A touch more restrained than with Caitlin, but it had not been a problem.

"Tell me, Shad. That pro you were with in China, was she as aggressive as you would like me to be?" I hated myself for asking; didn't really want to know. Even if she had been, why should he admit it?

"Veronica," he said, "I don't want to talk about her. I told you, it was an emergency, without any meaning or emotional involvement. I can't even remember what she looked like."

He hadn't answered my question, of course, but I decided to let it drop, even though I felt sure he had deliberately avoided saying yes.

We were getting tired. I was still worried. Perhaps more so now than before, but there was nothing else I could do at this point except to work on myself to change, to become more like Shad wanted and had—I suspected strongly—found in that whore. At least I hoped that's what she was.

Suddenly he surprised me. "You know what, Veronica? As long as we are on this subject, I do have one wish you could make true."

"Oh, oh. I am not sure I want to hear this," was all I managed to say. "But tell me anyway."

"I wish that sometimes when we make love—or maybe it would be more appropriate to say when we fuck—you would talk dirty to me. Or let me talk dirty to you. It turns me on."

I didn't know what to say. It had never occurred to me. I had never thought about it. We didn't even do it when we were with Caitlin. "I don't know if I can, Shad. It wouldn't feel natural to me. I don't know how I would react if you did it. Perhaps it would depend on what you would say."

His only response was to shrug, and we left it like that, unresolved. I needed time to think. I didn't believe I could do it, at least not without sounding like an idiot to myself or feeling as if I were some cheap whore.

The next morning after Shad had left for work, I continued thinking about what we had discussed. I was still glad I had brought my concerns out into the open, but I couldn't tell how Shad felt. He hadn't appeared uncomfortable and I wanted to believe what he had said. What worried me was that he would be going back to China shortly and I wondered if he would try to meet the same girl again. She had obviously been good to him, and even if I thoroughly drained him before he left, I knew it would not take him more than a day or two to recover and he would start thinking about sex again. This I knew from experience. Caitlin and I would wear him out to where he would literally have to crawl home on his knees and a day later he was all over me again.

The answer was obvious to me: I alone had to so completely satisfy him in every way imaginable that he would not even be tempted to look for someone else. Would I be able to do it? I didn't know, but I was determined to try. Too much was at stake.

I made another resolution that day. I would get Shad to agree on a marriage date soonest. I didn't want to take the chance of letting him get away. I loved him too much.

20

Shad felt about Ruth's massage the way he felt about good food: absolutely fantastic, but only a great memory hours later. Just as his body craved for another meal, it wanted another massage all too soon. It occurred to him he simply wanted to see her again; wanted to feel her hands on him. The relaxation she had induced had penetrated deeper than his skin; his emotional well being had been taken care of.

He kept thinking of her and how good her ministrations had felt and the desire they had stirred in him. He wondered if the next time would be as satisfying. He was eager to find out but did not want to appear too impatient. He wanted to give her time to consider coming to his house. The sober atmosphere of the health club was a downer.

Her hands had succeeded in lifting him out of the lethargy that had crept up on him with the signing of his option agreement. Instead of starting to liquidate the necessary assets for the full payment of the apartment, he had fallen into a slump, despairing over both his uncharacteristic indecisiveness and his loneliness. He found it required a conscious effort to take care of himself. The most rudimentary necessities meant overcoming a sluggish willpower. He had to force himself to shower and shave and change attire. Even brushing his teeth thoroughly and flossing were work. He ate irregularly and too much junk food. He drank too much. His despondency gnawed at him. He knew he could not continue to live like this. He threatened to become slovenly when he had always been so fastidious. If he kept this up, he would not be welcome in the Towers, he feared.

Feeling so lonely, he thought, was ironic. Throughout his life he had been a loner, needing time off to be by himself. To think and daydream. Inner tension had built up inexorably if he spent too much time among others, including Veronica, until it reached the point where he *had* to go off by himself for a few days. That self imposed loneliness had brought on temporary depressions in which he wallowed with perverse pleasure. A life time of traveling and being alone—on long flights, weekends in hotels—had formed him. It had frequently been the most difficult aspect of getting used to retirement—the never being alone any more.

What he had not realized was that only a few days at a time had sufficed to re-establish his emotional equilibrium. Much as he had yearned for a few days without companionship, he now had to accept always being alone was too much of a good thing. Never being alone had been hard; always being alone was considerably worse.

Perhaps he might have gotten solitude mixed up with loneliness, he mused. He had not really needed the latter; only the former. He had all the solitude he wanted now; he had not anticipated the steady solitarian environment quickly leading to depressing loneliness.

Compounding his moroseness was the background check Sybil had initiated. It contributed significantly and negatively. He still had not heard from her. Before he could change his mind he called her.

"Oh, hi, Mr. Cooper," she greeted him cheerfully. "What a coincidence. I was about to get in touch with you. We have run into a little snag on your background check. The police want to know when and where you were born."

"I see. Is it enough if I tell you?"

"Maybe a piece of paper would be better. Less chance of an error being made."

"Okay. I will bring my birth certificate this afternoon."

His back was wet with nervous perspiration. Were his worst nightmares about to come true? He shuddered at the thought. He berated himself for having signed the option agreement, thereby precipitating the look into his background. Had he inadvertently awakened a sleeping monster? Wheels had been set in motion that could not be stopped.

As he pondered what Sybil's request might portent, he concluded he had to do what he should have done years ago: consult a lawyer.

Through the legal department of AmeriDerm he was given the name of a reputable one and he called for an appointment.

"What can I help you with, Mr. Cooper?" Mark Brooks, the lawyer, asked him the next day.

Shad had weighed carefully what to say and was determined to reveal as little as possible. "I am hoping you can get some information for me. Please consider the following: A teenager kills his grossly abusive stepfather in Los Angeles county, is convicted of involuntary manslaughter, sentenced to three years in prison and escapes while being transferred from a juvie facility to state prison. He assumes a new identity and is never caught. He never commits another crime."

"And this all took place when?"

"1958."

"In Los Angeles and such a long time ago. So what exactly do you wish to know?"

"First of all, would the police still be looking for someone like this, fifty years later? Secondly, is there an applicable statute of limitations? Thirdly, would the pertinent police file have been kept? And finally, what would be likely to happen if this individual were to turn himself in today or come to the attention of the authorities?"

"Well, you were right about the need for council," Brooks confirmed after some thoughtful reflection. "I need to contact someone where the crime took place. I do know there is no statute of limitations *per se* on breaking out of jail, but extenuating circumstances could conceivably apply. Technically speaking, one might be able to argue that this was not an actual jail break. Taking on a fictitious identity is a crime. Going to court would be unavoidable. It would obviously help to know the names of the persons involved, as well as other pertinent data, but I get the impression that is something you do not wish to divulge."

"That's correct. At least at this time."

"I understand. I will see what can be learned, but without names it may not be 100% reliable. I will get back to you soonest."

Although more apprehensive than ever before, Shad felt strangely relieved to have a lawyer find out whether he needed to continue worrying or could forget his criminal past. He hoped he had done the right thing. He knew he would be anxious during the coming days and concluded another massage was in order. As soon as he got home, he called Ruth.

"This is Shad Cooper," he said when she answered. "I don't know if you remember me, Ruth."

"Sure I do," she said after a brief pause. "The dirty old man from the Tranquil Towers." He could hear her laughter. "How have you been?"

"Not bad," he lied, "although I wish you would forget that dirty old man business."

"I'm sorry. I was only trying to be funny." She sounded contrite.

It made Shad feel better. "That's all right. I guess it's better than you not remembering me at all."

"What can I do for you, Mr. Cooper?"

"Please call me Shad. I need another massage and wondered whether you had had a chance to consider coming to my house."

He could hear her hesitate. He didn't think she had given it any more thought and she confirmed it. "Not really, I have to confess. When did you want to see me?"

"The sooner the better. Whenever your schedule permits."

"How about tomorrow afternoon? I am free at four o'clock."

"Sounds good to me," he said, then hesitated, almost afraid to ask. "So will my house be okay? You wouldn't have to bring your massage table. I have a twin bed in one of my guest rooms we could use. It's narrow enough so you wouldn't have to climb up to work on me. And I meant it when I said I would behave."

She laughed again. "I am not convinced I can trust you, but I am willing to give you the benefit of the doubt. I must warn you, however: I never go anywhere without my Mace. And by the way, I charge $75 for house calls."

"All right!" he nearly shouted, ecstatic at the prospect of seeing her at home, and added, "You won't need the Mace. The higher fee is no problem."

He gave her his address. Instructions on how to get to his house where not necessary, she told him.

He was jubilant; his lethargy and bouts of despondency magically evaporated. The Towers decision receded to the back of his mind and the memories of Apries that had been preoccupying him lost their significance. He finally had something exciting to look forward to. He had 24 long hours in which to get his house ready for a visitor.

*   *   *

He woke up early the next morning; could not fall back asleep. He tossed restlessly for a while before getting up and having breakfast. He knew it was ridiculous at his age, but he was so excited about seeing Ruth again that time stood still. He was as antsy as a teenager waiting for his first date. He would look up from whatever he was doing and discover no more than five or ten minutes had passed. He tried reading but could not keep his mind focused.

An extended walk along the coast took two hours off the clock. A leisurely lunch consumed another couple of hours. He vacuumed the floor for an hour.

He hoped he could convince Ruth to stay for a cup of coffee after the massage. If he could, it would be nice to have some cookies available. He went shopping and while at it, added what could be turned into a simple dinner. He surmised a four o'clock appointment probably meant he was the last customer of the day. Maybe he should invite her to stay for dinner.

He felt ten years younger again. He couldn't remember the last time he had so much looked forward to something—anything. It was completely unjustified; risky, in fact, in that he was setting himself up for a disappointment. He knew his eager anticipation was a symptom of how boring his life had become. How could the thought of a massage in the privacy of his house inspire such happiness in him? And why? Was it the massage, or was it Ruth; the thought of being alone with her in his house? Or the surely futile hope something above and beyond a massage would be given?

He immersed himself in these idle ruminations. He thought about what he should wear when she arrived. His street clothes? Just his robe, so she could go to work immediately? What might his neighbors think if they saw him opening his door to an attractive young lady? He was not in the habit of worrying about what they thought, and yet such a greeting could be embarrassing. More for Ruth than for him.

His doorbell rang. Right on time. He got up to open the door, his heart racing. He had decided his street clothes would be just fine; jeans and polo shirt, flip-flops on his bare feet.

"Nice house," Ruth commented when they had greeted each other and were standing in the foyer, with her looking around. She was carrying a rather large basket with what he assumed were the tools of her trade and wore a short white nurse's smock over her jeans and shirt, its sleeves rolled halfway up her arms.

"It is, isn't it?" he agreed, seeing no need for false modesty. "Would you like to come in and take a look around? The view is really quite magnificent." He did not wait for her to respond and walked towards the living room with its spectacular view of the ocean. She followed him.

If she was awed, she did not show it. "Yes," she said drily, "almost as nice as the view of the border I have from my apartment in National City."

He knew she was joking, but her voice was so neutral, so lacking in irony, that he wasn't sure.

It suddenly occurred to him he was being stupid, careless, in showing her the opulence of his surroundings. He did not know her, after all, and had no idea in which circles she moved. To her, based on what he was allowing her to see, he must seem very rich indeed. Who knew what ideas this might give her? Burglaries had always been a problem in the area and common sense should have made him more cautious with this very nice stranger. All he knew about her was that she gave an excellent massage. And that he liked her.

"Well," he said after his carelessness had dawned on him, too late, "I guess I should show you where you can massage me."

He led her into his guest bedroom. Its furnishings were sparse; the room seldom used since Caitlin had dropped out of Veronica's and his life years ago. It had twin beds, about two feet apart, a chest of drawers and a small closet. A second door led into the utilitarian bathroom, where he had hung his robe.

"It's not ideal," she pointed out. "The bed is too low and that's bad for my back. But I guess it will have to do. Why don't you go change so I can get started?"

He nodded, stepped into the bathroom and closed the door. It took only moments for him to get undressed and slip into his robe.

She had turned the bed down and spread a large towel over the sheet when he emerged. Another towel was in her hands. A tentative smile played around her mouth. She really is very attractive, Shad thought. He had always been partial to dark complexioned, smooth skinned women with black hair and exotic, slightly almond shaped deep brown eyes.

"You know the drill," she said. "Please lie down on your stomach."

He took off his robe, and when she saw he was naked again, she groaned. "Not again!" she said. "I thought you had promised to behave."

"I did and I will. I keep my promises, but a massage just wouldn't feel right if I were not nude."

She made some indefinable noise. Maybe resignation; maybe inevitability. When he had stretched out, his head turned sideways so he could breathe, she draped the second towel over his behind and set to work.

The massage oil she dribbled on his back made him shiver involuntarily.

"So when are you going to move into the Towers?" she asked after a while, her hands kneading his back, apparently unaware of the effect she was having on him.

"I am still hesitating," he admitted. "I think I told you I paid the deposit, but I just can't wrap my mind around moving into a little apartment."

"I thought the apartments there were large."

"They are, but it's all relative, isn't it? It is large—about 2300 square feet, but compared to what I have now, it's small. And with its low ceilings it feels a little stifling. Almost claustrophobic."

Silence met him. Her hands continued their task. Her fingers felt warm and indescribably intimate as they moved over his back.

"How come you are so silent all of a sudden?" he asked minutes later. He felt mellow; content.

He could sense her shrugging. "I was just wondering what it would be like to be so well off you can be unhappy at the thought of living in an apartment with *only* 2300 square feet. You should see my place. It's not even half as large, and yet I consider myself lucky. And I don't have the terrace or ocean view you would have in the Towers."

"I am sorry," he said quickly. "I didn't mean that the way it sounded. Believe me, I am grateful for what I have and appreciate it every day. I haven't always lived this luxuriously. I know I am fortunate and no doubt spoiled. But I am used to my surroundings here. It's home and the thought of a smaller apartment is just not that appealing to me."

He could see she was shaking her head. She must have known he was financially sound or he would not have been thinking of buying into the expensive Towers, but hearing what it meant practically must have made her envious. It had to remind her of what she would presumably never have. Or maybe it just made her aware of the differences between his and her lifestyles.

"If it's of any solace to you, Ruth, let me tell you I am not a happy person, despite the way I can afford to live."

"Then there must be something seriously wrong with you. You think you could be happier living the way I do? Just let me know. We can trade anytime. I think you are completely out of touch with reality."

It made Shad cringe. "No thanks. I am not interested in living with your boyfriend," he joked, covering for his discomfort.

"Ha, ha, ha! Very funny," she said and pushed her hands harder into his muscles. "You know exactly what I meant. Besides, how do you know my boyfriend lives with me?"

"I don't. I just assumed. Anyway, aren't you happy?"

He saw her shrug once more. She kept the pressure of her hands up and he felt his groin tingling. He was eager for her to remove the towel covering his butt. He wanted to feel her hands down there. He squirmed, trying to get unobtrusively more comfortable with his developing erection. She ignored what he was doing.

"I don't really think that much about it, I guess. I'm okay. I usually like my job. I make enough money to pay the bills. I meet lots of interesting people. I have a bunch of friends. I live close to my kids and see them regularly. I have a boyfriend. What more could I want?"

"Happiness?" he hazarded. "You don't sound as if you were."

"I don't really give it that much thought."

"How many kids do you have?"

"Two, and a baby granddaughter from my son. I used to be married."

"You are a grandmother already? I don't believe it!" He really couldn't.

"Don't you know what we Mexicans are like?" she asked, a note of bitterness barely suppressed. "We become sexually active early and don't have enough common sense not to get pregnant. That was me before I wised up. But at least the father of my children married me, even if it didn't last."

He wasn't sure whether she was being sarcastic or making fun of him or wrongly assumed he harbored biases against Mexicans.

"I still can't believe you are a grandmother," he reiterated. "You look much too young."

"Thanks! But I don't mind telling you I am forty four. I got pregnant for the first time while I was still in high school. After I graduated we married and I had my second kid."

"That I never would have thought," he said and hastily added, "I mean your age. You look at least six or seven years younger. When I first saw you I thought you were in your mid thirties."

"Don't I wish!" she exclaimed. Then, after a short pause, she added, "That's not really true. I don't have any trouble with my age."

"I would hope not. Look at me. I'm sixty eight already."

"Well, your age doesn't seem to affect your virility yet," she said drily. "If Pfizer depended on you for sales of Viagra they would be starving to death."

She had pulled the towel from his behind over his shoulders and had seen the effect her ministrations had had. He wanted her to touch him, even if inadvertently.

"Not a subject I want to talk about, Ruth, or it might become too difficult for me to keep my promise."

She laughed. "Maybe I should test your resolve. See how much willpower you actually have."

"Go ahead!" he encouraged her.

To his surprise, she did, but barely. He felt her hands between his upper thighs, barely below his butt, her thumbs like feathers on his shaft. She stroked his erection ever so lightly, a thoroughly titillating sensation.

He waited for more, but nothing happened.

"No, it wouldn't be fair of me to raise your expectations and then disappoint you."

"I don't believe you could do that, no matter what you did or didn't do. That little tenderness alone with your thumbs already made me feel good. But don't do anything you don't want to do. I would love it if you played with me, but not if you did it just because you thought I was expecting it."

She didn't respond. He was glad when she told him to turn over so that he could see her. He caught her unawares, looking thoughtfully at what she had caused.

"Tell me," he said, "are you ever tempted to go beyond giving a legitimate massage?"

She shrugged. "Not really tempted. Sure, once in a while I give a massage to some young, good looking guy and like what I see. I like sex and enjoy seeing a beautiful cock as much as you must like seeing a woman's tits. I have fantasized when seeing a man's tent pole sticking up, but that's only natural, isn't it? But it's no problem for me not to react. I focus on doing my job and ignore how attractive or ugly my customer is. Besides, I already told you, my clients are never completely nude, so I don't get to see what they have."

"And your boyfriend? Do you share those fantasies with him? Does he mind you seeing more or less naked men every day?"

"I just told you my clients are not nude. I insist they always wear shorts or panties, as the case may be, and I keep them draped except for the body part I am massaging. I don't know why I let you get away with undressing completely," she said, frowning. "Especially here in your house. I must be nuts."

"Because you like me? Find me attractive? Make you fantasize?" he ventured, leering suggestively and exaggerating so she had to know he was joking.

She studied him quizzically. "You aren't really serious, are you?"

"Of course not. I was kidding. But *I* do like *you*—a lot, and I think you sense that and as a result you let me get away with it."

"Hmmm. Well, anyway, you are right when you suspect my boyfriend isn't always thrilled by my work. It's actually quite ironic because that's how we met: through my job. He had suffered a work injury; problems with his back. I was still working in National City and he came for a series of therapeutic massages. I guess I let my guard down when he started flirting with me, and eventually we wound up in bed together."

"Lucky guy. In a way I like hearing you say that, because it tells me you are not completely immune to temptations. Since you let it happen once, maybe you will do so again."

"Don't hold your breath. You seem like a nice guy, but I am not even remotely tempted."

"That's okay. My time will come, I hope, and I can hold my breath for a long time."

"Yeah, well, they say hope is the last thing you lose as you get older. Anyway, it's really funny with my boyfriend. He can get jealous and mad at me, but when he does, I can calm him down quickly by sharing some imaginary dirty fantasy. That gets him so excited we wind up in bed or on the floor or wherever."

"I envy him," Shad sighed. "I think if I were your boyfriend, I would pretend to get jealous every day and let you soothe me."

"Then it would become so repetitive as to be boring."

"Hard to imagine. Does it get boring for your boyfriend?"

"You sure ask a lot of questions!" she consternated. "What's up with that? Are you playing games with me?" Suspicion was in her voice.

"Not at all. I just want to get to know you better."

"You already know more than enough, considering I am only here to massage you."

"Sure, but isn't it fun to talk while you work? Besides, you didn't answer my question about your boyfriend getting bored."

"I don't know. Maybe he does. He is younger than me and it's beginning to show. He gets mad at me more and more often. Not just about my work. He's a fireman and works shifts, so sometimes we don't see much of each other. When we do, we lately often argue and fight, and I have to work harder and harder at distracting him. But I am often so tired at the end of the day I just don't feel like making the effort. His sexual demands are becoming more outlandish and he gets mad when I don't go along with what he has in mind. Sometimes it's almost like he is raping me, and I don't like it. Maybe he is getting tired of me or has found another, younger lover."

"How old is he?"

"Thirty seven."

"Seven years don't seem like such a huge age difference," Shad said.

"Maybe not, but psychologically it's getting bigger all the time, and there is quite a difference between a man being seven years younger, rather than the other way around. When we met, he was thirty. Age was not an issue. Now it is. He has kindly pointed out to me a woman reaches her sexual peak in her mid to late thirties. He gives me to understand I am already over the hill, which isn't true. I enjoy sex today just as much as five or ten years ago, and am probably better at it than I was back then. But the age factor is there and who knows what will happen a few more years down the road?"

"I don't know," Shad admitted. "I have never had an older girlfriend. I can imagine where age could become a problem if the gap is too great.

But I think you are much too young to have to worry about that. If you have problems with your boyfriend after living with him for seven years, I think there are other causes than the age factor."

Ruth took the towel off and he was glad their discussion had served to diminish his arousal. She was pensive and paid no attention to him as he put his robe back on.

"How do you feel now?" she asked automatically.

"Very good. I really liked you testing my resolve."

She grinned back at him. "I was almost a little disappointed you didn't try to get me to do more. I was expecting you to encourage me or reach out for me or make a grab for my tits."

"Don't think I was not tempted, but I remembered the Mace you carry around."

"Oh, good. I was afraid I had lost my touch."

"No, but I am a person who keeps his promises. It had nothing to do with you. And if we don't change subjects I might try to make up for lost opportunities. Now that you are done I am no longer bound by my promise, right?"

This time she laughed outright. "I am glad you haven't changed. I was getting worried about you."

He was relieved she had not reacted negatively. "You don't have to worry. I want you to give me more massages and don't want to have to specifically promise to behave. Just think, you might pick up some fantasies to share with your boyfriend," he said and smiled, "and if you couldn't, maybe I could relate some of mine to you."

"I wouldn't do that," she said, and he didn't know what she meant. Not talk about hers? Not have any? Not want to hear his?

"You didn't answer my question," he reminded her.

"What question? Let's just see what will happen. Don't push me, okay?"

This sounded promising to Shad. Instead of slamming the door in his face, she had opened it marginally wider, and the thought of what he hoped she had implied electrified him. As she stood there, her arms crossed over her breasts, a slight sheen of perspiration on her brow, her lips sensuously parted, looking at him with an expression he could not interpret, he was severely tempted to hug her. He refrained.

"Listen, Ruth, I assume this was your last appointment of the day. How about a cup of coffee or tea before you leave?"

He could see the wheels turning in her head as she debated with herself. "Okay," she finally relented, "if it isn't too much trouble. I could actually use a cup of coffee. It's been a long day. But I don't want to have to be on my guard. You have to promise to behave."

He shrugged philosophically. A small price to pay. She had raised his hopes. He was willing to be patient. He went to get dressed while she gathered her things into her basket.

It took him only a few minutes to brew coffee and put cookies on a tray. He watched her through the open niche of the kitchen as she wandered around his living room, studying his souvenirs from his travels.

"Where are you going to put all this stuff when you move into the Towers?" she wanted to know when he joined her.

"You mean *if* I move. I have no idea. It's one of the problems I am facing. I am very attached to many of these things; each one holds a memory for me. I couldn't take them all."

"I don't want to sound presumptuous, but before you throw something out, maybe I could take the odd item off your hands?"

"Sure. No problem. I have also thought of eBay, but I don't really need the token money they might bring. Most of them aren't all that valuable to anyone but me. I would be delighted to let you have something you really like; what interests you."

"Oh, I don't know off hand. Maybe I could pick out something next time? I promise I won't be greedy!" She looked a little embarrassed. Perhaps she feared such gifts would be construed by Shad as obligating her?

She asked him about several items, and he told her how he had acquired them. She was genuinely interested and he found himself telling her about some of his trips and adventures. He didn't realize how much he was talking until he saw her glance at her watch. An hour had passed. The coffee was long gone. She started fidgeting.

"I'm sorry," he said, "I wasn't paying attention to the time. I shouldn't have talked so much, but you are a good listener. I hope I didn't bore you to death."

"Not at all, Shad. I love listening to you. It sounds like you have led an interesting life."

"I have. That's why it's so difficult for me to adjust to not having anything meaningful to do. I spend too much time alone, so when

I get a captive audience—like with you today—I can't seem to stop talking."

"Don't worry. I enjoyed it very much. It's all so exciting compared to the boring life I have had. Maybe you could share some more anecdotes with me when I come the next time?"

"I would love to. I spent a lot of time in Iran when I was in the Army. That was obviously long ago, but considering what is happening in the Middle East these days, perhaps you would like to hear a little of what I saw there."

"That would be great! I am sorry I have to run now. I hadn't planned on staying so long."

As he led her to the door, Shad draped an arm loosely around her shoulders. She didn't object. "I hope you don't get into trouble for being, so late."

She smiled at him. "Don't worry," she said.

When he pulled her against him before opening the door she didn't resist and quickly reciprocated his embrace. As he watched her leave he felt very happy.

He was attracted to her. He had to remind himself that he was a generation her senior. Was he an old fool, dreaming as he did? It wasn't just her looks or body he found so appealing. She had a good sense of humor and he admired the way she had inoffensively fended off his innuendos. She had poise and maturity and was easy to talk to. He imagined she liked him a little as well. He hoped he was right and that she did not have ulterior motives. His obvious wealth and availability could well be considerations for her, he reminded himself. But he wasn't sure he cared. He had been alone too long already, and her relaxed companionship elated him.

He thought about what effect his having met Ruth could have on his contemplated move into the Towers. If they were to develop a closer friendship, would she be a reason not to move? She definitely did not make his decision any easier.

21

Beijing, 1987

Shad scanned the crowd outside the terminal, searching for Apries as he left the Beijing airport arrival hall. Their friendly debate about who would recognize whom more quickly was on his mind. He had felt confident he would win. The confusingly similarly dressed multitude confounded him. Everyone was in heavy winter clothes, collars turned up against the cold, and with scarves and caps hiding much of their faces. He began to wonder if she had actually come to meet his flight when he could not find her.

He had learned when meeting someone under such chaotic circumstances it was best not to move around. It was too easy to miss each other if both parties walked around, searching. Therefore he stood still, waiting for her to find him. He would stand out more than she would.

"You did not recognize me!" She suddenly stood beside him, hugging him.

"Of course I did," he assured her straight faced. "I just pretended I could not see you because I wanted to know if *you* would recognize *me* again."

"Bullshit! You couldn't have seen me. I was hiding."

"That's not fair," he said as he put his hand under her chin to turn her mouth up to be kissed.

"I know. I just wanted to have some fun with you," she mumbled against his mouth. "Did you think I wouldn't be here when you couldn't see me?"

"No," he said. "I knew you would come, and if you hadn't hidden, I would have spotted you immediately. You can't believe how happy I am to see you again, Apries."

"No more than I am to see you. You were gone so long. I missed you."

"Let's go to the car. I am freezing." Despite his overcoat, the winter air made him shiver. Patches of dirty snow covered the open area beyond the road, and slush and ice made for hazardous walking. A dreary, heavy cloud cover obscured the sky. More snow looked imminent. He wondered if Beijing ever had clear skies.

The driver of the hotel car she had arranged had kept the engine running and the warmth felt good when they sat down. She unwrapped the heavy scarf from around her neck and took off her padded jacket, then helped him shrug out of his overcoat. He put his arm around her and pulled her closer. He could feel her trembling.

"What's the matter?"

"Nothing. Maybe I stood too long in the cold. Or maybe I am just so excited at finally being with you again."

Her lips were still cold when he kissed her again.

"I want to caress you," he said, "but my hands are so cold I am afraid you would scream if I did."

She laughed. "I know how to warm them," she said and took his right hand and put it between her thighs, up against her crotch, and squeezed her legs together. He could feel her heat. She did not object to the coldness of his hand.

"It feels good," she said, as if reading his thoughts. Her legs held his hand captive. "I am so hot down there. I think my pussy must be on fire. Can you please help me put it out?" The hunger in her eyes was unmistakable.

"Gladly. As soon as we get to the hotel."

"I don't want to wait. If you are worried about the driver, don't be. He is totally discreet and won't mind."

She spread her legs and pulled her skirt up higher, showing him her naked thighs and skimpy panties. He glanced toward the driver. His eyes were resolutely focused on the road.

Shad was tempted. Not only was she obviously more than ready for him, he wanted her badly. The very thought of doing it with her in the hotel car, weaving through traffic and subject to being stopped by an alert policeman, was strangely thrilling. And yet he couldn't bring himself to fulfill her wish. Maybe if they had been anywhere else but in China, he would not have been able to resist. As it was, he was scared of what would happen if they were to get caught. He could already see himself languishing in a Chinese prison for public lewdness.

"You don't want me anymore?" she asked plaintively when he did not react to her offer.

"It's not that, Apries, and you know it. It's just too dangerous here in the car. We'll be in the hotel in a few more minutes and have the rest of the day and all night." To underline his words, he pulled his hand back.

She pouted. She did not share his concerns. Whatever they might do in the car would only be a prelude; had nothing to do with what would come. She was ready to sit on his lap. She was not afraid of the police. She was not willing to give up so easily. She reached down and pulled her panties aside and started playing with herself. He stared, mesmerized. Her tongue moved lasciviously over her lips. He had to sit on his hands to keep himself from touching her. He worried the driver could see what she was doing. He reached over and pulled her skirt over her busy hand.

"You don't like watching me?" she asked archly, a lewd grin playing around her lips.

"I love watching you. I could do it for hours. But I don't want the driver to see you."

"Why not? It would excite me even more, I think," she admitted, and continued masturbating until she suddenly shuddered violently. She closed her legs and leaned back against the seat, very much relaxed.

Shad could only shake his head. He realized how little he knew about Apries. Although already having seen how open and direct she was, this exhibitionism was more than he had imagined possible.

He should have gone to the hotel by himself and met her there. Much as he wanted her, he was struck by guilt. When she had left him the last time to go back to Alan, he had been shocked by the ease with which she had jumped from one bed into another. Now he was on the verge of doing the same thing. Only the long flight separated him from the last time he had been with Veronica, and here he was, lusting after Apries and ready to go to bed with her as soon as they reached the hotel. He was powerless to stop, despite his earlier resolve not to continue this relationship. Was he not all that different from her? No. Not really. His weakness disgusted him.

Apries strode purposefully by his side as they entered the hotel and took the elevator to the executive floor. A moment of mutual embarrassment ensued when the receptionist inquired whether they were checking in together.

Apries saved them. "No," she said. "I will be translating for Mr. Cooper and had to meet him at the airport. I will wait in the lounge while he unpacks and freshens up."

Shad breathed a sigh of relief. So did the girl doing the check-in.

He had barely reached his room when a knock sounded on his door. It was Apries. He gathered her in his arms and asked, "What happened?"

"I went in the lounge and watched reception. When the girl left I came to your room. I saw your room number when she wrote it down for you."

She started to take off his clothes. "Wait a minute," he said, "my bag is going to be brought up any minute."

She stopped with undisguised reluctance. "Bad planning, Shad!" she said with a toss of her hair and stomped into the bathroom and closed the door.

Moments later, when the bellhop had left, the bathroom door opened and Apries emerged. She was smiling and naked. She was impatient and gave him everything and more he had fantasized about, and his earlier, troubling thoughts were forgotten.

$$* \quad * \quad *$$

Apries finally allowed him to take a long nap. Afterwards he insisted they go downstairs for dinner. He knew he needed a break. And he was ravenously hungry.

They lingered in the restaurant after they had eaten. He felt drained, and yet one look at Apries sitting across from him, her face relaxed, her eyes deep pools of happiness, her lips moist and slightly parted, and he felt his body responding. He stalled; wanted to talk. Wanted to get to know *her*, the person who lived and breathed and had a history, rather than just as the woman who knew no boundaries when it came to sex and was perennially insatiable.

"I remember Alan mentioning you had a degree in entomology, Apries. What made you study such an unusual subject and then not use it?"

She shrugged dismissively. "No particular reason. I did not know what I wanted to study, and some friend suggested I go into this bug business. I was actually quite a good student, but do you know how many job openings there are for an entomologist in China?"

"Not too many?"

"That's right. Only zoos and universities hire them and neither one interested me in the least. I found out I liked working with people a lot better than with bugs, so I thought I would try my hand at translating. My English was pretty good and China has a great demand for translators. This accidentally led to some tour guiding through people for whom I had translated."

"But surely you must have learned English someplace other than just the university. You speak it so fluently, including slang and idioms, and you have an American accent."

She hesitated. "I am not sure I should explain, but you are bound to find out sooner or later anyway."

"That sounds rather mysterious."

"Good. That's what I want to be for you. A mystery. A riddle you will never solve. But before I tell you about my English, I have to warn you: You must always remember that when I tell the truth, I lie. And when I lie, I tell the truth."

He sat up straight, thinking she was toying with him. "Huh? Are you serious?"

"Absolutely."

"I am afraid I do not understand. That makes no sense at all. It's a complete contradiction. What are you telling me?"

"I can't explain because you would not know whether I am telling you the truth or am lying. You have to accept me at face value. What you see is what you get. Isn't that what you say?"

He nodded. "Don't worry. I do accept you the way you are, but I also want to trust you when you say you are telling the truth. What should I think if you lie when you tell me the truth?"

"Poor Shad! Don't be so serious. I am messing with you. Can't you see that?" She was laughing at his confusion.

"Is that the truth or is it a lie?" he persisted.

"It does not matter. It is what you believe it is. You have to trust me no matter what I say, and then you can not go wrong." She was smiling sweetly at him, enjoying his utter bafflement.

"Okay, I give up. But you were going to tell me about your English."

She abruptly became so quiet he thought he had lost her. Her eyes had taken on a far away look. He waited patiently, thinking her inconsistency was part of her unique personality.

"I come from a very poor family," she finally said. "When I was still very young, maybe six or seven years old, I had to help my mother sell the stall food she had prepared at home and sold on the street. We made only pennies a day, and that was all we had. I hated it. But I did not hate it as much as when I had to start working in a whorehouse when I was only nine."

"You what?" he couldn't help exclaiming.

"I had to work in a whorehouse. Not as a prostitute, of course, but as what I think you call a gofer. If one of the girls or one of their customers wanted a drink, they would summon me and I would get them what they wanted. When a girl had finished with a customer, I had to bring fresh laundry to her room. I ran out for cigarettes. Sometimes go shopping for the girls. Change money for them with the Mama-san. Clean up. Escort customers back out. Whatever tasks the working girls didn't want to take care of themselves, I had to do."

"I don't believe it," was all he managed to say.

"What is there not to believe? Haven't you ever been with a prostitute and seen some kid running around, handling errands? As far as the work was concerned, it was not a bad job. I got many tips and most of the girls liked me and looked after me. What I hated, really loathed, was what I witnessed and the filthy atmosphere and despicable surroundings. Sometimes when customers were drunk they would be so mean and brutal I could have killed them."

"How could your parents have allowed that?" he asked in disbelief.

"I told you," she said, slightly exasperated. "We were very poor. We needed the money and there were no other jobs for me available which paid as well, and which allowed me to continue going to school during the day."

"Unbelievable. Didn't the authorities intervene? I thought prostitution was illegal in China, and then employing young children in one of those houses . . . that just seems like too much."

"Yes, it is illegal, but so what? The police get paid off and the girls are free of charge for them. You stay in business. No problem."

Shad didn't think he could still be shocked, but he was. He didn't know what to say. He realized how innocent he was and how different her world was from his own.

"Anyhow," she continued, "I wanted something more for myself and knew I could only get out from the life I had if I studied. Despite my night job I got decent grades in school. When I finished at age 17 with what you would call high school, I was accepted by a university. The problem I had was I had no money, and my parents obviously could not help me. I had to get a job; one paying me enough to study while leaving me with enough time to attend classes."

"Don't tell me . . ." he said, not liking where this was going.

She shook her head. "No, it's not what you are thinking. One of the prostitutes I had worked with as a young girl had taken a liking to me and stayed in touch. When I told her about my problem, but made it clear I was not willing to become a professional, she introduced me to the Mama-san of a bar catering to foreigners, where I was hired as a hostess."

"I am not sure I want to know what that means," he said. He thought he already did.

"Up to you," she said nonchalantly. When he remained quiet, she continued. "We hostesses were there to entertain. Like geishas in Japan. We received a commission on what our customers drank or bought us. I was one of the youngest and men loved a teenager who looked like a virgin. As a result I did quite well financially."

"And the customers were foreigners?"

"Yes, of course. We hardly ever saw someone who was not a *gweilo*. Not only Americans, obviously, but English was the common language, so if we wanted to keep them entertained, we had to speak the language. We couldn't get very far with the typical bar girl slang . . ."

"You mean like 'me like love you very much'. Stuff like that?"

"Yes. Besides, that would have sent the wrong message. Anyway, my English gradually became fluent. It also helped that I found a longer term boyfriend, a very nice American, who taught me a lot. Language wise, I mean," she said as she grinned rather lewdly.

He didn't want to hear about an old boyfriend. What she had told him was already more than he wanted to know. He was beginning to understand her behavior. "But there was no prostitution involved?"

"Not as such. A couple of rooms were available upstairs for emergencies, but the Mama-san did not encourage this. She didn't want to spend money on bribes. She made enough money with the bar. Nevertheless, if she knew a customer well enough and he insisted and the girl was willing, she would allow them to go upstairs. What happened more frequently was that a girl would take her customer to a booth if he pushed for more than a drink. She would close the curtain and give him a blow job. Mind you, no girl *had* to do that; it was strictly voluntary. The tips for this extra service were good, of course, and the girls could keep them. That Mama-san was happy with what she made off the drinks."

He was dumbfounded. He had suspected her wanton behavior and incredible expertise was no coincidence, but had not believed she had relevant professional experience. Now he understood why she was so fabulous in giving head. He was bitterly disappointed, and it must have shown on his face. He found it hard to believe her job had been limited to oral sex only.

"Did I shock you, Shad? You don't want me any more now?" She looked sad as she said this. "I shouldn't have told you."

"Yes and no. Yes, I *am* shocked. But I appreciate you being so open with me. And I still want you. Very much. It was almost ten years ago and you had to survive and get an education. I admire the fact you left that life behind you and have such a demanding job now. That transition must have been terribly difficult." Then he smiled. "Besides, I am now the beneficiary of what you learned in the bar."

"Believe it or not, I was highly selective in choosing customers. There were many evenings when I did not go into a booth."

He wondered what that meant, exactly. How often *had* she gone? How many customers had she taken in her mouth?

He was working hard at keeping a friendly grin on his face. "Is that the truth or is it a lie?"

She did not help him. "You decide."

He could not. "So you worked there the four years you attended university?"

"Almost. Towards the end, I got fired," she admitted, and he was surprised to see her smile somewhat wistfully at the memory.

"What happened?"

"The Mama-san was quite young herself and was married to a beautiful man. He liked me a lot, and I was attracted to him as well. So good looking! He spent a lot of time in the bar talking to Mama-san and the girls and helping out until the bar closed. Well, one evening the place was hopping and he got me to go upstairs with him. We thought Mama-san hadn't seen us, but of course she saw everything. I had just pulled my dress up and her husband was fucking me doggie style—my favorite position—when she burst into the room and caught us."

"Ouch!" he said, full of sympathy on one hand and amazed at her brazenness on the other.

"Ouch is right," she said. "Needless to say, I had to look for another job then. But you know what? Mama-san didn't hold a grudge. She blamed her husband more than me; she divorced him and we are still good friends. I still feel bad about what I did but it was soooo good."

Shad knew how *he* felt. He knew first hand how horny oral sex made her. She had admitted going upstairs with Mama-san's husband. There was no way he could have been the only one. But did it matter today, long after she had given up the life? He had not been joking when he had told her he was the beneficiary of her experience, and yet he could not help being jealous. How long had it taken her, and how many men had she had, to become so incredibly good? So unique? So wild and completely uninhibited? It also explained her outspokenness, her telling him so frankly what she wanted and how she wanted it. He wondered if there was more to her story than she had revealed.

"So you still see the Mama-san? In the bar?"

"Sure, why not? I only go there to visit her. You probably know the saying: You can take the girl out of the bar, but you can't take the bar out of the girl. That's me. I have to admit when I am there someone inevitably offers to buy me a drink. When I explain I don't work there and am not interested in more than talking, they are disappointed but accept it and I enjoy drinking and spending time there."

"Sounds kind of risky to me," he said, not at all happy at this revelation, harmless as she made it out to be. He was less than sure he could believe her.

"I see you don't believe me," she said, reading something in his eyes, "and you are right: I was lying."

"Meaning you were telling me the truth," he stated, and saw her smile in response. "Why are you smiling?"

"Because I am in a good mood and because I like being with you and talking. You are a good listener and it seems to me you are not passing judgment on me for what I did. I appreciate that very much. It shows me you are a good and understanding man. For some reason," she continued, "when I was telling you about going to the bar I remembered something and had to smile. I had this customer one time, a big, black American, and he had bought me several drinks before asking me to go into a booth with him. I had never seen a black man's cock, and I was curious. When he showed it to me and wanted me to take him in my mouth, I just couldn't do it. I was afraid of his size. He was huge; a monster. I had never seen anything like it. Had no idea anyone could have such a big tool. Probably very delicious, I thought and *was* tempted, but I just gave him a hand job. Sometimes I *still* think I should have done it because I keep wondering how he would have tasted. Maybe I would have liked it so much I would have screwed him. Just thinking about it now makes me horny."

"Well, isn't that nice?" Shad said, unable to keep the sarcasm out of his voice.

"Let's go back to your room, Shad." There was no doubt why she was suddenly in a hurry to leave, but he was reluctant. Having her think about a big black cock while he was making love to her did not appeal to him. How could she not mentally compare them?

They were still some ten steps away from his room, with her walking gaily in front of him, swaying her hips invitingly, when she suddenly took a quick look around, saw no one and pulled her skirt up around her waist and her panties down to her knees. She bent over and showed him her beautiful behind before reaching back with her hands and spreading her cheeks.

He was petrified. "Don't do that, Apries!" he almost shouted. "Don't you know they have security cameras everywhere around here? Security will be here in no time! Remember the last time?"

"Then you better hurry and open the door." He fumbled for his key while she tried to reach into his trousers to pull him out.

"Let me suck you out here in the hallway a little," she begged, but he pushed her aside, unlocked the door and quickly pulled her inside.

He couldn't believe she had started undressing in the hallway. What if someone had seen her exhibitionism? Were there no limits to what she would do?

Apparently not, he would find out.

Later, as they were lying in bed, recovering, he had to fight to stay awake. She had exhausted him. Jet lag was killing him. He needed sleep. He had appointments throughout the next day and would have to be able to concentrate. He got up to take a quick shower and kissed Apries good night before collapsing, barely conscious.

When he woke up he glanced at the alarm clock and saw it was only 4:00am. His eyes felt glued shut. It took him a moment to remember he was not alone, and that the mouth around his penis was not a dream. "Apries," he sighed, "I am dead. I have to work tomorrow."

"Me too," she mumbled, her mouth full, and resumed doing what she did so well. "Don't worry," she said the next time she took a breath, "I will leave you alone tomorrow. Go back to sleep please. I will be finished in a minute." He thought she had told the truth, which meant she had lied, and indeed it took longer than a minute before he fell back asleep.

*   *   *

If he had thought he could get up the next morning, shower, have a leisurely breakfast and then meet Ning Chang in the lobby, he was sadly mistaken. Apries would not let him shower alone. She insisted on washing him, and when he stepped out of the shower with her and she started tenderly drying his legs, her mouth moved up and he found himself between her parted lips again.

Her insatiability left him with hardly enough time for a quick bite and a coffee in the lounge before dashing downstairs to look for Ning. He was afraid she would be able to see immediately what a night he had had. He wondered how he could stay awake during the day.

To his relief, Ning was as impervious to his haggard appearance as she was to good food. She greeted him curtly and ushered him out to the waiting car.

"I have arranged a full program for you today, Shad," she said when they were on their way. "I hope you didn't make any other plans."

"No, I didn't. Are you going to be available tomorrow as well, Ning? I have appointments at the 402 and if you can't come with me I will need an interpreter."

"I should be free," she said, "but worst case, I can send Christina with you. She knows her way around now. You know her English is not too bad."

He didn't know whether or not to be disappointed. He remembered the pretty Christina well and wouldn't mind having her along, but he had hoped to have Apries translate, risky as her unpredictable behavior might be.

Upon entering Kang Ming's offices the ubiquitous tea was quickly served while Ning's staff was making small talk in broken English with Shad.

"If it's all right with you, Shad," Ning announced, "I thought it would be good if Christina gave you a run down on what we have learned since you left. Then we will discuss the terms of the draft contract you sent me after lunch."

"Sounds fine to me," Shad said, pleasantly surprised she had allowed time for lunch.

"Welcome, Mr. Cooper," Christina started out. "I am very pleased that I may talk to you this morning. If you have any questions please don't hesitate to interrupt me."

He only nodded his agreement.

"We selected six doctors in four different hospitals for the samples you sent us. Let me say up front we should have had many more. Everyone complained they needed more for a meaningful assessment."

"I understand what you are saying, but we were not looking for proof of efficacy. We already know they work."

"Yes, of course," Christina agreed quickly. "Perhaps I did not express myself well. I was referring to acceptance of the products and how they are perceived compared with what is already on the market."

"I see. And what did you learn?"

"As far as acceptance is concerned, both doctors and patients were satisfied. It was not clear, however, if the more generic ones worked better than what is currently being used. The initial results with *Melavict* look highly promising, but it is too soon, of course, to draw any conclusions, given the duration of melanoma treatment."

Christina went into more details; excruciatingly so. Shad had problems focusing. He wondered what Apries was doing; whether she was working and how she was feeling and what surprises she would have in store for him that evening. He caught himself shaking his head when he remembered the feats of sexual heroism she had elicited from him.

"You don't agree, Mr. Cooper?" Christina asked, a worried frown creeping over her face.

"No, no," he hastened to reassure her. "I am sorry. I was thinking of something else. Please continue."

She did and presented the pricing conclusions. It had been difficult to get the patients to pay the price Kang Ming had provisionally established. They were used to receiving local drugs with reimbursement through their workmen's insurance.

"We were not trying to make money off samples you provided free of charge," Ning interjected. "We simply felt that we had to ask for payment to determine if patients would be willing to pay the price we must charge once we start selling the products. I can tell you right now that based on the feedback we received, this will be a major stumbling block."

"Let me make sure I understand correctly," he said. "Is the problem that patients are not willing to pay for imported products when they can have local ones for free, or that the prices you wanted were too high?"

"Christina?" Ning said. "How would you answer that question?"

"I think it's a little of both. They are not used to paying anything out of their own pocket, but they believe foreign products are inherently better and would be willing to pay for them. But not the prices we wanted."

"How could we get our products on the reimbursement lists of the work combines?"

Christine looked to Ning for help. It was slow in coming. "It would be a long and tedious process, and money would have to change hands."

"Regardless of what price we wanted?" Shad asked.

"No. We would have to be much more reasonable. Probably no more than a 20% premium over comparable local products," Ning said.

"I think," Christina added, "we should forget about listing and simply establish a more affordable price. Many of the locally made competitive products are around one to two dollars, so even with the premium we could not make a profit."

Shad thought out loud. "What if we considered a multi-tier strategy? We could apply for reimbursement of one or two products; market a couple without reimbursement at a low price, and charge a profitable one for the balance. In other words, we would have to look at profitability of the whole line, rather than on an individual product basis. If we did this for, let's say, one year, we could make valid comparisons and decide what would be best long term."

This idea prompted a lengthy discussion in Chinese before Ning responded. "We think this is a good suggestion," she said, "subject to agreeing on which products we should be marketing under which scenario, and of course at which price you would sell us your so called low priced products."

"I can provide you with that information tomorrow. I need some time to analyze the range in light of our costs. Now then, if I gave you my recommendations tomorrow, could you provide me with a tentative sales forecast before I leave Beijing?"

"I think so," Ning said without consulting the people who would have to do the work.

Another hour was spent fine tuning strategic aspects before breaking for lunch. Then Ning took him into her office.

"It's a long and complicated agreement, Shad," she said as she tapped the pages of the contract in front of her. "Much more complicated than what I have with my other principals. I am not sure how comfortable I am with the wording."

"Is that a question?" he countered. "No, seriously, Ning, it's all boilerplate. We only have to agree on the few blanks in the document. If we agree on those, we will be fine. If you have questions as to the contract itself we would have to involve lawyers. Have you run this by yours' here? Or in San Francisco?"

She shook her head. "That would be unnecessarily expensive. If we start quibbling about wording now, we will never establish a solid working relationship. We need trust and respect mutual interests. I am eager to get started with your business and don't want to delay while the lawyers argue with each other."

"Makes sense to me," Shad said. "Talking about getting started, have you hired those sales reps yet?"

"Yes, they start on the first of the month. Christina is preparing a training course for them now."

"Good. Then why don't we see where we stand on the blanks of the agreement?"

They quickly resolved the issues of duration of the contract and termination notices, exclusivity, trademark and intellectual property right protection and ownership, liability, possible product recall procedures, expense reimbursements, inventory levels and margins for Kang Ming. More difficult to agree on was AmeriDerm's production requirement of receiving a six months rolling sales forecast, to make sure products could be supplied when ordered. The biggest sticking point was payment terms. Ning still wanted 180 days, patently unacceptable to Shad. The discussion became vociferous and unnecessarily personal when she accused him of being an insensitive, ignorant *gweilo* who cared little about the difficulties of doing business in China. She appeared close to tears.

Shad remembered what Dave Hardee had told him and finally reluctantly agreed on a compromise of 120 days. Equally reluctantly, Ning agreed. They had a deal.

Before he left Beijing for Hong Kong two days later, they had agreed on which product would be sold at what price, and Kang Ming's initial sales forecast was in his possession. This, together with his hospital visits, made him cautiously optimistic regarding their future business in China.

22

Hong Kong, 1987

Membership in the Mile High Club is free and confidential. Unless a member talks no one knows someone has joined, and there is no proof of membership. Total number of people belonging is unknown. Initiation is clearly defined, the act itself potentially dangerous, and tends to come about unexpectedly, as it did for Shad. While he had discussed it with Veronica when they had thought about taking a long flight together, and she had been as fascinated by the prospect as he was, nothing had come of it yet. It was the future; the flight to Hong Kong was now.

An hour into the flight, Shad excused himself to Apries when he had to use the rest room. He was about to close and lock the door when she squeezed in behind him. He wasn't totally surprised. Nothing she did could still surprise him. His heart was pounding and he glanced out furtively, hoping no one had seen her enter. He quickly locked the door.

Space was less than ample. By chance, they found themselves in a toilet equipped with a fold-down diaper changing table. Apries lowered the table. She did not appear to worry about it holding her weight. She pulled up her skirt and slid up on the edge of the table. She was not wearing panties. She drew him close and glued her lips to his mouth.

"Do it!" she whispered fiercely.

"I will," he said, "but I have to take a piss first." What a time to have to do it, he thought. He was already so hard it wasn't easy.

"Hurry up!"

When he was finished she managed to put her legs over his shoulders. She was ready for him, the awareness of where they were doing it lending excitement. The cubicle was tight and did not allow much movement, and he kept worrying the flimsy table would collapse under her weight. Or that a flight attendant would interrupt them. Maybe these concerns led to his feeling slightly disappointed when they had finished; he had expected something unusual from doing it up in the clouds; that it would feel radically different.

They made it safely back to their seats, apparently no one the wiser.

"Thank you for being so kind to me," she said and kissed him.

"Welcome to the Mile High Club!" He was grinning hugely, happily.

The evening before, in Beijing, Apries had been waiting for him in the hotel. She had drained him again. He felt confident she had not thought about the lost opportunity with her black customer from the bar. She had given him such a work out he was sure he had lost 10 pounds. He had been glad they would be flying and had thought it would give him a few much needed hours respite. He had not anticipated the interlude in the toilet.

"When were you in Hong Kong before, Apries?"

"About a year ago, with Alan." She did not elaborate.

"Maybe we should make some plans." He said. "Tell me, do you enjoy gambling?"

"I don't know. I have never done it. Why?"

"Well, I thought we could take the jetfoil over to Macao and visit a couple of casinos; maybe win a few dollars."

"It doesn't matter to me. If you want to go, it's fine with me. I just want to be with you. I would be perfectly content to stay in the hotel the whole time and order room service if we get hungry."

"You want to kill me, is that it?" he joked and smiled at her.

"Yes, with my love. I want to love you to death." She sounded serious.

"You are well on your way. You need to give me time to recover, or I will be of no use to you. I thought it would be fun to take in some sights; maybe go up to Victoria Peak for a late lunch or early dinner. Taking the funicular up to the peak and looking down on the city and across the harbor to Kowloon and seeing the lights come on is fascinating. Or we could go to dinner in one of the floating restaurants in Aberdeen. They are fun and a unique experience. I would also like to take you to a shopping center and see if we can find something you would like to have."

"As I said, whatever you want. You only have to leave enough time for us to make love," she said. "Isn't there a footpath all the way around the Peak?"

"Yes, but I think it gets a little lonely—almost scary—once it gets dark."

"Then I know what I want to do," she exclaimed. "I want to go up there when it's dark and we can stare at the Hong Kong and Kowloon lights while you fuck me."

"Are you crazy? Do you want us to get arrested? I am sure police patrol those paths all the time."

"Don't be so worried. We wouldn't have to get undressed. I will wear a skirt and no panties and you could just stand behind me and do it and no one would notice, even if they walked right by us." He could see the excitement sparkling in her eyes.

When he thought about it, he had to admit it *did* sound very enticing, despite—or because of—the danger of exposure. When he pictured being up there with her, having sex in public, he nearly squirmed with anticipation.

Upon landing Shad felt as if they had only been in the air for an hour, instead of three. He had not been able to nap, as he had hoped. Talking with Apries and the sex had made him lose track of time.

He was hungry and wanted to eat after they had checked into the Hilton; she wanted to have sex. She won. By the time she finally consented to have dinner with him several hours later he was starving and exhausted.

"Have you told your girlfriend about me yet?" Apries suddenly asked while they waited for their food to arrive.

"Why, no, of course not. I only admitted having been with a prostitute."

"Why didn't you tell her it was me? She wouldn't have to be jealous. You could have explained to her I am just a bad girl who will not take you away from her. Who only wants your money and that what you learn from me will make you a better lover for her."

"I think that would be a hard sell. I would get all tied up in knots if she started asking me how often we were together, and when, and how much I had to pay you. Then she would want to know how we met and whether I would see you again."

Apries shrugged, unconcerned. "You wouldn't have to tell her everything and she doesn't know how much a call girl in Beijing costs." She paused before adding: "But you know what? I would like to meet her. I think I would like her, based on what you have told me about her, and maybe she would like me as well once she realized I am not a threat to her. Just think if we could all get together and make love. Wouldn't it be wonderful? I have always fantasized about a woman going down on me, but have never found the right partner."

Shad nearly choked despite immediately thinking of Caitlin and Veronica taking him to bed. He was sure there was no way Veronica would tolerate sharing him with Apries.

"I don't believe that's likely to happen," he said drily.

"Too bad. We could all be so happy together."

"You never told Alan about us, did you?"

"Of course I did. Remember? But I don't know whether he believed me or not. He also knows that when I tell the truth, I lie, so he is confused."

"You are really something else, Apries," he said, shaking his head.

"I don't know what you mean."

"Sometimes I ask myself whether you are for real. What kind of a person you are. What drives you, and what you want. Besides sex, I mean," he said, and grinned.

"That's easy. I want a husband who loves me and accepts me the way I am. Who does not try to change me and understands me and makes me laugh and protects me and is not jealous and to whom I don't have to account for every minute of my time. And one who can satisfy me in bed every day or whenever or wherever I want him. Do you think that's asking for too much?"

"I don't know. I do know I would not qualify. I am very jealous. I would want to know where you are if you were not with me, because I would worry about you if you just disappeared. And I honestly don't know if I could have sex several times a day. On the other hand I would not try to change you; I would accept you the way you are. I know that sounds like a contradiction, but I really mean it."

"Good, because I am not like other girls. I am different," she said, as if he had not realized this yet. "But don't be worried. I am not interested in marrying you."

He did not know what to say; was not sure if it relieved or hurt him to hear her reject him as a candidate, even though he did not want to be one.

"Are you ready to go back to our room?" he asked, after he had asked for the bill and paid. "I need to get some sleep or I won't be worth shit tomorrow when I have to work."

She nodded and held his hand as they took the elevator from the Eagle's Nest back down to their floor. She had had a couple of glasses of wine with dinner and he was worried she would do something outrageous again before they reached their room. He knew she could lose control easily when she had had more than one drink, but she behaved.

He didn't get as much sleep as he needed, but what she gave him instead was well worth it.

*   *   *

"What are you going to do today while I am gone, Apries?" he asked the next morning while they were having breakfast in the executive lounge.

She shrugged. "I have no idea. I will think of something. Maybe I will just watch television."

He did not want to push it, knowing how sensitive she was about having to account for her time.

"I don't know what to tell Thomas if he invites me to dinner tonight or tomorrow. "I assume you would not want to come along?"

"Does he know I am here with you?"

"No. I saw no reason to tell him."

"Good. If you want to have dinner with him, go ahead." Her voice made it obvious she could not have cared less. "We will be alone this evening, won't we?"

"Yes. I will be back as soon as I can but it might be rather late. We have been friends too long and he is lonely these days."

He got up to retrieve his briefcase from their room, and when he returned some minutes later, ready to go to work, she was still at the breakfast table, studying a newspaper.

"Are you going to be in the room when I come back this evening?" he wanted to know. "Or where should I look for you?"

"I don't know yet. I may try to meet an old friend of mine, if he has time."

"I didn't know you had a friend here," he said, not very happy at this unexpected news.

She shrugged her shoulders dismissively. "I met him when he was in Beijing with some friends and I took them sightseeing. We liked each other and stayed loosely in touch. He is a nice guy, and I have not seen him recently. But don't worry. I am not going to fuck him, okay?"

"The thought never crossed my mind," he lied, making sure his eyes did not betray him.

If she had deliberately wanted to ruin his day, she had succeeded admirably. He could not think of anything anymore except her meeting this old friend and what they might do to celebrate their reunion. He wondered why she had not mentioned him before. He knew he had no rights, but he was seething nevertheless. Knowing her proclivity for sex, he was not at all convinced she would turn her friend down if he pushed her hard enough. And if she did let him, would he, Shad, be able to tell?

She gave no sign of having detected his change in mood. She raised her lips for a chaste good-bye kiss and told him, "One other thing I want to tell you. I feel a lot better after having told you my bad stories about my past. I love you and think maybe you love me a little too and understand how I am, and why. Thank you so much for listening to my silly stories."

He wanted to believe her.

He had barely reached the front entrance of the hotel when Thomas pulled up in his car.

"So how was Beijing?" Thomas asked after they had exchanged greetings and were heading towards Causeway Bay. "Have you made a decision on distribution?"

"Yes. I decided to give Kang Ming a chance. Much as I liked People's First, I just couldn't make myself take such a risk. Culture wise, I don't think they would have been a good match. We tend to be rather risk adverse, while they embrace risk and feel that if you don't take big ones, you can not win. I feel more comfortable with Kang Ming's slow but steady approach."

"Probably a wise choice, based on what I saw of AmeriDerm during my visit," Thomas said. "But I would caution you to monitor Ning Chang closely. She will test your patience, and unless you are tough with her from the outset, she will attempt to run all over you. Stay very much on top of what she is doing."

Once in Thomas' office, they reviewed the status of AmeriDerm's business in Hong Kong. The news was predominantly positive and Shad was able to relegate Apries to the back of his mind. He came to an agreement with Thomas to hire another fulltime salesman. They talked about whether it would make sense to cover Shenzhen and Guangzhou out of Hong Kong. Ning had the rights, but maybe he could pay her an override commission on sales in the economically strong south. She had no presence there whereas Thomas could send a sales rep from nearby Hong Kong.

It was only during lunch that Shad felt free to inquire how Thomas was coping with his loss of Jade.

"It varies," Thomas admitted. "I have good days and bad days. Between my work and the old boy's network here I generally don't have enough time to be depressed. I am always busy and get more invitations than I can possibly accept. But no matter where I go, eventually I return home to sleep alone, despite my friends' persistent efforts to fix me up with someone. That's when it hits me that Jade is gone. So I try to go home late, dead tired often after having had too much to drink to dull the pain. I try not to become morose or feel sorry for myself. Do you hear what I am saying?"

"I suppose. I can only guess as to how I would cope. Not as well as you seem to be doing, I suspect."

"Appearances can be deceiving. But anyway, overall I am doing okay. It also helps that I have taken a strong interest in that lovely secretary of yours, Pam," Thomas said, looking slightly embarrassed.

"Yes, I noticed she got your attention. Does this mean you will accept your new assignment in New York?"

Thomas grinned. "Yes. I have accepted and have also been in touch with Pam. She appears to reciprocate my interest in her."

"That's great, Thomas! I think it's the best thing that could happen to you."

"Yes, well, it is a bit of a challenge, of course, to nurture this mutual attraction over the great distance separating us."

"But you have thought about correcting this problem?"

"Quite a lot, actually. I am taking a week's vacation before New York and have made plans to visit Pam. If the time with her goes well I will try to persuade her to come to New York with me. I am sure she could find a good job there—especially with your good references, Shad."

"I don't believe it! Not only are you deserting me here in Hong Kong, but you are stealing my secretary!? And to top it off, you want me to give her good references? Pretty darn cheeky of you," Shad said and had to smile.

"Don't pretend you are all upset, Shad," Thomas said.

"Talking about Pam reminds me, Thomas. Where do you stand on buying a condo?"

"Well, I am seriously tempted. The only reason I am not rushing into it is that I want to give this friendship with Pam a chance to mature before committing to a significant down payment. But as long as I am going to be in La Jolla again soon, I plan on looking at what is available, and at what price."

"Just let me know if you want me to set up something with a reliable realtor for you."

Thomas nodded, looked at his watch and said, "I guess we better go on back. By the way, would you be terribly upset if I left you alone tomorrow evening? I do apologize for having to attend this horrible charity benefit gala. I could take you along, but I am afraid you would be bored out of your mind and might even be asked to make a generous contribution, as a presumably rich American businessman."

"Spare me," Shad pleaded. What a lucky break, he thought. He hoped Apries would be equally happy to learn he would be free.

*   *   *

Late the next afternoon Thomas took him back to the hotel. "Are you sure you will be all right?" he asked solicitously, and when Shad nodded, he added, "In that case, I will see you in La Jolla shortly. I will let you know exactly as soon as I have finalized my trip."

Whistling quietly, happily, Shad strode quickly to the elevators and up to his room. He fervently hoped Apries had returned from her afternoon meeting with her friend. The previous day she had been waiting impatiently for Shad when he had finally come back from his dinner with Thomas shortly after 9:00pm. Her friend had not been able to see her, she had explained.

Now, with the business part of his Hong Kong visit successfully concluded and the weekend ahead, he felt liberated and couldn't wait to take Apries in his arms. He wondered what delectable surprises she might have in store for him.

The first one he did not like at all. His room was empty; the bed undisturbed.

He frowned, but was not worried; he knew she was unpredictable when it came to the concept of time. He had not been able to tell her precisely when he would return. She most likely had not expected him back so soon. He changed into more casual attire and set out to find her. He looked in the executive lounge. No sign of her. He checked the lobby bar. He strolled through the many shops in the hotel. He thought she might not have waited for him to have dinner. But she was nowhere to be found.

He did not know what to do. He was getting worried and angry. Maybe, he fumed, she was having a leisurely dinner with her friend. Or maybe they were doing things he did not want to think about and had lost track of time.

He paced nervously up and down the lobby. Sat down and had a drink. Went up to the lounge and had two more. His hunger was gone, completely replaced by worry. Where could she be? He kept looking at his watch and when the lounge closed at nine, he walked back to his room. It was still empty. Thoughts of accidents entered his mind. He thought of calling the police, but what could he tell them? What if she had decided to stay with her unnamed friend? Her belongings were in his room; would she not have taken them along? What should he do now?

He was both mad at her and extremely concerned. He didn't know which was worse. His heart beat painfully fast; his chest constricted with his mixture of apprehension and anger. How could she be so insensitive and not let him know where she was, or when she would return?

After a while he took off his shoes and lied down in frustration, still dressed, his thoughts in turmoil. His alcohol consumption on an empty stomach soon caught up with him. He fell asleep.

Hours later he became dimly aware he was no longer alone. Apries was on her knees next to him, unbuttoning his clothes.

"Sssshhh . . ." she admonished him when she noticed he was about to say something and put a finger across his lips.

He was too groggy to fight with her. A glance at his beside clock showed it was after 1:00 o'clock. He could not recall when he had fallen asleep. He wanted to tell her how worried he had been. Wanted to ask her where she had been, but she did not give him a chance, disarming him by covering him with her body and taking him in her mouth and then loving him tenderly, straddling him.

Waking up dreary eyed and feeling grouchy on Saturday morning, he could barely recall the night. He had vague recollections of being used; of serving as her tool to achieve the satisfaction she craved. Or maybe it had been her way of trying to make up with him; a physical apology.

Now, with the light of a new day edging past the curtains of the windows, she was as cheerful as he was grumpy. He was aching for an argument and wanted to take her to task for having abandoned him the evening before. He was determined to vent his outrage, but she preempted him.

Still in bed, she snuggled against him and told him how sorry she was for coming back so late. Her hand cupped his face and she looked adoringly at him as she explained.

"I had too much to drink and lost track of time, Shad," she said. "When I met my friend, it was already late in the afternoon and he insisted we have a drink. I hadn't had much lunch, so I felt the whiskey immediately and that made me stupid enough to have another one. When he suggested we have dinner together, I could not refuse. Then he wanted to show me Wanchai, a bar he thought I would like. It must have been one of his regular hang outs because the moment we walked in, he was surrounded by friends. He left a couple of hours later, but I was a little drunk and having such a good time I decided to stay. There was dancing, and you know I cannot refuse when I hear music and someone asks me to dance. It was so much fun I never thought about the time. The men were all watching me; cheering me on. I put on a show for them, knowing what they were thinking as I gyrated provocatively on the dance floor. It was an incredible turn-on for me, I have to admit."

She kissed him and scooted over his body and started caressing him, obviously turned on again from relating her dance performance to him, and he was powerless to resist. His grumpiness dissipated and he gave in to the pleasure she provided, his recriminations forgotten.

Only later, as they were walking to the Macau Ferry Terminal, was he tempted to raise the question that had plagued him the night before. But questioning her fidelity was not something she would appreciate, he knew.

"Nothing happened last night, Shad," she volunteered, reading his mind. "Please believe me, okay? I love only you and would not do anything to hurt you."

"Are you sure?" he couldn't keep himself from asking.

"Yes. There were times when I was able to have sex without love and could not control myself. I used to be very weak and used men and pretended to love them, but it was just a physical thing. Emotionally meaningless. But not anymore. Now I love you and want only you, so please have pity on me."

He wondered how long ago she meant when she talked about her previous behavior, but he kept his mouth shut. She was in a good mood, and he wanted to keep it that way.

Her high spirits began to rub off on him and they talked about what he had planned for the day. He was looking forward to the jetfoil ride to Macau, where he had never been.

The more than one hour ride was not as exciting as he had anticipated. The water became choppy outside the sheltered harbor and the noise from the engines made conversation difficult. The sky was overcast and there was little to be seen, except the occasional distant island. He kept his arm around her shoulders as she snuggled against him.

He thought about what she had told him: that she loved him. It had been said so casually, but it had sounded sincere and he wondered how he felt about her. He intensely loved her body, the way she looked, her laughter and obvious intelligence, and certainly her uninhibited, direct nature and her sheer insatiable appetite for sex.

He was less certain of his feelings for her as a person. It was exhilarating to be with her. She was easy to talk to and her laughter was contagious. She was vulnerable and he admired the way she had escaped her past and had made something out of herself. Tough as she had proven to be, he had the impression she needed protection and positive re-enforcement and he liked feeling he was providing that for her. She was unpredictable to an extent he was not sure he could cope with longer term. He had to assume the previous night's events would be repeated and he knew he would suffer. Giving her space was one thing; having to constantly wonder whether she was being faithful or safe was another one entirely.

Inevitably, his thoughts turned to Veronica and how different she was. With her, it was the person he loved first of all, and all her other positive attributes only enhanced the love he felt for her. He tried to compare her with Apries and wondered how he would feel about Apries if he had met her before Veronica. Would he have fallen in love? He didn't know.

They docked in Macau and after having gone through immigration were undecided what to do. The skyline of the city itself indicated the heart of the enclave was too far away to reach by foot. They hopped into a waiting taxi. He told the driver to take them downtown and drive around to give them an impression of the colony. He was surprised how different it was from Hong Kong. The Portuguese heritage was quite evident in the ornate old buildings they passed; charming and rather quaint. Much more laid back and slow paced than Hong Kong. Casinos beckoned with their flickering, gaudy neon advertising.

Eventually they agreed to leave their cab and walk, soaking up the intoxicating atmosphere.

"What do you think?" he asked Apries, stopping abruptly, "should we go in there?" He pointed at a casino that reminded him of a royal palace. He could not explain why this particular one appealed more to him than the dozens they had already passed.

"Fine with me," she said. She sounded less than enthusiastic. "Do you think we can get something to eat in there? I am hungry."

"You are the one who can read the signs," he countered, "so why don't you check it out?"

She did and apparently satisfied with what she had learned, she told Shad there were three restaurants to choose from. "What do you prefer? Cantonese, Portuguese, or Continental?"

He knew what she wanted, so he opted for the Chinese.

Once they had eaten, they strolled through the various floors of the casino. The noise level was deafening with the predominantly Chinese gamblers shouting with glee or despair over winning or losing. Lights from the one armed bandits were flashing blindingly.

"Anything in particular you would like to try, Apries?"

She shrugged. "Not really. I don't know how to gamble."

He took her arm and led her to a row of roulette tables he had spotted. These he understood, whereas he was afraid of the unfamiliar table games.

She refused his offer of money with which to play. He felt he could not leave without having tried his luck a few times. The large bills being placed on numbers made him cautious and he restricted himself to only playing colors.

An hour later he was pleased to walk away with HK $150. "You brought me luck, Apries!"

"Of course," she agreed. "What did you expect?" She smiled up at him and gave him a hug.

"Are you sure you don't want to try?"

"I am sure. Let's go back. I have seen enough."

So had he and they found a cab to take them back to the ferry terminal.

They were both inexplicably tired upon their return to the hotel late in the afternoon, and after a quick shower decided to take a nap. At least he decided. She had different ideas. She prevailed. She coaxed him back to life.

In the evening, the ride up to Victoria Peak appealed much more to her than had their excursion to Macau. She was ecstatic about the view from the funicular as the car made its way slowly up the mountainside, passing within feet of the apartment blocks on both sides of the track.

The ever changing lights of Hong Kong Island shimmered below them as they emerged on the peak; a huge cruise ship on the Kowloon side was gaily illuminated by a string of white lights along its superstructure. It was breathtaking, and she thanked him for bringing her to this marvelously exciting place.

Apries said, "I want to go on the footpath around the peak."

She realized he could not find it in the dark and stopped someone to ask for directions. It was not far away and she led the way, holding his hand tightly. The path was nearly deserted and as they started walking it became even less populated.

She stopped. Aberdeen harbor lay below them, the shoreline in front of the floating restaurants teeming with people, a constant stream of small boats shuttling dinner guests from shore to restaurants and back.

On the path itself only the ambient light from the harbor provided minimal, ghostly illumination. She released his hand and stood facing the distant harbor, her hands propped on the rail fence running along the walkway.

"You know what I want," he barely heard her say, and when he sidled up behind her and put his hand under her skirt and moved it up her legs, he noted she had remembered not to wear panties. She was already wet and waiting. He was nervous, but not too nervous to comply with her wishes. He was unaware of their surroundings; aware only of how good she felt. Doing it illicitly, in public, with the risk of discovery, was exhilarating.

By the time they were back in the hotel, Shad was dead on his feet. Ready to collapse. But she would not let him. The Peak had not been enough for her; more like foreplay; she demanded a more thorough workout. After an hour he could do no more. She was still hungry and insisted he use his fingers until he fell asleep despite her strident pleas not to stop.

Hours later he woke up groggily. He fought his way out of unconsciousness. The room was dark. His mouth was parched; his limbs heavy. Something was wrong, he sensed, but it took time before he registered he was alone in bed. In the pale ambient light he discerned her pillow was still indented where she had slept, but Apries was gone.

His first thought was that she was already in the bathroom, but it was silent and dark, its door open. His last recollections of the night were blurry. He recalled her urging him on to keep stimulating her manually, but whatever might have happened thereafter refused to come into focus. It had been a glorious, wonderful day; their love making incredibly passionate and exceeding his wildest dreams. He felt so drained he was sure he would not need any more sex for the rest of his life.

He leaned against the doorframe of the empty bathroom and flipped a light switch. He tried to make sense of what his eyes told him. Her toiletries were gone. This made him turn around to check his room. He could not see anything that belonged to her. The closet was empty; her clothes and backpack gone.

As his eyes swept the room uncomprehendingly, he spotted an envelope propped up on the small desk in front of the window. He recognized his name and her handwriting. His hands were shaking uncontrollably as he reached for the envelope. It was not sealed. He was afraid to extract the sheets of paper he saw, covered with her meticulous handwriting. Sour bile rose in his throat as he unfolded the hotel stationary. The words swam before his eyes as he read.

> Dear my love Shad,
>
> I know this letter will hurt you, and I am sorry for that. Please believe me when I tell you that I love you very much, and always will. Our situation is hopeless, as I am sure you will agree, and I have to end it while I still have the strength to do so. I don't know how you really feel about me. I know you love fucking me, but there is more to me than that, and despite your assurances that you accept me the way I am, I don't think you can. No one can.
>
> I have been a stupid and naughty girl and have done bad things to Alan who loves me so much. I feel good about what you and I have done, but it was not the right thing for either of us. If our relationship were to continue it would become a big problem for us.
>
> When you fell asleep last night, I could not believe it. I felt like a failure. I could not sleep. We had such a beautiful day together, but for me, something was still missing. You had passed out; were useless to me; could not give me what I needed. I finally got up and took a taxi to Wanchai and the bar where I had been the night before. It was jumping, and I had the greatest time dancing. I realized this was something you would

never be able to understand or accept. I am not even sure I can understand it myself, but that's just how I am and always will be. How could you love a woman like me? Impossible. You will be so much happier living in your familiar surroundings with your bride and in the culture you know and embrace.

This is what I realized when I returned from the bar. You did not hear me leave; you did not hear me return. I thought about waiting for you to wake up so I could tell you this in person, but I was afraid I would change my mind; that I would not have the strength to go through with this decision if I had to look you in the eyes. So I packed my things, gave you a last kiss, and left. I will try to catch the first flight back to Beijing, but if this does not work, maybe I will call my friend here and see if he can look after me until I can leave.

Please do not try to find me. You would not know where to look. When you return to Beijing next time, you can call me and we can get together, if you want. I will always be there for you. You are the best lover I have ever had, but we have no future together beyond incredible sex, and both you and I need more than that over time.

I am a sensitive person, even if often stupid. When I am with you, I want you, but I need to be good to Alan and not do bad things to him anymore. If I say good bye to you now, remember I will always and forever keep the good memories of you. We can remain friends and occasional lovers. I also want to say thank you for what you have given and shown me, and for being such an understanding listener. I need not only a good lover but someone whose wife I can become and who needs more than sex from me. My eyes are full of tears. Can you please understand and forgive me?

I love you. I love you. I love you. Your sad Apries.

He started reading again from the beginning. As unbelievable as he found her message to be, there was no mistaking its contents. Irrationally he asked himself how she could have gotten up, left, returned, packed her belongings and departed again without him noticing anything. Could he really have slept through it all? Yes, he had been totally worn out; dead to the world.

By now he was awake enough to start thinking rationally. He read her letter a third time. It left no room for misinterpretation. He looked at his watch. It was barely 7:00 o'clock. It might not be too late to catch up with her. He dressed hurriedly and rushed downstairs to get a taxi to Kai Tek airport. He had no idea when the DragonAir early morning flight left for Beijing; he only knew he had to catch up with her. Even if she had decided to end their relationship, and even if he was unsure of how he felt about her, he was still responsible for her. After all, he had brought her to Hong Kong.

Nagging at the back of his mind were the stories she had told him about her suicide attempts. He didn't know whether she had actually tried, or how hard, but just the fact that she talked about it was reason enough for concern. But what could he do?

His search for her was hopeless. One flight to Beijing had already left. The airline refused to tell him whether she had been on board. She was not among the crowd of people lined up before the check-in counters. Without a boarding pass, he could not get to the departure area. Dejected and despondent, he was finally forced to give up. He did not want to think about her maybe having contacted her friend again and being with him.

23

La Jolla, 1987

Shad had never appreciated a long flight more than when he returned from Hong Kong. He needed time to reflect and digest this chapter of his life and its abrupt end. Hours of retrospection brought no relief and no answers.

Thinking about taking Veronica into his arms again made him acknowledge the truthfulness of Apries' good-bye letter, but it did not lessen the pain. He was devastated. He might not have been in love with her, but an emotional attachment was there. Part of it was a reflection of the incredible sex they had had, but it also related to her, the person. Her traumatic, unenviable background and complex personality had been hard to accept and he doubted he could have lived with her long term.

Could he have resisted the overpowering urge to try to change her behavior? Unlikely. Her free spirit was an integral part of her personality, and even if she would have given that up, how different would she have become? And he could not have changed her basic character. Changing her behavior was one thing; changing her character, developed over too many formative years and with too much emotional and physical damage was surely hopeless. Her past made her the woman she was.

His vanity had been severely wounded and still festered. Rejection was hard to take, especially considering their last days together. He had to remind himself how short their relationship had actually been; it felt more like years than months. But he had to admit she had solved a looming problem for him by exiting his life. How could he have continued with her while being engaged to and in love with Veronica?

Apries had been so right in telling him it was hopeless and needed to be stopped before it was too late. She had shown the strength he should have had.

And yet he felt sad. Demoralized and dejected. He struggled to accept that Apries was gone from his life. He thought about contacting her when he next visited Beijing but knew this would be emotional suicide. His physical longing for her was profound and as painful as a migraine that would not go away. Only her body could heal him, and this was not an option.

He was highly worried he would not be able to hide from Veronica the turmoil wracking him. He was sure his anguish would be evident. His face looked haggard. Deep lines of exhaustion circled his inflamed eyes. He debated endlessly with himself whether or not he should confess to Veronica but decided it would serve no useful purpose. If she were to ask, however, he would not lie. Maybe not share all of the more salacious details, but not deny having been unfaithful.

He brought Veronica up to date on Thomas's interest in Pam as they drove home from the airport and told her to expect Thomas to visit shortly and perhaps purchase a condo. She was delighted. "If it's not too soon," she said, "why don't we get married while they are here? Thomas could be your best man, and I would ask Caitlin to be my bridesmaid."

"Hmmm. Great idea, but wouldn't you be worried I might fantasize about her while going through the ceremony with you?" he teased her.

"You probably do that anyway. Besides, as long as you include me in those fantasies, I will be fine."

Looking at her, Shad marveled at her generosity and wondered how much time the two friends had spent together while he had been gone.

He called Thomas some days later, advised him of the planned wedding and asked him to be his best man.

"Nothing would please me more, Shad. Congratulations! I am so happy for you and Veronica, and I am glad you finally decided to go ahead and legalize your relationship."

"Yes, I think the time is right and I am looking forward to having you here. Do you want me to start looking around for some condos or will you leave this up to Pam?"

"Let's let Pam do it. I assume she could always call on you if she needed help or advice."

"Certainly," Shad assured him, and they spent a few more minutes catching up on business.

Shad left the planning of the wedding to Veronica. She had her heart set on getting married at Whale Point, a small grassy knoll between two beaches in La Jolla. It was to be a small ceremony, they agreed, with just family members and a few close friends attending. A party service was hired to provide chairs, flower decorations, music, mini pulpit and a small white gazebo under which their vows were to be exchanged. The Skyroom of the La Valencia Hotel, overlooking the famous Cove, was reserved for their subsequent reception, to be followed by a sumptuous sit down banquet. Thomas had been booked into the hotel with Pam.

The weather cooperated when the day arrived. Bright blue sky, with a mild breeze ruffling the radiant Veronica's flowing white wedding gown. The ocean was placid, with small waves gently curling towards the shore greeting them as they descended the stairs to the lush green lawn late in the afternoon. The normal contingent of several dozen spontaneous spectators were lined up on the sidewalk above them and applauded when they exchanged rings and he kissed the bride.

With Veronica on his right and Caitlin on his left, Shad was embraced by happiness and contentment as they sat down for dinner. The champagne toasts during the preceding reception had given him a slight buzz. Or maybe, he thought, it was just the excitement of having gotten married again. He was crazy about Veronica and couldn't wait to go home and consummate their marriage. He wondered if it would feel different somehow as husband and wife.

Glancing over to his side at Caitlin, he tried to imagine what she was thinking. The last time he had spent a night with her and Veronica was not that long ago. Did she remember it as vividly and as exciting as he did? Was she already picturing the next time? Would there even be a next time, now that he had married Veronica? He hoped so but didn't know how Veronica felt. These speculations prompted the memory of Apries confiding her dream of making love with Veronica and he shook his head to rid himself of the thought.

He saw Veronica deep in conversation with Thomas, her partner on her right, and turned towards Caitlin. Her deep décolleté could not be overlooked and he made no secret of his admiration.

"Does that turn you on, Shad?" she asked, catching his stare with a twinkle in her eyes. "Maybe I could join you when we leave here?"

"Not tonight, Caitlin. This night should belong to Veronica and me, don't you agree?" he said, but she had been right that he was lusting to have her join them.

She shrugged ever so slightly. "Up to you. You know what you will be missing."

He did indeed, but he didn't think he would need the extra stimulation this particular evening. He was sure there would be plenty of opportunities for the three of them to be together again to delight in what they all found so gratifying.

"Listen, Shad, it's really none of my business," Caitlin said, "but with your long stretches away from home, do you mind my asking what you do when you get really horny?"

"Try not to think about it. Masturbate, if it gets too bad."

"What about girls? There must be plenty of them available where you go."

Shad found himself squirming. He had no fundamental problems discussing his sex life with Caitlin after all they had done together and knew it would turn her on, but doing so now made him undeniably uncomfortable. What if she told Veronica before he could? It could well cause resentment.

"There are," he finally said, "but why don't we talk about that when the three of us are together the next time? It might even add a little spice, not that I need more when I have both you and Veronica."

"I hope not."

On the way home later that evening, he told Veronica about Caitlin's suggestion that she join them and that he had turned her down.

"I am glad you did," Veronica said. "As much as I love her and want to continue having the occasional threesome, I feel the same way you do: tonight belongs to us alone."

*   *   *

With Thomas visiting them, Veronica and Shad had agreed to forgo a honeymoon for the time being. He had promised to take her along on his next trip to China instead, stopping off in Hawaii on their return to celebrate a delayed honeymoon.

He had another reason for taking Veronica with him to China. He did not trust himself to go back to Beijing without trying to see Apries. He knew this would be wrong and felt by inviting Veronica to come with him, all temptations would be blocked. He knew Apries' idea of meeting Veronica was suicidal. No way could the two of them become friends, as Apries had hoped. Neither of the two women was the jealous type, but sparks would surely fly if they were to get together. Veronica would detect the history Shad shared with Apries.

Still, he could not get the thought out of his mind. He continued toying with this absolutely crazy idea. It would not be ideal to see the city on their own and Apries worked part time as a tour guide. Should he hire her to take them sightseeing? Wouldn't that be a wonderful opportunity for them to meet, without any preconceived ideas, and to find out how well they got along? And if they did, could he have the best of two worlds by substituting Apries for Caitlin in their triangle? He shivered with excitement at the fantasy.

He forced himself to concentrate on the workload facing him. Thomas used the occasion of his visit to try and convince him to start distribution in Taiwan and Korea. Thomas had commissioned some market research on the dermatological business in the two countries and would be happy to share the gathered data with Shad, he said, providing AmeriDerm would use Pan-Asia as their distributor.

"We know how to handle the biggest hurdle you will face in these countries," Thomas said.

"Which is?"

"Corruption. Both markets have an extensive network of private clinics, and you can not sell anything there unless the doctor benefits personally—financially."

"You mean through direct cash contributions?"

"That's the most popular method, but also providing free goods they can sell, sponsoring their travels, donating to family events like weddings, funerals, anniversaries or what have you, or underwriting so-called clinical studies."

"Sounds like a lot of fun, not to say minefield," Shad mused. "And if we worked with Pan-Asia, you could keep us from engaging in these nasty customs?"

"Yes. We know how to work our way through these obstacles, and you would simply pay us an appropriate commission. No one would question whether you grant us a 15%, 20%, or 25% distribution margin, and this would allow us to adhere to the prevailing business methodology."

It was a non-issue for Shad. He had enough experience working in Asia by now not to be shocked. Thomas had outlined reality and elucidated a way of AmeriDerm operating cleanly. Thomas' help had proven invaluable in China. Shad felt comfortable in agreeing to Thomas' proposal and spent an afternoon with him working out the details of their best course of action. Thomas would prepare the groundwork through his subsidiaries in Taipei and Seoul for a visit by Shad. He promised Shad to try and accompany him. In the meantime, Shad would begin to develop an appropriate business plan for management approval, based on the data Thomas had provided, while Thomas would calculate the margin he would need to handle both extraneous and actual expenses as well as to generate a reasonable profit.

"Would you have a couple of hours tomorrow to look at some condos with me that Pam has identified?" Thomas asked, changing subjects when they had concluded their business discussions.

"Sure. How about right after lunch?"

The three of them—Thomas, Pam, and Shad—set out the next day to look at the properties of interest and were able to quickly reject three of them. They agreed it was difficult to decide between the remaining two. What finally determined their choice was that Thomas' promotion had brought him a significant salary increase. This would allow him and Pam to keep the unit for their own use only.

Shad thought the two bedrooms/two baths penthouse condo was a good buy. Excellent location in the village itself, close to restaurants and shops and within a five minute walk of the ocean. It had been recently remodeled and offered state of the art appliances and décor, as well as an adequately sized balcony on its third floor location. If it had a drawback, it was the lack of an ocean view, but both Thomas and Pam were sure they could live with this shortcoming.

Their offer was accepted just before Thomas had to leave for New York and Veronica and Shad took Thomas and Pam out to dinner to celebrate.

Veronica put them on the spot. "So now that you will be La Jolla homeowners shortly, are you planning on living in sin, or do I hear wedding bells ringing?"

Shad saw Pam and Thomas glancing at each other. Thomas seemed slightly put out but recovered quickly. "We have talked about our future together, obviously, but I think it's a little too soon after Jade's death. It would not feel right to me to get married again so shortly after she passed away. Where we are right now is that we will move to New York and wait a few months to see how things shape up. Pam and I haven't really spent a lot of time together so far, you know."

"Makes sense to me," Shad said. "And if by chance the home office does not work out for you, maybe AmeriDerm could find a good job for you, and you could live here full time." He ignored the reference to their personal issues.

"Wouldn't that be something?" Thomas said, and Pam added, "I certainly wouldn't mind. Much as I am beginning to love Thomas, I hate the thought of living in New York."

Shad could tell from the thoughtful expression on Thomas's face that he had struck a nerve. He wondered if he had gone too far by voicing possible employment with AmeriDerm before having first discussed it with Dave Hardee. But then, it was unlikely to happen anyway. Thomas had been with Pan-Asia too long to change companies lightheartedly.

Thomas and Pam were eager to get back to their hotel; they had a morning flight to New York and wanted some time alone. Shad and Veronica went home for a night cap.

"I have been meaning to ask you, Shad, what you and Caitlin were talking about during our wedding dinner," Veronica suddenly asked as they were sitting on their terrace with a glass of wine, enjoying the balmy evening.

"Nothing much, actually. I told you she wanted to know if she could spend the night with us, and that I turned her down."

"I have the feeling, the way she was looking at you and you were staring at her boobs that more was said. Don't worry, okay? I am not trying to pry. You know how I feel about Caitlin. I was just curious, not jealous."

Shad debated with himself whether or not he should confide his sex life had come up and if so, how open he should be. He didn't know where this might lead. He had already regretted having told her about his transgressions in China before and the discussion it had prompted. And yet, Veronica had proven to be broadminded and understanding.

"It was quite harmless," he said. "She was curious how I cope with being away from you, without sex, for extended periods, when girls are readily available."

"And what did you tell her?"

"Nothing. None of her business, don't you think?"

"Not entirely. I think considering what the three of us have done together, she has some legitimate rights to know what you do, and with whom. Just like I do. Think of safe sex and all that stuff."

Shad thought of how to respond. She was right, of course, but how far should he go in enlightening her? Was it necessary to admit he had been with the same woman once again? That she had ended it? Should he shade the truth enough to be forthright without revealing how deeply he had been involved?

"So was that a question?" he said, stalling for time.

"Sure. I think both Caitlin and I should know whether you have been screwing around over there, and if yes, with whom."

"Well, before answering that, I want to remind you of what you told me before I started traveling, namely that you would understand if I paid a professional if my needs became too urgent, and you didn't seem too worried when I told you about the time it happened."

"Yes, I remember, and I am not being critical or going back on my word. I just don't want to have to worry about you falling in love with some whore. If you did fuck some floozy, you have to tell me. As long as your heart belongs to me, and only me, you can have sex with a pro when I can not take care of your emergencies. You could even enjoy it as long as you did not fall in love and it remained strictly physical, with no emotional involvement. I couldn't tolerate you setting up a steady girlfriend."

"I hear what you are saying. I can assure you nothing like that has happened," he equivocated.

"But you did have sex," she stated and added, "with the same woman?"

"Yes," he reluctantly conceded, "but it was a purely physical thing." He looked Veronica in the eyes and saw she did not feel as comfortable as she pretended.

"How did you know where to find her again?"

"I had her telephone number and called her."

He could tell she was less than happy. "Did you go down on her?" she wanted to know.

"Are you kidding? On a pro?"

He was relieved she interpreted his deliberate ambiguity as being a no and did not ask how many times he had strayed, or what it had been like, and what he had paid. Maybe she was smart enough to know better than to ask.

For an agonizing moment he was afraid more questions would follow, but all she said was, "I guess I am okay with that. I assume you were careful."

"Of course," he assured her, thinking carefulness could mean many different things.

"And how was it for you? Was it different with an Asian woman?" she asked, her inherent curiosity overcoming her need not to know.

He couldn't help grinning. "Sure," he said, "after all, we are talking about a pro with lots of experience. She knew what she was doing and what would make her customer feel good. But there was no emotional satisfaction. It was the draining of a release valve and served its purpose. As for the Asian thing," he went on, "well . . . what can I say? She was tender and didn't seem to *pretend* to enjoy it; she made me feel as if she really did. She made me forget she was a professional and behaved like a girlfriend. There was none of that 'hurry up' business; no rush because she had another customer waiting. I had the feeling she would have had all night for me, so it was fine."

"You bastard," she said, but there was no reproach or jealousy in her voice. "Come on, let's go to bed. This talk has made me horny."

24

La Jolla, 1993

Shad was happy. Happily married. Happy with the life he led. The world in which he moved could not have been better. AmeriDerm had been good to him and recognized his performance in promoting him to President of Far East/Latin America. He assumed it would turn out to be the pinnacle of his career; ascending to managing all international operations seemed unlikely in light of who was ahead of him in the organizational hierarchy and their ages. He had no problems with this. He had as much work as he could cope with, was successful, and enjoyed his new assignment.

AmeriDerm's decision to go public coincided with his expanded responsibilities. Their initial stock offering had been hugely successful and Shad knew he would eventually become rich through the options he had been granted. They were a powerful incentive for him to continue contributing to the growth of the company, presumably leading to steadily increasing share values.

Given his expanded responsibilities, Shad had persuaded Dave Hardee to recruit Thomas Grady as their vice president of Asia, reporting to Shad. Thomas, having married Pam in 1988 shortly after his relocation to New York, had never felt comfortable in the city, and both he and Pam were eager to move. Thomas had accepted Dave's job offer with alacrity. He was a natural to succeed Shad in Asia and had been delighted to settle down in La Jolla. They had discussed Thomas managing his area out of Hong Kong, but Dave Hardee was adamant he should be based at the home office.

As Shad had pointed out to Thomas originally, the proceeds from the sale of his condo were enough to cover the down payment for the house Pam and he found on the hillside above La Jolla shores. They were ecstatic about their new surroundings and grateful to Shad for having given them such good advice.

A solid friendship had developed between Pam and Veronica.

"Since you are so close to Pam now, Veronica, did you ever tell her about Caitlin?" Shad asked her one evening.

"No. I came close once, when the three of us had dinner. I was concerned Caitlin might let something slip, so I was on the verge of clueing Pam in ahead of time on our special relationship with Caitlin, but I didn't. I don't think she would have understood and was also afraid she might share our secret with Thomas."

"That could have become interesting. I am glad you didn't. And I assume you never tried to make a move on Pam?"

"No," Veronica said, shaking her head, "I like her tremendously, but she does not tempt me sexually. Caitlin is enough for me, and besides, I am so happy with you and our love life that I see less and less of her anyway. I think if you were home all the time, I would not need her at all."

"Well, as long as I have to travel so much, I am glad you have her. Who knows what trouble you might get into otherwise?"

"None, I can assure you."

Shad believed her. He thought back to their honeymoon trip to Beijing and Hawaii and was still thankful he had avoided the temptation of getting Apries together with Veronica. It had not been easy. He had thought so much about it he hadn't known if he could relax enough to enjoy the city with Veronica. He had, but it had been a struggle. Knowing Apries' work with the Sheraton, he had been so concerned they might run into her accidentally that they had stayed in the newly completed Shangri-La.

By now he rarely thought of Apries, and when he did, it was with gratitude. Her decision had been the only right one, and who knew where he would be now if she had not finished with him? He was perfectly content with Veronica, who gave him everything he desired, and no other woman had seriously tempted him since they had gotten married. He intended to keep it that way.

What did periodically intrude on his overall equanimity was his guilty conscience for not feeling more remorseful about how he had started adulthood. After thirty five years as Shad Cooper, he had all but forgotten Roger Stevens and the events leading up to his transformation as the individual he now was. He still carried the scars on his back and had concocted a plausible story about events in Vietnam for Veronica when she had first asked him for an explanation. The pain associated with them had receded far into ancient memories. He thought what he had made of his life at least partially vindicated what he had done to his abusive, cruel stepfather, but it should have weighed more heavily on him than it did. He was more bothered by his nearly complete lack of remorse than by the knife attack itself and its consequences. The stabbing had been buried in his sub-consciousness and he had to periodically remind himself no amount of rationalization could ameliorate his having killed, no matter how justifiable. His future had been built on another man's death, and he felt he should regret this constantly.

He didn't. It was too late to change history. Looking back, with the wisdom of hindsight, he had often asked himself why he had tolerated his stepfather's tyrannical punishments for as long as he had. Why had he not simply run away? Even after having decided to no longer submit to the beatings, why had he not considered alternatives? In retrospect he had rationalized he had done it for his mother's sake. He could not have left her behind, and she would not have come with him. That he knew from discussing it with her. Although an equally suffering victim, her loyalty to her second husband transcended the beatings she endured. It was the same reason she had refused to accompany him to the authorities to file a complaint, and without her support in bringing a non-violent end about, he had implemented the most radical and final solution to their problem. He had been unable to think of a realistic alternative.

Because of his escape he was still a wanted man, he had to assume, and would cringe involuntarily whenever face to face with a law enforcement official, never losing sight of the possibility of being brought back to justice. Unlikely after so many years, but with the huge strides in computer technology and the police converting their paper files to electronic ones, who could tell what might be inadvertently discovered about his true background? This was the fear he could never completely suppress.

He could not recall how often he had wondered if it had been smart to have fled when he had the chance. He had not come up with a satisfactory answer. What would prison have made him? Could he have joined the military as an ex-felon? Where would he now be if he had served his term?

With the manslaughter conviction on his record it would have been unlikely any reputable company would have hired him for a meaningful position. Would a college have accepted him? What could he have expected as an ex-con? Very little, even though his innate abilities would still have been there and he might have succeeded at something if he had been able to overcome the felon stigma. As it was he had been lucky twice: not to have been convicted of premeditated murder, and then to have escaped and never getting caught. He needed to count his blessings.

His escape and subsequent assumption of a fictitious identity had changed everything. Predominantly for the better. Had permitted him to build a successful life, one from which he could not step back voluntarily. Realistically, it was too late to turn himself in. The thought had periodically crossed his mind; to throw himself on the mercy of the courts, but he feared the potential consequences too much. Better to continue living with the steadily decreasing likelihood of being apprehended.

*   *   *

Shad's overall contentment with his life was rudely interrupted with an early morning call from Thomas.

"Shad? I need to see you. We have a problem."

"What's going on?"

"I will tell you when I see you. I just wanted to make sure you stop by my office first thing."

Thirty minutes later they sat across from each other. Thomas was visibly apprehensive, his normally calm demeanor in tatters. "Look at this letter," he said, passing it over to Shad.

It was from the legal department of their main competitor and accused AmeriDerm's sales staff in China of violating the Foreign

Corrupt Practices Act by allegedly paying money under the table to doctors and hospital purchasing agents to solicit sales. They threatened to notify the Justice Department and the Securities and Exchange Commission immediately unless AmeriDerm would not only cease and desist at once, but would furthermore notify them of what action plan they would implement to avoid this clear violation of the law in the future.

"Don't they do the same thing?" was Shad's first reaction.

"Sure, but it would be impossible to prove. And besides, even if we could, it would not give us the right to follow in their footsteps."

"Bastards! They must be bluffing. There is no way they could have proof. No one in China would admit to taking money. They would kill the goose that lays the golden egg, if I may use this trite analogy. Besides, we don't have any employees in China. Our Chief Representative is an employee of Pan-Asia in Hong Kong and does not engage in sales activities. His office is provided by Kang Ming. The sales people are all employees of Kang Ming, so we don't really have a legal presence in China, do we?" Shad said, thinking out loud.

"You may be right technically, but since we reimburse Kang Ming for all expenses and basically control their AmeriDerm activities, I think we are treading on thin ice."

"Still, if Washington were to get involved, it seems to me they would have to go after Kang Ming, to whom US law does not apply."

"Oh, come on, Shad. If they tried hard enough they could certainly prove we manage their sales force. There is ample documentation in our files."

Shad frowned. Thomas was right of course, and it was both too late and illegal to purge their files.

"Have you consulted our legal department yet?" he queried.

Thomas shook his head. "I wanted to discuss it with you first. I am afraid that once we get legal involved, it will be out of our hands."

"True enough. But I don't think we have a choice. There is too much at stake; for us personally, for Dave Hardee, and the company. My thinking is we go into complete denial. Have legal write to this outfit they are mistaken; we would never participate in or condone such payments, and we demand they prove their allegations. Maybe even mention we have heard the same thing about them."

"I suppose it might work. Should I set up a meeting?"

"Yes, please. But do it for this afternoon. I need time to brief Dave. I wouldn't want him to be blind sighted."

Shad considered how much to tell Dave. He thought the less he knew, the more convincing his mandatory denials would be. There was a significant difference between Dave knowing corruption in China was endemic and hearing from him, Shad, that he was aware of Kang Ming making illicit pay-offs.

He gave the letter to Dave to read. He said, "I assume this is all bullshit. We are taking too much business away from them and they are hurting. What do you plan to do about this?"

"We have a meeting with legal set up for this afternoon," Shad said and went on to explain how he proposed legal should respond.

"Okay. Sounds good to me. Keep me posted on developments."

As was to be expected, the lawyers agonized over the proper response. They quizzed Shad and Thomas thoroughly on possibly incriminating documentation in their files, especially anything from which one could deduce AmeriDerm management was aware of illegal Kang Ming activities or that the company had knowingly reimbursed its distributor for banned payoffs. No conclusion could be reached as to whether Kang Ming's employees were engaged in bribery and to what extent, if any, AmeriDerm could be held liable.

At Shad's request the lawyers agreed to draft a letter to Kang Ming clearly outlining AmeriDerm's unequivocal position on illegal payments, namely they were neither tolerated nor condoned under any circumstances and if it should come to AmeriDerm's attention that Kang Ming did this, the existing distribution agreement would be terminated for cause forthwith.

An official response to the letter of complaint was written in line with what Shad had recommended and the lawyers suggested a copy of the warning letter to Kang Ming be included.

Shad was not happy. Hours had been wasted; unproductive time expended on what he considered a non-issue. To succeed in international markets, local methodologies had to be followed, and it was clear what these were in China. If the lawyers started monitoring their operations in essentially corrupt countries, sales would suffer severely. He pointed this out to Dave Hardee, but Dave was adamant that AmeriDerm comply with the relevant laws. The potential liability to which the company would otherwise be exposed was too great. Shad understood Dave's position but knew it would not make his job easier.

Worse was to come. Shad was still contemplating how to expand their business in China with the restrictions being enforced by Dave when Ning Chang called him a day later.

"We have a problem, Shad," she advised, eerily mirroring Thomas' call from the day before. The tone of her voice underlined her concern.

"Okay. Have you discussed it with Thomas?"

"Well, no, I haven't. It's a highly sensitive issue, and since Thomas is new in his job and you and I have worked together from the beginning, I wanted to discuss it with you."

"I am sorry, Ning, but that's not how it works. Please call Thomas, who you know is in charge of Asia now and is certainly competent to handle whatever issues come up. And he and I talk and work closely together, so nothing is going to happen without my knowing about it."

Silence met him. He wondered if he had been too hard on her. Confessing to him might involve less loss of face for her than speaking with Thomas. It was not normal for her to call and he did not want to discourage her from sharing whatever problem was important enough to phone him at what was already late evening in Beijing. But he had to establish Thomas as the man in charge or he would *de facto* continue running Asian operations personally. "Listen, Ning," he finally continued, "please call Thomas immediately. Tell him what's wrong and then he and I will discuss the problem and get back to you expeditiously."

He didn't hear from Thomas for more than an hour. He speculated whether this was due to the length of the conversation he had had, or a delay on her part before calling Thomas, or if he had not been sure he needed to bring the issue to Shad. He was definitely curious when Thomas came into his office.

"You are not going to believe this," Thomas said. He looked deeply worried, frown lines running through his face, and before Shad could raise a question went on, "I just had a call from Ning Chang. She is beside herself. Our best customer, Dr. Hong, the oncologist from 402, has been arrested for massive graft. Apparently the government is in one of its crack-down modes to show the West it is ostensibly serious about eliminating corruption, and Hong got caught in the net they cast. We have to assume someone denounced him. Healthcare being a topical subject these days, he is in an ocean of trouble."

"Meaning what?"

"According to Ning, he is in prison and will be tried within a couple of weeks. If he is convicted, he may well face the death penalty. Ning is still gathering more information, but from what she has heard so far, Hong is apparently being accused of accepting hundreds of thousands of dollars in kick-backs, going back many years."

"You have got to be kidding," Shad uttered.

"Don't I wish. Do you remember me telling you about these periodic campaigns by the authorities to crack down? Well, this seems to be a prime example."

"But how could he possibly have siphoned off so much money? I mean the products he uses are expensive, especially the imported ones, but I don't see how he could have amassed such an amount."

Thomas shrugged. "You are thinking only of drugs. You have to remember, however, all the sophisticated equipment the hospital has purchased for his oncology center and where he decided what to buy and from whom. Although the hospital is required to solicit bids for capital equipment from multiple qualified suppliers, the bidding process is rigged. The competing distributors agree up front who will receive a particular order, and the losers then get cash back from the winning bidder. They take turns submitting the low bid, which is obviously highly inflated to cover the pay offs to their competitors, the doctor, purchasing agent, and whoever else needs to be taken care of. It's really quite elaborate, even if apprehensible and sheer inconceivable to the western mind."

"This is the reality? I can't believe it! Are you sure?" Shad persisted. "I have never heard of such patent crookedness."

"Of course I am. Everybody in the business knows the system. Or a slight variation of what I described. Sometimes the price quotations are slewed by the supplier working with the customer up front to define the specifications of the equipment to be purchased in such a way that only one supplier's machine meets all technical requirements. The kick-backs involved in this process are then included in the price being submitted."

"That just boggles my mind," Shad admitted. "I can see where the bribes rendered can add up over the years."

"Exactly. So our friend Hong is in deep yoghurt."

"What about the companies or individuals who have paid him off? Are they being named?"

"Not so far, at least, and I suspect they won't be because nothing could be proven. These distributors work with parallel accounting. They keep two sets of books; one for the authorities and a real one, which you will never find in their offices. Everything is in cash and off the official books, so unless someone would be stupid enough to confess, they are pretty safe."

"And if Hong tries to drag them into this mess in order to save his own neck?" Shad asked.

"Apart from the fact I don't believe it would help him, it would be his word against theirs. As I said, it's all cash and transpired in the utmost secrecy, so what could Hong say, let alone prove? Besides, even if you take the worst case scenario and he names names, he would still remain guilty of accepting the bribes. He was not forced to accept them."

"So what does this mean for us? I mean, why did Ning call you? Is she involved? Worried?"

"She did not expressly say so, but from what I gathered her primary concern at this point is the loss of business for us with Hong out of the picture and his colleagues so scared nobody wants to make a purchasing decision. Sales will definitely suffer, at least for some time."

"I assume she was involved in this pay-off scheme with Hong. Is she concerned about that as well?"

"I don't think so. First of all, what she paid was peanuts. Secondly, if she were to get into trouble, her husband, the general, should be able to help. Since we are talking about a military hospital and PLA doctors, the general should be quite influential."

"Let's hope so. I just wonder whether that bloody letter we received yesterday and these events are somehow related."

"The thought occurred to me," Thomas said, "but I really don't see how. The only thing I can think of is that they found out about Hong's arrest before Ning did, and wrote to us in order to cover their asses, just in case. It seems unlikely though, since Ning must have her ears closer to the ground than they do, given her husband's status."

"So is there anything specific Ning wants us to do, or not do?"

"Not right now. I believe she wanted to give us a heads-up on the sales impact and let us know what is happening just in case our name should somehow come up in the trial which will commence shortly."

Shad was not sure he could agree with Thomas' assessment. Ning had sounded too worried when she had called him, but there was nothing he could do. He knew a period of tense waiting was ahead of them.

When Shad related this story to Veronica that evening, she was flabbergasted. Could not believe business could be conducted in such a manner anywhere. And she was extremely worried about Shad getting into major trouble over the incident. He did not admit to sharing her concerns. She did not know his past and would not understand why he had his own, additional reasons to be nervous.

25

Ruth had no sooner left than Shad missed her. His house seemed unnaturally empty and eerily quiet; a reminder he had been spending too much time alone since Veronica's death. Perhaps another woman, and one so much younger than he at that, should not have set off a chain of fantasies in him after less than a year of widowerhood, but while Veronica's presence could still be felt throughout the house, he was painfully lonely. Ruth had addressed that problem. He tried to remain realistic. After all, they had only spent some pleasant hours together and those in a client/service provider relationship, but the magnetism she radiated would not let him go.

It was hunger that brought him back to the present. He had hoped—believed—Ruth would accept his invitation to stay for dinner. When she hadn't, he was left alone with a growling stomach. He didn't feel like leaving the house for a lonely dinner in a restaurant where his thoughts would be intruded upon. He was not in the mood to cook just for himself either. Paradoxically it occurred to him that it would be convenient if he could simply walk downstairs to the dining room of the Towers and have a selection of food ready and waiting for him. But that was the future—maybe. Right now he was at home, alone and hungry.

He set about making an omelet with bacon, an onion, mushrooms, a potato and three eggs.

He felt better after having eaten. A couple of glasses of wine also helped, as did the comfort of his recliner. If he had to spend yet another evening alone, this was as good as it was going to get.

His sense of urgency about whether or not to buy into the Tranquil Towers had mysteriously receded, as had his fear of the background inquiry. No longer were they his only priorities or the sole subjects on his mind. Thoughts of Ruth and moving into the Towers had become interlinked. By seemingly reciprocating his own interest in her, she had inadvertently introduced a significant new consideration into his deliberations. He was cognizant of the time pressure generated through his deposit, but he was trying to convince himself that Ruth could become an alternative to moving. An end to the extreme loneliness that had driven him to make a preliminary commitment was conceivably in sight if things worked out as he hoped.

As his mind thus wandered he was suddenly brought up short by memories of the crisis of 1993, as he had come to call it. Why these should intrude on his mellow reflections just now, he could not fathom. What an unmitigated disaster it had been. It still seemed like a miracle to him that he had escaped unscathed. When word of Dr. Hong's conviction and subsequent execution three short days later had reached him, he had recoiled with horror and guilt. Dave Hardee and Thomas had been understanding and supportive and had tried to talk him out of his uncalled for guilt trip, but Shad was convinced he carried some measure of blame. He had known up front that in order to get Dr. Hong's business, Kang Ming would have to pay him off, and he had tacitly condoned these payments. They had not been Hong's downfall, but they had been part of a pattern which ultimately led to his death, and for this Shad could not forgive himself. Even today he was unable to completely absolve himself of the role, no matter how minor, he had played in this tragic event. It had taken him a long time to recover, not least because it had been a stark reminder of how he had once before directly brought another man's life to an abrupt end.

He pushed these morbid recollections aside by forcing himself to concentrate on Ruth's entry into his life.

She had succeeded in rejuvenating both his body and his emotional well being, but he was practical enough not to forget what had brought his interest in the Towers about. He was still essentially alone with plenty of time to brood. The hours between Ruth's visits would be long and drag on interminably.

A few days of intermittent deliberations led him to the conclusion he had to play it safe. While continuing to pursue winning Ruth's affection, he also wanted to keep the option of moving into the Towers open. For this, he had to do more research; get more information on what life in the Towers was really like. He had to talk to Thomas again, and follow up on the Radford's invitation to see their unit.

Thomas was on his mind for other reasons as well. Despite his preoccupation with Ruth, the time between her visits had let his thoughts drift back to Apries, where they had been before meeting Ruth. Even after so many years he struggled to understand what had happened in Hong Kong, and why. He still had her letter, tattered now and almost falling apart from unfolding and refolding it over the years. He continued to think there had been something between Apries and Thomas and he wanted to make an effort to find out what Thomas knew. Before he could procrastinate any longer he gave both Thomas and the Radfords a call. Neither was at home. He left messages for them, asking if he might stop by the next afternoon to see them.

*　　*　　*

Returning from his habitual morning walk along the beach the next day, he had a message from the Radford's that they would be pleased to see him anytime after 4:00pm.

"It's good to see you again, Shad," Kenny said when he opened the door in response to Shad's knock.

"Same here, Kenny. I appreciate you letting me come by."

"Don't mention it. We are happy to see you again. Come on in."

Shad's first impression was that the apartment was over-furnished and the ceiling too low. Used to the open floor plan of his house, with its soaring ceilings and panorama windows, he felt boxed in; almost claustrophobic. It did not help that the walls were painted dark red. A large LCD TV dominated one wall, and the couch in front of it was too overbearing for the size of the room. A life size, extremely well done sarcophagus replica stood upright in one corner, its imitation gold and bright blue colors and decorative scrolls and hieroglyphics demanding to be admired.

Jerri caught him staring. "Isn't that the most marvelous thing you have ever seen?" she gushed. "We bought it in a museum store years ago."

"Yes, it's very impressive. It catches your attention and you found the perfect spot for it."

Kenny walked over. "Come on out and let me show you our balcony," he said.

When Shad stepped through the sliding glass door Kenny had opened, he was impressed. Probably sixty feet long and thirty feet wide, it looked more spacious than the whole apartment. A lot bigger than his own terrace at home or the one attached to the apartment he had optioned.

"It's by far the largest balcony of any of the units here," Kenny said. "It's a result of the building's design, with the driveway underneath leading into the underground garage. It really sold us on this particular apartment. I think we spend more time out here than inside, even though you can only see a sliver of ocean off to this side," he explained, pointing towards one corner of the balcony.

"The famous peek ocean view the realtors love to talk about."

"I guess so," Kenny said and laughed. "But we wouldn't trade this balcony for a smaller one with a better ocean view. Look how wonderfully lush the hills are. The palms and bougainvilleas. The flowers and shrubs. We can never get enough of this view. It's so quiet and peaceful here, and by not facing the ocean directly, we get a lot less traffic."

"I made us some coffee, Shad," Jerri said as she came out to join them, a tray with cups and a pot of coffee and a plate of cookies in her hands. "Why don't you sit down?"

He did. It was a beautiful late afternoon. The balcony was in the shade and was sheltered from the permanent breeze coming off the ocean. Perfect climate; warm enough to be comfortable in a short sleeved shirt, not too hot to perspire.

"I guess you feel right at home here," Shad said.

"Absolutely. We are happy and wouldn't trade it for our old house," Jerri said.

"What is it that you *don't* like about living here, if anything? Or what would you change if you could?" Shad inquired.

Kenny and Jerri looked at each other. They really had to stop and think, Shad noticed.

"Well," Kenny finally ventured, "I suppose we wouldn't mind seeing a little more of the ocean, but as I said, we enjoy the view as it is and only have to walk around the building to be right on the beach."

"I think the ocean view is overrated anyway," Jerri said. "I much prefer to see the flora and fauna that is so abundant and beautiful here. Some flowers are always blooming brightly throughout the year."

"Well, I guess what both Jerri and I would agree on is the ceilings could be a foot higher, and an extra five hundred square feet would be nice," Kenny volunteered. "We have too much stuff, and because it all means something to us, we couldn't bring ourselves to throw things out, as the size of our unit demanded. As a result, it's more crowded than we would like. But we have gotten used to it and it's large enough for two and the clutter doesn't bother us any more."

"Do your neighbors intrude on your peace and quiet at all?"

"No," they both agreed. "We hear nothing. The building is well constructed. Even the folks living above us can't be heard. We actually enjoy being surrounded by people. We run into folks and stop to talk. It keeps us in touch with others."

Shad wasn't sure how he would feel about having neighbors next door. It was fine as long as everyone got along, he thought, but what if they were the nosy type, always keen to know what he was doing, where he was going, who was visiting him? He pictured Ruth coming into his apartment and the whole building gossiping about it within hours. Not necessarily harmful, but certainly no one's business. Would the talking bother him? How much privacy would he have to give up and how much would he be willing to?

"What about your privacy?" Shad asked. "When we sit on your terrace like this, don't you have to assume the people above you overhear you? That they could watch you without you knowing?"

Kenny shrugged. "I don't know. I have never thought about it. I guess they could, but then they would probably be bored to death. As it is, if we are sitting out here and our upstairs neighbors come out, they wave to us or say hello and we exchange a few words, but that's it. It's certainly never been an issue for us."

Shad concluded the Radfords lived in a world different from his own; with different sets of values and priorities. Plus, they had each other. There was nothing more he could learn from them that would make his decision easier. As soon as he could gracefully do so, he finished his coffee and made his excuses.

"Any time you want to visit," Kenny said, "please do so. We would love to see you. I know you and Thomas are good friends, so when you

26

The next evening Shad had one of his frequent dinners with Thomas. Shad had had to reluctantly postpone his scheduled massage because in his impatience to see Ruth again, he had completely forgotten his date with Thomas. They met at their favorite restaurant, Roppongi, and ordered a selection of tapas. Sharing several of these generously large 'appetizers' appealed more to them than ordering individual dishes. The special this evening was a lobster roll with Kobe beef that turned out to be divine.

In the course of their meandering discussion, Shad recalled Jerri's comment about so many lonely women being available at the Towers and the possibility of these coming after him.

"Thomas? You remember what Jerri said the other day about ladies in the Tower waiting to pounce on you?"

"Sure. Why do you ask?"

"Because I was wondering what your relevant experience has been."

"It's been rather ambivalent, I would say. I have been in situations where I thought a woman was interested in me, but nothing ever came of it."

"Why not?"

"I guess because I don't want to have to get used to another fulltime companion. I am too set in my ways. I would inevitably make comparisons to Pam and would find these women lacking. As it is, I enjoy taking one or another out to dinner occasionally, just to have someone to talk to, but I make sure it never goes beyond that."

"And they accept that?" Shad asked.

"They don't really have a choice, do they? If I find my dinner date starts expecting more from me, I don't ask her out again. Some of them resent this, of course, and a few have asked *me* for a date, but when I decline they give up. Admittedly, since we are all living under the same roof, it can get somewhat awkward at times."

"You don't want or need the sex they might offer you?"

"Not really. Besides, these women may be fun to be with, but they are not exactly objects of sexual desire."

"I assume then you did not see the *Playboy* issue with the pictorial featuring sixty plus year old women in the nude?" Shad teased.

"No, I didn't, and if they were in Playboy, I doubt they would be living in the Tranquil Towers."

From what he had seen so far, Shad had to agree with this assessment. He changed subjects to the one that had been on his mind whenever his thoughts returned to Apries.

"Thomas, I have to ask you something. Think back to the first time I visited Beijing. Do you remember Apries Xie Hsu?"

"Why, sure. I even recall how surprised you were when we met her at the Ministry of Health to translate for you. The expression on your face was priceless."

"It was, eh? Well, it seems to me that you were caught off guard as well. I was surprised you knew each other," Shad said.

"Yes, well, I had actually known Apries for a number of years and had hired her at times when I had needed a translator. What are you trying to get at?"

"That I never completely forgot her, and for the first time in many years found myself thinking about her again. Maybe because I have been alone for a while now and spend too much time reminiscing about the past. And in thinking about her, one of the things I recall is that evening we all went back to the hotel after our Ministry meeting. I thought I detected you knew each other better than could have been expected from just having worked together."

"What makes you think that? And why now, after so many years?" The puzzled expression on Thomas' face looked genuine, even if a little wariness was discernable. "It's not like you and I haven't seen each other a million times since then, and you never once raised the subject."

"Because I stopped thinking about her after Veronica and I got married, and when I now think back to that particular evening . . .

well, let's just say there are more memorable occurrences from that night than the time we spent together in the lounge," Shad said.

"Really. Do tell." The Brit in Thomas came through again. Cool. Relaxed. Sovereign. Even haughty. Maybe just a little too disinterested in light of their decades' long friendship. "You are saying you fucked her that night," he added bluntly.

Shad tried to hide his embarrassment. "So what if I did, Thomas?" Thomas' unvarnished statement indicated to Shad his friend knew Apries' character. "The point I am trying to make is that something was in the air that evening, which, in retrospect, makes me believe you knew each other better than I assumed at the time."

"And?"

"It's hard to put my finger on it, Thomas. There was a certain wariness between you two. You seemed to be treading very lightly and took care in choosing your words when you said something to her. You also ignored her a lot. And yet I sensed an unusual familiarity between you two; a greater one than a strict, occasional working relationship. Am I right? It doesn't really matter anymore now that we are old and good friends and only have our memories to sustain us, but I am curious."

Thomas became pensive. Then he appeared to have made a decision. "Well, in that case," he said, "I suppose there is no harm in telling you that yes, I had met Apries before she started working as a translator." He did not look entirely comfortable. He was staring into the distance, lost in thought.

"That's it? That's all you want to say?"

Shad could see Thomas was reluctant to add anything, but he persisted. "Are you going to tell me about it?"

"I am not sure I should. It would serve no useful purpose."

"Why don't you leave that up to me to decide?" The more hesitant Thomas was to explain, the more curious Shad became.

"Look, Shad, this was all so long ago. What possible difference could it make to you today under what circumstance I had known Apries before?"

"Probably none," Shad admitted, "but for reasons I can not even begin to understand, she has been on my mind recently, maybe because I am bored. She was such an enigma and I am making a new effort to figure her out. I'd like to understand and make sense of what happened.

Anyway, I remembered the evening in Beijing and your behavior and it made me think."

"In that case, why don't you tell me what kind of a relationship *you* had with Apries, Shad, so I can understand you dragging up this old stuff."

"Okay. You go first, and then I will tell whatever you want to know," Shad said. "Something had gone on between you two and I would like to know what it was."

Thomas was shaking his head. "Don't go there, Shad."

"Why not? What are you hiding from me? What are you afraid of?" Shad couldn't let go. Why had his desire to know become all consuming? It should not matter after so many years.

"Hurting you, Shad. Maybe shattering your illusions."

"What? You can't be serious. Not today, twenty five years later. Besides, I would rather have a painful ending than endless pain. The pain of not knowing."

"Okay," Thomas said, "Let me ask you this. Are you a jealous person?"

"Jealous? With regard to Apries and what happened a generation ago? Of what she might have done? After I have not heard from her in decades? No, I don't believe so."

"But?"

"But nothing. There is no but."

"I am not sure I believe you. But anyway," Thomas sighed, "you seem to be obsessed with digging up history, so I will tell you. But remember I warned you. I first met Apries years before you did, on my first trip to Beijing, in 1981. There weren't many western visitors so soon after the Cultural Revolution, and the ones who were there tended to escape to a certain girly bar in the evenings, a sort of disco cum nightclub in the Holiday Inn near the airport. It was *the* place to go if you were in the city by yourself and wanted to have some fun. A little off the beaten track because the authorities wanted to keep this symptom of western decadence away from the city center. Anyway, I came back from an early dinner one evening with nothing to do and facing a long evening alone. I decided to grab a cab and check out the action in this joint."

"I seem to recall you telling me in Hong Kong," Shad interrupted, "you did not like bars like that and avoided them like the pest."

"I did say that and it was true. But I didn't tell you I was a weak man when it came to women. If I went into a bar where I absolutely knew women were available, I could not resist. Then I would regret what I had done and castigate myself for having succumbed. Besides, I didn't know what to expect of such a place in Beijing."

"Don't tell me," Shad mumbled.

"Yes, Apries was working there as a hostess. I assume you knew she used to work in a bar?"

Shad merely nodded. He had never been able to reconcile this seedy past of hers with the sophisticated woman she had become, despite her explanations of how she had been driven to accept such a job.

"Well, I had not been in the bar very long when she joined me. Customers were staring because she had this certain something about her. She exuded a radiant sexuality; an animalistic, erotic magnetism. You knew she was hot. She was probably the youngest hostess there, and she managed to combine blatant sensuality with a virgin like, youthfully slim body. She was wearing blue jean hot pants, I remember very clearly, really short and tight and these silly pink cowboy boots."

"Go on," Shad encouraged, fearing Thomas was too lost in the past to continue.

"On top she wore a tight sleeveless white undershirt coming barely down to her midriff, with plastic spaghetti straps. A silver charm dangled from her bellybutton. Her hair was pinned up—sort of like that girl from "I Dream of Jeannie" from the old TV series. Her walk was like a determined slouch. She was pushing her pelvis ahead of her, as if she were stalking prey. She looked at me with veiled eyes as she sat down and started talking. Her English was still poor then; mostly bar girl talk in fragmented phrases and poor grammar. But she was funny and I found her charming, her smile irresistible, and she made me feel special. All part of her job, I had to assume, but it seemed genuine. I had the distinct feeling she liked *me*, that I was not just another customer willing to buy her a drink. That she found me attractive or handsome or whatever."

"She must have made a hell of an impression on you if you can recall these details so vividly."

"She did. She appealed to me. She was very attractive. Not beautiful in the classical sense, with her big black eyes a little too far apart and her somewhat too full lips. But I can still see how dazzling white her teeth were and she had a naturalness about her I found quite irresistible."

"And you fell in love with her," Shad guessed.

"Not quite. Or at least not then and there. But an instant, strong attraction was certainly evident. Anyway, with her, what you saw was what you got. There was nothing artificial about her; no pretensions. She told me she was working her way through university and was divorced and had an infant daughter. She was living with her mother and a sister. Working in the bar provided her with a livelihood and allowed her to learn English in the process."

"Yes, that's what she told me as well," Shad said.

"Well," Thomas continued, "I don't know if you have ever been in one of those Asian girlie bars, but I was given to understand by the Mama-san that the girls were available. If you bought a girl enough drinks and she liked you and danced with you for a while, you could take her into one of the booths lining the bar, with privacy curtains, and for a modest tip get a blow job."

"Just that?"

"Yes, at least in the booths. The subject of sex didn't come up. I suppose if I had pushed they might have provided a room for us upstairs. I found out later from Apries that they had some facilities available for sexual emergencies."

"So she gave you a blow job?"

"No, although she was more than willing, I dare say."

"Tell me about it!" Shad could not control the idiotic impulse to flagellate himself.

Thomas gave him a strange look, as if trying to figure out why his friend wanted to be punished with details of an encounter so far in the past.

"We had danced a couple of times," he related, "when she maneuvered me against the wall off to the side of the bar, where customers couldn't see what she was doing. She crowded against me, her back to the bar, and pulled up her shirt. She wasn't wearing a bra and pushed her breasts in my face. I was momentarily dumbfounded; mesmerized. Before I could react she was telling me—no, ordering me—to bite her. Hard. She had long nipples on small, firm breasts. I had never seen anything like it."

Thomas had this dreamy expression on his face. Shad felt himself being torn apart. Thomas' description was an uncanny mirror image of his own first experience with Apries. He had thought it had been he who had turned her on so ferociously, and it pained him deeply to now learn it had just been part of her behavioral pattern. Merely one of the odd pleasures she sought when she was horny. It had not been because of him. It had been because of her twisted needs.

"She made me suck her breasts," Thomas continued, "and bite her nipples until she came, telling me again and again to bite her harder. I was petrified I would hurt her, but she obviously relished the pain."

"And that was enough to make her come?"

"More than once," Thomas said.

"And you?"

"I was also highly aroused, of course, but still had a measure of control. She couldn't seem to get enough. It excited her to the point where she appeared to be in a state of perpetual orgasm. Later, when I was alone again and was reflecting on what had happened, I wondered if she was masochistic. How could a woman otherwise get off so quickly by getting her nipples bitten so hard? She was as much of an enigma to me as you said she was to you. Still is, for that matter."

Shad was speechless. Not over what Thomas had described, but that she had done with him exactly what she had previously enjoyed with Thomas of all people. What he had revealed about Apries and himself was too much for him. It wounded his pride terribly. It was an utterly unexpected side of staid Thomas, one he never would have guessed or thought possible. He felt Apries had betrayed him, even though the event had occurred years before he had met her.

"And you didn't drag her into a booth?" he finally managed to ask, disbelief in his voice.

"I was sorely tempted but I wanted more from her. The booth didn't seem right. I liked her too much. I didn't want to go to one of the rooms upstairs and didn't dare take her to my hotel. I was more than a little apprehensive about going with her to one of those sleazy one hour hotels—which she offered to do—and maybe getting nabbed by the police. For all I knew, I was just being set up, you know?"

Shad nodded in understanding. Bile kept rising in his throat. "So then what happened?"

"Nothing much," Thomas said. "If she was disappointed, she hid it well. In fact, later on she told me she had been oddly pleased I had not done anything. I gained her respect in that I was content just being with her, talking, rather than trying to get her to do what was expected of her by nearly every customer. There couldn't be any doubt in her mind that she had succeeded in turning me on and the little breast episode had satisfied her immediate needs. That is why she accepted my offer to take her to dinner the next evening. She saw I was interested in more than just her body; that I was interested in her as a person."

Shad nodded dolefully. "So then what happened?"

"She came to the hotel the next evening. I was consumed with jealousy. The thought of her spending time with another man, doing whatever, drove me crazy, even though I knew, of course, that she was doing this every night and probably with more than a single customer. Anyway, I didn't know whether she had the night off or simply did not go to work. I was waiting for her in the upstairs lounge. But she had a hard time getting past hotel security. I suppose they recognized her as a working girl. She finally reached me on the house telephone, and I went down to get her."

"I can't believe any of this," Shad said. He was devastated; could hardly believe what he was hearing. And yet, strangely enough, it also helped him get over what had happened in Hong Kong and re-confirmed what her personality had been like all along and why she had been so incredibly good in bed: she had the experience. "Let me guess. You took her to dinner and then you smuggled her into your room and slept with her."

"I wish you wouldn't put it that way. You make it sound so coarse, so profane, when in fact it was very beautiful and what we did was make love."

"Call it what you want," Shad said, unable to suppress his bitterness. "Making love. Having sex. Screwing. Fucking. Sleeping with her. It's just semantics. At the end of the day, it's all the same, isn't it?"

"No, it isn't. Or wasn't, I should say. At least not for me. We really had something beyond sex. It was much more than that. I thought I had fallen in love but eventually it dawned on me that for her I was just one more in an endless string of lovers. She was using me as she would apparently use you later."

"Could be. I thought I might have been in love with her as well," Shad confessed. "I still don't know whether she was sincere when she told me she loved me. I think she had a really screwed up personality. I could not figure her out. Just when I thought I had, she would do something totally unexpected and inconsistent with what she had said or done previously. No wonder, I suppose, given her history of being raped and sexually abused and the circumstances under which she grew up." He was despondent. "Well, at least she appears to have been consistent in what she told her lovers about her past. And she never pretended to be anything other than permanently, ravenously hungry for sex."

"I guess so," Thomas concurred. "I couldn't understand her anymore than I guess you did when she took you as lover. Maybe she shared with you what she told me one time when I confronted her with a gross inconsistency in something she had related. I will never forget her words: "When I tell the truth, I lie; when I lie, I tell the truth.""

"Yes, that's what she told me too," Shad snorted. "I couldn't understand what she meant and I still don't. Those words stick in my mind as well and still puzzle me."

"I know what you are saying. I don't know whether they reflected her thinking, or she had picked up this gem of contradiction somewhere. I also thought a lot about what her message implied. It makes no sense and yet I spent a lot of time trying to understand. Maybe her personality was a lot more complex than we gave her credit for. Maybe it was a reflection of how confused she was about herself. Perhaps she simply meant she would never reveal her true self to us. Or she wanted to make sure we wouldn't take her for granted. I have lived in Asia all my life and was married to a Chinese, and still I could not begin to understand how they think. Jade once told me her heart consisted of five or six chambers, and that she would never be able to tell me the secrets buried in the deepest one. She just couldn't. There was a block she could not overcome."

"Rather strange," Shad said. "With Apries I never knew what to believe. When I caught her in what I knew was a lie, she was never embarrassed. She would point out to me I had been warned and with that she was in the clear."

"I guess that was the beauty of the whole thing," Thomas concurred. "Anyway, all this was years before you met. And surely you did not think you were the first man she loved, apart from her former husband?"

"Of course not. I knew about her having worked in the bar and occasionally taking a customer into a booth, and she told me about her fiancé and her Mama-san's husband, but it never crossed my mind that you two had been lovers."

"It had not occurred to me either—about you and her, I mean," Thomas said. "After all, what were the chances of us both meeting the same woman in a city the size of Beijing, and then both of us taking that woman to bed? And what difference does it make now?"

"None, I suppose," Shad admitted reluctantly. "And yet it is oddly disconcerting to find out we have almost identical histories with the same woman. Knowing she had a bunch of lovers before me is one thing. Knowing you were one of them is an entirely different matter."

"Don't think it makes me feel any better," Thomas said, "to find out you, of all people, followed in my footsteps. I think we both have to just accept it. It's history."

He knew Thomas was right. He had to accept that his best friend had not only preceded him, but that they shared exactly the same behavior and events. And yet, how could he not be thoroughly upset?

"You know, Shad," Thomas said, guessing at Shad's devastation, "if anyone was going to be upset about this, it ought to be me. After all, I had her first. Do you think it was easy for me to see you two looking at each other in the Sheraton the way you did after what I had had with her, and knowing how she was and strongly suspecting what you would be doing the moment I was gone?"

"Why didn't you keep her then?"

"I was tempted. I was also newly married to Jade. I didn't have enough time for Apries; couldn't be with her often or long enough to keep her sexually satisfied. I knew if I didn't see her for a couple of months she would be taking someone else, and that thought drove me crazy, as I am sure it did you too. I thought she would make the ideal mistress, or number two wife as we call it in Asia, but to be married to her? Impossible to imagine!"

"I think you are right," Shad admitted. "She swore she was being faithful to me while I was gone, and I wanted to believe her, but it was hard. I don't believe she had to be in love with a man to go to bed with him. I am convinced she could love one man and still have sex with someone else—no love involved—as long as she could still her overpowering craving for sex. I don't think she would even consider that being unfaithful. She could use a man with no more emotion than using a dildo. She was so complex in many ways and so simple in others. I know for a fact she jumped from my bed into her fiancé's and back into mine within twelve hours without any apparent hesitation. Whom did she love, and who did she simply use? Her fiancé or me?"

"You are joking, right?" Thomas said incredulously.

"I wish I were," Shad said ruefully, and proceeded to share with Thomas what had transpired with Apries in Beijing.

"Wow! That's absolutely unbelievable. As capable and willing as she was to do anything, anytime, I shouldn't have thought she would go that far."

"Well, she did," Shad said.

"And you accepted that? Made love to her knowing she was coming straight from her fiancé's bed?"

"What could I have done? You know how she was. I was helpless. She controlled me completely. She knew how to make me forget where she had just come from. I lived for the moment and had no time to think. Can you tell me why I am suddenly thinking of her again at all?"

"Because you have never been this alone before. All you can do is dream about the past. You have too much time on your hands. Or you think it was a mistake to have broken up with her."

"Not really. We had no future, and she recognized this before I did. In fact, *she* was the one who broke up with *me*." Shad said and told Thomas the story.

Thomas shook his head. "You don't have enough to do to keep your thoughts occupied. I am telling you, you need to move into the Towers to get out of this slump you seem to be in."

"Could be. I don't know. I am working on it. The last few days have already brought a dramatic improvement. I met this woman, you see, who gave me a massage, and I find her incredibly attractive and am trying to convince her to have dinner with me. For the first time in months I am actually enjoying life again and look forward to what the future might hold for me."

"That's great, Shad!" Thomas enthused. "It's high time you took an interest in someone again. Maybe we could have dinner together with her one evening?"

"Sure, providing I can get her to go out with me at all."

"I am sure she will. Just give it a little time. How old is she?"

"Too young for me," Shad said. "Only forty four."

"Don't even think about her age. Besides, if she succeeds in making you forget our common history with Apries and helps you get over Veronica, you will have something to be thankful for, regardless of what may develop between you."

"I know what happened back then doesn't matter anymore. Hasn't, for a long time. I am not going to dwell on it any longer. In a strange way you telling me about your involvement with Apries has really helped me."

"Good. I am glad there is a positive side to this sordid saga."

"Still, if you had mentioned your affair with Apries when we met in Beijing I would have stayed away from her and thus spared as both a lot of grief."

"Do you think you would be happier now if you had never known her intimately?"

"No," Shad admitted. "She gave me memories I will cherish until the day I die."

"I am glad to hear that, Shad. I can say the same thing. And I am sure this will not harm our friendship, knowing we have even more in common than we did before," Thomas grinned.

"I agree," Shad said, deep in thought. He knew he needed to see Ruth again quickly and bring her more deeply into his life before he could forget Apries once and for all despite what he had vowed.

27

Contrary to what he had told Thomas, Shad felt shell shocked by Thomas' revelations about the intimate relationship he had had with Apries. He viewed it as an inexplicable betrayal on both their parts. But it also led to a positive turn of events for him. A shadow looming over his long ago affair had been lifted and he felt strangely free, sure now Apries' professed love had not been as profound as he had thought. An inner peace settled over him.

Several days passed before he received the good news he had been hoping for. Sybil called to advise him the results of his background check had come back in good order. He breathed a long sigh of relief. One more hurdle eliminated, leaving him free to dwell on Ruth—and on whether or not he should move.

He tried to analyze why he was so attracted to Ruth, and why this feeling appeared to be reciprocated. He knew next to nothing about her. What little she had told him during her visits were only fragments; minimum facts. He could only guess what hardships she must have endured growing up and how hard she had had to fight to establish a solid foundation for her life. He wondered how bright she was, much as he had done years ago with Veronica. In this regard, he had not changed. He still could not spend a lot of time with a woman who was not his intellectual equal.

He wondered again if it had been foolish to introduce her to his comfortable life style. Was she more interested in what he represented than in him? Given her circumstances he could imagine being an attractive target for a woman desiring a sudden, dramatic improvement in materialism.

How important was their age difference, he mused? The winter/ summer romance cliché was inevitable. He wasn't sure he cared how people might react. Let them think what they wished. Veronica had also been younger than he, by more than ten years and should have outlived him. They had never been cognizant of their age difference; had never discussed it as a negative until, suddenly, her advanced colon cancer had been diagnosed. At that point her younger age had not made any difference; had not helped her and had not slowed down the rapidly growing malignancy. Neither her age nor her lifestyle, nor regular exercise and never having smoked had made the slightest difference, so why should he worry about Ruth being so much younger than he was? Shouldn't he simply accept whatever positive relationship, if any, might develop between them?

Twenty four years. Anyone who saw them together would think more years separated them. She looked so youthful and he more than showed his age. He knew he should be looking at women more his age rather than be attracted to someone so young. But he had not deliberately set out to find a young woman. Their meeting had been coincidental, unplanned, but could turn out to be fortuitous. Her age, he told himself, had nothing to do with why she attracted him.

Still, he felt there was something fundamentally wrong with him. A basic disconnect between his brain and his emotions and body. The three were in need of synchronization. While his brain told him to stop taking an interest in Ruth, that she did not see him as anything other than what he was—an old man and a client—his body and his emotions reacted to her inexorably.

He rationalized age was a matter of perception. She had indicated her boyfriend already found her to be too old, but for Shad she was definitely young. He struggled to accept being a member of the old generation and kept dreaming that Ruth still found him handsome and desirable. Intellectually, he knew how foolish this was. Emotionally, he could not change his thinking.

He had seen Ruth only a few times and strictly professionally at that, even if she had seemed to like him. As a customer only, he kept asking himself? Or as a man as well? He deluded himself into minimizing their age difference; didn't dwell on there being one or that she might be much more cognizant of it than he chose to be. It was seen as a non-issue by him; not important. The time they had spent talking over coffee in his house had lifted his spirits and sent his imagination soaring. He could easily picture seeing more and more of her privately, going on dates and having endless, interesting discussions. And an eventual romantic involvement.

Was it merely his loneliness that had made him so vulnerable to her kind and gentle ministrations? Had her massages been no more than a band aid for his soul? His arousals an automatic reflex?

He might have thought so if she hadn't stayed for coffee and engaged him in conversation. She had been such a good listener and seemed genuinely interested in what he had related and the souvenirs and art objects he had collected. Or had she only been courteous? He prided himself on always having been good in assessing people during his long career, where his success had depended on his people skills, and he didn't think she had been playing a game just to impress him.

The decision he would have to make shortly on moving into the Towers or not intruded on his reflections. If the bond he imagined developing between Ruth and himself was more than just wishful thinking, his whole rationale for considering moving could be undermined. The loneliness driving him would no longer be an issue. Time with Ruth could be better spent in his home than in the Towers, where immediate neighbors crowded in on them. On the other hand he found the possibility of living in the Towers enticing, sitting with Ruth on the broad balcony, watching and hearing the ocean and seeing people strolling along the beach. One thing was certain: having met Ruth and becoming interested in her was not going to make his decision any easier. At least not until he had a better feel for how their relationship progressed.

He did not know what to do. Not with the move and not with Ruth. Getting old was a bitch, he thought; being old was worse. He recalled reading somewhere that the only good thing about being old was that you were still alive.

He wanted another massage from her. Even more he wanted to take her out to dinner. He wanted to get to know her; to find out what kind of a person she was. What she wanted out of life. What motivated her. Her family circumstances. About the situation with her boyfriend. Destroying whatever relationship she had with him was not his intention, despite the emerging strains to which she had alluded.

Shad was uncertain of what the next massage might bring. He knew he could not control reacting to her physically. Would he be able to restrain himself as he had done the last time? He did not want to send the wrong message; did not want her to think he was only interested in her masturbating him. He was eager to show her he was interested in *her*, the person. He wanted to tell her he had been fantasizing about her; that he wanted to spoil her and make her feel good.

He had too much time to think. He was alone and had no one with whom he could talk about his emotions. No one who could give him meaningful advice. He only knew Ruth had the ability to make him feel alive again, and for this alone he was almost excessively grateful.

Before meeting her he had been nearly exclusively preoccupied with whether or not to move into the Towers. This had now been pushed into a more distant space and become a function of what kind of association he could establish with Ruth. Although still quite aware of the clock he had set in motion with his deposit, his perspectives had changed. Ruth's potential availability could mature into an alternative to moving. If he could have her, why would he need the Towers? She would be the answer to his loneliness.

He pulled himself up short when this far out thought crossed his mind. He was making light year jumps and had to get back to the here and now, instead of losing himself in wild, unfounded and unrealistic dreams.

He waited three interminable days before calling Ruth to set up another massage. To his great delight, no cajoling was needed to get her to agree to come back to his house. She did not even extract another promise from him to behave. He hoped it had not just been an oversight. He was not sure what it meant when she said she would come at 4:00pm. No other time available? Or was she anticipating being invited to stay afterwards and would accept? That was certainly his hope.

The first thing he noticed when he opened the door for her was that she was wearing a rather short skirt instead of her usual jeans. He liked the looks of her bare legs. The second thing he noticed was that she looked even lovelier than she had in his imagination. And finally he saw she was wearing more make-up, making her look yet younger than before.

"What's wrong?" she asked when she noticed how closely he was studying her.

"Nothing," he assured her. "I am so glad to see you again. You look absolutely stunning. I was staring a bit because I saw you wearing a short skirt, and with my fertile imagination, I immediately thought of what this could mean." He smiled, telling her not to take his remark too seriously.

"Forget what you are thinking, Shad. The only reason I am is because I am going out for a drink with my colleagues after I finish here and didn't want to go back to change."

He was disappointed, and it showed. He had been looking forward all day to spending more time with her.

"How come you suddenly look so sad?"

"It's nothing," he said. "Come on in."

She followed him silently; waited while he undressed and slipped into his robe.

"So how have you been?" she asked as she began massaging him.

"Pretty good. How about you? Are you keeping busy?"

"I can't complain, even though we seem to be getting more competition all the time. We are lucky to have a solid base of repeat customers, but it's tough to go up against all the spas and health clubs offering massages in addition to their standard services."

"I can imagine," he said. "People want to combine a massage with working out or getting a spa treatment, I guess, especially the women. How do you set yourself apart from the competition? I would have to assume it would be difficult to differentiate yourself, since all therapeutic massages are about the same, right?"

She frowned. "Not really. The basic principles apply, obviously, but there can be significant differences from one masseuse to another. It's a skill, after all, and not everyone is equally adapt. Or willing to do their best all the time. Or have the same experience level, which translates to quality. Then there is the range of massages. Plus we are specialized; massages are our only business, our livelihood. We pride ourselves on that. So we do and can differentiate."

"Do you do any advertising?"

"Oh, sure," she said. "But you know how expensive that can get. We girls share the costs and only put small ads in the local papers. Our customers tend to come from here, and most of our new clients come through personal referrals. I hope you will be kind enough to refer me to your friends too."

He tried to grin at her, but had to twist his head awkwardly so she could see. "Well, let's not jump to conclusions," he cautioned playfully. "After all, you have just gotten started, so I don't know if you will impress me enough to recommend you. The last ones were so long ago I forgot how good they were."

A little slap on his butt was her answer and he cried out in mock pain. "You better be careful," he warned, "or I will tell my friends you slap your customers around!"

She was not intimidated. "That's okay. If your friends are anything like you they would flock to me then."

"You are probably right," he said. "I guess what you are really telling me is that a slap on the butt is a sexual turn on."

"You don't really expect me to answer that, do you?"

"Sure I do. Because if that is the implication, I would assume you find a little slapping of your butt during sex exciting."

"You are incorrigible!" she admonished. "And don't think I am going to tell you what I like or don't like in bed."

"You don't have to. I am just curious whether your boyfriend does it."

He could sense her smiling, but she kept quiet. "I knew it!" he said.

"You don't know anything," she said as the pressure of her hands on his back suddenly increased noticeably.

"There is nothing wrong with admitting reality, Ruth," he told her. "I think it can be a great pleasure enhancement."

"So you enjoy it?" she asked, curiosity in her voice.

"Sure, but not in or by itself. Only when it turns the woman on and heightens her pleasure. Then it makes me feel good."

"Very noble."

He did not react when she moved the towel from his butt to his shoulders. He could not prevent getting hard from her touch, but he made no move to encourage her or to give her a better view. He waited to see what she might do.

She moved her hands down between his legs, working on his thighs. He was certain she could see him clearly. Perhaps she was a little surprised he did not offer her easier access. Her hands brushed against him, touching him ever so lightly. It didn't seem accidental.

"Look," she said suddenly, "I really appreciate you behaving, okay?"

"You noticed that, did you? Good. It is not easy for me."

"I know, and I know what you would like me to do," she said, "but I am not ready yet. I may never be. And certainly not while I am here on business. I like you and you are fun to be with, but it's hard for me to cope with the expectations you always seem to have. If I did what you keep dreaming about it would confirm what you thought all along, namely that you can get more from me than a massage. But I am not like that. *If* I ever did what you would like, it could not be while giving you a massage. I told you that is strictly business for me, and I meant it, and you must see it the same way. You pay me for a clearly defined service. Anything else would make me feel cheap and demeaned. I could not live with the thought you were paying me because of the extras."

He nodded; let her continue. "What may happen in the future I don't know. I suppose anything is possible. If it ever came to that it would have to be completely outside our professional relationship, under which you implicitly contract to get a massage, and nothing else, for a fixed fee."

He turned half way around, propping himself on an elbow, so he could look into her eyes. "I truly understand what you are saying and have no problem with that. I admire and respect your principles."

"Good. Then we understand each other," she reiterated and gave him a dazzling smile. "Get back on your stomach so I can finish. I don't want you complaining I didn't do a thorough enough job. And sorry for the long speech."

"Don't worry," he said, "The clarification was in order. Or was it a warning? Maybe a promise? I can't make up my mind."

She shrugged. "You decide."

He had a hard time hiding his elation over what she had implied. Her principles told him that by not succumbing to his wishes, despite how friendly they had become, she would adhere to her professionalism with other customers as well.

He tried to restrain his dreams but felt confident a more intimate relationship was on the horizon. The key, he thought, was to have her accept his dinner invitation.

He could see her legs as she stood by his side. They were strong yet graceful, perfectly proportioned; tanned and smooth skinned.

Despite his best intentions, he could not resist stretching an arm out and running his hand over her naked knee, caressing its sensitive crook ever so lightly with his finger tips. She pretended not to notice at first, but when his hand began slowly moving up her leg, she stopped him.

"Please don't do that," she said. Her voice lacked conviction and so he kept his hand where it was, about halfway up her thigh. But she brought her legs together sharply and repeated, "Please don't. I mean it. Haven't you heard anything I said?"

"I am sorry. I heard you all right, but why do I get the feeling you like it anyway?" he said, but pulled his wandering hand away.

"That makes no difference. I can only repeat what I already told you. I am here to work, Shad. To give you the best massage I can. I can't do that when you caress my leg, okay?"

He nodded, appreciating she must have liked his touch enough to have distracted her.

"I do have one question," he said after a long silence. He had been daydreaming of being with her, hardly registering what she was methodically doing to his body.

"Namely?"

"What would be a reasonable number of massages for me to get from you in, let's say, a week or a month?"

She shrugged. "I have no idea. It's up to you. Most clients don't come more than once every two weeks, and a lot of them only monthly. There are no rules. I think it's mostly a question of money. It becomes expensive if they come too frequently. I don't give quantity discounts."

"Maybe you should. Have you ever considered offering package deals?"

"You mean like 'get six massages and the seventh one is free'?"

"Something like that. You could also offer some kind of cash discount for buying five or ten massages in advance."

"Hey, that's a great idea. Let me think about it and discuss it with my colleagues to see what kind of plans we could come up with."

"I have another idea," Shad said, now totally into his old marketing mode. "Why don't you offer a free massage to anyone who brings you a new customer? And then you offer those your package deal. I bet you would become so busy you would have to work ten or twelve hours a day."

"What makes you think I would want to do that?" she asked, but he could tell the additional revenue it could generate appealed to her.

"I just took for granted you wanted to make more money. But anyway, to get back to what we were discussing before, no one would think it strange if you gave me one twice a week, for example?"

She smiled. "I doubt it. Besides, who would know other than you and me and maybe my co-workers? But could you afford it since I haven't decided on a quantity discount yet?"

He grinned at her. Eight hundred dollars a month would be well worth it to keep him out of his recent doldrums. "I can afford it."

"Well, then let me know. I wouldn't mind the additional business and if you are serious, I can plan accordingly. But I may not always have 4:00 o'clock free."

"It does not matter. As far as I am concerned, you could come even later."

"What is that supposed to mean?" she said, immediately suspicious of ulterior motives.

"Just what I said. I normally have no plans for the evenings except for an occasional dinner, so you could come however late would suit you. In fact if you did come later, maybe we could have dinner together one of these evenings."

He was glad she did not immediately turn him down. "I don't know. That's really something I would have to think about. It would make keeping a strict business relationship awkward. It would be hard to keep the two separate. Besides, what would I tell my boyfriend?"

"I don't know," he admitted. "Maybe we could do it when he has the late shift and would not notice what time you came home. Or you could tell him that you have a good customer who insists he only has time for a massage in the evening. Don't you have clients like that? People who have to work late and then still want a massage?"

"Not very many. We try to discourage them. They are usually the ones difficult to control; the ones who think they can get more than just a massage."

"Well, you don't have to decide right now. My invitation is open ended. And I don't see a conflict between you treating me like any other paying customer and us having dinner together. We could even go out Dutch once in a while if you were worried that my buying you a meal would imply some kind of obligation on your part. It wouldn't,

I can assure you. It would simply be a great pleasure for me to invite you."

She nodded non-committally as she finished her work and sent him off to the bathroom to get back into his street clothes.

"So when would you like me to come back?"

"Tomorrow," he joked. "No. Better yet, why don't you just stay? Just kidding," he hastened to add when he saw how consternated she looked. "Three or four days from now would be fine; just tell me when and what time would be convenient for you."

She didn't accept his invitation to stay, reminding him her colleagues were waiting. He took her to the door. "Thank you very much for coming, Ruth. I really appreciate what you did and said."

She smiled in response, and he hugged her. As he did, she turned her face up and kissed him lightly. He was so surprised he could not react before she left him and hurriedly walked to her car.

He savored the lingering taste of her lips as he strolled into his living room. He was mellow and thought about what she had said and what it could mean. He was presumptuous enough to now think more about the *when* than the *what*, there no longer being any doubt in his mind they would become intimate at some point.

The more he thought about being with her, the harder it was for him to remember that he did not have all that much time to decide what to do about the Tranquil Towers. It occurred to him once again that Ruth could resolve his dilemma of being alone in his house, but he restrained himself from jumping to conclusions. For the time being he would be content with taking her out to dinner and he felt confident this day would come soon.

Veronica suddenly intruded on his thoughts. He was shocked to realize he had hardly thought of her for hours, for the first time since she passed away, and he felt guilty. What would she think if she knew he had become so fixated on another woman only nine months after she had left him? He himself had not thought it possible, and yet here he was, unable to get Ruth out of his mind. Would Veronica understand? Would she want him to be happy again and not feel so perennially desolate? He hoped so and wished he could ask her.

28

Ruth

The drive from Shad's house to *Su Casa*, the restaurant where we had agreed to meet, was too short to allow much deep thinking. I had to hurry; was already running late. I hadn't planned on staying so long with Shad.

Narissa Doost, Andrea Penny and Marilyn Cole, my three partners, were waiting for me at the bar. We exchanged perfunctory hugs before taking our drinks to the table Narissa had reserved. We felt comfortable in this venerable institution of Mexican food and relaxed ambience. We used this venue regularly for our informal bi-weekly meetings. The food was inexpensive and good, the Margaritas fabulous, and the service excellent.

Although we ran into each other sporadically between customers in our institute, we had learned we never seemed to have enough time to get together and talk. Having dinner together every two weeks to review what happened, problems we were encountering, what the competition was doing and just gossiping had proven to be beneficial.

I kept thinking about the suggestions Shad had made on expanding our revenue base, and I shared these with my colleagues. Momentary silence greeted me when I stopped speaking. Then Narissa, the senior partner, said, "I wonder why we never thought of this ourselves."

"Because we are too busy to stop and think," Marilyn offered.

"Or because we already have as many customers as we can handle, and even if we had the time to handle an increasing number, where would we accommodate them? We only have our four rooms, and they are utilized most of the time," Andrea said. She was prone to consider the glass half empty, I had observed more than once.

"I don't know about you guys, but I am not sure I can work more than the eight or nine hours I already do. My hands start cramping up towards the end of the day as it is," Narissa confessed.

"Same here," I admitted, "which means we would have to come up with different solutions to handle a bigger customer base. Any ideas, anyone?"

Helpless glances all around greeted me. "As I said," Andrea repeated, "with the four of us and only four stations, I just don't see how we could accept more clients, much as making more money appeals to me."

I saw Narissa and Marilyn nodding in agreement. "I have some ideas," I said.

"So let's hear them," Narissa prompted.

"Okay. The first problem is there are only four of us, and we are all pretty much booked fulltime. This we could overcome by hiring someone . . ."

"What do you mean, hire someone?" Narissa interrupted. "Bring in another partner?"

"No," I said. "I mean hire a masseuse. We charge $50 for a one hour massage. What if we could find an advanced trainee who needs more practical experience? We would pay her a flat $30 an hour. That would be good money for someone, and we partners would pocket $20 per customer."

"Hey, I like that! If we could get ten more customers per week, it would mean an incremental $200 for each of us," Andrea said, quick with her math. "Maybe we could even hire a man. I have had any number of clients who have told me they would prefer being massaged by a man."

"I can just imagine why," Marilyn interjected, smiling suggestively.

"Forget that stuff," Narissa said. "It would not be *our* problem, and I agree with what Andrea said. I have also had women who wanted a man to massage them. We lose customers because we don't have a male partner."

More thoughtful nodding from everyone. We had all had this request. Then Narissa resumed. "Let's assume for a minute we could find somebody —maybe even two, a man and a woman—and we would then have the capability for an additional six to twelve massages a day. What could we do about the lack of space?"

"Yes," I said, "that's the second problem, isn't it? The most obvious answer would be to lease bigger facilities, of course, which I am sure we could find."

"But wouldn't that be too risky?" Narissa asked. Her black, exotic Indian eyes were veiled. "Our overhead expenses would probably go up by 50% before we would even know if such an expansion would work, and before we knew if we could find suitable employees."

"Exactly right, Narissa," I concurred. "We need to find the additional customers and hire someone before looking for more space."

"Sounds to me like the old chicken and egg conundrum," Marilyn said, tossing her blond mane.

"Perhaps there is an answer to that dilemma," I said. "Let's take for granted, first of all, we could recruit staff and that we could attract a sufficient number of new clients. Then we need to accommodate them without physically expanding. To me, the answer is simple: the four of us have to make more house calls, thereby freeing the stations we have for our new employees."

"You have to be kidding!" Marilyn said. "That's asking for trouble, and you know it."

"I understand what you are saying," I mollified Marilyn, "but it would not have to be permanent. We would only have to do it until we have established that this expansion is basically viable. Once we know it is, we can look around for a new, bigger facility. Maybe even one which would give us eight stations, if we generated enough business to hire more employees. I look ahead and see the four of us gradually making fewer outcalls and again concentrating on our in house business. Further down the road we might consider offering additional services. We could contemplate transitioning from being just masseuses to becoming a full fledged spa. Why not? Let's think big and long term. I mean, do any of you wish to simply give massages for the rest of your lives? Don't we all have the secret ambition to rise above our present totally predictable future?"

I saw my partners looking at each other, eager expressions on their faces.

"That would be a dream come true," Narissa said. "Please don't laugh, but when I first brought you three in as partners, my vision was to eventually establish a broader business."

"It would certainly be appealing," Marilyn added, and even conservative Andrea concurred.

"In the meantime," I continued, "if we set ourselves an objective of making three house calls a day each, our two hires would be able to handle up to twelve new customers daily. We would just have to coordinate schedules carefully, but that should not be an issue."

"Well," Marilyn said, "that sounds great in theory, but are there enough potential customers around with the competition we have? And as to outcalls, I am not exactly enthusiastic, based on my personal experience."

"I know what you are worried about," Andrea said, "and I have been avoiding them for the same reasons. But I wonder if we could minimize the risks by concentrating on well known customers only. We all have long term clients we believe we know well. Who we can presumably rely on to behave, don't we?"

"True enough," Narissa conceded, "although I am not so sure that just because someone has always behaved, he or she would do the same under house call conditions."

Marilyn threw in, "I have another idea. There are so many retirement homes here. Maybe we could actively pursue setting up massage services with them, if they don't have one already. That should be pretty safe."

"Excellent idea!" Narissa said.

"Okay, let's go for that," I said. "Look, we all have a lot of experience with different customers and have learned to deal with them. I like Marilyn's idea and we need to follow up on it. We need to think about these various scenarios for a couple of days and then reconvene to see where we stand and what we need to do if we go ahead and implement."

"Sounds good to me," Narissa said. "I do think prior to meeting again you should sit down with our accounting firm, Ruth, and have them run some numbers for us. If business were to expand the way we hope, we might also need a receptionist to handle appointments, station assignments, answer the phone, and so on."

"And we have to calculate what other costs might hit us," Andrea added, "including car expenses for house calls."

"I don't think we could clear $20 per massage through an employee either," Marilyn said. "Wouldn't we have to pay social security and unemployment tax, and maybe even health insurance?"

"A good point, Marilyn," I acknowledged. "I'll find out. Maybe we would have to try and get someone for only $25 an hour. The other thought I had applies to our fees. We should consider different prices for different massages."

"What are you talking about?" Andrea asked.

"About the fact that all we provide today is a straight forward therapeutic massage, which we promote to make sure there are no misunderstandings about our institute. Most clients seem to be happy with this, but I have also had questions about whether we offer anything else. When I have to say 'no', I risk losing a customer."

"You mean like Thai, or Swedish, or whole body, or whatever?" Marilyn asked, her eyes wide open with what looked like mild shock.

"Precisely," I said. "Haven't you all had the same inquiries?"

My partners concurred reluctantantly. "So why don't we offer a range, at different prices?" I said. "And instead of only providing a standard one hour massage, how about adding a 30 minute or two hour one? I can see us coming up with a price catalog for various types and lengths. Maybe we could eventually stock some products to expand our repertoire . . . body lotions, massage oils, that sort of thing, as a prelude to becoming a spa."

"I guess we could," Andrea said, "but we are only qualified to give therapeutic massages and I don't like what those other massages could be construed to imply. As to selling over-the-counter products, we would probably need some kind of license."

"That should not be difficult to get, and regarding what clients might think, that couldn't be helped," I said. "Remember that a lot of people already hope for more anyway. As to the skills needed for different massages, I am sure we could learn easily enough. There must be relevant schools for that in San Diego."

It was getting late. Our dishes had long been cleared away and the hovering waiters seemed eager to see us leave. When I looked at my watch I was surprised it was nearly 10:00 o'clock.

"Look guys, I have to leave," I said, and we stood up and moved towards the exit after splitting the bill four ways and paying.

As I drove away, my thoughts lingered on our discussion in the restaurant. I was excited at the panorama of possibilities we had explored and was grateful to Shad for having provided the impetus to think about expanding our business. I was confident the basic concept could work and wondered if Shad would be willing to help us with developing a business plan. I sensed he had considerable experience and hoped he would share his knowledge with us. I wanted to discuss this with him and on the spur of the moment decided to accept his next dinner invitation. I did not doubt he would invite me again.

I was surprised when I realized I automatically thought of him when I needed help. What did it mean that he was the first person to come to mind? I felt comfortable in his presence, even if he never let me forget he wanted more from me than I was willing to give. I had to be cautious, I told myself, because despite his advanced age I found myself more attracted to him than I should have. I was used to men reacting physically to my massages and did not appreciate it, but Shad's responses had somehow been easier to take. He managed to remain inoffensive while being openly suggestive and I had not found this as unpleasant as I would have thought.

Contrary to what I had told him, I had actually caught myself fantasizing what it might be like to have this mature man make love to me. I knew his body was still okay; slim and with only moderate sagging of his skin. Not as smooth and muscular as my boy friend Brandon's, of course, but would that make a significant difference to me? More importantly, would he be as selfless as he had claimed? As unhurried? Focused only on giving me maximum pleasure; making me feel good? What a contrast that would be to Brandon's behavior, who was only interested in taking care of himself and had developed an utter disregard for what I wanted.

If asked, I would have had to admit I had reached the point with Brandon where I often hoped he had night shift and would not be home when I returned from work. Then I would not have to fight off his increasingly outrageous sexual demands and avoid the loud arguments that inevitably ensued. Just thinking of his latest insistence—that I participate in a threesome with him and his best friend—made me shudder. We had argued and fought when I refused to even consider it. I was tempted to tell Shad about my escalating personal problems with Brandon, knowing I would find sympathetic ears if I did.

I was thankful I had not married Brandon as he had proposed during our first years together. I had been very much in love with my handsome young fireman, and he had gone out of his way to make me happy. The only thing initially keeping me from marrying him had been our age difference. It had always worried me. I had sensed he would eventually tire of me. Over the past year, as he became less considerate and at times nearly abusive in bed, it had occurred to me he was taking advantage of me because of the age factor. He assumed I had to be grateful to him and acquiesce to anything he wanted simply because I was so much older and therefore had no choice. But I did not agree. I was not too old yet to find someone else. Shad's interest in me seemed to confirm this.

It was ironic to be drawn to a much older man. From one extreme to another. A role reversal. Thinking of Shad's nearly seventy years reminded me of my parents' age and I wondered if they still had sex. It seemed inconceivable; they *had* to be too old. And yet I had seen how quickly and easily Shad had become aroused, despite his years. Because of me specifically? Because he found *me* attractive and sexually desirable? Or merely because he had been alone too long and, as far as I knew, hadn't gotten laid like forever?

For Brandon, seven years my junior, I was already too old. He had stopped pretending otherwise. For Shad I was still young and desirable. What a dichotomy; too old for one, too young for the other. I wasn't sure how I saw myself. I didn't feel I was 'over the hill', but there was no getting around I was middle aged and a grandmother. I wished no more than ten or fifteen years separated me from Shad. Much easier to contend with. But maybe he had only developed into the kind of person he was now later in life. It was so academic and I wanted to stop thinking about it, but couldn't. Ten years from now he would be approaching his 80th birthday and presumably the end of his life, while I would be in my early fifties. Where would that leave me? The age difference was there and would not go away and would become more pronounced.

As these thoughts flitted through my mind I wondered why Shad seemed to have great problems making up his mind about the Towers. His uncertainties appeared much easier to resolve than my troubles with our age difference. I had seen one of the model apartments and knew the penthouse he had optioned was noticeably larger and appealing than what I had admired, apart from the magnificent views it offered. So what was his problem, if not affordability? To me it seemed like a mere question of time before he would have to move into assisted living facilities in any case. It should not be a question of *if* for him, but rather of *when*, and penthouses were rarely available. His house would inevitably become too much for him alone and in the meantime it reminded him constantly of what he once had had and the wife he had lost. Was a fresh beginning not better, in new surroundings unencumbered by daily recurring memories of how married life had been? I thought perhaps I should encourage him to exercise his option. I had the impression he could be influenced by my opinion.

And if he did move, would this impact what might happen between us? Would he behave differently if he met me outside the shadow his deceased wife cast throughout the house? Would he be even less inhibited in neutral territory? It would mean either having more of a fight on my hands, or succumbing to his advances. What did I want? I was not sure and realized I needed to make at least as major a decision as he did. I should just let events unfold, both with regard to his apartment and our relationship.

But the dinner question could not wait. I asked myself how I would feel if I accepted it and we walked into a restaurant together. How would other people perceive us? See me? Given my Mexican heritage and looks, there was no way I could be mistaken for his daughter. Age wise he could well be my father. Would people think I was his trophy wife? Probably not; I was too old and not blond. Would they speculate I was a professional escort? Would people wonder why I, young looking and maybe even considered attractive, would go on a date with a senior citizen? Would any of this bother me? Embarrass me? I concluded probably not; I had sufficient self confidence. I felt inexplicably excited when I realized I might already have made a subconscious decision.

29

Ruth

Still lost in these thoughts I pulled up in front of my apartment. I must have sighed unhappily when I spotted Brandon's pick-up parked at the curb. I hoped he was already asleep. I was tired and wanted nothing more than a quick shower and to go to bed.

It was not to be. "Where have you been?" Brandon scowled when I came in. A beer was in his hand and the TV was on; some kind of sport show.

"Nice to see you too," I said, not wanting a fight but unable to keep the reproach out of my voice. "Weren't you working the night shift this week? What are you doing at home?"

"Watching TV. Having a beer. Waiting for you. I traded shifts with Percy and got off at 10:00. You are pretty damn late."

"Yes, and you look sick with worry. You could have called me on my cell phone. We had our partner's meeting tonight and had so much to discuss it became later than expected."

"I am hungry," Brandon stated.

"There are some leftovers from last night in the fridge. You can nuke them in the microwave. I already ate."

"I can remember the days when you used to do that for me," he grumbled.

"And I can remember the days when you were much nicer to me," I retorted.

"Okay. Okay. Okay. I got the message." He got up to go to the kitchen.

I did not wait for him to return; tossed my handbag on the couch and walked into the bedroom. I undressed quickly and, grabbing my nightgown, went to take a shower. I luxuriated under the hot water and felt the day's exhaustion draining from my body.

As I stepped out of the shower and reached for my towel, I saw myself reflected in the mirror. I paused to study myself critically. I wasn't twenty five any longer but I thought I still looked okay. My body did not reflect my true age. It occurred to me the years had been kind to me. Despite my age and two kids, my breasts were still reasonably firm, with minimum sag, my prominent nipples still pointing forward. My stomach was flat; my butt round. No flab under my arms or on my thighs. My job required strength and stamina, and my body reflected this.

I was sure Shad would be more than pleased if he could see me like this, and I felt a rush of adrenaline as I imagined showing myself to him. His hand had felt good when he had sneaked in a quick caress. Maybe I should not have stopped him, just to see how far he would have gone. But I was afraid of what would have happened and I had not been ready.

I stopped reflecting and finished drying off. I slipped the nightgown over my head and brushed my teeth, then worked night cream into my face and brushed my hair.

When I emerged from the bathroom, Brandon was standing next to the bed, getting undressed.

"Have you given any more thought to doing it with Percy and me?"

"I didn't need to. I told you it's out of the question. I think it's disgusting. How can you even entertain the thought of sharing me with your buddy?"

"You shouldn't be so narrow minded," he admonished. "You don't know what you are missing. I bet it would be a lot of fun and very exciting, and if you didn't want Percy to fuck you, you could at least give him a blow job."

"That's revolting! Would you please shut up?" I said. My voice was dripping icicles.

"No, I won't. You should be grateful two young guys still want to do it with you, instead of pretending to be grossed out."

"I don't have to pretend. I am. I am going to bed."

"Oh, come on, Ruth. Don't be like that. Talking about a threesome makes me horny. I need you. Badly. Just the two of us, okay?" he said and climbed into bed next to me.

"Leave me alone, Brandon," I said when I felt his hand cupping my breast. I turned over on my side, my back to him. "I am tired and absolutely don't feel like it tonight."

I thought he had accepted this verdict when he took his hand away, but a moment later I cringed involuntarily when I felt his hand pushing into the crevasse of my butt, massaging my cheeks none too gently.

"Come on," he whispered hoarsely, "turn around on your stomach. I want to take you from the back."

Instead of complying, I wanted to slap him but forced myself to only shouting vehemently "NO!"

He wouldn't leave me alone. His hands were all over me as he tried to force me onto my stomach. I was beginning to fear him. He was strong and determined. For just a second I considered giving in, getting it over with so he would leave me alone and let me sleep. But I was deathly scared of him entering me as he wanted; I was absolutely so not ready it would be more than painful and no good for me at all. His wish to have Percy join us had turned me off completely.

"Go to sleep," I said. "I am going to spend the night on the couch." With that I got up, went to the closet to pull out a blanket, took a pillow and walked into the living room to make myself as comfortable as I could on the couch. He did not follow me. I was glad.

It took me a long time to fall asleep, despite my exhaustion. Did I really have any kind of acceptable or desirable future with Brandon? Hard to believe. Maybe now was as good a time as any to end our relationship before I could not stop him from raping me. It was my apartment. I could kick him out any time. But before I could pursue this thought further the day caught up with me and I fell asleep while speculating about what would be best for me.

*   *   *

No matter how long I brushed my teeth the next morning I could not get the foul aftertaste of the previous evening out of my mouth. The fight with Brandon had drained me. It wasn't that I was categorically opposed to what he had wanted—without Percy's participation—but

I had definitely not been in the mood, and how he had tried to force himself on me and bringing Percy into the picture had been the ultimate turn-off. Where had the romance gone? The prelude to making love? How could he possibly love me if he wanted to see me screwing or sucking another man? I knew he was not a jealous person, but what he was pushing me to do could not be explained by lack of jealousy. To me it was sick. Perverted. I wondered if these gross fantasies of his were something new, or if he had always harbored them. I didn't know and did not care. The world he wished me to enter was definitely not one I was willing to be a part of.

I was glad he had still been sleeping when I left the apartment. I could not have coped with sitting across from him, eating breakfast. I already dreaded coming back home in the evening. How had I gotten myself into such a mess? The timing could not have been worse, with the opportunities for expanding our business to be explored. Thanks to Shad I had found a promising way to break out of the largely boring routine my life had become. And now, instead of being able to totally focus on what I wanted to do, I had Brandon and my future with him to deal with as well, instead of enjoying his unqualified support.

First things first, I decided as I headed towards La Jolla and my first client. I needed to call Shad to see if he was willing to help me draft a business plan. I had to make an appointment with the accountants handling Massage Mahal. And I thought I should consult our lawyer to determine if the articles governing our current limited liability partnership adequately covered the expanded scope we envisioned for our venture.

I was in the process of parking when my phone rang. A quick glance at the caller ID told me it was Brandon, and I was tempted not to answer. But that would be childish and would not solve any problems, and so I activated the connection.

"Hey, Babe, it's me," he greeted me. "How you doing this morning?"

"I'm okay," I answered, my voice reflecting I was less than delighted to hear from him.

"Look," he said, "I know you must be pissed at me, and I don't blame you. I want to apologize for last night. I don't know what came over me to make me behave so badly."

I was caught by surprise. Brandon was not known as the apologetic type. In fact, I could hardly remember him ever having apologized for anything.

"Ruth? You there?" I heard him ask.

"Yes, I am here. I just wasn't sure I heard right," I couldn't resist saying.

"Ha, ha, ha. Very funny."

"I'm sorry, Brandon, it's just that you caught me by surprise. I am glad you called, and I accept your apology."

"Good. But I don't want us to have any misunderstandings. My apology was for how boorish I behaved, not for what I wanted from you."

"Gee, thanks, Brandon. That really makes me feel better. An apology with restrictions. Forget it. I don't have time to talk with you right now anyway. And as far as I am concerned, there is really nothing to discuss. Not if you persist with wanting to do that group thing."

"I guess I caught you at a bad time. Maybe we can talk about it tonight; clear the air. I don't have to go to work until ten."

"If it's about Percy and you and me, there is absolutely nothing to discuss. Listen, I have to go." I clicked the phone shut, furious at him and that he had ruined the beginning of my day.

The short walk to Massage Mahal helped calm me. I was the first one on site and set to work immediately by calling our accountant to set up a meeting. Then I did the same with our lawyer. I saw I still had a few minutes before my first customer was scheduled to arrive and, on the spur of the moment, decided to Google Shad. I was curious to see if Google had information on him that I did not.

The image icon I clicked on brought up a photo showing him receiving an award for his efforts on behalf of the Chinese Dermatological Society. I thought he had not aged drastically since the ten year old photo had been taken. His hairline appeared to have receded; the wrinkles around his eyes were deeper. Other than that, he had not changed noticeably. The text references to him did not reveal much more than I had already learned from him personally. I could not find anything relating to his source of income or the extent of his wealth, and after browsing through the short references for some minutes, I closed the site.

I thought of calling him to ask him for the help I wanted, but there was little point. He had made it clear enough he had time on his hands and would be happy to spend more of it with me. I would ask him following the next massage.

Narissa arrived and I told her about the meetings I had set up.

"That's a smart idea, including the lawyer," she said. "I'll tell the others when I see them."

"I think we should go together," I said, "and if we agree on our business plan by then they should be able to tell us what other aspects we might have to consider."

"Are you going to need help on the plan?" Narissa asked.

"Not right away. Based on our discussion I have a pretty good grasp of what needs to be addressed. I also know a guy who can help me. When the draft is finished, we can all review it and make whatever modifications the group deems necessary."

"Well, I am glad you volunteered. I wouldn't know where to begin," Narissa confessed.

"I am not sure I know either. I am going to rely on my friend to guide me and who knows all about writing business proposals."

"Anything I can do to move our project along?" Narissa asked. She had apparently decided to defer to me in assuming leadership.

"Yes, I think there is. Could you find out where we could learn those other massage techniques we discussed? How long relevant courses would take, and how much they cost? I expect you could get preliminary information through a computer search and then a few follow up phone inquiries. And now that I think about it, why could we not specify in the 'Help Wanted' ads we need to run that we are looking for someone with experience in giving the other massages we want to offer?"

"That's a super idea, Ruth. But that would not cover our increased house calls. At least I assume we would want to offer a menu of different massages irrespective of location."

"You are right," I said. "I hadn't thought of that."

"Well, let's just see what happens. I'll research the training courses. Meanwhile, I have my first client coming in."

"Yeah, me too."

*   *   *

Shad was visibly delighted when he opened his door for me two days later. He had called and apologized profusely for having to postpone his massage. He had forgotten the dinner engagement he had with

Thomas Grady and was loathe to break it. I had managed to hide my disappointment and rearranged my schedule.

The easy comradeship we had established set the tone. I was no longer apprehensive about massaging him at home, and his expectations, or hopes, had been brought into realistic perspectives. I was not afraid I would have to fight him off; wasn't sure I would if he did try something. The latent tension I had felt previously had dissipated.

If he was unhappy at seeing me back in my uniform of jeans and polo shirt, he did not show it. I did not tell him I had debated with myself as to what to wear when I speculated about accepting the dinner invitation he would surely extend. He did not know I wanted to discuss the plan for which I needed his help. If we were going to have dinner I had wanted to wear proper attire and shoes instead of sneakers, but I had rejected this as being perhaps misleadingly provocative.

As if we had settled on an unspoken agreement, we both remained largely silent during the massage. He was evidently content and so relaxed that at times I was not sure he was still awake. He made no effort to get me to touch him sexually and did not reach out for me when my legs brushed against his arms. I was almost disappointed as I remembered studying myself in the mirror, standing nude in the bathroom, thinking about Shad seeing my body. Was he no longer interested in me? Had I been too harsh in rejecting his innuendos? I was not at all sure what I preferred, he trying to seduce me or like this, seemingly indifferent.

"I want to apologize for canceling yesterday on such short notice, Ruth," Shad interrupted my train of thought.

"Not to worry. It gave me a chance to reflect on a business plan I want to write. How was your dinner?"

"A lot longer than I had expected; with Thomas Grady, my retired ex-colleague, who lives in the Tranquil Towers. That's what I wanted to discuss with him, to see how he likes it there after eight months, but then as we were talking I also remembered events from many years ago that I wanted to clarify concerning someone we had met and worked with in China."

"Oh?" I said, my eyebrows no doubt arching. "Did you succeed?" My curiosity had been piqued.

"Yes, but it's a long and complicated story. It goes back twenty five years. Maybe I will tell you about it one of these days, if you are interested. But you mentioned something about a business plan?"

"I did, but let me finish your massage before I get started. And I am curious about that bit of history you mentioned."

He nodded his acquiescence and let me do my job. A business discussion—or his conversation with Thomas—would only distract him from my massage. I wondered if he was testing me by not flirting with me. I was surprisingly disappointed he had not even tried.

"How about a glass of wine?" he asked when I was finished and he had gotten dressed again. I was relieved he had returned to normal.

"Sure. Why not?"

"Hey, that's great!" It seemed he had not expected me to agree so readily.

I settled into one of his easy chairs, staring out at the ocean while he brought our drinks.

"So tell me what you meant by working on a business plan."

"It goes back to those ideas you were airing the other day about us expanding our business," I said and went on to share in some detail the discussion we had had and what we had concluded. "I was elected to draft a plan we could run by our accountant and lawyer to see if this thing is feasible, and since you gave me the initial impulse and must have a lot of experience in writing such a plan, I thought maybe you could help me."

"Well, sure, I would be happy to. But keep in mind I can only assist you with the technicalities. I know absolutely nothing about the massage or spa business. I do like the ideas you came up with. You have gone way beyond what I had suggested, which is good. Your thinking is innovative and it sounds achievable to me. What exactly is it you would like me to do?"

"Get me started properly, I suppose, and provide me with an outline of what I would need to incorporate. I have never seen such a proposal, let alone written one."

"You want to start on it right now?"

"If you have the time, yes."

"I do, but I hope you won't be shocked when I tell you what it will cost you," he said, a sparkle in his eyes.

I sat there for a moment, dumbfounded. It had never occurred to me he might want to extract a payment. "What were you thinking of charging us?" I finally squeezed out, trying to smile, but my lips were too compressed.

"You would have to let me invite you out for dinner and accept."

I laughed with relief. "I should have guessed. It's a deal." I was pleased my assumption had been correct.

He went to his office to retrieve a scratch pad and pens and started outlining what I would have to include. "You need to start by summarizing where you are today, the scope of your business and the competitive environment. Some market research needs to be carried out for the latter. Then you identify the problems and opportunities in conjunction with what you are planning to do. Formulate the strategies and tactics you wish to employ in your expansion, together with your long range perspectives. A cost/benefit analysis needs to be done, based on your assumptions, together with an estimated profit and loss statement. And finally, you have to spell out what your goals and objectives are."

"You make it sound simple," I said, somewhat enviously, "but I am not sure I know what you are talking about."

"I don't know if simple is the right word. It's certainly not rocket science. It is a lot of work and time consuming. It's easy to spell out the chapter headings. The hard part is developing realistic numbers and correctly identifying the underlying assumptions. I can't do that for you, but if you start filling in the blanks of this outline with what you and your colleagues know, then I would be happy to go through it with you and help you make whatever corrections or changes might be appropriate. I could challenge your numbers and assumptions and get together with you as a group to make sure everyone agrees."

"Fantastic. I'll get started tomorrow. But what's with this research you mentioned? I have no idea what that might entail or how to go about it."

"I may be able to do some of that for you. Visit some spas. Surf the internet for relevant information and data. But keep your payment obligation in mind."

"You drive a hard bargain!" I said and smiled.

"Yes. And since payment is upon demand, what do you say we go and have dinner now?"

I protested feebly, pointing out I was hardly dressed for dinner, but he was adamant. We would go to a casual eating establishment, he assured me.

He took me to a little Thai restaurant he liked, and after we had spent some time discussing details of the business plan while we were eating, I reminded him of what he had said about telling me about Thomas and the individual in China with whom they had worked.

It took quite a while. He was surprisingly frank and included what he was not proud of and seemed hesitant in sharing with me. But I appreciated his openness and showed as much understanding as I could. I hadn't realized he had meant a woman. I felt a sense of pride that he trusted me enough to reveal this background so freely, which could not have been easy for him.

It encouraged me to unburden myself as well; to share my frustrations with Brandon. I respected Shad and his opinions, and hoped another man's perspective might help me with the struggles I faced.

"I have problems with Brandon, my boyfriend."

He acknowledged this with a slight nod. "Somehow I am not surprised. Do you want to tell me about it? It's none of my business, but I will be glad to listen."

"You already suspected as much?" I asked. His perception validated my raising the subject.

"Yes. From how you reacted when we talked about him during that first massage you gave me. There were things left unsaid which I thought pointed to some issues you have apart from the age factor."

"Well," I said, "you were right. I do think it's mostly related to the age difference, however. I told you he has started to take me for granted and believes I should do whatever he wants; that I should be grateful to him for putting up with me, an old woman."

"Which means what?"

"I am embarrassed to talk about it," I admitted. Should I really discuss my sexual problems with Shad? Was I not being foolish?

"You don't need to be. I doubt if there is anything you could say that would shock me, and you can depend on me that whatever you tell me goes no further."

I became pensive, still unsure of my ground, but having started, I could hardly stop. "We used to have a very romantic relationship. Sex with Brandon was fabulous, and he was kind and considerate. But lately he gradually changed. He has this good friend at work and whether it was this Percy or Brandon who came up with the idea I don't know, but bottom line is Brandon wants me to get into a threesome with his friend. Brandon wants me to screw Percy and watch us doing it. Or have Percy watch us, and I just can't do that. It's physically impossible for me. The mere thought dries me up completely; makes my vagina cramp so tightly I can't even do it with Brandon alone once he has raised the subject. And then Brandon wants to do it anally, sort of as compensation for me not being willing to comply with his other wishes. Fights and arguments become inevitable then and I wind up sleeping on the couch."

I felt relieved at finally having shared my misery. I felt sure Shad liked me a lot and it occurred to me he might become jealous when hearing my bedroom secrets; that he could not possibly view my problems dispassionately; that his own feelings would intrude on his objectivity.

I studied him closely, searching for either understanding or condemnation in his eyes, but all I saw was studied neutrality.

"Have you talked to him about it?"

"I have tried, but he doesn't attempt to understand me. Or simply can not believe I can not do what he wants. As a man, do you think it's unreasonable for me to turn him down? That I am being too narrow minded in this era of sexual enlightenment?"

"No, not at all. I think sex can only be as good as it should be if both partners thoroughly enjoy what they are doing, without pretenses. You could call it compatibility, which doesn't appear to exist between you two anymore. Having said that, also keep in mind that to achieve compatibility some compromise might well be necessary in any relationship. But compromise has to be a two way street; both partners must be willing. You must determine how far you can or are willing to go to maintain a healthy sexual relationship, and it sounds like you can not do what he wants. If he has decided he can not do without the things he desires, and you are not able to accommodate him, you can not achieve happiness any more, in my opinion."

I nodded forcefully. "I don't know what to do. If he had broached this subject when we first met, I never would let him move in. Why does he come up with this now, after we have been together for years?"

"No idea. Maybe he didn't feel comfortable raising it earlier. Maybe he thought you would come up with the idea yourself. Or his tastes have changed. People do change you know. Or maybe he thinks this is the best way to keep you both from getting bored with your sex life. Perhaps he feels sex has become routine; an obligation. That extra stimulus is required to bring back the fierce passion you had. What if he had an affair instead? Would you find that easier to accept than what he proposes to have you do?"

"Of course not. But I don't believe one has anything to do with the other." I paused, thinking. "Please help me understand how men think."

"I can't speak for men; only for myself. Based on what you have said, I believe you have to assume that if you don't succumb to his demands he will start looking for a woman who will. There must be enough of those. Maybe doing it one time would get it out of his system. Maybe he would become addicted to it. But one thing is sure for me: he is not going to drop the subject until he has tried it, either with you or someone else," he said, painfully blunt.

I couldn't disagree with his assessment. I knew he was right. "Could you imagine ever asking your wife to have sex with another man? Or having someone watching you having sex with her?"

"Not with another man, no. Under no circumstances. It would drive me insane with jealousy."

It took me a moment to understand what he had left unsaid. "What do you mean not with another man?"

"Exactly what I said."

"So am I right in assuming you think it would be okay with another woman?" I asked, caught by surprise.

"I am not saying it would or would not be all right. All I know is I would not object to my wife having sex with another woman. In fact, since we are in this confession mode, let me tell you another one of *my* secrets, if you can handle it and at the risk of you freaking out."

"Oh, oh, I am not sure I want to hear this," I said, but of course I did.

"Fine with me. I just thought we had reached a point where we could share our deepest secrets openly so we would begin to understand each other more thoroughly."

"I do wish that." It crossed my mind I might never have another opportunity of learning about this part of his past. "Go ahead. Tell me what you meant."

He did, going back to when he had met Veronica and discovered her bisexual personality and how he had accepted this and occasionally participated in a threesome with her and her girl friend Caitlin.

"I don't believe it!" was all I managed to say when he had finished. I was flabbergasted, to put it mildly. Could he be telling the truth? Was I shocked or revulsed? I didn't know; needed time to digest.

"Up to you, but it's the truth. Why won't you believe me?"

"I guess I do. I didn't mean that the way it sounded. I just find it so unbelievable; so incredible." Then another thought occurred to me. "Is that why Veronica and you never had any children?"

"No. We really wanted to, but try as we might it never worked out. There was nothing physically wrong with either one of us, but for some reason Veronica could never conceive. We talked about artificial insemination, or even a surrogate mother, but neither option appealed to us, so we gave up and just enjoyed ourselves. Maybe it was an age issue. Veronica was already in her mid thirties when we got married."

"That must have been a heavy burden for you," I commiserated.

"Yes, it was. But we were happy nevertheless. Anyway I am sorry if I shocked you. Haven't *you* ever fantasized about getting it on with another woman?"

"Of course not!" I said, but I could not stop the blush suffusing my face that made a lie out of my words.

"I rest my case," he said and smiled. "And just in case you are interested in knowing, I was never the driving force behind our little games. It was always Veronica and Caitlin who wanted to get together and insisted I join them periodically. So I did, and not too reluctantly, I have to admit."

I found the silence that settled over us awkward. It was too late for me to admit to the fantasies Shad had mentioned. I had had more than one opportunity through my profession, but I had never been seriously tempted and had found it quite easy to resist making these fantasies come true. The desire had been missing. It had been idle speculation; plain curiosity about how it might be.

I didn't know how I felt about Shad's pertinent experiences. It would take some time to come to grips with what he had revealed. I could not picture such a scene.

"So how long did this go on with . . . what was the name you mentioned?"

"Caitlin. I don't remember the exact date, but it ended sometime in the mid nineties," he said. He paused, as if overcome with old memories, before continuing. "I sometimes wonder what Caitlin is doing now and how she is. She gradually moved out of our lives. Not because we didn't enjoy our threesomes any more, but because she sensed the slight discomfort I always experienced. I was too much in love with Veronica and knew Caitlin really wanted her, not me, and I didn't have enough emotional space to include Caitlin as additional partner. I was happy with Veronica alone, despite the sexual thrill our threesomes provided. When I traveled she saw Caitlin at times, to which I never objected because I knew it had nothing to do with how she felt about me, but eventually Caitlin met another woman, fell in love with her, and severed her relationship with Veronica. She wanted to be faithful to her new lover. I haven't seen her since and Veronica never took up with another woman. I guess Caitlin was an episode in her life, and she put it behind her. We never discussed the reasons."

"Were you ever alone with Caitlin?"

"No. Caitlin was lesbian and only accepted me so she could have Veronica, and I was very satisfied with my wife and did not cheat on her."

"I am not sure these revelations about your past help me with the problem I have with Brandon. They don't seem relevant or comparable."

Shad shrugged. "Probably not. But they do illustrate that people have different desires. I don't want to be judgmental. Brandon's obsessions and what I told you about Veronica and me simply mean our concepts of good sex may be different from yours. To me it's not a question of perversion or one thing being better or not as good as the other; they are merely different. You should not feel bad about turning down Brandon's demands, any more than I feel bad about what Veronica and I had with Caitlin. You have to decide what you want and whether you might be willing to make concessions to make your partner happy. If the situation is non-negotiable, meaning neither one of you can change, you have to accept the inevitable consequences."

This made sense to me. "What would you do if you were in my place?" I was hoping he could help me more specifically.

"Hard to say. I am not a woman. I am also biased. I have a vested interest. I like you a lot and would love to see you free of the relationship you have, but I also don't want to be responsible for you breaking up with Brandon. You might eventually hold it against me."

"I would not do that," I said and believed it. "Whatever decision I make is mine alone and in what I feel would be in my own best interests."

"Maybe, maybe not. You can't really predict how you might feel a few years from now. It seems to me you first have to decide whether you could ever comply with his wishes. If you can't and he continues to insist you really have no choice, do you?"

"I suppose not," I found myself reluctantly concurring. "But let me ask you this. If instead of Caitlin another man had become involved, could you have lived with the situation?"

"Absolutely not. I already told you. Totally impossible."

"Sort of strange in a way, I would think, that you tolerate another woman but not another man. After all, sharing is sharing."

"Perhaps, but all I am saying is I can do one but not the other. That's the way I am; you can be—are—different. Again it's not a judgment call but rather a matter of personal likes and dislikes."

Shad had given me a lot to think about. Given what he had revealed about his sexual history, I wondered if he secretly harbored visions of a threesome with me and a second woman. But then I thought how could he when he could by no means be certain I would ever be willing to go to bed with him under any circumstances? Or had he concluded it was going to happen? Had I? I was thoroughly confused.

In any case, I was grateful for his frankness and advice and wished I could talk this openly with Brandon. I wondered why I couldn't. Was it because Shad was more mature and understanding? Or had he ingeniously pushed me into breaking up with Brandon, thinking he could then have me? I couldn't tell and needed time to ponder what I wanted out of life.

"I hope some of what I told you proves to be helpful and that I didn't upset or shock you too much, Ruth," Shad said as he reached across the table to take my hand.

I reciprocated his pressure automatically and smiled at him. "Thanks for being so patient with me," I told him. "You were indeed very helpful, but as of now, I still don't know what I should do."

"That doesn't surprise me. You have hard choices to make with long term consequences. So I suggest you take all the time you need and think it through."

30

The long discussion Shad had had with Ruth made him thoughtful long after she had left. He had hoped to entice her to have a nightcap with him at home, but she had adamantly refused. It occurred to him she might have been worried about what would happen if she had accepted. She had not looked too upset about what he had revealed, and yet he was concerned it might have been premature to tell her about Veronica's and his history with Caitlin. Had it scared her off? Or was she so engrossed in her problems she had wanted to be alone? Whatever her reasons had been for leaving could not be changed, and he stopped dwelling on them.

Talking about Veronica had saddened him, retroactively. A flood of memories washed over him as Ruth drove away. At home, renewed loneliness enveloped him. Could Ruth fill the void Veronica had left? He did not think about his deceased wife constantly any longer, and when he did, it was often not for long. It was the frequent, fleeting reminder of her at unexpected moments that depressed him. Something as trivial as seeing her favorite mug could unleash the realization his life had changed forever. He missed her easy going presence. She was everywhere and nowhere more than in his bedroom. No room felt emptier without Veronica than his bedroom.

He had thought of moving into the guest room, but it felt too small and constricting and he loved his king size mattress and the spaciousness of the master bedroom. And yet the emptiness of his bed had become more pronounced since meeting Ruth. She was an inadvertent reminder of how good it had always felt to go to bed with Veronica, but somehow he could not imagine sleeping with Ruth in this room, despite the fact that he desired her and dreamed of making love to her.

He had become fixated on Ruth and knew this was ridiculous, given the short time they had known each other. Was it simply his desperation? His urgent need for sex? Or was he falling in love with her?

He enjoyed being with her and fantasizing about her but she could only distract him for a few short hours at a time. Between her visits it still took an effort to keep from feeling sorry for himself. Ruth could lift him out of his despondency, but she could also be the cause. What they discussed or how she behaved made old memories inevitable and precipitated comparisons between her and Veronica. They were very different in every aspect except one: their ability to make him relax and feel good. He felt guilty for being so attracted to Ruth when Veronica had only been gone such a short time, but these feelings were beyond his control and he hoped Veronica would understand. Certainly he would have wanted the same for her if it had been he who had passed away. As it was, he caught himself talking to Veronica, telling her about Ruth and what they had discussed and how good she made him feel.

He debated with himself whether or not it had been right to have told Ruth about Caitlin. There had been no good reason to divulge this unusual aspect of his marriage, and he doubted it had helped Ruth in coming to grips with her own issues. She must have been shocked; might well decide she wanted nothing further to do with him. What he had done with Veronica and Caitlin would no doubt scare her. Should he call her, try to explain and reassure her she had nothing to worry about? Or should he give her time to work through her problems? He couldn't make up his mind and finally called Thomas. He had always been a good listener and was a wise man who might be able to help and would be happy to hear from Shad.

The irony of consulting Thomas for reasons similar to why Ruth had confided in him did not escape Shad, but it did not deter him.

"What's going on, Shad?" Thomas greeted him.

Shad decided not to beat around the bush. "I am a mess, my friend. Do you remember my mentioning that I had met this masseuse?"

"Sure. I didn't give it much significance though, I must admit."

"Well, I have been seeing more and more of her, both for a massage and socially."

"Good for you. Is she attractive?"

"Very. But more importantly, I like her as a person. Her personality. Her sense of humor and her maturity and ambitions."

"So what's the problem?"

"I am wondering if I am making a fool of myself. If I have told her too much about myself already. Whether it was right of me to show her how and where I live, which makes me wonder whether she likes me or what I represent."

"You mean you worry she might be a gold-digger?"

"Not really. I can't see her being that materialistic, but my financial status could definitely influence her, I suppose. It might be enough to make her look at my shortcomings, especially my age, more favorably."

"So what? If she can make you happy why not enjoy life? You aren't planning on marrying her, are you?" Thomas asked.

"I hadn't thought about it. My conscience plagues me. I still see Veronica everywhere and even find myself talking to her, and here she is, not even gone a year, and I am chasing another woman. It doesn't seem right to me and unfair to Veronica, and yet I can't seem to stop myself."

"Well, if you are looking for advice, I am hardly in a position to give any. You know how quickly I fell in love with Pam after Jade died. I felt the same way you do now, I suppose, and all I can tell you is that it was beyond my control and looking at it retrospectively, it was the best thing that could have happened to me. Who knows what would have become of me, or where I would be now, if I hadn't met Pam? Years of moping and feeling sorry for myself? Seeking treatment for ongoing depressions? Becoming a social outcast and recluse? How would that have helped Jade? Or me coping with my grief?"

"I guess you are right," Shad sighed.

"Don't force the issue is all I can say. Take it easy and see what happens. Which reminds me, where do you stand on buying in here?"

"Nowhere. My option is about to expire, and I am still hesitating. On one hand, I need new surroundings to get away from the shadows Veronica still casts over the house. On the other hand, when I am with Ruth—my friend's name—my feelings of loneliness evaporate. If I could get her to stay with me my main reason for contemplating moving would be gone. But I need time to see what kind of relationship might develop between us, and that I don't seem to have."

"Why don't you talk to Sybil Delatour and see if you can negotiate an extension? After all, economic times are tough and from what I hear, the Towers is not selling apartments as fast as they would like, so they may be flexible."

"Good idea. It's certainly worth a try. Thanks, Thomas."

"Listen, Shad, I would love to meet this Ruth. Why don't you ask her if she would be willing to have dinner with us?"

"Fine with me, as long as this doesn't turn into an Apries situation in reverse!"

"That I can not promise. I am pretty lonesome myself at times," Thomas said but quickly added, "I am kidding, Shad. Don't be worried, okay?"

*   *   *

The message light on his answering machine was blinking when Shad returned home. It was Mark Brooks' office, the lawyer he had consulted about his distant past. He had obtained some answers and asked Shad to call to set up an appointment.

Hearing this, Shad felt himself breaking out in a cold sweat. Between his pre-occupation with Ruth, the business plan she wanted him to help prepare, his looming decision regarding the Towers and his recurring memories of Veronica, he had nearly forgotten Mark Brooks. Now all his latent worries and deepest fears rose to the surface and he had problems sleeping. His apprehension was so great he reluctantly canceled his scheduled massage, knowing he was too nervous to enjoy it and fearing he would not be able to stop himself from confiding his origins in Ruth, something he had not even done with Veronica.

"I hope you have some good news for me, Mr. Brooks," Shad ventured when they greeted each other two days later.

Brooks shrugged. "That's something you have to decide. I can only transmit the information I was able to gather." He consulted some notes on his desk before continuing. "Through my contact in LA we were able to access the Sheriff's data base. We could not find anything relating to the questions you posed. Given the sparse information you provided, the base would seem to be irrelevant."

"How can you get into that data?" Shad interjected.

"Through well connected contacts I can not divulge. Believe me, our information is solid. Anyway, as previously explained, there is no statute of limitations for jail break as such. It is dealt with on a case by case basis through the courts which may or may not consider mitigating circumstances, including when the escape took place, how it was effected, whether anyone was hurt, the original crime of the fugitive, age factor, and the individual's life since escaping, i.e. has he been a model citizen or continued with a life of crime. Even the subjective impression the judge gets of the fugitive when he appears in court is an important factor, as are character references."

"You mean things like showing regret, apologizing, etc.?"

"Yes. All of that is potentially important. But an appearance in court is inevitable, and turning himself in could be another factor in his favor."

Shad saw Brooks studying him closely before he heard him say, "Mr. Cooper, you must remember that everything we discuss here falls under client/lawyer confidentiality. It will not leave this room under any circumstances, so please permit me to say that I believe you have been less than open with me, and it is therefore next to impossible for me to answer your original questions definitively, let alone advise you. The more I have thought about your request, the more convinced I have become that you are the individual we are reviewing. Whether you acknowledge this or not is entirely up to you, of course, but as I said, if you want meaningful advice, I need more background than you have provided."

"Like what?" he asked, knowing he had paled as he listened and not at all sure he should comply.

"The name of the fugitive, to begin with, and under what name he has been living. I have to assume he took on a new identity, or he would have been caught long ago. When and where the jail break took place. The exact circumstances. How the fugitive escaped re-capture. Where and what he is today. This would at least allow me to get started."

Shad felt the pressure rising inexorably. He did not want to reveal his real identity, but he was also tired of living in constant fear. The lawyer was sworn to secrecy; what was the worst that could happen to him, Shad asked himself? He would not be turned in. At worst the lawyer would not be able to help.

"All right," he finally said. "You are right. I was talking about myself. I have lived under an assumed identity since 1958." And then he proceeded to bare his soul.

Silence greeted his detailed confession. Brooks had listened attentively; was ruminating.

"So what do you think?" Shad finally asked.

"I can only give you an off the cuff response at this point. I need to do additional research and go back to my contact in LA, if we decide to pursue this. First off, in addition to your escape, you have since then broken a number of laws. You lied to government officials—the Army, CIA, FBI—a federal crime. You obtained legal documents fraudulently—birth certificate, passport, social security card, draft card, voter registration card, etc. Another crime. The relevant sheriff's files probably still exist somewhere. When the department computerized they only went back approximately forty years except for so called major crimes, which would not include yours, in my opinion. So while your record could still exist in paper form, it should not be in any computer base. It would certainly be hard to access; deeply buried. I seriously doubt anyone is actively looking for you. The original conviction was not grave enough; no one was hurt; you were essentially still a juvenile. The guards must have been acutely embarrassed at having let you escape. Even a cold case squad would not waste time looking for you today. You did not commit what we would call a major crime. The original circumstances would not justify it. There was no central reporting or tracking system of a death in those days. By and large, only capital murder cases and kidnappings are pursued forever, and other particularly violent or heinous crimes. I suspect strongly no one would be interested in digging into your crime after fifty years. Current crime rates are simply too high for that. If someone were to look into your escape today, because you turned yourself in, they would be opening a can of worms. Like your social security payments, for instance. Since Shad Cooper paid his taxes throughout the years, and it is he who gets the benefits now, where is the crime? I don't know. It would be a gray area, in my non-researched opinion. You served your country honorably during an official time of war. One could argue you redeemed yourself."

"That sounds like good news to me."

Brooks shrugged. "I am not sure I would go that far. Technically, you remain a fugitive and are subject to arrest at any time. Is it likely to happen? More than extremely unlikely, I would say, but we can not totally eliminate the risk."

"So based on what you know today, what is your best advice?" Shad asked.

"As an officer of the court I am obligated to do everything in my power to get you to turn yourself in and throw yourself on the mercy of the court."

"But?"

"Don't ever quote me on this, but if I were you, I would do nothing. Keep your fingers crossed. Given your age and status, why would you have to show your fraudulent documentation to anyone? Who would have reason to question it? Continue to keep a low profile and hope for the best. Since you have not gotten caught in fifty years, there is no reason to fear the years you have left will be any riskier."

Shad nodded. "My thinking exactly. I can not see myself at age 68 surrendering to the police, going to court and risking jail."

"Do you want me to pursue this further, or should I drop it?" Brooks asked.

Shad hesitated only momentarily before concurring that the matter be dropped. "I do have one other question as long as I am here. I am a widower. I recently met a woman I rather like and she seems to feel the same way. I don't believe I want to marry again but have thought of asking her to move in with me, as a paid fulltime caretaker and companion. Let's say until I died or became too infirm to remain at home. Could she then make a case that she had become my common law wife?"

"You would pay her a salary, but she would also be your lover?"

"Hopefully yes. I am working on it. I have no idea whether she would accept such a proposal."

"It would certainly be unique, I must say. Off hand, I suspect the answer to your question is no, but regardless, I recommend you think this through carefully. If she were to become your lover, and you pay her, what would that make her? You know what I mean? Not to put too fine a point on it, but there are words to describe such a woman."

Shad blushed. "I hadn't thought of it that way. Nothing is further from my mind."

"Well, anyway, to avoid misunderstandings the employer/employee relationship must be so clearly spelled out it would outweigh any other consideration, including a potential common law possibility. To underline the employment status you would have to deduct/pay social security taxes for her, and it probably would not hurt to provide medical insurance as well. You might also consider some kind of retirement benefits, or leave an appropriate lump sum amount to her in your testament. But, as indicated, you should decide whether you want a lover or an employee. Wanting her to be both sounds like a disaster waiting to happen, speaking strictly as a man rather than as your lawyer."

"You are probably right. I need to give it more thought."

"Well, if you do go ahead, I would be glad to draw an employment contract up for you. Whatever you agree to, you should have it in writing. So should she, for that matter," Brooks advised. "You might also want to keep in mind that if you did decide to marry her, the false identity issue arises. Shad Cooper is dead, remember?"

Shad sighed dolefully as he left, not sure how he felt. The definitive resolution of his fugitive status had not been achieved as he had hoped, but he felt reasonably secure in continuing to live with the status quo. The idea with Ruth he had been mulling around needed more consideration. Marriage sounded less than prudent. There was nothing he could do at this point. What he could and had to address was the apartment issue, and this he resolved to do expeditiously.

31

Recognizing the urgency of making up his mind about buying the penthouse was easy; making the best decision was difficult. The crazy idea regarding Ruth he had mentioned to Mark Brooks was up in the air. Brooks had dampened his initial enthusiasm considerably. He needed to crystallize his thinking and find out if Ruth would even consider such a proposal. Her answer would be the fulcrum on which his decision balanced. He could not expect an immediate answer from her. He still had to find a way to approach her.

He had not heard from Sybil Delatour. This meant she had not found another viable buyer and he hoped she might agree to extending his option until she did.

He walked to the Towers and was in luck. Sybil had time to see him.

"How have you been, Mr. Cooper?" Her smile was as dazzling as always. "I have been meaning to call you to find out when you would sign the purchase agreement."

"That's what brings me here," he said. "Not to sign, but to talk to you about extending the option."

The smile left her face. "I am not sure I understand. I thought we were more than generous in agreeing on the three months option."

"I appreciate your accommodation. On the other hand, if you could have sold the unit by now, I am sure you would have. You see, my personal circumstances have changed somewhat and might lead me to reconsider. A more extended evaluation period is necessary for me."

"Okay," she grudgingly conceded. "How much more time do you anticipate needing?"

"I wish I knew. Perhaps very little, but it depends on someone else. What I was thinking was that we could leave the option in place, but make it open ended."

"I am not sure I understand what that means." A puzzled look was on her face.

"It means we would go from month to month, or day to day. My option would remain in effect until either I make a decision, or you find someone else. If you do find someone ready to purchase, you give me a call and I would have the right of first refusal. The option fee of $100,000 I deposited remains with you in escrow until then."

"Hmmm, I am not sure we could do that. It has certainly never been done before, but we want to work with you and continue to be as cooperative as possible. I tell you what: why don't you let me run this by my management. When I stop to think about it, I suppose we would be no worse off than we are right now."

"Okay," he said. "Think about it; get whatever authorization you need and let me know. Keep in mind it wouldn't cost you anything. If you want to make a change to the contract, I can come by and sign it."

Sybil agreed and a day later she called to confirm the new terms had been approved.

Shad was elated. A deadline avoided. With luck he would come to an understanding with Ruth before Sybil came up with another purchaser.

The problem for him now was Ruth. It was she who would determine his fate. Without her, he would move. He had to be ready. Sybil might call at any time advising him he had to make up his mind immediately. He could not delay outlining his thinking to Ruth.

He had established a promising relationship with her. Not long after their dinner in the Thai restaurant she had kicked Brandon out of her apartment, with less acrimony than she had feared. If she hadn't, she told Shad, he would have left anyway. She had not budged on her refusal to meet his outrageous demands and he had already been looking for a replacement for her. At the end, she had not shed a lot of tears.

He had been hard pressed to hide his happiness at this turn of events. She was now free. With her unencumbered, he felt confident it would only be a matter of time before she would sleep with him. He refrained from pushing her as hard as he would have liked. He wanted her to be ready; to come to him of her own accord. But despite their frequent dinners, the many hours they spent on her business plan and the regular massages, she had not been willing to become intimate.

He wasn't sure why she continued to resist. His age, perhaps. Whenever he had gently let her know he wanted her to come to bed with him she had said "no", and he had immediately backed off, taking her at her word. He felt she had been tempted more than once and it had taken considerable self control on his part not to persist, but it had been the right thing to do. Their good relationship and easy companionship might not have come about if he had behaved differently.

Admittedly, heavy flirting had become the norm. Her massages had become more intimate. She was not teasing when she lightly stroked his penis. More than once she had brought him so close to the edge it had been physically painful for him, but she had backed off at the last second. He had cupped her breasts as she leaned over him, but when she told him to please stop, he had. He had run his hand up inside her thighs until he touched her panties; felt how wet they were, only to have her ask him to take his hand away. He had reluctantly followed her wishes. She had never kissed him as long as he was on the bed, but after dinner, when they said good bye, her passionate kissing was promising and maintained his optimism. He was sure she would become his. He was determined to remain patient because he wanted more from her than just her body.

He thought back on how their relationship had blossomed. The turning point had been the evening she had asked for his help and he had eventually told her about Apries. After that it had become easy to talk about Veronica and her death and the kind of marriage they had had and about the role Caitlin had played in their lives. He had gone on to share details of his career and his travels and a strongly edited version of his years in the military.

She had reciprocated by relating more of her background, how her parents had commuted from Tijuana to work in San Diego and the hardships they had had to endure in raising a large family. She had told him more about her first boyfriend and her subsequent pregnancy; being talked into becoming a masseuse by a girlfriend. That decision had changed her life. To underline her new beginning, she had legally changed her Spanish name Condolencia to its Anglican version, Ruth. She had been open about the few serious boyfriends, other than Brandon, she had had and why they had not worked out. None of what she said changed his conviction that she was wonderful, a keeper.

In the process of exchanging backgrounds, he started falling in love with her, and for the first time since he had met Veronica, this strong feeling for a woman went beyond mere physical attraction. Ruth and he were on the same wavelength, despite their age difference, and talked animatedly for hours and laughed at the same jokes and felt comfortable with each other. There were no awkward silences and no attempts at keeping secrets or spreading falsehoods or pretensions. They were their own, natural selves. They had their private histories and accepted them.

He wanted to tell her what she was beginning to mean to him, and yet he hesitated, afraid she would think he was telling her only because he wanted to make love to her. He assumed she could sense how he felt about her, just as he was sure she more than liked him.

It was time to speak with her. "Hi, Shad," he heard her say when he called. "What's up?"

"Not much, Ruth. I wanted to cancel today's massage because I would like to discuss a couple of ideas with you. I can't do that while you are massaging me, and since restaurants are so noisy I thought we could spend a little time alone here before going out to dinner. Is that okay with you?"

"I guess so. Anything I need to know before I see you?"

"No. Is there any place in particular where you would like to have dinner tonight?"

"Up to you. I'll see you later. I have to go."

While waiting for Ruth to arrive, Shad mentally rehearsed how he could sell her on his idea. Some aspects were still unclear to him. He would have to improvise based on her reactions.

She greeted him with a kiss. Not just one with which to say 'hello', but one with a message. He embraced her tightly before leading her into the living room.

"So how is the new guy you hired working out?" he asked.

"Not bad. We are using him with women specifically asking for a man and also on some clients who are indifferent. Our customer base is increasing gradually, so he is pretty much busy all day. We are paying him $25 per hour to start with, with the promise of more when his probation period is up, but with the tips he is getting—which we hadn't considered—he is probably clearing more like $35. So he is happy, especially since I am sure he doesn't pay taxes on his tips. He isn't gay and is thoroughly enjoying the working environment."

"I am not sure I like hearing that," Shad admitted. "About him being straight, I mean. I would not want him to make a move on you!"

"A little jealous, are we?" She was smiling hugely. "Good. I like that."

"Ha, ha, ha! Anyway, your plan seems to be working."

"Thanks to you and the conservative approach you pushed. We are really happy with the way it's shaping up. We are now interviewing a girl who we hope to have on board by next month."

"And your colleagues are okay with the house calls they have to make?"

"Well, sort of," she said, her voice reflecting the reluctance the girls must be overcoming every day. "Don't worry. They will get used to it, and it has brought us new, very happy customers. But I am sure that's not what you wanted to discuss with me, is it?"

He smiled. "No, it's not, glad as I am the plan seems to be working." He saw Ruth looking at him expectantly and continued. "I have been thinking, and wanted to bounce a couple of ideas off you. Just food for thought, mind you. I am not expecting any kind of commitment or decision."

"That sounds rather mysterious. Go ahead. Tell me."

"All right. The first one is this: By working with you on your business plan, I think I got a pretty good feel for your set-up. I am convinced your idea of expanding into a full-fledged spa is viable, but I see two potential problems. The first one is that you—I mean the four of you—can not do everything yourselves. You lack both the time and the necessary expertise. You need qualified staff for each of the various spa services, including a part time dermatologist nominally in charge of treatments requiring medical supervision—laser applications, for example. A lot of thought has to be given to how many people you need, how to compensate them and their experience level. The second one is capital. You will need money to get started—for staff, operating expenses, leasehold improvements, purchase of expensive equipment, more comprehensive insurance, and various overhead expenses. And you have to anticipate running a deficit for at least a year or two."

"You are not telling me anything we don't already know."

"Good. I am glad you are thinking along these lines. Perhaps you have also thought of a solution?"

"Not really. We have been so busy we haven't been able to think of how much capital and cash flow the envisioned expansion requires."

"I don't know either. It's not actually an expansion, but rather a completely new business into which your present operations would be integrated. I expect we are talking about hundreds of thousands, but not millions of dollars."

She was nodding thoughtfully. "A lot of money, either way."

"Yes. More than the four of you have, I assume. But I could provide these funds. I think I have enough cash available, but even if I don't, I am sure I can get a loan, based on my net worth. And if I don't buy the apartment I will definitively have enough. I suspect your start-up costs will hardly exceed what I would have to invest in the Towers."

"Are you kidding? I had no idea they were that expensive."

"Believe me, they are," Shad said.

She was shaking her head. "Unbelievable! But what do you mean with you could provide?"

"I mean I would like to propose we go into business together. The four of you plus me. We would create a limited partnership, with me as the majority shareholder. Maybe 75%, with your three partners holding 5% each and you 10%. You would all draw a salary approximately commensurate with your current gross income, and at the end of every quarter, or year, we split any profits along ownership lines."

"Five or ten percent don't seem like all that much."

"Maybe not in percentage points, but when you consider we might need half a million to get started, it would mean an investment of $25,000 for each of your partners and $50,000 for you."

This made Ruth sit up. She had become pensive at Shad's unexpected proposal and the cash it would require. He could virtually see the wheels in her head turning, trying to come to grips with the scope of what he had outlined.

"And where do you think we minority shareholders could come up with our part of the capital contribution?" she finally asked. "Those are huge amounts for us."

"Of course they are, but I have an answer to that." He was relieved she had not burst out laughing at his idea. "We won't have exact sums until we know our total start-up costs, but assuming you would not have what your share would come to, you have several options: Borrow the money from friends or relatives or from a bank; sell some assets you might have; or I could loan it to you at a nominal interest rate, to be repaid out of the profits we will eventually make."

"Whoa," she said, overwhelmed. "Slow down. This is more than I can absorb so quickly. What in the world gave you this idea?"

He shrugged his shoulders dismissively. "You know me pretty well by now, and have seen what a boring life I have been leading since Veronica passed away. From the day she left me until I met you, Ruth, I was adrift—mentally and emotionally. Fighting emptiness with which I could not cope. Almost like merely waiting to die. Not that I was eager to, but I certainly did not worry about it. I had no purpose in life. My brain has been atrophying from lack of activity. I need challenges. You have given them to me. You have restored my will to live meaningfully."

"Oh, come on, Shad, you are exaggerating. I didn't give you anything except some massages."

"You really believe that? I don't think so. You made me come alive again, directly through your interaction with me, and indirectly through the ideas I have had because of you and what you do. I wouldn't want to work again full time, but being intimately involved in a start-up business in which I have a personal financial stake really appeals to me. I wouldn't interfere with day to day operations or management and wouldn't draw a salary, but would always be available to provide whatever counsel you deem worthwhile. I am sure this would be a win/ win situation, if the enterprise is going to be as successful as I think it will. Good use of my money, something for me to be involved in from a distance and to occupy my mind, while you stand to make money from profit sharing with practically no risk."

"That doesn't seem quite true to me. We would risk the capital we put in, and could be without a job or a business if it didn't work out."

"Sorry, but I don't see it the same way," he said. "The risks lie with me. If I loan you the capital, and the business fails, you could not repay me. The loss would be mine. As would the 75% or whatever I would put in. And worst case, you could always go back to having a modest but successful massage institute, but I would be back at square one."

"I don't know what to say," Ruth admitted.

"I don't expect you to say anything right now. I told you I am just bouncing an idea off you for your consideration. Once you have given it some thought and have discussed it with your partners, we can get together and work up some concrete numbers."

"Would you be willing to meet with us and present this to them? I am sure they would have a lot of questions I could not answer."

"Sure. No problem. Just tell me when and where."

"How about the next time we girls have our regular meeting?"

"That might be too soon," Shad said. "I need a couple of weeks to do the research we discussed before I can generate solid numbers. And then it would be better to have a formal meeting where I can make a power point presentation covering marketing and the business structure I will recommend. I would want this to be professionally done and comprehensive. We could do it in my house."

"Fantastic! Let's do it!"

"I'll let you know when I am ready."

32

Shad's proposal to the Massage Mahal partners was based on the data and information he had gathered over several weeks. He had immersed himself enthusiastically into the project, delighted to have a meaningful task to address under some time pressure. Conducting his on line research had not been difficult, but it had been years since he had set up and given a power point presentation and this made him somewhat nervous. He wanted it to be faultless and persuasive, and just as during his working days, he thought a dry run would benefit his objective.

When he was finally satisfied with what he had put together he called Ruth to invite her over.

She came the next afternoon after work. As he opened the door for her, he hesitated momentarily, studying her. He liked the way she was dressed with a short dark skirt and a sleeveless white blouse. Simple but elegant. When she moved, enticing cleavage became visible. He had to force himself not to stare. She looked so different from her normal jeans and polo shirt attire, and he wondered if she had deliberately dressed up for his benefit.

"I am glad you were able to come, Ruth," he said as he led her into his small office where he had his computer set up. "I haven't made a power point presentation in years, so I'd really like you to tell me very frankly if this one is okay before sharing it with your partners."

She did not comment as he scrolled through the slides and talked. "Looks fine to me," she said at the end. "I am amazed with what you pulled together. The group will be impressed, and if we can get the financing part resolved, I am sure they will be as eager to get started as I am."

"Well, good. Have you checked when they will be available?"

"Yes. If it's not too much of an imposition on you we would like to have the meeting Saturday afternoon, after we have closed for the weekend."

"You mentioning weekend reminds me. Opening hours is something I did not include but we need to discuss. Saturdays—including afternoons—are apparently one of the busiest times for a spa, with everyone desiring to look good for their evening's social activities. We would have to stay open until at least 9:00pm, and possibly Sunday as well, if we want to be competitive."

"But that would mean working shifts. We can't expect our staff to be there twelve hours a day, six or seven days a week."

"Correct," Shad agreed, "which makes staffing and its costs even more critical. We should hire some part-timers; maybe some "retired" treatment specialists who would be happy to work for a few hours per day but could not do so full-time anymore."

Shad saw Ruth nodding, thinking about what they would need to do. He made a note to himself to address the subject of opening hours with the group.

"So are we good to go with this on Saturday?"

"I think so. I can't think of anything you left out. We will have to see what questions or concerns will arise."

A short silence settled over them. They were lost in thought, in no hurry to leave for dinner. Shad remembered the other idea he had wanted to broach with her but had not gotten around to earlier.

"Didn't you tell me the other day there was something else you wanted to discuss with me?" she asked unexpectedly, as if reading his mind.

"Yes, I did. I still do, but I am not sure you are ready and even less sure how I should put it. It falls into the personal sphere. Both your's and mine."

"Why don't you just try?" she said, a questioning look in her eyes. "I am a big girl. You can be open with me. We have talked about everything and I doubt there is anything you'd like to raise that would be too personal."

He thought for a moment. "Okay. I'll give it a try. But don't get upset or think I am taking something for granted."

"Like what?" she asked, truly curious now.

"Well," he started to say before hesitating once again. "Maybe it would be better to discuss this with you after we have spent a night together."

Even to his own ears he sounded too presumptuous; too blunt. What a stupid thing to say! He kept his eyes resolutely focused on her, challenging her, and saw her face turn red. But she did not appear to be angry or shocked. She simply said: "You are assuming that is going to happen. Taking it for granted."

"No," he assured her. "I am neither assuming nor taking anything for granted. I am merely eternally optimistic. Hopeful, if you will, based on the time we have been spending together, how we have gotten to know each other, and how I think we feel about each other. I would like to have the chance to show you that what I told you about old men is true. That I would be totally committed to spoiling you." He paused, waiting for her to react, but she did not. "You see, Ruth, given my age, my sexual needs have changed. I am more interested in quality than quantity, if that doesn't sound too trite. Making you happy is more important to me than my own gratification. Your happiness, in fact, would become mine as well. Having an orgasm is no longer paramount to me, as long as I can satisfy you in every way. I don't need sex with you for sex's sake. I need it to show you what you mean to me and to make you feel better than you have ever felt. Age makes for patience, and that I would like to prove to you. I sincerely believe it is inevitable that we will make love. What I don't know is *when*, because that is entirely up to you."

She was smiling now. Rather dreamily, he thought and wondered what she was thinking.

"An interesting perspective," she finally said, "not to say problem. I am not sure I appreciate the pressure you are exerting on me. I would like to know what you want to tell me, and I don't want you to wait until we have slept together—if we ever do. It's by no means as certain as you seem to think. Maybe I wouldn't want to go to bed with you *before* I knew what you wanted to discuss with me. Has that ever occurred to you?"

Shad had to laugh. He was very happy. She had admitted she was considering sleeping with him. This was more than he had dared hope.

"That wouldn't be your style, Ruth. You would not have sex with me if you felt your curiosity was coercing you."

"You are right. I can wait. I will sleep with you when or rather *if* I am ready. That could take a long time."

"Okay. Chicken or the egg, I guess. How about going to dinner now?"

It was only while they were lingering over dessert that Shad concluded he should not wait any longer. "Let me tell you what I have been dwelling on for weeks but have been hesitant to share with you, Ruth."

"Finally. I am all ear."

"It's hard for me to know where to begin, so be patient if I sort of skip around a bit and stumble," he said. "You know I have been wrestling with the thought of buying the penthouse. My option was originally for ninety days, which have now passed, but since they haven't found another buyer they have agreed to maintain my option until further notice. This means I may still have months to decide, or only days; possibly only hours if someone else suddenly wants to buy the unit."

"So what's the problem?"

"That I have been considering the purchase off and on for months now; almost ever since Veronica passed away. I was so lonely I couldn't stand it anymore. I thought by living in the Towers, I would be among people again. I could have as much of a social life as I wanted. I could eat there. I could participate in the activities and events they organize. My best friend, Thomas, lives there. In short, I thought I would become a full fledged member of the human race again, instead of the vegetable I was turning into at home."

"Sounds pretty reasonable to me, even though you seem to be dramatizing your present circumstances."

"I can see why you would get that impression. I am always happy when you are with me, so you never see the flip side of my emotions, which come out whenever I am alone. But it is there and it is real. I have lived in my house for more than twenty years. I know every nook and cranny. It is home to me and holds a thousand good memories. I still feel young and fit enough to take care of myself. I agonize over the thought of having to move into an apartment, despite its size and conveniences. If I moved, I couldn't very well leave my house vacant for any length of time. I would have to sell it within the foreseeable future. But what if I didn't like living in the Towers? What if living there was disappointing? What then?"

"I don't know. Having lived in an apartment all my adult life I find it difficult to relate to this being such a major issue for you. You must have lived in one before at some point in your life."

"Sure, but never in a retirement community, where you are sort of just waiting to die, surrounded every day by a bunch of senile old people shuffling down the hallway in their wheelchairs or walkers. How could I stand witnessing that all the time? I would despair; become totally despondent."

"Now that I can understand," Ruth acknowledged. She didn't think it was necessary to point out to him he could well join the ranks of the physically impaired within a few short years. "So if that's how you feel, why not stay in your house?"

"Two reasons, primarily. First of all, if it did become necessary for me to have care and I would have to move, this penthouse I like would surely be gone and I would have to buy a smaller unit—assuming one would be available. Secondly, what if something were to happen to me while I am home alone? A heart attack. A stroke. An accident. I could be laying there for days without anyone being the wiser, and I fear the thought of not being able to drive any more; Alzheimer's sneaking up on me without my noticing and no one around to tell me. Or being mentally alert but physically incapacitated, maybe having to have my diapers changed. These possibilities scare the hell out of me."

"I suppose none of those doomsday scenarios are impossible, even if unnecessarily pessimistic," she agreed. "So you don't know what to do. You are afraid to move and afraid to stay, is that right? But knowing you the way I do by now, you must have thought of a solution to this dilemma."

"Well, I don't know if solution is the right word, but I did have an idea."

"Which, I take it, concerns me," Ruth stated, "and brings us to what you were reluctant to discuss."

Shad found himself smiling. She was making it easier for him. Did she already guess what was coming?

"Go ahead. Tell me," she prompted.

"Well, okay. All other things being equal, I would definitely much rather stay in my house. If I do that I would have to find a way of eliminating this fear of physical or mental debilitation on one hand, and the loneliness on the other. So far I have only been able to think of one way of accomplishing both objectives."

"Getting married again, or have someone like me move in with you," she observed.

"Not someone *like* you, but rather *you* specifically. But I have to warn you: I have no intention of ever getting married again. I have been down that road twice; the first time I got divorced, the second time I became a widower. Neither was a lot of fun or to be repeated."

"You never told me about your first wife."

It wasn't phrased as a question, but Ruth left no doubt she wanted to hear more. His revelation of an earlier marriage must have surprised her, Shad realized. He didn't know why he had never mentioned Nellie before; it had not been deliberate. He didn't think now was a good time to get into the subject, but recognized he owed her something of an explanation. "Suffice it to say I was still young; 27, to be exact, and I was working as a soldier in the Middle East, in Iran. A very difficult environment and as far as women were concerned, an absolute desert for foreigners. Eventually I met this lady and we fell in love. We rushed into marriage just before I moved back to the States, but as soon as we had settled in Texas, where I was based, our problems became insurmountable. The differences in culture, her and my upbringing, and most of all her Moslem religion were hurdles we could not overcome, so we agreed to go our separate ways."

"Do you still love her?" she asked.

"Sure. But not actively; only as a vague memory. It was so long ago I can hardly remember what Nellie looked like. It was a mistake to have gotten married and I have not been able to forget the error in judgment I made with her."

He waited for Ruth to say something, but she remained silent. He couldn't tell whether she was still dwelling on Nellie, or the option of moving in with him. She hadn't appeared to be as shocked or surprised as he had feared about the latter, and this emboldened him to continue.

"I have given this—you and I living together—a lot of thought, and I see many mutual benefits in such a scenario. You wouldn't have to pay rent anymore. You would be living close to where you work. You would save money on food, since we would be eating together most of the time. You wouldn't have to take care of an apartment; I have a good cleaning lady who takes care of the house. You would be living in what I believe are beautiful surroundings and could look at the ocean every day and enjoy the patio and the garden. And finally, I would be happy to pay you an appropriate monthly salary in exchange for looking after me."

"You mean in addition to what I already make off you with the massages?" she joked.

"Sure," he said, "although I would propose to roll the massage fees into your overall compensation."

"What about my job? The idea for the spa?"

"Nothing would have to change, as far as I am concerned. You could work either as an employee or as manager of the spa, once we get it up and running. The salary I would pay you for living with me and taking care of me would be extra."

"I think you are nuts," she said. "I don't believe you have thought this through. It would be more than a really weird arrangement. You would be better off with a qualified full time nurse or caretaker. But apart from my lack of qualifications for the job you have in mind, just what specifically would you expect from me? How could I hold down two full-time jobs?"

"It's a question of time. Right now I don't need regular care, so you could devote all day to the spa. As that business matures and becomes firmly established and I get older and less able to look after myself, you would gradually transition to spending less time in the spa and more time with me. I don't believe you would have a conflict. The days in the spa, the nights at home with me. As to what I would be expecting from you initially, it's companionship. Someone to talk to and who would listen to me. The occasional massage. To periodically check my pulse to make sure I am still alive. I am not looking for a nurse; I need you around me to feel totally comfortable, knowing you feel about me the way I feel about you and reciprocating my emotional involvement. And—if worst came to worst—you would be there to call an ambulance for me."

"Well, hopefully that day is a long way off. You are in good health and great physical condition. Or you better be if you try anything."

"Thanks," he said, returning her smile. "You give me hope."

"I assume sex would not be part of the deal, correct? No way would I consider this scenario for one second if you thought you could buy me."

"I absolutely don't. I know this crazy idea sounds awkward, which is why I have been procrastinating about broaching it with you. If sex were to come up, it would be entirely your choice. No obligation whatsoever. If you find a boyfriend and decide to leave me, you would be free to do so. I would consider that my fault for not meeting your expectations. The only condition I would make, if you did find someone, is that you would not sleep with him in my house. I couldn't stand the thought of you with another man under my roof while I am alone in bed, thinking of you and what you are doing."

She playfully jabbed an elbow into his side. "I didn't know you were such a jealous person," she said.

"Well, now you know." He was dead serious.

"I don't know whether your proposal is an honor or an insult," she finally confessed.

"Neither one. It's a job offer."

"Well, it sounds to me like you are trying to hire a wife, because despite of what you said, I am sure you would expect me to sleep with you. The only difference I can see between a wife and what you envision is we would not be married and I would get paid. For what exactly is still not quite clear to me."

"I guess you could put it that way, looking at it from your perspective," he admitted reluctantly, "but that's not what I am thinking. A wife would have a lot of obligations, at least morally. I don't want this to sound too chauvinistic, but would it be totally unreasonable to hope a wife would cook, do laundry, grocery shopping, housekeeping, etc.? And a wife could have liability issues, if—for example—our spa would go belly up. None of that would apply to you as an employee."

She made some kind of strange noise deep in her throat. It didn't sound good. He worried he had overplayed his hand. Did she think he was trying to buy her affection? The concept had sounded so good when he had first thought of having her move in, but now he realized that his proposal was presumptuous, and—to her—probably demeaning.

"Listen," he said after a while, "I am sorry. This did not come out the way it should have. I thought it was a practical approach benefitting us both. Nothing was further from my mind than for you to feel in any way insulted. I realize now how harebrained my idea is. I should not have raised it with you. Please consider it as the ramblings of a senile old man. A grasping at straws, born out of desperation. It must seem asinine to you; forget I mentioned it."

"That's okay. I do appreciate what you are trying to accomplish and understand your reasoning. You just caught me by surprise. You have to admit it's a highly unique proposition."

"It is, and I doubt I would have made it if I weren't so old and you so young. You are an unbelievably desirable woman. Beautiful and intelligent, and I know there is a younger man somewhere out there eager to meet and marry you. If *I* were to marry you, on the other hand, we could optimistically look forward to maybe ten or so years of happiness, if I stay healthy. Then what would happen? I would be gone—mentally or physically—unable to satisfy you, and you would be a widow—actually or practically—in her mid fifties, and where would that leave you? Spending years alone? You would have given me the best years of your life with nothing to show for it. I couldn't do that to you."

"What if I wanted a choice between marriage and employment?" she asked plaintively. "Did that never occur to you?"

He looked up, startled. "Quite frankly, no. If I haven't even been able to persuade you to go to bed with me, how could I hope you would want to marry me? Keep in mind that if you worked for me you could resign any time, without complications or legal hassles."

"And by the same token," she answered drily, "I assume you could fire me just as easily."

"Oh, come on. Rather than firing you, the bigger risk for you would be that one day I might ask you to marry me after all," he said, and smiled broadly.

"That doesn't sound very likely," she said, "since you said you didn't want to marry a third time. Look, I told you I understand where you are coming from. I have to give this a lot of objective, dispassionate thought; digest the idea. It's too unusual and unexpected. Right now, I have enough problems thinking about the spa we want to open."

"I know. It was a mistake to hit you with both issues in one day."

"So how much time are you giving me to think this over?"

He shrugged. "I don't have a deadline. Take as long as you need. I am not going anywhere. But in a way it could depend on how long the Towers maintain my option. When that expires I will have to decide very quickly, and my decision would be strongly influenced by what you are willing to do. If you accept my offer I wouldn't have to worry about the Towers."

"So in effect *I* have to make the Towers decision for you," she summarized succinctly.

"Not really. This silly idea of mine could also work if I did move. Depending on timing, and how we got along until then, we could very well live in the Towers together."

"Well, I don't know about that; one more complicating factor for sure. I think I am too young to live in a retirement home, and I could just hear the tongues wagging if we lived there, regardless of the circumstances. Anyway, you are certain you would not expect me to sleep with you? And I would be free to do what I wanted if I fell in love with someone?"

"Yes, but I would do everything in my power to keep that from happening."

She was smiling uncomfortably. He could understand her doubts. He hoped he could live up to his promise. He was honest enough to admit that while not *expecting* her to share his bed, he would keep hoping, and he told her as much.

They decided to call it a night. The restaurant had emptied.

"Well, I certainly appreciate your openness," she said as they walked to his car, "and if I do take you up on your offer, and get horny enough, I might just consider sleeping with you—at least until someone better came along."

That hurt. He wasn't sure she was teasing. Her smile was gone. But then they were in the car and she leaned over and kissed him, taking the sting out of her comment.

He drove back home, where Ruth had left her car. He wanted her to come inside, but she unlocked her vehicle and opened the door.

"I have to leave, Shad. I know you'd like me to come in, but I am tired and confused and have too much to think about."

"I know. That's quite all right. Look, I can often express myself better in writing than orally. Why don't I take a stab at putting my idea in writing? It might make it easier for you to understand and would give you something to stare at as you consider your options."

"You mean sort of like a written job offer? With a position description?"

"Exactly."

"Okay. Go ahead, if you think it might help," she said and got into her car and waved him good-bye.

As soon as he was in the house and had gotten himself a drink he sat down at his computer and began writing.

33

It was Friday afternoon. Shad was engrossed in editing his brainchild to Ruth, re-reading and correcting to make sure all salient points were covered when the ringing of his phone interrupted him.

"Mr. Cooper? This is Sybil Delatour."

"Well, hello there, Sybil. What's happening?"

"I'm afraid you have to make a decision on the penthouse. I have received a commitment from another customer. As per our agreement, you have 48 hours now to exercise your right of first refusal."

He was flabbergasted. Timing couldn't be worse. His proposal to Ruth had not been sent yet and the meeting with the Massage Mahal partners was scheduled for the next afternoon. Now what?

Sybil said, "It's the best I could do. But in all fairness, you have had an extraordinarily long time to make up your mind."

"I know, and I appreciate your cooperation. The problem is that I have been unable to decide and the next two days will be critical for my conclusion."

"Well, what can I say? The ball is in your court."

"Okay, I will get back to you in time."

This totally unexpected curve ball came close to panicking him. He felt helpless; completely undecided. His first instinct was to call Ruth and tell her how urgent her reaction to his idea had become, but what could she tell him, and what would that change? He couldn't expect her to make the decision for him.

He forced himself to get back to what he had already drafted, laboring over the exact wording for another hour before feeling comfortable enough to email Ruth his summary. He thought it was accurate and comprehensive. He had highlighted the fringe benefits she would enjoy as employee, including paid time off and retirement entitlements. He awaited her response eagerly.

By the time evening rolled around she had acknowledged receiving his message. She looked forward to seeing him the next day, she had added. Nothing in her email indicated which way she was leaning. He thought about asking her to come a little earlier the next day so he could share the latest penthouse developments with her but quickly concluded this would put additional unfair pressure on her. She had to make up her mind without feeling she would effectively push him to buy or not buy the apartment. That dilemma he would have to resolve alone. It did not make for a good night's sleep and he had to concentrate on not showing his resultant irritability when the four partners arrived the next afternoon.

He had rented a LCD projector so he could throw his slides up against the wall in his living room, and started by sharing background information with them.

"I have done my homework," he said. "I have identified a number of websites covering various spas to see what services they offer and their price structures. I have visited the largest and reputably best spa in La Jolla and indulged in a number of treatments for men and engaged the women providing them in probing conversations to learn as much as I could about the workings of a successful spa. I have picked up brochures outlining the services and prices of different spas. Through Amazon, I purchased and studied a slew of magazines covering the spa industry, and I logged on to websites of companies selling both mundane and sophisticated, electronic equipment and checked out their prices and general terms of sale. Leasing, rather than purchasing equipment is an attractive option. And I studied facility and space requirements."

Shad noted he had their undivided attention. He continued. "Two important aspects are still missing. One is the number of customers needed to make a reasonable profit, and two is which treatments are the most profitable. While I firmly believe in the old adage that 20% of them will bring 80% of our profits, I was unable to calculate specifics. I do not know how to determine gross margins per treatment. These two unknowns will be critical for our ultimate success, and I need your help on the answers."

The women listened attentively as Shad presented his slides and talked. He was frequently interrupted, as expected, and remained patient as questions and objections were thrown at him. He had to remind them that he was not familiar with the spa business and was only sharing with them what his informal investigations had brought to light.

"One thing is clear," he said as he came to the end. "We need insider information before proceeding. We will have to recruit an experienced manager to get started, and with her input determine which services to offer."

"What are you thinking of so far," Marilyn wanted to know, "based on your research?"

"Hard to say, since I know so little. From what I have gathered, we would at least have to provide skin resurfacing, photo rejuvenation, laser acne therapy, micro-sonic skin therapy, bio-visage, dermabrasion, various types of peeling, a range of facial treatments, massage and body therapies, body wraps, and waxing and sugaring."

"I have never even heard of half of those treatments," Narissa confessed, and her partners nodded in agreement.

"I hadn't either," Shad said, "until I started looking into this business. Our mutual ignorance leads me to suggest that all of you make some modest investments by personally undergoing different regimens. Perhaps, Narissa, you could assign who would have which one to give us a better understanding of what these buzz words actually mean?"

"Yes, I can do that. What about the no doubt high fees we would have to pay for our treatments?"

"I suggest you keep track of your expenses and then we divide the total among the five of us. Would that be agreeable?"

He saw them nodding somewhat reluctantly. None of them had money to spare.

"Now then," he continued, "at some later point we could add manicures and pedicures, eyelash and eyebrow tinting, make-up applications, exfoliation and what have you. All of these could be combined into various package deals. Gift certificates would be offered and perhaps all day relaxing, beauty enhancing treatments with in house lunch service could be added. I am convinced the key success factor would be to have the best trained technicians. In order to have these we must identify and recruit an outstanding trainer. This would set us apart from the competition and allow us to charge higher prices."

"The option range seems extraordinarily extensive to me," Narissa said, "just to get us started."

"You are right," Shad agreed, "but if we don't provide a wide range of services, we will not be competitive and would not stand a chance of succeeding. We can't risk having only selected therapies and then having our customers go someplace else for the rest. I firmly believe we have to become a 'one stop shopping' spa from the beginning."

"I may be able to help," Marilyn volunteered. "I have a good friend working in a big spa, and she might be willing to share what she knows."

"We could also question some of our present customers as to what they look for in spas," Ruth added. "I know a number of them go regularly, and I bet they could tell us a lot."

"Good idea," Shad acknowledged. "Interviewing experienced job applicants will be another excellent source of information."

"Shad," Ruth said, "I notice you don't show a total investment number."

"That's right. I couldn't; I don't have enough information. If I had to make a guesstimate today, I would probably say around $500,000. But I want to sit down with an architect and have him draw up a tentative design. I learned we would have to spend a substantial amount of money on a representative reception area. We would need a break room for the employees. The infrastructure has to be costed out, including toilets/showers, hydro tubs, sinks, etc. Then we would have to decide what equipment is required and how many stations. The latter would be a function of the specific treatments we want to offer. At this point I don't know how many total square feet are needed, let alone their cost."

Andrea had been rather quiet, but now she spoke up. "With so many unknowns it seems rather difficult to make a commitment. I wonder if it would make sense to simply try and buy an existing spa, rather than starting one from scratch."

No one had thought of this possibility. It was Shad who responded. "I think it is worthwhile considering. We would know definitively how much we would have to invest. The downside I see is that I am sure it would be drastically more than setting up our own spa, simply because the greatest value of a service business is not the facility, but rather what is called "goodwill"—their existing customer base. If someone was willing to sell, they would want a multiple of their annual revenue in addition to their leasehold improvements and equipment. And if they were selling a profitable, successful business, it would beg the question of why."

"Well, I guess we can forget that idea," Andrea conceded.

"I wouldn't go that far. Someone might just want to exit the business for personal reasons and be willing to sell for a reasonable price. And the upside of the goodwill value is that we would have a solid, established client base from day one. But we have to assume nothing is on the market, or we would know."

They agreed to continue evaluating the feasibility of building their own spa. Shad was to find an architect willing to do the preliminary design work so a cost estimate could be developed. The partners would gather as much relevant information as they could before meeting again.

"When we cost this out," Shad said, "we have to consider another element. The spas I checked out all have long opening hours. They open anywhere from 8:00 to 10:00am and remain open until 8:00 or 9:00pm, including all day Saturday. Some are even open on Sundays, at least in the afternoon. We will have to do the same, so think about this as far as personnel requirements are concerned."

"Maybe we could recruit part-timers?" Ruth offered. "You know, we have discussed this whole scenario at length, Shad, and generally speaking like it. What worries us most right now is the capital question. If you are anywhere close to correct with the $500,000 estimate, and we go with the partnership percentages you displayed, we would each have to contribute $25,000, or in my case $50,000, and none of us have that kind of money."

"I hear you, but I am sure we can work out something. Personal loans at favorable rates are a possibility, or one or the other of you might not want to be a part owner but would rather be satisfied with plain employee status and a profit sharing plan, which I think we should have anyway. So why don't we postpone the investment decision until we have a better feel for how much money we will need?"

They all agreed this made sense.

The partners looked ready to break up—it had been a tiring afternoon—but Shad raised one more issue. "I would also ask you to give some thought to a good name for our enterprise. Massage Mahal would obviously no longer be appropriate."

"That's a good point," Andrea said. "I can't think of a name off the top of my head. Do you have any ideas?"

"Only one so far. SKIN & BEAUTY CARE INSTITUTE. Or maybe INTERNATIONAL BEAUTY CARE INSTITUTE. They would cover whatever services we will provide and would connate seriousness and hint at something more than superficial spa treatments."

To his disappointment, the names did not elicit immediate enthusiasm.

They were ready for the dinner to which Shad had invited them. They were eager to continue talking; brainstorming. The spa idea had captured their imagination, and it seemed they would be hard pressed to wait until the dream could be converted into reality.

Shad found the partners' excitement contagious. He had only met them briefly before and had not quite known what to make of them. By the time dinner was finished and a little more alcohol consumed than he deemed safe, they had become true partners in spirit and engagement. Like a family, Shad thought, and he assumed his wise father role naturally. He was sure together they would succeed.

If only Sybil had not called him, with the deadline now less than 24 hours away. He had not been able to speak with Ruth alone. Not about his imminent decision and not about the proposal he had sent her. The two were fundamentally related and he wanted to get Ruth away from the group so he could talk privately with her.

It did not seem possible. It was apparent the ladies would continue with their extended good-byes in the parking lot beyond his willingness to stick around. He would be better off going home. He waved one last time as he got into his car and left. He wanted time to think about Sybil's phone call and Ruth.

As he turned into his driveway, his cell phone rang. It was Ruth, he noted with surprise on his caller ID. It was well past 10:00 o'clock and he had not expected to hear from her again so soon.

"Shad?" she said, "do you have a couple of minutes for me? Or are you too tired?"

"No, not at all. I am fine. Where are you?" He could not imagine what she wanted to see him about but was elated she had called.

"Just turning up into Nautilus. I will be at your place in a few minutes."

She was, and by the time Shad had pulled into his garage and walked through the house to the front door, Ruth was stepping out of her car. He let her come inside before taking her in his arms. He could feel himself responding as she clung to him tightly, pressing her body against his. Did he dare hope she wanted something other than talk from him? She remained silent and raised her lips to be kissed and his excitement grew.

"Please don't say anything," she finally said as she maneuvered him towards the guest bedroom, still clinging to him, and silently started undressing. The ambient light threw provocative shadows over her shapely body and he kissed her breasts while he slipped out of his clothes. She helped him; caressed him with a sense of urgency. It was just light enough to show him how wonderfully she looked undressed, but she left him little time to admire her body.

He had never asked her about her personal life since separating from her boyfriend. The question flitted through his mind whether she was simply starved for sex after a long period of abstinence, or whether she needed *him*. It didn't matter what motivated her. What mattered was what she was doing to him, and he gave himself in to the arousing pleasure she provoked. She was obviously hungering for love and affection and her sense of urgency was contagious. He stopped thinking and concentrated on making her feel good, doing all the things he had described to her; wanting to meet or exceed her expectations.

He must have succeeded, he thought an hour later, when she murmured, "Not bad, for an old man." She was cuddled against him, spent and sated. He could hear the contentment in her voice and knew she was satisfied. He was perspiring from his exertions and started to shiver. She pulled the covers over them and they stayed there, entwined, giving in to their post coital bliss. He could hardly believe it had really happened, but her naked breasts pressing against his chest reassured him. He wanted to talk to her, thank her, tell her how good it had been for him, what a fantastic lover she was, but he was reluctant to break the spell of contentment that enveloped them.

"I only hope you won't regret this tomorrow morning," he finally said.

"I won't. Not at all. It was the right thing to have done. It was fantastic and I am glad we did it. Maybe it wasn't the smartest move or the right timing, but it certainly could not have been better for me."

"For me neither," he assured her. "You were incredible."

He felt sleepy but fought to stay awake, caressing her tenderly, lightly running his fingertips down her back until she purred with pleasure. He was surprised when he found himself wanting her again so quickly. He took his time getting her ready and when he finally entered her again, she groaned deeply and wrapped her legs around his waist, pulling him deeper into her. They were making love, not merely having sex, and it was more beautiful and thoroughly satisfying on both the emotional and physical level than he could have imagined.

"I'm so thirsty," she said when they had calmed down, "could you please get me a glass of water, Shad?"

He had to laugh. Not the most romantic words she could have uttered, but he loved her honesty and fetched her water. He needed some himself.

"Are you sure it was okay for you?" she asked, smiling at him when he returned.

"Not too bad," he teased and ducked when she hit him with a pillow. "You were unbelievably fantastic, Ruth," he added truthfully. "Out of this world."

"This is the first time I had sex since I kicked Brandon out. I had almost forgotten how good it can be."

He kissed her in response. "I thought this day would never come," he admitted, "despite what I told you about my optimism. I have been dreaming about it for a long time. You can't imagine how I have had to restrain myself to wait for you to be ready."

"I appreciate you did. I have to admit that in a way, I have been ready for quite a while, but I was afraid. I didn't want to sleep with you just because I needed sex. It had to mean more, and I had to be sure you wanted me for more than just my body."

"You mean you didn't seduce me only out of curiosity? To see if an old man would really be better, more patient?" he asked with mock surprise in his voice.

"You are the one who has been subtly seducing me for weeks now. Or at least trying to. But no, that's not why I made love to you. I did it because I needed you and because . . . well, maybe I shouldn't say it, but I think I might be falling a little bit in love with you. Is it okay for me to say that?"

"Sure. I feel the same way. I am very honored."

"How come you never told me?"

"I didn't want to put more pressure on you, Ruth, or make you think I was telling you only to get you into bed with me."

"I don't think it would have made any difference. I had to be ready. Clear in my own mind." She paused for a moment. "Do you mind that we didn't go into your bedroom?"

"Not really. I hadn't given it any thought."

"Well, if you do, remember I didn't want to do it where you had been with Veronica all those years. If you ever wanted to make love there, I think you'd need to buy a new bed—or at least a new mattress and sheets, and maybe redecorate the room so that there would be no reminder of Veronica for you."

Shad understood. He liked her sensitivity. It occurred to him that now might be a good time to tell her about his true identity. He did not want to continue living a lie and felt a sense of urgency to unburden himself with Ruth. She deserved to know the truth if they were going to enter into a long term intimate relationship. On the other hand, he had kept his secret from both Nellie and Veronica during the years they had been together, so would it not be more prudent to wait before confessing to Ruth? To perhaps take his darkest secret into the grave with him?

"I'll get started tomorrow," he answered. "Can you help me pick out the right things?"

"Sure. Let me get back to you on the best time. But tell me, have you gotten over Veronica now?"

He thought for a moment. "I have gotten over her death, more or less. You have helped me tremendously with that. But I will always love her."

"If that is so, how can you even think you are falling in love with me?"

"Because loving someone and being in love is not necessarily the same thing. You can, of course, love and be in love with the same person, but you can also continue loving someone while being in love with someone else."

"Aren't you splitting hairs?"

"I don't think so," Shad said. "If you picture your heart as being like a chest of small drawers, you can have different ones for different people you love. One for your parents, let's say. Several for some lovers you might have had. One for siblings or a good friend. Other drawers for people you will always love but who are deceased or otherwise gone from your life. I don't think it's impossible to love many people, each in their own way and for their own reasons. But I don't believe it's possible to be *in* love with more than one person at a time."

"Pretty convoluted," she said, "but I guess there is some merit to what you are saying. I have never thought of it that way. Anyway, now that we are clear on this subject and have done the deed, how about telling me where you stand on your Towers issue?"

"Well, contrary to what I expected, it is not any easier to decide now that we have had sex. Maybe even more difficult, in fact. What you don't know yet is that I had a phone call yesterday from Sybil, the marketing manager. She told me she had found another buyer and that I had until tomorrow 4:00pm to decide if I wanted to exercise my option."

"Wow! That's an unwelcome surprise, isn't it?"

"Sure is. I wanted to call you right away, but I didn't want to distract you from the email I sent you, and I also thought you would be utterly pre-occupied with today's meeting."

"Very considerate, but I wish you had let me know nevertheless."

"Would it have changed anything?" he asked. "Would you still have come to me tonight?"

"Quite honestly? I am not sure. It wasn't something I had planned in advance. It was completely spontaneous. I even surprised myself by being so bold. I have never done anything like it before."

Shad found himself nodding. "Well, in retrospect I am glad I did not let you know if that might have risked you not coming here this evening. That was immeasurably more important to me than the twenty or so hours I sacrificed."

He could just make out her smile in the shadowy room. He thought about asking her to get up with him to have a drink while they continued talking, but it felt so good to be laying in bed with her, feeling her snuggled up against him, that he remained motionless.

"So what do you think about that employment offer I made you?" he asked after a while.

"I shredded it."

"You what?"

"I shredded it. It was insulting and undignified. You can't buy me. Not as a girl friend and not as an employee. I was surprised that you, at your age and with your maturity, would still be so dense as to believe your offer would appeal to me."

Shad felt devastated. Nothing had been further from his mind than to make her feel insulted. He thought he had outlined a fair and practical approach, and she had destroyed it? And then come to him to make love? What was that all about?

"I don't understand," he finally said. "If that's how you feel, why did you come and see me tonight?"

She sighed. "Oh, Shad, how can you be so slow? I am just not willing to move in with you as an employee, for money, that's all. That whole crazy idea of yours has become irrelevant now, hasn't it? We have made love and confessed how we feel about each other, and that is your answer."

"I am still not sure I understand what you are saying," he admitted.

"I am trying to tell you I am happy and willing to move in with you and provide the things you want and need. But not for money. That would be cheap. Demeaning. Make me feel I am being kept. I want to move in voluntarily. No strings attached by either one of us."

He smiled happily. "It's a deal! I would be absolutely delighted to have you living with me—freely and unencumbered."

"And what does that mean regarding your penthouse decision?"

"That I will call Sybil tomorrow to let her know what I will do. For now let's just think about what we need to do to get you established in my house. Our house."